D.L. BLADE & C.M. LOCKE

A STANDALONE DARK ROMANCE

D.L. BLADE'S DEDICATION

I dedicate this book to my co-author, C.M. Locke. From friends of seventeen years to writing partners, creating these delicious stories together has been one of the most fun experiences of my life.

To partners in smut.

Love you to pieces.

C.M. Locke's Dedication

I dedicate this book to D.L. Blade, who gave me the opportunity to achieve a dream I never thought possible. Words cannot express how much happiness writing with you brings me.
Love you, my partner in vampires and smut.

In Loving Memory of Annabelle Lee
Beloved cat and best friend

CONTENT WARNING & DISCLAIMER

From the authors

We, the authors, care about our readers and their mental health. We do not condone or approve any action or behavior between the main characters. This is a work of fiction, so read it at your discretion. This story is intended for an 18+ audience. It is dark and contains situations that may be disturbing to others. The MMC is unapologetically unhinged, possessive, and dangerous. This standalone does have a happily-ever-after, and it will conclude at the end of the epilogue with no cliffhanger.

CONTENT WARNING

Drowning the FMC during intercourse
Murder, violence, and gore

Graphic sexual content

Attempted sexual assault - not by MMC

Mature language

Sexual asphyxiation

Dubious consent

Kidnapping

Mentioning the death of a sibling

Mention of suicide

Anxiety/PTSD

Rape fantasy roleplay

Touching without consent

Domestic Abuse

Childhood physical abuse – off-page/memory

Mental and physical abuse by a parent – to the FMC as an adult, on-page

Social Media

To follow D.L. Blade & C.M. Locke, visit:

D.L. Blade

linktr.ee/dlblade

www.dlblade.com

C.M. Locke

linktr.ee/cmlocke

www.cmlockebooks.com

CHAPTER 1

Sadie

Burbank, California, October 10, 2023

"Miss Ryan, please tell the jury if you witnessed Keelan Blake kill Richard Wertz in the warehouse on the evening of April fourth?" the prosecutor, Melissa Madison, asked.

She drew out that last question, clearly aware of how visibly uncomfortable I was up there. It was the fifth day of the murder trial, and it seemed as if tension was now seeping into the room—all eyes on me—leaning forward, eager for my response. If fear didn't have its icy grip on me, anger would have me instead. They weren't the ones horrified by what I had seen. They weren't the ones struggling to sleep at night while the image of blood and death haunted my thoughts. The case had now fallen upon me to recount what I had seen so the prosecution could seal Keelan's fate.

This can all be over soon. Just tell the jury what happened.

A bead of sweat trickled down my back as I sat on the witness stand. It had only been twenty minutes since my testimony began, but God, it already felt like hours. I was the star witness in the murder trial of my now ex-fiancé, Keelan Blake. Melissa was the prosecutor I had worked with alongside my family attorney, Hamilton Jones, for the last five months. Hamilton's presence was to advocate on my behalf as a "victim" and supply the prosecution with information for the case.

I kept telling myself that I could hold it together during the trial, but I was losing control. Keelan's haunting, deep-blue eyes had been staring at me the entire time, making it difficult for me to speak.

I just want this to be done so I can go back to hiding.

My eyes had fallen on Keelan again, causing my heart to feel like it was being submerged in acid. His dark hair was unkempt, and parts of it were falling over his right eye. It was longer than when I last saw him. He styled it differently, too. Now, it brushed against the back of his ears, and the right side that usually stayed neatly trimmed had grown out. He wore a dark blue button-down dress shirt, keeping the sleeves rolled up to his elbows. Keelan never dressed up like that, but he had to, of course, to look good for the jury. He didn't attempt to cover up his tattoos, though. The art he created was always on display, never shy to show off each design he came up with.

Prior to being arrested, Keelan Blake was Los Angeles's most sought-after tattoo artist. Clients heralded his work as the "modern-day Rembrandt with a tattoo gun." Even before he reached the legal age to work in the shop, he was already tattooing his friends from the comfort of his kitchen.

But his dad, Arthur, had other plans for him. He immediately introduced Keelan into the criminal underworld when he turned eighteen, taking on the role in the family enterprise as a tattoo artist. His father and mine teamed up years ago to create a network of secret-keeping for corrupt politicians, law enforcement, and anyone who had the money to bury their sins. My father, Finnegan Ryan, was a well-known software engineer and graphic designer. He specialized in converting documents and images into code, which were then placed into whatever digital art piece the client requested.

The program my father had created was one of a kind; no other technology company held a candle to his data conversion software, making him highly valuable to anyone who needed to hide their secrets. Arthur Blake was a renowned painter who took the newly converted art and created beautiful canvases for his clientele. Both men thrived in the dark realm of blackmail, extortion, and concealment, carving out empires that made them two of the wealthiest men on the West Coast.

Arthur was a monster, and his sons were no different. Especially the man I was trying to put behind bars. The one whose eyes hadn't left mine since I entered the courtroom.

"Miss Ryan," Melissa spoke again, pulling me out of my thoughts.

"Yes," I said, redirecting to her. "I had just walked into the warehouse's front door when I heard two men arguing. As I approached, I watched Keelan grab Richard by the hair and swipe a large knife from left to right across his throat." I used my thumb to demonstrate the method of how he killed the man.

My stomach clenched at the memory, but my eyes returned to Keelan as if on impulse. He didn't look upset by what I was saying. His face was blank, cold even, like a psychotic devil.

A beautiful devil disguised as an angel.

"And then what happened?" Melissa asked. I felt every pair of eyes in that courtroom on me, burning into my skin. My head turned toward the jury box on the left side of the room. There were seven women and five men. Some looked bored, others leaned forward with elbows resting on their knees, and a couple looked concerned for my well-being rather than the murder victim. I wondered if they believed me at all.

They have to believe me. If Keelan goes free, I'm dead.

"Tell the court what happened next," Melissa urged. "Please, Miss Ryan."

Nodding, I took a steady breath and sat upright, allowing the last vestige of self-confidence show. This time, I kept my eyes on the jury, not Keelan.

"My body went into shock and I dropped the magazine I had been holding into a puddle of water. It had been raining that day, and there was a small leak in the ceiling," I recounted. "Keelan heard me and turned to look. He was smiling, still holding that knife with blood all over it as the man he killed fell at his feet." Courage took root in me, making my voice strong and clear. The images were vivid in my mind, each detail as stark as they were when it happened six months ago. "Keelan stepped toward me, and I bolted out of the building. I didn't hear him coming after me when I reached my car. I got in and sped off."

Melissa nodded. "That must have been difficult for you to see."

No shit.

"What happened next?"

"Honestly, I was in such a panic that I didn't know what to do. Our families are close, and I wasn't sure anyone would believe me. All I knew was that I witnessed something I shouldn't have. After three days of hiding in a hotel near Sherman Oaks, I drove to the Burbank police station and told the officers what happened."

After the prosecutor gave me a small smile, she said, "Thank you, Miss Ryan. No further questions, Your Honor."

I eased back as my anxiety faded, and I started to stand. Judge Benjamin Russell leaned forward and lightly tapped his hand on his desk. "Miss Ryan, I haven't excused you yet," he said. "There's still cross-examination by the defense."

"Please," I said. "I need a break."

"Your Honor," Melissa called out. "Motion for a quick recess so my witness can regain her composure?"

"Objection!" Keelan's lawyer, David Swanson, shouted. "It's crucial for this case to cross-examine the witness while her testimony is fresh in her mind."

"Counselors, approach the bench," Judge Russell replied.

Melissa, Hamilton, and David walked up to the bench and spoke quietly with the judge while I waited.

After a minute, Judge Russell nodded and addressed the courtroom. "We will adjourn for a ten-minute recess. Miss Ryan, you may step down."

I released all the air I had been holding. *Thank God.*

Hamilton helped me down from the stand, leading me back to our side of the courtroom. I kept my head down, avoiding the eyes of Keelan's family and mine.

"The court is now adjourned for ten minutes. Please return here no later than eleven o'clock," the judge ordered, banging the gavel once.

The jury rose and exited to the back room while several murmurs moved through the crowd.

"Melissa, I need to use the bathroom," I said, my voice trembling as I spoke.

Melissa placed her hand on my back and leaned in close to my ear. "Take a breather. Don't speak to reporters or the Blake family members if they try to talk to you. Come right back in ten. Okay?"

I nodded and hurried down the aisle toward the door, avoiding Keelan's gaze. I couldn't bear to look at him then.

Exiting the courtroom, I rushed down the hallway toward the bathrooms, dodging a few reporters who shouted at me. Luckily, no one was inside when I went in.

I turned on the sink and splashed some cold water on my neck and face. After wiping my cheeks with a paper towel, I looked up, inspecting myself in the mirror. My light-blonde hair was a curly, frizzy mess. I had taken my time on it that morning, but the heat of the courtroom and my nerves spiraling had turned it into a rat's nest. The time on the stand had left my dark-pink blouse creased, with noticeable armpit stains, and my black skirt felt damp and uncomfortable against my legs. I looked so tired. My green eyes were bloodshot and swollen from crying the night before.

As I tried to smooth out my hair by pulling and brushing it with my fingers, I heard the door open behind me. I looked at the reflection of my father, glaring at me with hatred and fury, and a cold tremor ran through my body. When he raised his hand, I instinctively tried to move away, but his fingers found the back of my head, yanking the strands at the scalp. I bit my lip to keep from shrieking.

"You're treading on thin ice, Sadie. Be very careful about what you say on the stand when Swanson asks you questions."

The warning was clear. My asshole father had already threatened me a thousand times before the trial. But I wasn't going to take it anymore.

It ends now.

The door opened again, and my mother, Aisling, sauntered in. Her Louboutin shoes clicked against the linoleum floor as she came to my dad's side. "Finn, let her go," she whispered. "Not here, for God's sake."

After today, not anywhere ever again, you coward. There was no chance that my mother would ever protect me *here*. She knew what that punishment would be.

"Finn," she started again, swaying a little as she held Father's arm. God, she was day drinking again. It had gotten so much worse since my older brother Patrick died of an apparent suicide earlier this year.

"What?" he said sharply, but his eyes never left mine.

"Alex Thatcher just arrived. He'll join us in the seats once they start again."

My head snapped over to look at my father, and my eyes widened.

Hold your tongue.

Alex made my skin crawl, like cold steel pressed against my neck. Following the families' merger, he had gained the trust of both our families, becoming the new Chief Financial Officer. Six years ago, when I was fifteen, my father introduced him to my brother and me. Despite being half his age and a minor back then, he would stare at me in the foyer of our mansion as if he wanted to devour me for lunch.

Fucking pedo creep.

My parents didn't give a shit when I told them how uncomfortable Alex made me. Being here today, what business did he have with this trial? However, arguing with him about it now wouldn't do me any good.

"Look, I need to get back," I said, my scalp burning. "The ten minutes is almost up."

"We're not done," he seethed, releasing my hair.

Oh, we are so fucking done.

I turned to face him and said, "I already told you. I won't say anything about the family business or elaborate on our relationship with the Blakes outside of that *engagement.* But I can't allow that man anywhere near me again. Keelan is a murderer. Fuck that deal you made with Arthur. I'm out." I tried to push past him, but he reached out and grabbed my wrist, squeezing so hard his nails cut into my skin through the fabric. This abuse was tame compared to all the other times he'd put his hands on me, starting at the age of four. But it didn't lessen the pain or my anger.

My father's dark brown eyes blazed as he leaned toward me. "You know I don't give a fuck if that boy goes to prison. If anything, he was the perfect one to take the fall. You had to open your stupid mouth and get the attention of the police on us, on *my* business. So, we're now forced to deal with this shit. But let me assure you, little girl, the deal I made with his family to unite our businesses still stands. If Keelan gets locked up for life, then one of his two brothers will gladly take you to their bed."

I raised my gaze to meet him, staring defiantly into the bastard's cold eyes. For once in my life, I felt brave. "After this trial is over and they put that monster away for life, I swear to you, *Finn*, you will never see me again."

I headed out of the bathroom and into the courtroom, my right hand still trying to fix the mess my father's grip left behind. My gaze automatically fell on Keelan, who was staring at me again. His eyebrows creased as I headed down the aisle to my attorney's table, a strange look crossing Keelan's eyes.

He's probably enjoying the fact that he got me rattled and looking like a mess.

After the judge returned and resumed the trial, they directed me back to the witness stand. It was time for David Swanson to cross-examine my testimony. Despite my act of bravery against my father, I felt anxious about what questions he would ask me.

David was a shrewd man who liked to nitpick every statement made during the trial. When the police officer who interviewed me was on the stand, he tried to find holes in the statement by painting me as a hysterical woman who imagined the murder. Melissa objected so often that Judge Russell had to reprimand David for speculation.

My hands fidgeted in my lap as David approached the stand in his sleek gray suit and yellow tie. Once he stood directly in front of me, he began his line of questions. "Miss Ryan. Is it true that you were engaged to Keelan Blake?" he began, likely establishing a timeline for the jury.

"Yes, we were engaged for over a year."

"And you remained engaged until the alleged incident on April fourth? Is that correct?"

I nodded grimly. "Yes. After Keelan *murdered* Richard Wertz, I thought it would be wise not to marry a killer and ended our engagement instead."

"Allegedly, Miss Ryan." David smiled. "But let me ask you this…. Your father, Finnegan Ryan, is in business with Keelan's father, Arthur Blake, correct?"

My stomach twisted. Before coming to court, Hamilton had thoroughly coached me through what to do when this line of questioning came up. He ordered me to deny and divert everything if they went there. It would paint a massive target on my family. I wouldn't just face the wrath of Arthur and my father but everyone employed by our families. That included the dirty cops in Los Angeles County and even the goddamn mayor that my father was running against. The election was five months away, and the news coverage focused *a lot* on my family. My father had been a city council member for years and was now vying for the mayor's office. He aimed to gain significantly more political power and get his claws into new clients and *resources.*

If he had more power, no one could touch him.

If I fucked this up and revealed anything, he would make me disappear for good.

"Yes, they are," I answered truthfully, but I knew how to deflect from there.

"Please elaborate on the business relationship," he asked, but I found that question odd. Why would Keelan allow his lawyer to ask about that? Clearly, Arthur would have warned his son, as my father warned me.

'Keep your fucking mouth shut, or you'll be at the bottom of the ocean by dawn,' he had said.

"I don't really pay attention to that stuff," I said. "I prefer to get my nails done and read a book by the pool. As far as I know, my dad orders pretty paintings from Mr. Blake's galleries and refers his clients for their custom pieces. He's also done a few jobs for their galleries' websites, but that's it."

He smirked again. "Your parents forced you into an engagement with my client, didn't they?"

"Unfortunately," I replied coolly. "What's your point?"

"Were you upset about it?"

"Objection, Your Honor," Melissa called from the desk. "Relevance. How does her engagement with the defendant pertain to the murder?"

David threw up his hands. "Understandably, an arrangement like that would upset Miss Ryan. Her father forced her to marry a man she didn't choose, so she came up with a lie to have him sent to prison. The marriage can't happen if he's locked up."

"Bullshit!" I yelled.

Fuck! Calm down, Sadie. You know what he's doing.

"Miss Ryan, mind your language," the judge scolded. "Overruled, Ms. Madison. Please answer the question."

"Yes, I was upset about the arrangement. Keelan and I never got along growing up, so it didn't make sense for us to get married. But I know what I saw in the warehouse. I saw Keelan brutally kill a man. The evidence shows that as well."

Swanson stepped closer to me. "Your family owns the warehouse where the alleged murder took place. Is that correct?"

My stomach pulled into another knot. I knew what was going to be asked next. I rehearsed my reply in my head before speaking. "Y-yes," I said, but my voice stammered. *Shit.*

"And is it true that you were heading to the warehouse to grab paperwork from the office for your father?"

Everyone knew I was my father's little errand girl. He often sent me to the warehouse's office to pick up sales forms, order receipts, or correspondence with his overseas partners. But not that day. Keelan was supposedly at the warehouse picking up new tattoo machine parts that had arrived earlier in the week. That day, I went there to show him the magazine I had posed for as an engagement gift. I wanted to build a more stable relationship with my new fiancé that didn't involve fucking late at night and slipping out the front door the next day. He had tattooed my body three months before, and what better gift than modeling the art for him, showing that I appreciated what he had done? Maybe it would bring him more business, not that he needed the help. Ultimately, I didn't want to be as miserable as my mother was. I wanted whatever our relationship was to work.

After calling Keelan's older brother, Aiden, he mentioned that Keelan had been on his way to the warehouse. When investigators asked if he had told me where Keelan was to corroborate my story, he denied everything.

"No, not that day," I answered. "I went to see Keelan since he was there picking up some parts for his shop."

"Did you know Richard Wertz?"

"No, I didn't know him." I started sweating again, my nerves fraying at the implicit accusation.

The attorney smiled so widely this time that it touched his eyes.

Again, with the creepy smile. Jesus.

"Richard Wertz worked for your father's IT company. You've seen him before and—"

"I didn't!" I raised my voice that time. All that preparation was going right out the window as my temper grew close to snapping.

"Objection!" Melissa called. "Badgering the witness."

"Sustained. Mr. Swanson, that's enough."

"Permission to rephrase the question?" David asked.

"Granted," Judge Russell said with a nod.

"Let's say you didn't know Mr. Wertz. The accusation that you're making is that my client, your *fiancé*, killed Wertz in cold blood. But his prints were nowhere near where you said he killed the victim. There was no supposed magazine, no blood, and no murder weapon. Your story would imply speculation and fantasy, to be perfectly honest."

That's because Arthur hired a cleaning crew to scrub the place and destroy the evidence. At the time, even my father wanted to protect his reputation for being tied to a murder inside a building that our family owned, but later backed off as evidence piled up. Unfortunately for them, Richard's body ended up washing ashore in the Hollywood Reservoir. Whatever ropes they tethered to his ankle had loosened, and his corpse floated to the surface.

"I believe what happened was you were angry with your family for arranging this marriage. You and Keelan were physically involved, but you were tired of him treating you like a sexual object. The only thing you could think of was framing the man for murder so you could rid yourself of him. You killed Richard yourself, didn't you?"

My jaw dropped, and my hands clenched into fists.

This motherfucker!

I looked up and stared at Keelan again. His sapphire blue eyes were as arrogant as they always had been, but there was something else. He almost seemed angry with his attorney for talking to me like that. Keelan's nostrils flared, and he gripped the arms of his chair. He broke his gaze with me and bore it into David's back instead.

"Objection!" Melissa shouted, her cheeks flushed deep red with anger. "The defense is speculating and accusing the witness of murder with no basis in reality."

"Sustained."

"No further questions, Your Honor," David said smugly, walking back to the desk and sitting next to Keelan, who wouldn't even look at him.

The judge finally excused me from the stand, and I went to sit beside my mother. My father was nowhere to be found, which was fine with me. The defense just tried to suggest that I killed a man just to break my engagement with Keelan. I did everything I could to control my breathing, but I was pissed.

The prosecution and defense presented their closing statements over the next few hours. The defense reiterated that all the evidence was circumstantial at best. It was a coincidence that Keelan's prints were inside Richard's home and that the neck wound was consistent with the Buckhorn knife Keelan kept inside his car. They attacked my character as the 'crazy, desperate woman who wanted out of her engagement' and questioned my motives for being at the warehouse that day.

But the prosecution did their research though, offering a strong rebuttal with several pieces of evidence that were damning to Keelan's defense. After presenting their case to the court, it was clear that the defense had no grounds for blaming me for the murder. On top of that, my father had already paid off one juror, so if something didn't go according to *his* plan, it meant there was a mole in the jury, and someone would take care of them later.

At four-thirty, the judge sent the jurors to deliberate, and within an hour, they came back with their verdict.

"We, the members of the jury, find Keelan Blake guilty on all three counts. First-degree murder, improper disposal of a corpse, and tampering with evidence." A gasp went through the crowd, and my chest pounded despite my relief. The guilty verdict carried a sentence of twenty-five years to life in prison. Keelan was going to rot away for a very long time.

Keelan rose from his chair so the bailiff could handcuff his wrists behind his back. Before they led him away, he turned and looked in my direction.

The world seemed to slow to a deadly crawl as he mouthed five words to me—*I am coming for you.*

CHAPTER 2

Keelan

Burbank State Penitentiary, One Year Later

The cool wind brushed softly against my lightly tanned, inked skin, and the California sun warmed my cheeks. I had to enjoy it now before I was back to looking at the world through a tiny window at the end of my cell.

I spent most of the morning studying the image my cousin, Gavin Sanderson, had drawn for me and mailed to the prison. Before the signal to head outside came for my cellblock, I sat on the bed and stared at it intently before shoving it under my mattress.

I'll look at it again in a few hours.

It was my cellblock's turn to spend time in the yard, getting fresh air and exercise. The drawing was safe for now, but even if found, the guards would never figure out what it meant. Gavin and I shared the same talent in art, and the clues within the drawing were a signal only I understood.

The drawing was something I had created years ago when I sat down to work on my first client, but when I looked further, I saw he had altered it—just as we had discussed before they locked me up. It was my signal; I had about forty-eight hours before leaving this prison—the drawing, instructions, and who to trust for my escape.

It was about fucking time.

If the guards were to find the drawing, as far as they would be concerned, my cousin thought I'd enjoy a lovely little painting of a blue Morpho butterfly to hang on the wall.

Everything was in place—the three correctional officers on my uncle Byron Sanderson's payroll and the carefully scheduled roadblock. Of course, that also included the unmarked getaway car stashed in Wildwood Canyon to get me the hell out of the city.

Byron was married to Gavin's mom, Serena Blake, who was my dad's younger sister. When I started drawing as a kid, Serena was my mentor, passing on the tattoo shop Gavin and I now owned once we turned eighteen. Byron was a high-ranking investigator with the Los Angeles County's Internal Affairs department, but he moonlighted as an art dealer for my father's more "coveted" pieces. He had connections throughout law enforcement, including those he hired from within the prison system, and it wasn't hard to get a couple of officers to aid in my escape, especially if he had the power to wipe away their discrepancies.

When your family can grease the right palms, you don't stay imprisoned for very long. My family had a talent for collecting scandalous details on corrupt cops and politicians. Though we had a long history with the warden, he was careful with his secrets. He knew the moment we got access to his sick world, we could twist and pry, making him do whatever the fuck we wanted. Unfortunately for him, the warden hired men who were easily manipulated by money or promises of secrecy, weakening the security of his prison. By exploiting their fetishes and lewd affairs that could taint their reputation, we soon had several officers in our back pocket. That included the most recent recruits through Uncle Bryon, who had ties to the hiring process. After he assigned them to work at the prison, we manipulated them into becoming little puppets in our twisted game.

Serve the Blake family, and we'd protect your image.

Fuck us over, and we'd bury you six feet under.

A movement in my peripheral broke my train of thought, and I looked over my shoulder. Andrew Wright, my cellmate, was holding a dumbbell out to me. I shook my head and returned my gaze to the guard pacing outside of the gate. The yard was a small dirt lot on the southern side of the prison, with thirty-foot-high barbed-wire fences and a single patrol tower equipped with two snipers at all times.

I noticed a subtle change in Andrew's expression as his lips contorted into a frown. "Come on, Keelan," he urged, his rich brown skin catching the afternoon sunlight as sweat beaded across his forehead. "You have two sets left, and we only have a few minutes before we go inside to the showers."

The guard heard Andrew and glanced at me briefly before another guard came over to talk to him and switch shifts.

"What the fuck are you doing?" Andrew whispered, lowering his hand and dropping the weight on the dirt. He knew *something* was up, but he couldn't tell what. That made him nervous.

"What time is it?" I asked, not answering his question. I continued to scan the yard and the perimeter of the prison itself. They only gave the inmates an hour a day out in the yard, a respite that I was going to lose in a few minutes. Not that it mattered. By Wednesday night, I would be long gone from this shithole.

"I don't know. I'm guessing about noon," Andrew replied, his dark brows pinched together.

Judging by the shadows on the worn concrete walls and pillars and the glinting metal of the wires, I'd say he was correct.

"Why?"

I shifted to look at him. "I'm done lifting for the day."

Andrew opened his mouth to speak when an inmate, Greg Donovan, came into the yard along with three of his dickless cronies. I rose to my feet, but Andrew pushed a hand against my bare chest, his palm covering the face of my grim reaper tattoo that climbed to my throat, the scythe pressed against my Adam's apple.

"Don't be a fool, Keelan. If you beat up Greg now, everything will go to shit. I know you have something on your mind that's agitating the fuck outta ya. Why don't you tell me what's going on in your head?" he said sternly. "This isn't just about the—"

"I don't want to talk about it," I cut him off. "I'm still two seconds away from snapping that fucker's neck and adding another life sentence to my name. Drop your hand, or I'll break it." I wasn't going to, not to Andrew. He was the only person I could call a friend in this dump, and I didn't want to break *his* bones. But the threat did its job, and Andrew pulled back.

"That magazine has been making the rounds for almost a year. It's not like you didn't know about its existence until now. Are you more upset because of who is in it, and it slipped into the prison?

Or that almost every inmate has likely jacked off to it, and Greg keeps rubbing it in your face?"

I jerked my head at him and scowled. Rightfully, he glared back.

"Easy," Andrew said. "Unless you plan to pluck out every eyeball who has seen that photo, you need to let it fucking go. You can't change what's happened. No one knows where she is, not even you."

Veins of red filled the borders of my vision. I was half tempted to burn the prison to ashes and charred flesh, but considering what I had to do, I shelved the idea ... for now. My plans for Greg were enough to take the edge off. That pasty-looking fucker had been a thorn in my side for months now, and there were only so many warnings I could give before my patience wore out. Greg was on his last fucking strike.

It also didn't help that the bastard was a woman beater. A jury had found him guilty of attempting to kill his ex-girlfriend and her daughter. The sick fuck even laughed about the night they'd caught him, bragging about how he "was going to teach those bitches a bloody lesson if the neighbor hadn't stuck his nose in personal business."

I may be a ruthless murderer, but he was something far, far worse.

I glanced back at the rookie guard. Even if Andrew disagreed with me, I knew I could count on him to have my back in a fight. "Just make sure Donovan and those three motherfuckers who cling to his pockets don't come within two feet of me right now. I need everything to go smoothly so I can get out and find my wife."

Andrew chuckled. "You still call her your wife, huh? Even after she testified against you and got you locked up in here?" he asked. "I mean, you guys never walked down the aisle ...."

I smirked as I imagined how shocked Sadie, my little princess, would be when she discovered I had found out where she had been hiding and stepped back into her life. The look on her beautiful face would be priceless. She was my *prize*—a gift from her father. It's what's been my motivation to keep surviving in this dank, godforsaken place.

"It's complicated, but what can I say? Obsession is never easy."

It was true we never actually got married. We didn't even like each other. Since childhood, we had fought like cats and dogs. I bullied Sadie relentlessly, and she grew up despising me.

But our parents made a deal to unite our families. What better way to tip the scales in my father's favor against his enemies than an arranged marriage for his youngest son to the daughter of the most powerful man in Los Angeles? He needed her family's empire; for that, she and I were the bargaining chips.

Sadie, of course, hated the arrangement, avoiding me like the plague unless it was in bed. *Fucking* is how we managed to tolerate each other's shit. We didn't have to fall in love, but we had to get something out of the messed-up deal. Even her mother's parents forced Sadie's mom into a marriage with her dad, and they hated each other. Sadie didn't *want* to hate me. I think part of her believed that if she gave her body to me, we'd somehow connect and create a relationship that wasn't so bleak.

We never got the chance.

There had been a glimmer of hope at one point, a chance for us to *like* each other. But that went to shit when Sadie saw me do the one thing I knew would send her over the edge; slicing open a man's throat and letting his blood pool at my feet.

Like a scared little mouse, she stood at the doorway, gripping a magazine between her fingers, trembling ... and then ran away from me.

"You're even more delusional than I thought, Keelan," Andrew scoffed. His hands were the only sign of nervousness as they fidgeted at his side. I knew he would follow through with my plan, but that didn't mean he wouldn't question every decision I made going forward. He was a good man who didn't belong in prison. His wife was all alone, raising their two-year-old son, Ben. I'd promised Andrew that if he helped me with the escape, I would do everything in my power to ensure my family took care of them for life and get him out.

If not, I would do what I do best: use violence and threats to ensure my will is obeyed. Andrew was an ex-FBI hostage negotiator who had worked with the Bureau for ten years. He claimed his fellow agents framed him—dirty operatives who wanted him out of the way. They had set him up to take the fall for the murder of their director—who had found out about their deceit. The dirty agents silenced Director Rodrigo by tying his legs to a cinder block and tossing his body into the Hollywood Reservoir. Andrew took the fall. No, he didn't deserve to be in here, and someday soon, I would help him get out and put the real criminals behind bars.

"Alright," Andrew sighed heavily. "Make sure the message gets passed to your connection here." He wiped a bead of sweat dripping down his forehead. "Oh, and Keelan, don't forget me when you get out."

I gave him a single nod. "A promise is a promise."

After dinner in the mess hall, Andrew and I headed to the chapel. This was part of our "normal" routine; the guards weren't the wiser. We sat in the sagging wooden pew near the front and looked up at the cracked painted cross above the pulpit. The scent of old wax candles and dust made my nose itch, and I tried not to laugh at the irony of a holy place falling into neglect.

We waited.

"How much longer?" Andrew whispered, keeping his voice low.

"It took me a while to decode the painting, but my cousin has three officers ready. I'm just responsible for making the illness look believable enough." I smiled, feeling a flicker of hope. Fuck, I couldn't wait to take a hot shower without seeing three to four dicks next to me while I washed. There was a price to pay for that simple pleasure, and I was ready to pay it.

"I'm not going to hold back, Andrew. If I can't trick them, I will kill someone to get out of here. Are you okay with that?"

His face was unreadable. Andrew had been my cellmate for close to a year. He knew *some* of my secrets and what I had done to get put away, but he never judged me for it. After seeing countless people locked up for shit they didn't do, his views had changed. While I *did* do it, I told him the reason why.

He also had a particular understanding of those who commit crimes under a family name, especially mine—one of the most prominent mafia families in Los Angeles. Our wealth protected us ... well, not me. The feds were practically feral over the evidence

and perfect testimony to put me, the heir, behind bars. They wanted to tie up loose ends and send a warning message to my family to
stay in line.

Message received.

No one from my family tried to get me out of here a year
ago—not even my goddamn father. He'd pay for that, though.
They all would, one way or another. The only people in my corner
were Andrew, Uncle Byron, and my cousin Gavin.

Someone cleared their throat behind us, and Andrew immediately dropped his eyes and began mumbling some prayer. Only I
turned around to look at the officer. Andrew wasn't allowed to
see who the guard was that my source paid off. Those were my
instructions—for his protection, of course.

The officer handed me a Bible and gave me a brief nod. "You
have fifteen minutes; then I expect both of you back for the lineup
at the cells," the guard said, his tone low and thick with a fake
Southern accent, keeping his identity secret from Andrew's ears.
"There'll be another officer to escort you back to the cell block.
Am I clear on that?"

I quickly nodded before placing the Bible on my lap. "Yes, sir."
The sound of leather boots on the worn carpet faded as the guard
left the chapel room. That was when Andrew lifted his head and
looked at me. I cracked open the leather spine to the middle of the
book. There was a thicker page with something solid bulging, a slit
at the center. I wedged my fingernail into the paper and pried it
apart like an envelope, revealing what lay hidden within it.

"A hacksaw blade, huh?" he asked. "That'll get messy."

I shrugged, turning the blade in the dimmed light, the tarnished
silver gleaming. "You've known me long enough to know I never

do anything easy. But if all goes as planned, I won't have to spill blood."

We got up and exited the church. An officer immediately met us and escorted us back to the second floor of our poorly lit cell block. I looked around the entire wing, taking in the decrepit scene. The place deserved to be burned to the fucking ground. Decades of rust, dirt, and blood were embedded so deeply into the walls that no cleaner could get them out. The air was rank with the smell of male bodies, shit, and piss. There was no fresh air aside from our one-hour rotation in the yard. Simply put, it was a cage for monsters.

And I was going to break free.

As the guard radioed to open our doors, I saw another officer escorting Greg and three of his loyal followers to their cells, only a few spaces down from mine.

Although I wanted to kill the asshole, I had to be smart about this, or the plan wouldn't work, and I'd be fucked. It wasn't necessary to overcomplicate things, so I had to rein in my boiling temper.

"Officer Johnston," I heard Greg say as they approached. "Mind giving us a second before you lock them up?"

Johnston turned to look at me, and I shook my head. If Greg pushed me too far, I wouldn't have the control to walk away.

The officer smirked and gave Greg a quick nod, ignoring my protest.

Now, I can't promise I won't spill blood. Goddammit, Johnston.

With a broad smile forming on Johnston's lips, he casually leaned back against the wall and folded his arms. The second guard followed suit. The prison staff was well aware of Greg's crimes and knew he was due for some prison justice. Though this was the wrong fucking time, they just made me the executioner.

"Andrew, will you put this on my bunk?" I asked, handing him the Bible. The whirrs of the cell doors echoed in the block.

"Walk away, Keelan," he pleaded. He didn't want to deal with this shit, not now. That was what made us so very different.

He was a man wronged. I was the wrong man.

"Come on," I purred, holding my hands out wide. "Where's the fun in that?"

Andrew shook his head and entered the cell, sitting on the lower bunk's mattress. I'd rather he stayed clear from this unfolding chaos.

A high-pitched voice broke my thoughts. "Oh, is the little pussy scared of me?" Greg taunted. The sound of raucous laughter from his devoted followers and those watching bounced off the cell walls. We were already drawing an audience with the other inmates, their ugly faces pressing against the bars, ready for a show. I saw a single drop of sweat roll from Greg's bald head to his expansive forehead. He was a few inches shorter than me and about fifty pounds heavier, yet he felt entitled to think he owned the prison.

I turned on my right heel to face him, a sinister smile plastered on my face. "Greg, up until this point, I've spared beating your face in. Unlike last time, I don't think I have as much self-control as you think I do."

Greg advanced a few steps. "Easy, boy," he said, holding up his hands. An ugly smile crossed his pale face, making him even more hideous, which I didn't think was possible. "Actually, I have a gift for you." He reached behind him and pulled something from his belt loop. It was a half-folded magazine, and he handed it to me. Before unfolding it, I knew what magazine it was and *who* was on the pages. But what was surprising was a disgusting cloudy white substance oozing from the folded pages. It took little brain power to know what that was, too. That sick cunt had the audacity to cum all over Sadie's images.

I tossed the soiled magazine into my cell, landing near Andrew's feet.

Give me another reason, you motherfucker. I needed one push—one excuse.

It physically hurt me to hold my tongue, but I had no choice. I shook my head while fury gripped me and turned on my heel, heading into my cell.

Unfortunately, with Greg's ego and blatant stupidity, he had to open his fucking mouth. "God, Sadie's so stunning, isn't she?" he said, and I turned slowly to face him again. "Last night, we passed it around. You know how it is. We share things, and we don't mind it when things get a little messy. That present right there,"—he pointed toward the cum stained magazine—"that's from me and the boys, just for you. Some of the other guys with only a few months left said they planned on finding her and paying her a visit. Get a close look at those beautiful tattoos and then force her pretty mouth on their fat cocks. Hell, I'll visit her too, teach her how to be a good, submissive *whore*."

My spine locked up, blinding rage racing down my limbs as I digested those vile words. A cool darkness painted my vision.

When I was a child, my father said I was a loose cannon, a feral beast of rage. I always got into fights, even shattering a few bones in elementary school. Having older brothers and cousins taught me the harsh reality of surviving in my family; it was them or me. I was the enforcer who left others quaking in fear of my family name. We were unstoppable—*no one* could touch us, especially not Greg or the officers watching us. Sure, they wanted to see Greg get his due, but they wanted me to fight, to punish me for my family's sins. We were everyone's worst fucking nightmare.

Without blinking, I threw my right fist out, connecting with Greg's jaw, relishing the sound of bones and teeth shattering upon impact. When his head shot back, I lifted my leg and slammed my foot down on his shin, right below the knee. I was met with another satisfying crack. Greg fell to the ground, blood spewing from his ruined mouth as he screamed. His body knocked into the other spectating guard, and he, too, fell over.

It wasn't enough. There was no way I could refrain from killing him. The reins on my control fell apart. I wanted to strangle the bastard until his breath caught in his crushed windpipe and then hunt down anyone who dared to even *speak* of Sadie in that way.

As I sprinted toward Greg's prone body, I was able to deliver a few sharp kicks to his ribcage before a pair of hands grabbed my elbows and yanked me back. I felt the press of something hard before a Taser dropped me to my knees. Suddenly, I found myself thrust forward, my face slamming into the grated floor, while they swiftly restrained my wrists with cuffs. The guard, a third unnamed man, leaned down, pressing his lips near my ear, and whispered, "Have fun in the Hole for thirty days, you piece of shit."

Seeing another opportunity, I snapped my head back, connecting with the guard's nose. When I flipped onto my back, I kicked both feet into his gut, sending him flying. Before I could leap on him and bash his skull to pieces, Andrew yelled for me to stop.

These men are lucky sons of bitches.

I allowed myself to go limp, letting Johnston and the other two men seize me and drag me away. Greg's shrieking echoed off the walls, and it was music to my ears.

I had been in isolation for over three days, waiting for someone to check in on me as I sat on a concrete floor in the corner of the cell. No one came. No one cared.

But that was what I wanted to happen once plans had changed. It was easier to deprive myself of water and force myself into dehydration while in isolation than it would be if they poked their heads into our cells.

By now, my skin had become dry, brittle, and pale.

"Come on," I whispered as footsteps came down the hall. My window was rapidly closing, so it was now or never.

Clutching my stomach, I shoved my finger down my throat, inducing vomit. I strained as I puked, making the sound as loud as possible. There wasn't much coming out, but it was enough to paint the scene.

Footsteps paused, and I hurried over to my door. I hastily moved backward as the door swung open. As soon as the guard entered the room, the officer's eyes darted downwards, and the pungent smell of bile assaulted my nostrils.

"What's going on, Blake?" he asked, but when his eyes met my face, he pressed his lips together. "Fuck, are you sick?"

I scrunched up my face. "It's my stomach," I lied, pressing down on my right side. "It fucking hurts, and I haven't been able to eat or drink while you animals neglected me for the last three days." I put on the show, looking disoriented and keeping my hand on my lower stomach. I swayed a little and fell on my knee for added effect.

"Shit. Alright," he cursed. "Just give me a second." The guard pressed down on his two-way radio. "This is Officer Farmer. I need to transport Keelan Blake to the infirmary. Send someone up to clean his cell." He released the button and gestured for me to stand. I struggled, keeping my hand on my lower right side as I clambered to my feet.

He escorted me to Medical, and I dragged my heels, moaning weakly.

"Come on, Blake. It's not that bad. You're probably just a little dehydrated or have some damn stomach bug. Take a painkiller, and I'll put you back in there to ride it out."

The walk to the infirmary was quiet, except for my loud groaning every thirty seconds.

Nurse Rita Martinez was sitting at the desk, typing something on her computer and brushing her straight black hair behind her ears. Her back was turned away from us when Farmer cleared his throat.

"He needs something to drink," the officer said.

The nurse turned on her swivel chair and then stood, gesturing to the bed while she hurried to the fridge to grab me a bottle of water. Only one other inmate was inside the room by the back wall, and another medical professional was tending to him.

"What's going on, Keelan?" she asked, placing the water on the table beside the bed.

I gripped my stomach again. "Sharp pain," I said, keeping my intense gaze on hers. She gave a subtle smile as the officer released my arm, and I walked over to the bed, propping my feet up.

"Right there?" Rita asked, pointing to my lower right side where my hand pressed. Once I lifted my hand, she pulled up my shirt, and her fingers grazed over my bare torso. "Lie down flat," she instructed. "I'm going to apply some pressure. Alright?"

Once flat on my back, she slightly pressed down and released quickly. "Fuck!" I cursed and scrunched up my face. "That hurt ten times worse the moment you released that pressure."

She lowered her brow. "Let me take your temperature. What other symptoms are you having?"

"Nausea."

"He puked in his cell," the officer added.

The nurse grabbed the thermometer and ran it over my forehead, then reached behind her, grabbed a blood pressure cuff, and wrapped it over my right bicep. "A hundred and two," she said, placing the thermometer on the table after clearing the number so the officer wouldn't see. "How long have you been having abdominal pain?"

I shrugged. "It started yesterday—a couple of days after they threw me in the Hole, but this is the worst."

"Did you guys not bother to check on him?" she accused, glaring at the officer. "I don't have the equipment to know for sure, but I think we need to transport him to St. Peter's Hospital."

The guard lowered his brow. "Are you serious? What for?"

"Well, if this is appendicitis, it could kill him if we don't. He needs a CT scan to know for sure. I don't even have enough supplies to do a blood and urine test. We can't have a potential lawsuit from the Blake family for negligence." She let out a breath. "You know what they'd do."

I gave Martinez a look when she turned back to face me, and though the nod was minuscule, it was there.

And hopefully, the guard didn't see it.

"Alright, fuck. I'll call it in."

As the correctional officer made the call, I met her eyes again. "Sorry. I got a little sidetracked with another inmate. Is everything still set?" I asked in a whisper, then followed it with a wink.

She gave me a tiny smile. "We figured there might be a mishap. I'll let them know you're ready, handsome. Give Byron my regards."

Chapter 3

Sadie

Chester, Vermont

"Mason," I called, standing at the center display table inside the quaint little bookstore where I worked. "Do you think this space is enough, or should I put the new releases closer to the front of the store?" I gestured to the round wooden table we salvaged at a garage sale last weekend. Now, the table was covered with books I expected would sell quickly in our small town.

Mason looked up, adjusting his thick, blue-rimmed glasses. Coming around the checkout desk, he walked over to me, running a hand through his wavy silver hair. After looking things over, he said, "No, this is perfect." He met my gaze. "This is exactly why I hired you, Tess. You always know the best way to set up the book displays. It was such a mess a year ago."

I offered a small smile. No matter how hard I tried, I couldn't forget the night I arrived at Mason's bookstore. "It's been a year already?" I asked.

"One year this month."

While the details of that day were still perfectly memorized and tucked somewhere in the back of my mind, it was as if I had lost all sense of time. It seemed like it had happened both yesterday and eons ago. But Mason's mentioning it brought everything back in stark detail.

I remember how painstakingly slow the taxi driver drove through Main Street in Chester, Vermont. A thick layer of snow already covered the streets, and my driver feared getting stuck. I had a black duffel bag in my lap, which held a thick envelope of cash I had stolen from my father's safe. The bastard trusted me too much, using my birthday month and year as the code to open it. That was just one of the many mistakes he made and one of the times he had underestimated me.

His little girl got the jump on him, I had thought wildly as I fled from my family's mansion and headed to the train station. It was only two weeks after the trial had ended. Before I testified, the police kept me under twenty-four-hour surveillance to ensure my safety, as they knew who Keelan's family was. But after that, I had no one. They got the testimony to put away at least one of them, and I was no longer their priority. My father had plans to pass me off to one of Keelan's older brothers within days, so I *had* to escape.

"Hey, right here's fine. It's probably safer for your car. You don't wanna have to drive down that road and get stuck," I'd said. "The motel is right up the street, anyway."

The man nodded, pulling over in front of a bookstore and a clothing boutique. I handed him two twenties and hopped out of the cab, pulling the strap of my duffel bag across my back. The snow quickly soaked my hair when I stepped out of the car, and I knew the red dye would drip if I didn't find a place to wait it out. It was so cold that November night, and I started shivering almost immediately. I glanced around, and given that it was eight-thirty at night, I saw that most of the small shops were closed for the day. Except for Mason's bookstore, Hughes's Book Nook, its sign displayed on the sidewalk. I chuckled a little at the sign because it read: "Slay Your Book Ennui, Pick up *To Kill a Mockingbird* by Harper Lee."

I pulled open the door and was met with warmth, the smell of paper, glue, and coffee wafting in the air. The door chimed at my entrance, and a man with peach-toned skin and bright silver hair looked up from behind the counter, his eyes on mine. "Hey, welcome. Come on in!" he said with a bright smile. "That snow is coming down pretty hard, isn't it?"

"I'm not used to this cold," I stammered, then realized I probably shouldn't mention that I was from California. "I grew up in Arizona."

No one can know who you are.

"If you don't mind, maybe I can hang out here until this slows down a bit before I get to the Sapphire Motel," I said, but my voice once again stammered as nerves hit my gut. "I saw that it's a bit more of a walk than I thought."

Mason frowned. The fear in my eyes and the hesitation in my voice made it pretty damn clear I was a woman in trouble. But as he walked around the counter and toward me, he smiled warmly and held out his hand. "Well, welcome to my store. I'm Mason Hughes, the owner. Please stay for a bit while the storm passes, Miss ...?"

"Uh, Tess. Tess Larson."

The expression in Mason's eyes was somber, and he hesitantly smiled. He probably knew I was lying, refraining from asking any questions. I was grateful for that.

For the next hour, we chatted about our favorite books until the snowfall stopped. He insisted on driving me to the motel, where he gave me his phone number and told me to come to the store the following day.

After that, Mason helped me move into a second property in a secluded part of the Vermont forest just outside town. He let me pay the discounted rent in cash and offered me a full-time job at his store. Of course, I couldn't turn down an opportunity like that.

Over time, Mason and I developed a very close friendship. He had a daughter who lived in Illinois, but they had become estranged, so it felt like he had replaced the loss of her with me. I did the same. My father was such an asshole, and I felt like Mason and I were supposed to meet to heal the broken part of our hearts stamped with "Family."

"Tess," Mason said, jarring me out of the memories. "You're daydreaming again. What's going on? Everything okay?"

I quickly smiled and tucked a strand of hair behind my ear. "Of course, I'm just excited we got the shipment of L.M. Lewis's new release. Thank you for considering it."

"How could I not? The sales have picked up over the last twelve months because of your recommendations. You've done such a phenomenal job here, and your opinion is valuable." As he spoke, the wind outside picked up, rattling the windows. Mason's brows furrowed, concerned. "The storm isn't supposed to hit until Wednesday, but yesterday's temperature dropped so fast. I may consider closing the shop for a few days until it passes and the roads are clear."

"They're saying it'll be that bad?" I asked, watching his warm brown eyes meet mine again.

He answered with a nod.

"I guess I can get caught up on some reading," I said, picking up L.M. Lewis's new book, *The Shadow Hunter.* "This one."

I reached into my pocket, pulled my wallet out, and headed to the register.

"Absolutely not," Mason said, quickly rushing over and shutting the register drawer. "Stop trying to pay for books from my store, Tess. You know your money isn't good here."

I wrinkled my nose and laughed. "Fine, but I'm bringing you coffee in the morning," I said, grabbing a plastic bag from under the counter and placing the book inside. "See you tomorrow."

I pulled into the driveway just after sundown and climbed out, seeing Brian Danon, the guy I had been dating on and off over the last eight months, waiting on the porch steps.

I wasn't expecting him tonight.

This wasn't the first time he'd shown up unannounced. It had taken me a while to agree on a first date eight months ago. I wasn't even remotely ready then, but he was persistent. One thing he loved to do, though, was show up without notice. I had been running into him occasionally on Main Street and exchanging hellos at the local coffee shop before he had asked me out on a date. To say I was terrified would be an understatement. I knew I wasn't ready. But I wanted to move on, and so I agreed.

The date was at a small wine bar two blocks from the bookshop. Over appetizers and a couple of glasses of Malbec, we discussed our hobbies and what we liked and disliked.

Small talk.

The wine must have eased my fear, because Brian and I chatted for three hours. At the end of the date, Brian asked for a second date, and my wine-fueled bravery said yes. Since then, we've had a casual, physical relationship. It was my way of seeing where things could go without the labels.

The only frustrating part was that we only got to see each other once a week, mainly on weekends when he wasn't in the office or traveling for work. It was better that way, though. Given my past, I wasn't ready to commit. I had too many secrets I needed to keep hidden for his safety ... and mine.

Brian was a contract lawyer for several large investment firms on the East Coast. While he lived in Vermont, he often had to travel to New York, Boston, and New Haven to meet high-profile clients. Occasionally, I would spend a weekend at his apartment, but he stayed at my house most of the time.

When I stepped out of my car, a few flurries hit my forehead. I moved around his charcoal gray BMW before making eye contact with him. The wind whipped at his usually nicely combed, dirty blond hair, leaving it mussed. The automatic porch lights cast an orange glow on the front entryway.

"Hey," I said, walking up the front stairs to the house. "I thought you were in meetings all week and couldn't leave the city."

Brian stood and smiled at me, his six-foot-two stature leaning down to kiss my lips softly before pulling back. "After hearing about the storm coming through this area, I was concerned about you. I didn't want you to be alone."

I smiled subtly at the thoughtful gesture, though I wished he had called first.

A distant rustle of leaves rolled in behind us. "Come on. Let's get inside before we get covered in this snow," he said, holding his hand out for me to take.

Once inside, I felt the heater's warmth over my chilly skin and let out a contented sigh.

Quietly, I watched him remove his loafers and hang his coat on the rack. Then I went over to the fireplace and placed the book, still wrapped in the plastic bag, on the bookcase Mason helped me build last fall. Since I started working at the store, I amassed quite a collection.

I need to read that J.D. Linton novel before adding another book to the pile.

"Why are you so quiet?" Brian asked, his blue eyes looking worried. Since Mason mentioned my arrival a year ago, my mind replayed those memories for the rest of my shift. Suddenly, a prickling sensation crawled up my neck and into my scalp—an eerie feeling I couldn't shake off. The damn storm was making me jumpy.

Only one person knows I'm here, and they swore to secrecy.

"What do you mean?" I asked, wrapping my arms around my waist as I glanced out the window at the dark sky.

"Well, I don't know. Maybe the fact that I haven't seen you in a week, and you're acting like I'm a stranger."

With an apologetic shrug, I motioned toward the window. "Come on. This is only my second winter out here. I'm not prepared for a storm rolling in. If the roads are icy, I won't be able to drive to buy groceries after work." I turned from the window to meet his gaze. "Trust me, I'll crash."

While the storm made me uneasy, it wasn't the only reason. But I wasn't going to tell Brian that. The secrets of my past was mine to bear. Alone.

He smiled and walked over to me, taking my hand. "It's only supposed to last for a day. You'll be fine."

"Yeah, but the winds are supposed to be near blizzard levels. It could knock over my fence or snap the trees." Alright, so maybe I was exaggerating a little. "I might get blown away."

Brian's charming smile lit up again, making my stomach flutter, and I bit my bottom lip slightly.

"Tell ya what?" he said. "I don't have any meetings tomorrow. How about I stay here, work from home, and stock up the fridge while you're at work?"

"Really?" I asked, arching a brow. He was just full of surprises today. "You're always in meetings. What changed?"

"Some contracts need to be reviewed, so I'm clear for two weeks while that happens," Brian said, wrapping his arms around me from behind. "I'll adjust a few meetings so I can stay put. Just text me a list; you'll have a fully stocked fridge and pantry waiting. I'll even get your fireplace going so you come home to a warm, crackling fire." He leaned down, kissing me softly again. "And bed."

I grinned against his lips. "I love the sound of that, but why wait on the warm bed?"

Right then, the lights in the living room flickered as the wind took up a keening howl outside. I was thankful I made it home in time and wasn't alone, but there was still something ominous in the air.

"Maybe I can take you up on that bed offer now," I said, looking over my shoulder into Brian's deep-blue eyes. He smiled, took my hand, and led me upstairs.

While Brian pulled off his button-down shirt, I couldn't help but look at the giant oak tree outside my bedroom window. I watched the branches sway under the moonlight. The atmosphere was shifting even though the worst of the storm wouldn't arrive until tomorrow night. I couldn't see any of the lights from the neighbors or the street—only the faint glow of the moon through broken clouds shone in the bedroom.

The house was in the perfect location for me. Contrary to the chaos and pollution of Los Angeles, Chester provided the serenity that my soul craved. I thrived in the seclusion of the forest and the untainted night sky, where I could see the stars. My favorite thing in the world out here was to sit on my rocking chair on the porch. I would read a thriller novel or watch the stars fall across the sky once the sun had set—wishing I had been born into this life instead.

A life free from lies, blood, torment, and betrayal. One that didn't force me to run.

Brian slowly wrapped his hands around me from behind again and squeezed me against his bare chest. The heat radiating from his body embraced me like a blanket. "Why aren't you undressed yet?" he murmured in my ear, his lips lingering against my neck. Goosebumps rolled over my skin at the teasing touch of his lips.

I turned slowly and placed my hand against the center of his chiseled stomach. "Because I want *you* to undress me."

There was a creak at the door, and my cat, Poe, walked into the bedroom. He greeted us with a purr before sauntering over to the bed and rubbing his tuxedo body against the blue comforter. Satisfied, he went to his window perch and curled up for a nap.

"Sorry," I said with a soft chuckle. "I can grab some allergy meds for you."

Brian let out a dry laugh. "I already took two before I got here," he replied, his hand moving to the hem of my shirt. In one swift motion, he pulled it over my head and flung it across the room. "Tess," he whispered against my skin as he drew me closer, his eyes full of worship as he looked down and cupped my chin with his fingers. His gaze continued to roam over my body, drinking in the sight of me.

At that moment, when his eyes looked back into mine, I could see a subtle shift on his face. It was barely noticeable but undeniably there. I'd become good at spotting details, even with the dim moonlight coming through the window.

I swallowed. "What's wrong?"

I watched his Adam's apple bob before he said, "Nothing. It's just ... you're beautiful, Tess." He moved even closer, pressing his lips against my forehead. "So damn beautiful."

Discomfort roiled in my stomach. It wasn't the first time Brian said those words, making me feel ashamed. Brian calling me Tess was a lie. Tess was a character I had to play, a falsehood to present to a guy whom I was dating.

He has no idea who I truly am.

Brian wasn't saying these things to *me*. He was telling them to a lie made of flesh. He would never know that I was Sadie Ryan from Los Angeles, with blonde hair and bright green eyes—the woman who carried such a dark past that he would run screaming from the house and never return.

If Brian knew the real me, my family would track him down and flay his skin from his bones.

The man in my arms knew me only as Tess Larson, a redheaded cocktail server from Tucson, Arizona, with sparkling blue eyes, courtesy of the colored contacts I wore daily.

As Brian's large hand pressed against my bare stomach, it pushed away my guilty thoughts. He walked me back until my ass hit the bed, then he slowly lowered me to the mattress and climbed on top, straddling me with his knees.

He unhooked my back strap and stripped my bra free from my body. Lowering his lips to my nipple, he took it into his mouth, swirling his tongue over the nub. I moaned and tilted my head back as I felt his finger trace the tattoos between my breasts and my stomach.

The permanent reminder of *him* and the chaotic, painful life I once had. Sometimes, I wished I could scrub this ink off me to forget entirely. But I couldn't. Not even now.

"God, Tess, you're perfect," Brian said as his lips touched the constellation tattoo that started above my navel. He reached into a pocket, pulled out a condom, and held it between his teeth. Then he slid down his pants, ripped off the wrapper, and took it out, moving it over his cock in one roll.

Brian's fingers clutched my underwear, sliding it down my smooth legs before he positioned himself against my already wet and heated core. With one smooth motion, he entered me. There was no foreplay or anything to help me accommodate his girth as he slammed himself to the hilt.

I winced at the sharp burn. It had been almost two weeks since we last fucked, and I wasn't ready for his intrusion. Brian's chest met mine, holding me down on the mattress.

A small gasp escaped my lips at the feeling of his cock filling me up. It felt good, but I wanted more. I wanted more of him. I wanted him to take me rougher, to silence the continuous chaos in my mind.

As his lips crashed into mine, I wrapped my legs around his waist and moved with him. It was more difficult to reach my orgasm with Brian, no matter how hard he tried to get me there. It was as if our bodies knew each other well enough by now, but something was missing. I felt we weren't entirely in sync.

"Oh, God, Brian," I mumbled against his mouth, desperate for more. "Harder ... please. Fuck me harder," I cried out. My body was aching for release, and I wanted to ride that pleasure on his cock. I reached for his wrist and pulled his hand to my throat, hoping he'd understand.

But he didn't.

He never did.

Brian lifted his hand and gently glided his finger down between my breasts instead, against my moon phase tattoo. Though it felt so good with him moving inside me, all I wanted was a bit of pain—just a little—enough to help me get there. He continued to thrust, beckoning me closer, but I knew it wouldn't be enough.

For once, I wanted him to let go, to give into the more primal side of him I *hoped* was buried beneath his usually perfectly polished self.

Just remind him what you want. Clearly, he wasn't picking up on my hints. Maybe I'd have to be more forward.

I reached out and placed his hand on my throat again, tipping my head back to expose more of the delicate skin there. I licked my lips, my eyes pleading with him.

"You won't break me, Brian," I told him softly, my words melting with breathy grunts as he continued to thrust. "Squeeze your fingers around my throat ... please. It won't be enough to hurt me." I pointed to the places on each side that would be safe, figuring some guidance may help him feel more secure. "Right here. Please. I just want ... more of you."

We were panting by now, and I could tell he was close as his cock pulsated inside me. Brian's head tipped lower, and his mouth lingered against the corner of my lips. "I've told you before. I don't want to hurt you," he whispered, increasing the pace of his thrusts. This time, he didn't pull his hand back, which was an improvement.

"You won't," I said. "I promise."

He gave me a slight nod before he clutched my throat and rammed himself back inside.

"Oh, fuck!" I cried out right as my breath escaped me.

He may never do some of the wilder things I fantasized about, but this could be enough. I could get used to this.

"Fuck ... fuck." The pleasant tingle had overcome me, making it hard to think as my eyes rolled back into my skull. Fuck, this was good. So damn good. I could feel my body climbing to the peak

... but then Brian let go of my throat and leaned down, kissing me where he squeezed, as if he thought he had hurt me and his tender kisses would heal the wounds. His body tensed on top of mine, and I knew he was almost there, but maybe there was still a chance for me, too.

"Brian, please, do—" My words cut off as he groaned, his cock pulsing hard inside of me, and my sensation fell away into nothing.

Fuck.

I tightened my legs around him, anyway, and let out an exhausted breath. My chance was now definitely gone.

"Shit. I'm sorry," he said into my ear, showering my skin with soft kisses. Though I didn't mind them, I wished he'd sometimes give me a little more than vanilla. "I've told you a hundred times before. I just ... don't want to hurt you. In any way. I worry I'll squeeze you too hard, and you won't be able to let me know."

That's valid.

I nodded against his neck, ignoring the disappointment that flooded me. "It's fine," I said, catching my breath as he rolled off me and stripped off the condom, tossing it into a trash can beside my bed. I thought about finishing the task myself, but honestly, I was too tired now to care.

"I gotta use the bathroom," I said. "Give me a minute."

"I have to get up, too. There's something in my briefcase I need to bring up."

Smirking, I thought about that burgundy briefcase he always carried. I made a joke once that only lawyers on TV had those. He laughed, saying it gave him the advantage in meetings because of its disarming presence.

I closed the bathroom door and switched on the lights. Looking in the mirror, I felt even more like a stranger. I turned on the water and grabbed my rose-gold electric toothbrush.

All this acting could get me an Oscar, I thought bitterly as I brushed my teeth.

The wind still howled outside, and I felt the house shudder with its force. The chaotic energy was making me feel out of control. What would I do if I had to escape again? How would I explain that to Brian? What if I—?

Stop it! Breathe. I spat out the minty foam and rinsed my mouth clean. I leaned against the counter, drawing deep breaths until my body abandoned its panicked state. But my eyes went to one of the star tattoos on my stomach, and I ran a finger down the ink.

"Sadie, try not to move," he said to me. *"We're almost done."*

The face I can't seem to forget. I desperately wanted to forget him so I could live without fear. Even his name scared me.

"This hurts," I said. *"But I'll try to stay still."*

His tattoo gun moved against my skin, and I looked down. I suggested something related to the stars and the planets. I never intended to get a tattoo, but his artistic piece of constellations below a trail of moon phases suited me perfectly.

"Done," he said after forty-five minutes. *I looked down, and my breath caught. It was a masterpiece.*

"Thank you," I said. *"It's beautiful."*

I blinked away the memory, staring again at my reflection. I had to go back to the bedroom. Brian couldn't see me like this.

Afraid.

I opened the door and found Brian in his boxers, sitting at the edge of the bed. He had turned on the lamp on the nightstand and was holding something in his lap.

"What do you have there?" I asked playfully, walking to bed and sat down next to him. Brian grinned sheepishly and held up a small white box with a pink bow. The box bore the stamp "CHARMED." My hands shook a little as I took the box. "Brian, what is this?"

"Happy birthday, Tess," he said, kissing my cheek.

"Birthday?" As I tilted my head to the right, Brian's face creased in a slight frown.

"Uh, yeah. November fifteenth, right?" he said, shifting on the mattress. "Fuck, did I miss it?"

I should have put it on my calendar app.

I offered an apologetic smile. "Oh, no. Sorry. Today was such a busy day that I completely spaced the date."

"I get it." He smiled. "Well, don't just stare. Open it."

Nodding, I pulled the bow off the box and opened the lid.

The gasp that escaped my lips was soft and breathless.

Inside was a silver bracelet with a tiny charm resting on the black velvet lining. I lifted the bracelet and turned it in the low light of the lamp.

This was the first time he had given me a gift like this. Was this too soon? Or was this his way of saying he wanted to make our relationship more serious, something I could never give him?

"Brian, it's gorgeous," I said, my chest sinking into unease. This was too intimate. I felt my cheeks heat. "You didn't have to get me this."

"You deserve it," he said, taking the bracelet and fastening the clasp on my right wrist. I held it up, running a fingertip over the charm.

"It's a book," I whispered.

"To commemorate your work anniversary at Hughes's. That's this week, too."

He remembers everything today.

"Thank you," I said, leaning in and giving him a soft kiss on the cheek.

"You're welcome," Brian answered with a charming grin that reached his eyes. "Now that we've warmed up this bed, let's actually get some sleep." He winked. "I have to be up early to get your storm supplies once the store opens."

We turned off the lights, and Brian quickly drifted off to sleep. I watched him as he slept. Brian was so handsome, well-spoken, and kind. He had his life sorted out, and even though I didn't get to see him as often as I'd like, we aligned in our values. He could give me the life I wanted once I was ready ... *when* I was ready.

But the passion was missing where I needed it the most.

After setting my alarm, I pulled the blanket to my shoulder and turned to face Brian. As if he could sense my presence, his hand extended toward me, wrapping around my frame and drawing me closer. I basked in his warmth, still observing his features.

He was so beautiful as he slept. Peaceful even, as if his dreams offered a perfect escape from the world. It was something I wish I had.

My dreams were nothing like Brian's. Mine were haunting images as I quailed in fear at the faces looking back at me. My dreams were of running from my family and the life I never asked to be a part of.

Running from him ...

Keelan Blake.

CHAPTER 4

Keelan

E ven though the nurse recommended I get to the hospital as soon as possible, the prison delayed transportation until the following day.

Now they had put my *condition* at risk.

It was nearly sunrise when two officers escorted me to the bus. As we walked toward the loading dock, I doubled over, panting. Thanks to the sweltering heat in solitary confinement, it helped drench my clothes in sweat. Once inside, they handcuffed me to the seat, and the officers sat both in front and behind me. The door slid shut, and the bus driver pulled the vehicle toward the main gates. Although I had worked this plan out to perfection, regardless of the delay, there was a nervous twitch in my gut. If someone fucked up or became afraid and confessed, they would leave me to rot in that damned cage.

A glance revealed two other inmates seated at the back, and we exchanged a look before I turned my head away. The main gates slowly opened, and the bus rumbled through. I carefully exhaled as we departed the prison and headed toward the highway that would take us to the hospital. Once we passed the bottom of the mountain, the total travel time was about thirty minutes.

I leaned back against the seat and closed my eyes, my hand still gripping my right side to sell the lie. I heard a shuffle against the seat as the officer in front of me turned around, and I cracked an eye open.

"Blake, when we get to the hospital parking lot, I'll run in and grab some security guards to help me get you inside. Bradshaw will be with you during the examination."

Sitting behind me, Officer Bradshaw tapped on the back of my seat, letting me know that's who the officer was referring to. I gave a curt nod, and one of the inmates began to hum a soft tune. I felt myself relax a little.

Only ten more minutes. It'll happen in ten minutes.

The Burbank State Penitentiary was on top of a mountain overlooking the city, so the bus had to navigate down a switchback road before reaching the highway. There were several checkpoints along the way, and after we passed the final one, the driver pulled the bus to the right lane, which took us on a shorter route and avoided rush hour traffic.

Opening my eyes, I shifted to the window and looked ahead at the road. As we crested the hill, I spotted a black SUV parked on the shoulder near an adjacent suburban neighborhood. A smirk pulled on my lips.

It's showtime.

The ambush would happen quickly, and once the people in those nearby houses heard the commotion, they would call the cops. When we passed the SUV, there was a loud pop, and the bus began leaning to the right. Instantly, the guards started cursing while I held onto the bar they attached my handcuffs to. The bus then swerved and hit the curb before rolling into a grassy field and coming to a jarring halt.

"Everyone, stay put!" Bradshaw shouted from behind me. He got up and walked to the front.

"Where the fuck would we go, Bradshaw?" I replied, rattling my cuffs against the bar.

I knew the spike strip had done its job, shredding all four tires, but they would realize within minutes that it was more than a nail. As the bus doors opened, Bradshaw reacted swiftly, pulling out his pistol and jumping out while I settled in my seat, ready. Bradshaw's yelp rang out before a loud thud, and I heard boots against the concrete. The noise grew louder before a hooded man entered the bus and fired two shots into the driver's head, killing him instantly. *Fuck.* The men Byron hired were only supposed to injure the cops.

The officer ahead jumped into the aisle, ready to fire his gun. But I lifted my left leg and slammed my heel into the side of his knee. There was a sickening crunch as tendons tore and his kneecap dislocated. The officer screamed and fell onto the floor, dropping his gun. As he scrambled for it, the hooded man strode toward him and stomped on his outstretched hand, breaking the bones. When the gunman looked at me, I shook my head, reminding him what his duties were.

The gunman lifted his weapon, and I turned away, avoiding the blood splatter as the bullet shattered the officer's knee completely. One more shot destroyed the walkie-talkie that had fallen to the floor.

Though my goal was to escape, I didn't need dead cops on my record if I were to get caught.

"Oh, fuck!" one inmate shouted from behind me.

Once the officer inside the bus was down, the hooded man grabbed the handcuff keys from his belt strap and unlocked my cuffs. "Thanks," I said.

I had no fucking clue who my uncle had sent, and it would stay that way. The less I knew about this man, the easier it would be to keep our identities safe.

"What about them?" the man asked, pointing to the two inmates from behind me. The inmate with the bright green eyes was in the cell across from me, serving a ten-year sentence for petty theft and arson. The other one, a bald man with pale skin and dark brown eyes, had hurt children.

"Take that bald one out and release the other guy."

I moved past the hooded man, exiting the bus while two more gunshots rang from inside. Bradshaw lay flat on the grass with a nasty bump on his forehead.

Right then, I took a moment to breathe and glanced at the open space around me. God, it had been a year since I had seen the world outside those prison gates. I wanted to take more time enjoying the scenery, but a faint sound of sirens echoed in the mountain, letting me know it was time to leave.

I ran to the SUV and hopped in the backseat. The hitman followed right behind me, sitting on the passenger side. He turned to the driver and signaled for him to get going, but to do it slowly. If we took off too fast, we would leave tire marks in the dirt.

Once we were clear, the driver sped off, leaving behind a bloody scene in a cloud of smoke and dust.

CHAPTER 5

Keelan

A fter the SUV dropped me off at the getaway car near Wildwood Canyon, I drove a few miles north to the tattoo shop. As I traveled down the road, I heard several sirens behind me, making their way up the mountain. Then, twenty minutes later, a helicopter passed overhead. The authorities were aware of the crash now and that I was long gone. I reached for the police scanner Gavin had left and switched it on. While I navigated the city with trepidation, I listened to every call the cops radioed to each other. So far, they were searching nearby neighborhoods and woods, so they hadn't reached town yet. My instructions were absolute from Gavin: get in the car left at the mouth of the canyon and get the hell out of town. There was no time for a family reunion.

Gavin had months to plan this for me and prep the car for my escape. Hidden beneath a suitcase of clothes in the trunk's floor panel were a couple of weapons, stacks of cash, and fake IDs. Though he had thought about everything, there was one more thing I had to do.

After parking the car in the alley connected to the shop's street, I quickly crept onto the sidewalk, the cool breeze brushing against my cheek. I stood there a moment, taking it all in. It was finally silent—no sound of helicopters flying overhead or sirens blaring down the main road, only cars and people walking. I felt the tension in my body slowly ease, a moment of relief washing over me.

Even though the prison didn't keep me locked in my cell twenty-four hours a day, I knew now the air I breathed was mine and mine alone.

It meant *freedom*.

The block was already teeming with city folk. I knew it wouldn't be long before the cops came here. Since it was November and unusually cool that morning, I shoved my hands into my pockets, hurrying down the row of shops toward mine.

Once I spotted Sinful Marks Tattoos, I moved to the back alley and lightly tapped the steel door by the dumpster.

Within minutes, it cracked open, revealing Gavin's bright hazel eyes, wide with shock at the sight of me. "Jesus, Keelan! Get the fuck in here," he said, gesturing for me to come inside, but he wouldn't let me pass him in the hallway that led into the shop. His light-brown skin flushed, and he visibly tensed. "You weren't supposed to come here. I gave you specific instructions to—"

"I know, but I need the box and a few other supplies you didn't put in there," I said, watching his body go still. "Please tell me you still have her box?"

Gavin swallowed nervously and nodded. "It's in a safe inside my apartment. I moved closer to the shop a year ago after you got locked up. I'll grab it and meet you somewhere else."

I shook my head. "Maybe it's better if I get it and you stay behind. Your apartment might be the first place the police go looking for me." He didn't respond to that, only his dark brows pinched together. "I won't get caught," I added.

Gavin scoffed. "Yeah, that's what you always say, and look at what happened a year ago." There was a long pause before Gavin's lip pulled up into a grimace. "It won't matter. The safe is fingerprint-coded. I'm the only one that can get inside. Just give me an hour."

After a moment, Gavin reached out and pulled my muscular frame into his lanky arms. His curly golden-brown hair was shorter now, barely touching the top of my shoulders when he pulled me into a hug.

"Good to see you, cousin." I hugged him tightly. "How's Mia?" We pulled back, and he gestured with his head into the shop.

Fuck.

I glanced over his shoulder and saw my half-sister, Mia, busy sanitizing a table at the front right as she prepped for the shop's opening in a few hours. "Gav, please tell me she's your assistant or, better yet, just visiting?"

Gavin shook his head. "Naw, she's the real deal, man. Mia's getting good, too. Mom says she's almost as good as you. A few more months, and she won't have to be my apprentice anymore."

I swallowed down my nerves. This wasn't the life I wanted for her. Ever.

"Don't worry," Gavin said, seeing the look on my face. "She's not doing that other shit. What she draws and sells is legit. I won't let them drag her into this."

That didn't calm my nerves one bit. The fact that Mia was even inside that tattoo shop made my stomach clench.

"You need to get out of here," Gavin said while my eyes stayed on my sister. "One hour, and I'll meet you at Roma's Cafe."

Before leaving the shop, Gavin gathered a few more items for me I had requested, and I slipped through the back alley and into the getaway car. I kept Gavin's hoodie zipped high on my neck and the hood over my head. The thing barely fit, but I was too recognizable with my tattoos.

Once at the café, I slipped inside the front door, brushing my shoulders with a customer exiting through the doorway. No one paid me any mind. They all had lives and jobs that were too important to notice beyond that.

I chose the table farthest from the door but stayed alert, observing each person entering to order their drinks. I lowered my hands, concealing the tattoos that stretched from the top of my knuckles to my wrist. If anything, my tattoos alone would identify me to every officer in the city. I couldn't stand out. Gavin had to take his precious time, so I tapped my fingers on my thighs, waiting.

My body tensed over the next hour as I watched people come in and out to order their drinks. There were even a handful of officers at one point, but they never looked my way. Thank God it was the breakfast rush, so there were enough people to obscure my presence. "Come on, Gavin," I whispered. "Where the fuck are you?"

After a middle-aged woman in a black blazer ordered her drink, she spun on her heel and rushed toward the door, as if she were late for work. The moment she grabbed the handle, Gavin walked in, almost knocking her over with the door while his head was down, his ball cap low and covering most of his face.

After Gavin spotted me, he moved to the back and sat down. He pulled his backpack off his shoulder, unzipped it, and reached inside.

"Thank fuck," I cursed as Gavin retrieved the metal box and set it down between us. "That's all I have to go on."

Gavin gave me a strange look, his dark brows pinching together. "Do you honestly think you'll find out where she's hiding from the contents of this box?"

I shrugged. "Sadie hated her life. She kept everything that meant anything to her inside this box. It was a sacred gem she kept locked inside her closet on the top shelf. She didn't let anyone look inside, not even me."

"And what makes you think you can open it? You need a code."

I smirked. "Because I know the code. I just gave Sadie the respect of never using it."

Gavin let out a small chuckle. "And now?"

I smiled as I reached for the box, my fingers curling around the handle as I pulled it closer to my chest. I tapped my thumb on the cold, metallic lid, eyes narrowing on the numbered buttons. "My little princess put me behind bars, Gav. You think I give a shit about losing her respect right now?"

Entering the numbers, I sucked in a breath. Even though I knew it was her first dog's birthday, Sadie could have easily changed it before she ran from me. But when 1203 worked, I smiled to myself.

The first thing that surprised me was her wallet. I flipped it open, and there was her driver's license, a wad of cash, and even her passport below it. There was also a photo of a white house with black shutters and a cream-colored picket fence surrounding wildflowers. It looked aged, like she had taken it years ago while traveling across the country during one of their family vacations. It was one of the few times she felt like her father loved her.

"Well, she's not using her name wherever she ran to. She didn't bother taking any of this shit."

I sifted around the box, pulling out more items and placing them on the table.

Most of it looked like letters, written in black pen and folded several times until you could fit them in the palm of your hand. I opened the first one and found a letter from her mother tucked inside, which took me aback.

She wrote it six months before authorities arrested me.

"Sadie hated her mother," I noted. "They never talked, let alone wrote each other sentimental letters."

Gavin leaned forward as I looked at it. "Well, what does it say?"

A decent man would have respected her privacy by folding it up neatly and placing it back where he found it. Except, I wasn't a decent man.

Sadie,

We miss you. I know moving out and getting your own place was best for you. You've always had people taking care of you, and we never gave you the independence you needed to become the woman you were meant to be. But that doesn't mean I don't wish you well because I want you back. Maybe we can catch up and have dinner at your favorite restaurant, Bella Cucina, and have a glass of wine together. Please call me.

-Love, your mother

I leaned back in my chair and stared at the letter, tapping my thumb on the table rhythmically.

"What is it?" Gavin asked when my brows furrowed.

"This letter," I said. "None of it makes sense."

"What do you mean?" he questioned.

I looked at him, my eyebrows raised. "Come on, Gavin. You knew Aisling and Sadie weren't exactly on friendly terms. Aisling is trying to tell her daughter something. Something she'd want to keep from Finn. *Especially* Finn."

Everyone on both sides of the family knew nothing was safe around Finn. If you had secrets, you better find a damn good way to keep them hidden. Finn had control over everything Sadie did.

"True. Even if Sadie kept that box hidden, she'd be a fool to say something outright," Gavin noted.

"Exactly."

"So, what are you suggesting?"

"I'm suggesting that Sadie and her mother were much closer than Sadie made it out to be."

I moved more contents from the box around and found a copy of one of Sadie's favorite books, *Under the Yellow Sun*, a gift from her best friend, Cait, when they were younger. She took that book everywhere and read it at least a handful of times. I stared at the cover a minute longer before putting it back. But as I turned the book with the pages facing down, something fell out, and I caught it before it hit my lap.

"What's that?" Gavin asked, leaning forward slightly, but I didn't turn it toward him. I was almost speechless by what I saw.

"A bleeding heart flower," I said. "A laminated, pressed flower Sadie used as a bookmark." I quickly slid it into my back pocket before setting the book back into the box. "It's nothing."

Irritation ran through me, but I swallowed it and cleared my throat.

"Alright, besides a few other letters, not much else is in here."

"What now?" Gavin asked.

"Now," I started, "I track down her mother. Because I promise you, she knows exactly where her daughter is hiding."

CHAPTER 6

Keelan

In this crouched position, the muscles in my calves and quads began to burn and cramp, but I couldn't risk moving from the hedges, or Finn's men would spot me. The sun had set a few hours ago, shrouding the manicured landscape in darkness. Once the shift started, I could move freely.

As newly elected mayor of Los Angeles, Finn Ryan had access to the Getty House, but he felt the home was beneath his powerful status, so he only went there for appearances. He spent most of his time in his mansion in Hidden Hills. There was no sign of any additional police presence on the property. I only assumed that Finn was overly confident in his security and didn't want cops skulking around his pristine home.

From Gavin's information, Finn had men on rotation across the grounds every hour. There would be a small window of opportunity to sneak in, roughly around eight o'clock. When the third shift of guards went to exit the compound through one of the access roads on the east wing, there would be a two-minute gap where the backyard was unguarded. That would be my chance to cross the yard and get to the back door that the house employees used. Finn would never allow those beneath his status to use the front entrance.

I snorted. *Your worst nightmare is coming inside, Finn.*

The crackle of static on my left had me crouching even lower to the ground. The indistinct murmur of a man's voice told me it was time to move. I waited for the guard to pass the hedge and turn the corner. The security shift was starting, and it was time to move.

Now.

I crawled free from the hedges, my skin itching from the fucking branches, and made my way to the wall of the house. Cameras were everywhere, so I wore dark grays and blues to throw off the video feed. When I reached the door, I blew out a breath.

Almost there.

Suddenly, it swung open before I could grab the handle, and a blond-haired man stepped out. Before he turned, I wrapped my hands around his head and jerked hard. There was a sharp crack, and his body fell toward the ground, dead. I quickly tucked it into the shrubs next to the door, ensuring nothing stuck out for someone to see.

Seeing an opportunity, I stripped him of his jacket and pants, pulling them over my clothes. I tugged the collar high on my neck to conceal my tattoos. Luckily, the guy was roughly the same size as me, making the disguise easier. That was what I thought until I tried on his clothes and realized they were a bit too snug for the amount of movement I'd be doing. But if any staff spotted me, I'd at least blend in.

After double-checking my surroundings, I opened the door and snuck inside. The room was empty; from a glance, it was the laundry room. The smell of linens and detergent hit my nose, triggering an itch that threatened to devolve into a sneeze. I tugged on the collar that scratched around my throat. I needed to get moving.

Slowly, I crept out of the laundry room toward a narrow set of stairs leading to the upper-level offices. Finn conducted all his business from home. Sadie had once mentioned that her dad "felt like the true king of California, meeting his lowly subjects in his castle." The thought made me smirk.

The king needs the guillotine. But first, I need to find his queen.

Reaching the top of the stairs, I looked around, my ears honing in on the silence. According to my intel, Finn was in Vegas for a business meeting. So, it was just the evening house staff and Aisling.

One of Finn's larger offices was down the hallway, along with the primary bedroom. Assuming Aisling was in there, I headed that way. God, I could barely move in these tight-fitting clothes.

Hopefully, I'll be in and out within the hour.

It was then that I heard a heavy thud coming from the office. The mahogany door was slightly ajar, so I crept closer and listened.

"Oh, fuck! That's right! Right there! Fuck me, just like that ...."
A woman moaned in pleasure, her breathy sighs floating from the doorway. I slowly peered around the doorframe. Aisling perched on Finn's black marble-topped desk with an empty bottle of wine beside her.

Her skirt had hitched up around her hips, and she had splayed her legs wide, resting her black Louboutin heels on a man's bare ass. Her head tipped back, eyes shut. The man wore a white chef's coat, and his black pants pooled around his ankles. His close-cropped brown hair glistened with sweat as he fucked Aisling relentlessly on that desk. He was really going at it—the desk underneath her squeaked with every thrust.

That's most definitely not Finn. Wicked delight pulled at my lips. *The dirty bitch is fucking the personal chef. And on her husband's desk, out of all the places. She has style.*

I let her have a few more moments of her filthy pleasure before I slipped inside and cleared my throat loudly. "Well, well, what the fuck do we have here, Aisling?"

They both jerked, and Aisling's eyes widened in absolute horror when she met my gaze. The unnamed man jumped back and yanked his pants up before holding his hands out in front of him in a placating gesture.

"I'm not looking for any trouble—" was all he said before bolting for the door. Before he could pass me, I snatched the nearby bronze lamp and smashed it against the back of his head. He went down with a thump. A small pool of blood rapidly spread around him, but he was still breathing. Or he looked like he was, anyway.

"James!" Aisling shrieked, bringing her hand to her mouth while the other quickly pulled her blouse together to conceal her bare chest. "Oh, God, you killed him!"

"Relax, Mrs. Ryan. Your little chef is just out cold. He'll nap peacefully while we have a chat." I shoved the door shut and turned the lock.

Aisling stood, now yanking her skirt back to cover her long, slender legs. She tried to grab the phone, but I pulled out a hunting knife.

"Ah, I wouldn't do that. I'm just here to talk," I said, waving the knife toward an empty chair. "And you know better than to scream. You'll be dead before any of your guards can make it upstairs. Sit." I readjusted my collar with my other hand. *This fucking shirt.*

Aisling's hands trembled as she nodded in agreement and sat in the chair. She stumbled a little, clearly intoxicated.

"What do you want, Keelan? Finn's not here. And neither is Sadie."

I raised a brow. "You don't seem all that shocked to see me. Word spread already?"

Aisling pressed her lips together. Of course, the Ryans would be the first to learn that I had escaped. Every cop on their payroll would make sure to seal up this case real quick, sending an army out there to find me on their own, most likely to kill me instead of sending me back to prison. But Aisling clearly missed the memo—dismissing most of the guards on the floor so she could fuck her chef boyfriend.

"I know he's not fucking here," I growled. "But I need information ... like where Sadie's hiding."

Aisling's face paled. "You can't be serious. Why the hell would I tell you anything about her?"

I sat in the chair across from her and waved the knife at her face, the silver metal gleaming in the dim light. "Because," I drawled, "I need to find her before some very, very bad men do."

Aisling snorted derisively. "You *are* the bad person, Keelan. You slaughtered a man in front of my daughter, forcing her to run away. Because of what you did, Finn's violence toward me has kicked up a notch. If he can't have his daughter to beat, too, he gives it to me tenfold."

I found myself clutching my hand into a fist. Finn was always a fucker. I knew he had been hurting Sadie since she was little. We grew up together; I saw the bruises. Since Aisling wasn't willing to let go of the wealth, she pretended it wasn't happening, only accepting her fate that met the back of his hand.

So many times, I wanted to kill the bastard for putting his hands on his family, but my father would stop me. Telling me to mind my fucking business so I wouldn't ruin the chance of our families working together someday.

"Not as violent as I'm going to be with you if you don't start talking," I threatened.

"Right," she scoffed. "So that you could what ... find and kill her for what she did? I might not be the mother of the year, but I sure as hell know better than to send a viper her way."

"Goddammit, Aisling!" I shouted, jumping to my feet. Although I knew I needed to keep my voice down, the rage in my chest felt like it was about to explode. I pressed my knife against her throat to make a goddamn point. This little back-and-forth chat annoyed the shit out of me, as did the clothes I wore. "You and your husband signed an agreement to give her to me. That makes her my *property* now, not yours. I don't give a fuck if we aren't married yet. So, I'd be careful about what you *don't* tell me. I'm not going to kill her."

Aisling blinked, confused. Her lips parted as she tried to process my words. They seemed to have more of an impact than the knife to her throat.

"What are you talking about?" she asked, her eyes growing like saucers. "Her testimony put you behind bars for the rest of your pathetic life. How can I trust you won't punish her because of that?"

I stepped back and pulled the knife away from her throat. Running a hand through my messy hair, I felt a rush of satisfaction. "I never said I wouldn't punish her," I said, my lip turning up. "I just said I won't kill her."

On the desk, I spotted a small metal device near an ashtray and snatched it. I closed the gap between us and gripped her right wrist, yanking her off the chair and onto the ground. I drove my knee into her back and pulled her arm behind her body.

Aisling let out a wail as I leaned down to murmur my threat against her ear. "Do not scream, or I'll kill the next person who walks through that door before I fucking kill you. And it won't be a quick, painless death. If you don't talk, I'll use your beloved husband's cigar cutter to snip off every single finger on your hand and force-feed them down your throat. Tell me where she is." I touched the cold metal to her thumb.

"Chester, Vermont! She's in Vermont." Aisling broke down in tears. So, that was all it took for her to break down? A surge of rage pumped through me. Sadie was lucky someone else didn't come knocking on her childhood home before me because her mother would've spilled her location before they even started with the fun, painful part. "She's been living there this entire year."

"How do you know?"

"Because I was the one who helped her escape. Once she settled, she began writing me coded letters. Never with any details, just in case Finn figured it out. All I know is that she's working at a bookshop near the main town. Sadie leaves clues in the letters, hidden messages her brother taught her. There's a P.O. box she sends them to, so Finn never finds them. Please, Keelan, don't hurt her. I'll do anything you want. Sadie has suffered enough between our two families."

I cocked my head to the right and studied her. Yeah, it was pretty clear she and Sadie weren't the mother-daughter rivals they pretended to be with everyone around them, and though her spilling Sadie's details made me question if there was something she was hiding or if she was lying, I didn't have any other choice but to follow up with the information she gave me.

I released Aisling's arm and stood straight. Aisling scrambled to her knees and grabbed hold of my pant leg. The smell of wine rolled off her in waves, and I wrinkled my nose at her.

"You can't blame her for running away from you. From us. All of this shit. This life was never meant for her. Sadie deserved to have something better than *this*. The least you can do for Sadie is to let her live. Let her be *free* from all this ... filth. If you ever felt anything for her, anything at all, let her go."

I looked down at this blubbering woman, this absent parent who contributed to Sadie's loneliness and cowardice. I bared my teeth in a savage, mocking grin.

"Dear Aisling, I can't leave my wife alone," I said. "She's far too valuable to me. I have to protect what is mine. But I do agree with one thing. Once I have her again, she will never, ever look into her pathetic father's eyes again. Perhaps yours, too."

Aisling released my leg, clutching her stomach as tears streamed down her cheeks. Her eyes scanned my face for any mercy. "My sins will never be forgiven. The damage already done to Sadie will forever burn inside my soul. She's too good for you. She's too good for all of us. You'll *break* her!"

"Maybe that's the point," I said, staring at the woman pathetically begging at my feet.

My body felt like I had fallen into icy water at those words. Though, I didn't give a fuck. I'd bury that nagging guilt inside my head as soon as I walked out of that door.

"If I were you, I'd find a way out now. The next time I step into this city and face those who didn't do shit to help me get out of that hellhole, I'm going to burn them and everyone they love to the fucking ground." That was my *one* courtesy to my wife's mother. There wouldn't be another one. The next time I returned to the town, everyone would pay.

I spun on my heel, walked past James, who moaned softly on the Persian rug, and unlocked the door. I peered over my shoulder, and Aisling drunkenly climbed to her feet, tears mixed with mascara running down her face like inked scars.

"Oh, and if you ever mention I was here, I'll return and fulfill that promise of snipping those dainty fingers. I'll also tell Finn you were fucking the cook. Then another person's blood will be on your disgusting family name," I warned her, and then I was gone.

Time to reclaim my prize.

CHAPTER 7

Sadie

It had been a little over two weeks since the snowstorm had moved through Chester, dropping a foot of snow in just one night. We were lucky to have only minimal damage to the trees and roads near my house and in the town where I worked. Mason closed the stop for a few days to be safe, and as soon as the snowplows cleared the roads, he reopened.

The clouds hung around for a while, but the sun finally broke through two days ago, melting the snow and leaving a sparkling frost on the tree's branches and leaves scattered on the ground.

I sipped my chai while watching the trees bend and sway in the breeze through my kitchen window. Fall was finally here. Though the leaves had lost most of their color, the beauty of Vermont was still so breathtaking.

Brian, who stayed with me for the two weeks, had gotten up two hours before me and was already deep into work at the table when I came down the stairs. While I knew he was a contract attorney, he was pretty secretive about it, especially with the high-profile clients that kept him on the road most of the year. I had asked him once about what all he did during his trips, but he'd shut the conversation down, citing confidentiality agreements and NDAs.

Alright, so I get it. I respected his privacy, given my own secrets, but I missed him when he had to leave.

Brian stood from the table, went to the coffeemaker, and poured another fresh cup. I ogled him while he took a sip. Seeing him work without wearing a sleek, expensive suit was still strange. Brian was shirtless, his chiseled muscles and tanned skin on display, complemented by red plaid pajama bottoms. His hair, normally styled, was tousled and slightly damp, meaning he'd showered in the guest room while I slept.

Brian returned to the table, and when I went over to him, he held up one finger, silencing me while he typed. It was as if my voice would shatter his concentration and destroy the email. I tapped my fingers impatiently against my blue cat-shaped mug.

After a series of clicks on the keyboard, Brian turned to me and smiled. "Sorry, babe, I had to get that email out before eight o'clock. Now, time for a proper good morning, beautiful."

I leaned in and kissed him on his temple, smelling the cedar-scented shampoo he had brought. "I have to head out to open the bookshop in thirty minutes," I said. "What time are you flying out tonight? Will I see you when I get home at five?"

"Unfortunately, as soon as I send a few more emails, I have to get in the car and head to the airport. My client from Japan will be in New York earlier than I expected. I can't miss this meeting. I'm sorry, Tess."

"Mm, well, that's unfortunate," I purred, running my fingers through his blond hair. Brian stilled in the chair, looking up at me.

He knew what I wanted without words. "Maybe ... maybe we can make it a little *less* unfortunate."

I trailed my fingers from his hair, down his face and neck, gliding slowly over his chest and cupping his crotch.

"Tess," he moaned, the resistance evident in his tone. I knew he wanted this as much as I did. Who knew when we would see each other again and spend time like this? His work was so unpredictable.

"Come on," I pleaded, leaning down a little and slipping my fingers underneath his pant's elastic waistband. I let my nails graze against the warm, thick heat that twitched at my touch. Smooth and powerful. Male in every sense of the word. I needed his cock inside of me now.

"Tess, I need to get these emails done—"

"Those emails can wait. You won't see me for who knows how long, and I just thought you might want to fuck me on this kitchen counter before you go."

That did the trick. The last of Brian's resistance melted away, and he stood, grabbing my hips and lifting me onto the counter. His lips pressed against mine, and his tongue ravished me. "Fuck," he growled against my swollen lips, yanking my pink and white pajama shorts down my legs, along with my panties. "You're such a bad influence."

He pulled away from me only long enough to grab his wallet and pull out his "emergency" condom—neither of us could be bothered to go upstairs. I tugged at his pants, sliding them down his hips, and then pulled out his cock as the kitchen filled with the sound of foil torn. As soon as he rolled the thin layer of protection over his cock, he rammed himself deep inside of me, hard and rough. There wasn't even any foreplay, only his desperate need to give me what I begged for.

"Fuck!" I cried out, tipping my head back. God, it felt good. This was what I wanted from him: to take me mercilessly.

Brian pulled his hips back, only straying from my pussy for a moment before his entire length was back inside me—more brutal this time. My back arched as I leaned my palms against the cold marble, supporting my weight against it. Brian's gaze locked on mine; his eyes filled with the most primal lust that drove me insane.

"Is this what you want?" he demanded, his tone low. "For me to lose control like this, Tess?"

"Yes ... God, yes," I managed to muster between my heavy breaths. Most of our clothes remained on us—yet this was the closest and most intimate I had ever felt in his presence.

Especially as his hand grasped my throat, giving it a tight squeeze.

Thank you, Jesus.

There was no time to prepare for the sudden restriction, no time for my lungs to supply themselves with the much-needed oxygen as he pounded himself into me. I tried to tell him that the grip was too tight and that his fingers weren't entirely on the safe areas of my throat, but no words would leave my lips as my vision blackened. And then, in a heartbeat, my orgasm hit me.

Hard and fast, all at once.

Stars burst in my eyes as I came. It hurt and not in a good way.

I whimpered in Brian's grip, but he didn't ease his hold—not until I felt his own release hit him. He came with a groan, tensing against me before finally letting go of my throat. I drew in a sharp gulp of air. Then another.

Then I just stared at him.

What the hell just happened?

Brian removed the condom from his cock, tossing it into the trash before he tucked himself back into his pants.

"Fuck, I'm definitely going to have to shower again and change before I leave," he murmured, leaning in to plant a soft kiss on my forehead. I, on the other hand, remained seated on the kitchen counter, soaked in cum and sweat. "If I'm late, you're the one to blame because I can't resist you."

My brows furrowed. "I'm sure your client will want to hear all about it," I said half-heartedly.

A small, snuffed laugh escaped him. "I'm sure he would, but some things are for me to keep." The softness in his eyes heavily contrasted with how he had just fucked me. He didn't know *what* he was doing, but he tried. Bless him. That would be a conversation for another time. Despite my efforts, I coughed a little.

Brian's blue eyes lowered from my face to my neck, and he frowned. I knew there were red marks that would bruise quickly, and I'd have to wear a scarf to work today. It was a good thing it was cold outside.

It might even hurt to swallow.

"Oh, shit. I'm sorry." Guilt washed over Brian's handsome face as he looked at the reddening marks on my throat. "I didn't mean to. I was just ... trying to do it the way you liked."

My smile faltered, a sharp prick of guilt hitting my stomach. "I know."

Of course, it was my fault for pressuring him over the last two weeks to do something that he clearly wasn't comfortable with. Now, I had bruises, and he felt awful. It was *my* fault.

He may never want to try this again, and I wouldn't blame him.
Maybe it was a good thing.
Maybe this was something else I needed to leave behind.
To bury with *him.*

CHAPTER 8

Sadie

Having Brian sleep in my bed for two weeks made coming home to an empty house feel strangely unfamiliar. While it wasn't a permanent living arrangement, I had gotten used to it. I liked it. Regardless of where we were in our relationship status, Brian made me feel ... safe.

Since I had stayed longer than usual at the bookstore, I no longer had the energy to cook dinner, so I threw a frozen Buddha bowl in the microwave. After grabbing a bottle of mineral water from the fridge, condensation immediately formed on its surface before I poured it into a tall glass. I tossed the bottle into the overflowing kitchen trash can, but it bounced out and hit the floor with a loud clatter.

"Shit," I cursed, standing up and heading to the trash. As I tightened up the strings to pull it out, I stilled.

Wait a minute....

Slowly, I lowered the trash bag and opened the cinched plastic top, sifting through the contents. When I moved everything around until I reached the bottom, I blinked.

This was the trash can Brian threw the condom in. I saw him do it.

This was by far the most unusual rock bottom a woman could encounter—rummaging through her trash to find a discarded, *used* condom.

My mind replayed the images of everything that happened after we fucked in the kitchen, having memorized the encounter almost perfectly. The condom *should* have been right on top. I stood straight, and my eyes darted around the trash can, thinking maybe it fell out, too, but it wasn't there.

Where the hell is the goddamn condom?

A chill ran down my spine as my eyes looked around the kitchen. Maybe someone robbed me. Maybe I should call the police and—*And what,* the more rational part of my mind questioned, *tell them that the only thing the robber took was a used condom? Stop freaking yourself out.*

It *had* to have been in another one.

Quickly, I rushed into the bathroom, popping the trash can lid open and rummaging through that one as well. *Nothing.*

Did he take it with him?

As bizarre as Brian, of all people, taking a cum-filled condom with him before his trip was, I allowed my body to relax, accepting that as the only explanation. I thought about texting him, but that would have made me seem like a freak, so I sighed and gave up on the idea. Rubbing the sore spots on my throat, I turned off the lights.

As I stepped out of the bathroom, I heard a squeal and turned around quickly, my heart thumping hard in my chest.

"Poe," I yelped. "What are you doing? Sorry, sweetie. Did I step on your toe?" I leaned down and scooped him up, pressing his soft black fur against my chest as we walked to the couch. "Are you digging through my trash and pulling shit out again? If *you* took that condom ..."

Poe let out a soft purr when I squeezed him tighter before setting him down so I could grab my dinner.

I really hope I don't find it somewhere a month later. A shudder ran through me at the thought.

I propped my feet up on the coffee table while I dove into my meal, with Poe snuggling right by my side.

"It's just you and me tonight, bud," I told him. *And the mystery of a missing condom.*

After I finished dinner, I placed the plastic bowl in the trash bag, tied it off, and took it to the garage bin—out of sight, out of mind.

The wind howled, rattling the garage door and echoing loudly against the finished walls. I noticed the door hadn't closed all the way, leaving a two-inch gap at the bottom. I walked over to the wall and hit the button, but nothing happened.

Great.

Mason had done his best to upgrade his second home before I moved in, but it seemed like the breaker tripped at least once a week. If it wasn't the garage door, it was my bathroom, the kitchen, or the stove. He had been promising to have an electrician come out to repair it, but that was over a month ago.

I grabbed my phone from my back pocket and texted Mason to let him know I'd be flipping the breaker again. Maybe if I did this daily, he'd get sick of me texting, and it would force him to fix it. Or perhaps I would have to take matters into my own hands.

I went through the side door and over to the gray breaker box against the AC unit. After examining the switches, I found the culprit and flipped the garage breaker back on, along with the upstairs guest room lights that had also tripped. The wind suddenly picked up as I closed the door, tossing my long hair in my face. It was a cold, icy night, and I shivered in my thin tank top and shorts.

Maybe, someday, I'll get used to this frigid weather.

The side door to the garage was about to slam shut, but I caught it with my hand, slipping inside and locking the door.

After closing the garage again, I returned to the house and noted the time on the microwave.

Eight-fifteen.

I stretched my arms over my head and yawned. Though I'd usually stayed up until at least ten, watching television or reading a book, I felt like I had been awake for days. It didn't help that the wind rattled my windows at all hours of the night, preventing me from slipping into a deep sleep.

After splashing water on my face and changing into my silky black nightgown, I climbed into bed. I quickly adjusted my pillow before settling on the cool satin cover and glanced at my phone, intending to read for about ten minutes before falling asleep. Things rarely ever went according to my plans. I either fell asleep as soon as my head hit the pillow, or I would stay up reading for hours.

The book I was currently reading differed from the ones Mason sold in the store. Honestly, I felt a little ashamed to recommend these types of books. They were a secret part of my interests that I was too shy to share with anyone. It was a thrill for the heroine to be chased by a man who was morally ambiguous, possessive, and prone to violent behavior. But never to her. He'd treasure her even if she attempted to flee from him before he caught her, restraining her on a bed and fucking her raw while she screamed his name. I sighed. The memory of *him* popped into my mind, but I quickly did my best to chase it away. I couldn't allow myself to think about Keelan. Not after everything that had happened. And most certainly not now that I was with someone else. A good man, too, who treasured and treated me right in every way.

Though my mind tried to convince me that I only liked these things in fiction, my body didn't quite get the memo.

After flipping through a few chapters, I was already feeling myself growing wet between my legs. The heat inside me was unbearable, itching for a release. With a small sigh, I put my phone back on the nightstand, switched off the light, and allowed my hand to inch closer to my opening. I rubbed my wet clit in soft, slow circles, pushing my hips upward as pleasure tingled inside me.

"Oh, God," I breathed out softly. My pace quickened, now moving rougher and more demanding, to where my fingers left a slight sting in their wake. But it wasn't enough. Not even close. I reached over into my bedside drawer and grabbed my vibrator—pink silicone, almost eight inches. It was perfect for the blend of pleasure and pain I always craved. I flipped it on and pressed it against my opening. I was so wet already that it slipped inside me effortlessly. The little rubber rabbit-shaped nub stayed out to line perfectly with my clit, stimulating me in a way that had my entire body shaking. And my thoughts went into the darkest of my fantasies.

I slid down until I was flat on my back and looked up at my bedroom ceiling before closing my eyes, my breathing heavy as I spread my legs open wider. I pictured the face of the man from my book, the way I imagined him, anyway, straddling me and taking me as his. And I had no choice but to surrender to his mercy because I was *his,* whether I liked it or not.

CHAPTER 9

Keelan

S adie turned off the lamp on her nightstand, letting darkness into the room and allowing me to remain hidden. I was just another shadow in the closet. I waited until she was completely busy with her toy and then silently nudged the closet door open a crack and crawled out unnoticed. The soft creak was barely audible over the buzzing of the vibrator. I kneeled, and the moment my fingers touched the thick carpet, I stilled as I watched her body arch off the bed, the covers crumpling underneath. The moonlight through her window seeped into the darkness, allowing me to watch her touch herself. The sounds ... my God, the sounds she made were enough to stir my blood and whet my appetite.

For now, I can only imagine how her body trembles beneath the sheets.

I missed the way she reached her peak of pleasure beneath me as I held her down—crying my name as I fucked her relentlessly. We may have hated each other, but our chemistry between the sheets could set the world on fire. The memory of her wet tightness around my cock chased my dreams ever since they locked me up. One memory that never left me was the night we fucked on my tattoo table a few months before she saw me kill a man. It was an image that stayed with me.

For twelve months, I was away from her body. An entire year without her whimpers, moans, and breathless pleas. It was way too fucking long without making that little spoiled princess completely mine.

I arrived in Vermont just over a week ago and quickly tracked her down. I started learning her routine, watching her every move and following her home each night. *This right here has been my favorite sight yet.*

Aisling never knew her exact address, but she did know she worked in a bookshop. Once I spotted Sadie locking up late at night, I followed her home. Unfortunately, before I could make a move, I saw that a man was staying with her. But I soon realized he didn't *live* with her; it was only temporary. Not that it quelled my violent rage toward the fucker.

The bastard was a massive hitch in my plans. Instead of quickly getting into the house and waiting for the perfect moment to steal her away, I had to wait for the pretty boy to leave for good.

To say that I almost killed the motherfucker ten times was an understatement. I knew that if I slaughtered the man, Sadie would realize I was there and flee or call the cops. I couldn't fuck up my plans because he put his hands on her.

Hands that touched what was *mine.*

What was more infuriating was that Sadie *let* him. Perhaps she forgot who she belonged to, but no matter. I would remind her soon. Everything for my plan to work was in motion, and patience was the key. Tomorrow morning was when I'd make my move.

Earlier this morning, once Sadie had left for work and pretty boy had locked the house, dragging his suitcase to his car, I broke in through the side door in the garage. After scoping out ideal hiding spots and giving her cute cat a good chin scratch, I showered in her bathroom.

Thank fuck for the hot water. I was sick of the dirty motel outside of town and its abyssal water pressure. Not only that, but I felt tortured by the fact that Sadie was close yet so far away. So, when I was inside her home, I did what any sane man would do. I jerked off in her shower. Soon, I'd mark her body as mine all over again. But for now, the tile on that shower would have to do.

Life was about simple pleasures: a hot shower, the smell of ink, and Sadie's floral perfume, even if it made me sneeze. Being inside Sadie's home, taking in her scent, and seeing the knick-knacks on the shelves was all I wanted to do ... right before I shattered the perfect little lie that she built for herself.

I did almost fuck up this morning when I went around the house to the kitchen window over the back porch. The window was slightly ajar, so I could hear their bodies slapping and Sadie calling *his* name. The sound of her crying out made my blood boil. With the self-control I didn't even know I possessed, I somehow refrained from cutting his dick off right there and then.

Well, that man won't have the privilege of fucking my wife for much longer. She and I will be long gone when he comes sniffing around here again.

Another soft moan broke apart my thoughts in that dark bedroom, and everything else vanished as I watched her. Sadie was so beautiful as she was about to come undone. Her eyes were closed, slightly turned away from me as she pumped the hot pink vibrator in and out of her. My girl was fucking herself exactly how she liked it when I had her in my bed—hard and ruthless, with no mercy for her soaked pussy.

I turned my head and noticed the small wicker hamper on the left. A pair of dark pink lace panties peeked out, so I grabbed them and put them in my pocket. Once my prize was secured, I carefully moved toward her bed. Thankfully, the carpeted room muffled the sound of my hands and feet as I crawled along the floor. More than anything, I wanted to take her right then, but good things come to those who wait.

Once I reached her bed, I rolled onto my back and eased myself underneath, shifting quietly until I reached the middle of the bed. After adjusting, I found the perfect position to stay quiet and listen.

"Keelan!" she cried out.

My heart skipped a beat, and I held my breath. Had I been caught? I waited a few seconds to see if I needed to act, but I didn't hear her move, and the buzzing continued. If she had seen me, surely she would scream in terror and try to run. I did my level best to ignore the way my dick grew hard at the sound of her voice, let alone my *name*. What the fuck?

"That's it," she continued, louder this time. Her breathing was heavy, accompanied by the light squeaking of her bed as she moved her hips against the vibrator. "Fuck me harder. Please. Oh, God!"

A wide, wicked grin pulled on my mouth, and I had to bite my lower lip to suppress a groan.

Slowly, I reached into my pocket and pulled out her underwear, bringing it up to my nose and closing my eyes. As she cried out my name again, I inhaled her scent.

Jesus fucking Christ.

It was a scent that alone made me feral. Images replayed inside my mind, still embedded from when Sadie let me have her. Choking and pinning her down before I filled her up with my cum. No fucking condoms necessary.

"Yes. Yes! Oh God, Keelan! Right there. I'm going to—I'm going to come all over your big cock!"

"Fuck, princess," I whispered out loud while carefully unzipping my jeans. I pulled out my dick and rubbed myself up and down while my other hand held her underwear to my nose. By now, I was so fucking hard and aching for release that my hand was failing to provide. I needed her pussy wrapped around me, and soon, I would have it.

My little princess may have thought me a villain in her story, the man who sliced another man's throat. Good. I wanted her to be afraid. I *needed* her to be scared. Because deep down, it was obvious that even after everything I did, I was the one on her mind when she touched herself. Even when she betrayed me and had me locked away, I was still in her fantasies. I was her pleasure, the ecstasy that pretty boy blatantly denied her over and over.

Fear me, baby. I'm about to ruin this perfect little life of yours.

With a last cry, she released all the air she held in and flipped off her toy, placing it back on her dresser so she could clean it in the morning. There was a ruffle of covers, and Sadie soon fell asleep, unaware of the monster under her bed.

That's a good girl, Sadie.

Soon, it would be *my* cock deep inside her wet little pussy before she shut her eyes at night.

CHAPTER 10

Sadie

"Ah!" I cried out as cold water hit my back. The shower was still not as scorching hot as I liked it. I had to step out of the tub and wait a little longer for the water to warm up. When curls of steam crept across the rose-gold shower curtain, I stepped in again, my hair and back soaking in the hot water.

Today was my day off and God, did I need it.

With the hype of the new releases finally dying down, I wasn't working ten hours a day at the bookshop like I had been. Though I normally worked on weekends, he made the exception, given how many hours I had put in over the last month. I could finally catch up on my chores: cleaning my closets, deep cleaning all the bathrooms, and grocery shopping. I even gave Poe a bath, much to his chagrin.

After washing off a day's worth of ink, sweat, and grime, I shut off the water and stepped out. I grabbed my soft towel and wrapped it tightly around my body before something caught my eye on the bathroom counter next to my contacts.

Something I was sure was not there before.

Is that ... an earring?

Next to the sink was a silver star-shaped earring with a black gem at the center. It wasn't mine.

I picked it up to examine the trinket when something else sent cold fear skidding down my spine. It looked like the tip of someone's finger had drawn a small heart against the steamed-up mirror.

I swallowed, my hands trembling slightly. "Brian?" I called out, but my voice barely left my throat.

Did he cancel his trip and come to surprise me? I saw that he had returned the spare key he had been using these last two weeks under the mat.

I carefully placed the earring back down and pulled the bathroom door open slightly, the steam flowing into the cooler bedroom air. I scanned the area, taking deep breaths to calm my pounding heart.

"Brian?" I shouted, but this time, I let my voice carry.

I hurried over to my nightstand and grabbed my phone, pressing the home button—but it was off. Another wave of dread crept into my stomach. When I undressed for the shower, my phone still had at least thirty percent of battery life left. I checked for the charger I had plugged into my lamp, but it was gone.

"Shit," I cursed under my breath as panic joined the fear in a twisted dance. I looked toward the open bedroom door. "Brian, is that you?!"

Silence answered. The house was quiet. Way too quiet.

Dark ... *too* dark.

Someone's in the house.

As quietly as possible, I ran to the dresser and pulled out my underwear and black workout shorts before going to the closet. I carefully opened the door, checking for hidden intruders before snatching a red tank top from the wooden hanger. I quickly dressed and pulled my hair back into a wet bun before going back to the dresser. Opening the right top drawer, I found my black metal pocket knife that I kept close for protection. After picking it up and pulling the blade out, I wrapped my trembling fingers around the hilt tight enough to hurt. With how much I was shaking, I worried I would drop it.

Hurrying to the bedroom door, I looked around to search the dark hallway. "Brian, if that's you, you better goddamn say something!" I shouted as I stepped out into the hall. When silence greeted me, I swallowed hard against the icy fear coating my nerves. Brian wasn't here; I knew that. I had to get out. Climbing out the bedroom window was not an option, as the tree outside was too far away and the drop would shatter my ankles. I needed to get downstairs and out the front door.

I shut off the lights when I got home because I planned to crash after the shower. Now, I couldn't risk turning them on, as it would give away my location to whoever was inside. They would catch me before I could make it out.

Growing up, I learned how to avoid my father whenever he was in a foul mood and looking for a punching bag. I became adept at sneaking down hallways and stairs to avoid his wrath. But regardless of how quiet I was, I cried every time. Even now, hot tears were streaming down my face as I crept down the hall to the stairs. My eyes scanned for unusual shadows, and my ears strained for creaks in the floor.

I had lived in fear for over a year, knowing that I had put a dangerous man behind bars. Not only that, but I incurred the wrath of his family—his father, brothers, and cousins—who were far more vicious and ruthless than Keelan ever was. He may be in prison, but that didn't mean someone loyal to the Blake family couldn't act on his orders to kill me. I didn't want to believe they'd found me, but my mind's rational, cold side scolded me for thinking anything else. Someone left a star earring on my counter, and that was way too fucking personal.

My knife shook in my hand, but I steeled myself for the possibility that I would have to kill whoever was in my house. As I moved down the stairs, the wooden steps seemed to shriek my arrival through the house, signaling the intruder that I was close. The house was so old that every step moaned with age. My teeth ground together as I tried to hurry down without more creaks and cracks of traitorous wood. After what felt like an eternity, my feet touched the living room carpet.

"Poe?" I whispered, praying he'd listen for once and come to me. I couldn't leave my cat behind. I needed to make sure he was safe. "Come here, little man." Of course, Poe wasn't sleeping on the couch like usual. He may have been in the garage, where he liked to sneak into, which could work in my favor. If I could bolt to the kitchen and grab my car keys, I could catch him and get in the car. The house was too isolated in the woods for me to escape on foot. If someone were chasing me, I'd have nowhere to go safely.

I was not about to be hunted down in the woods and killed like some bimbo in a horror film.

As I eased toward the kitchen, I checked for movement behind the couch or curtains. I didn't need someone sneaking up behind me. The only light source in the kitchen was the moonlight beaming through the window by the sink.

They're hiding somewhere down here. I need to get to the mudroom now!

My keys were on the counter's edge, and the mudroom was a direct shot to the garage. Mason had been using it for storage, so I kept my car outside, but the side door opened next to it. I could escape that way.

I needed to move faster.

Suddenly, a low trill came from around the corner of the mudroom, and I had to clap my hand over my mouth to stifle the yelp in my throat.

Poe. There was the little sneak.

My heart was thudding so hard against my ribs that I couldn't catch my breath. I leaned down and scooped Poe into my left arm, slinging his slender body over my shoulders so I could keep both hands free. Once he and I made it outside, I could open the car and toss him inside before we drove off to get the police.

Ten steps to the mudroom ...

Nine ...

I calculated each step to go to the counter and then to the garage.

Two more quick steps.

Seven. My keys were within reach. I scooped them up, squeezing the keys between my fingers.

I took a long stride, covering the ground as fast as possible. The door to the garage was in sight, but when I crossed the threshold, Poe slipped a little, his black and white paw knocking into my arm. The knife fell onto the floor and skidded away from me.

"Shit," I cursed, carefully adjusting Poe back on my shoulders. I couldn't kneel to grab the knife, or Poe would jump off, costing me time. I turned back to the door, and all the air in my lungs left me as I stared into beautiful, familiar blue eyes.

Oh my God. No, it can't ...

"Keelan?" His name left my lips in a trembling whisper.

How ... he can't be here ... how?

My mind reeled as I took a step back toward the kitchen. Poe jumped down from my shoulders and darted off into the darkness. I squeezed the keys harder in my hand. At least Poe got away so that Keelan wouldn't hurt him. I couldn't see the knife anywhere on the floor, but I would go down fighting if I had to; I would gouge out his eyes.

"Easy," Keelan said, his voice low and eerily calm.

"Get away from me!" I screamed, terror leaking into my voice. "Now!"

The tears were back, leaving scorched marks in their wake, and I bit back a hard sob. Keelan was here to kill me; my peace was over.

Keelan lunged for me, and I shrieked again, swinging my keys forward. The house key slashed across his hands, but it didn't stop him. He wrapped his tatted arms around my waist, pulling me further into the kitchen. I frantically looked around before grabbing the pan I had used that morning, silently thanking my scatterbrain for leaving it out for later. I gripped the handle and swung it behind me. The pan cracked hard against Keelan's skull.

He cursed and fell back, releasing his grip on me just enough for me to slip from his hold and run to the front door. The door was locked, but not just the handle. The remaining three bolts that I had put in place were securely shut.

"Shit. Shit. Shit!" I frantically unlocked each one.

I had one left, but I didn't even touch it before Keelan wrapped his arms around my waist again from behind and hoisted me up in the air.

"Let me go!" I kicked my legs out, wriggling my body so I could slip out from the crushing hold he had around me. He didn't even budge or flinch; he was too strong. My nails dug into his hands, leaving behind thin trails of blood as I fought to break free. "Keelan! Stop!" My cries echoed through the hall as he forcefully sat me down, slamming my back into the wall. I felt trapped, pinned by his firm grip on my throat. He squeezed slightly, just enough to warn me to stop resisting. His body caged mine, and I couldn't slide my leg up to kick him in the balls. He had me trapped.

"My, my, sweet Sadie. You have some fight in you. Honestly, I'm relieved. Back in Los Angeles, you were aways so docile and weak. Afraid. I like this side instead. It's more fun when you fight against me."

"Fuck you!" I cursed, but that only caused his face to harden, his eyes turning dark, and his fingers seized my throat, cutting off my air.

"Hmm, that wasn't what you were saying last night when you were fucking your little toy. In fact, now that I have you pinned against me, maybe we can recreate that moment for you. The one you're going to pretend you didn't want. The one where you'll pretend you weren't picturing my face as you came."

My eyes grew wide with horror. Keelan was in my room. *Oh my God.*

I dug my nails into his wrist. "You're ... sick," I seethed as my air dwindled. All Keelan did was smile at my struggle, showing his perfectly straight, white teeth. He leaned closer, pressing his chest against mine. His intoxicating scent flooded my nose. The smell I remembered from so long ago, from when we first started hooking up. It was my weakness. *He* was my weakness. A beautiful devil painted like a canvas, drawing me into his dark embrace.

The grip on my throat lessened, allowing me to take a shallow breath. Keelan stroked a loose, damp curl that had come loose from my bun.

"I like the red in your hair; it suits you," he murmured.

I blinked. "Wha ... what?"

The way his voice flipped from cold and cruel to ... kind. Keelan's demeanor completely shifted into something else. For a moment, I found myself lost in the lie, drowning in his captivating voice.

The song of a monster.

"Are you going to kill me?" I asked, though I knew the answer. I was the reason why they locked him up for life. He'd been a prisoner for the last year. Of course, he was here to take revenge.

"Mmm," he growled. He actually *growled* while biting his bottom lip, making it clear that I was his prey and he could devour me at any moment. "Not yet," he said.

Right. Keelan came all this way to track me down just to talk about my hair color.

"What do you want, then?" I asked, pressing my hand against his chest—a feeble attempt to create more space, but he wouldn't budge. "I'm sorry, okay? I'm sorry."

No, I wasn't sorry. Keelan sliced a man's throat in front of me and deserved to be locked away. But I had to say anything to placate him. To walk out that door alive.

A million questions floated in my mind as he stared into my eyes. How did he get out of prison? Was he released? Was his family right outside the door, waiting for him to drag me out so they could help him dispose of my body?

Suddenly, the tip of his other hand, the one that wasn't wrapped around my throat, touched my chest, a ginger touch that sparked a warm, confusing feeling deep in my gut. He slowly dragged his finger down to the center of my sternum, and I stiffened.

What is he doing?

Keelan then slid my tank top straps down my shoulders, and my breath hitched.

"Keelan," I said, but my voice came out breathy, cutting off the rest of what I wanted to say.

"Yes, princess?" he said. That was the nickname he gave me after our parents forced us to get engaged. He annoyingly used it often, typically preceded by the words "spoiled little," belittling me as a brat who always got her way.

How little he knew. I never had a choice in my goddamn life.

My fucking family made every choice for me. Every decision was in the hands, or fists, of my asshole father. Until my escape, my mom did little to stop his tyranny, and my brother was long gone.

Keelan's grip tightened a little more when I moved my head to the side, trying to ignore the growing wetness between my thighs. His finger moved lower, pausing at the hem of my shorts.

"Don't play fucking games with me, Keelan," I snapped, despite the lack of air. "What the hell are you trying to do? If you're going to kill me, just do it. Don't touch me like you missed me."

Keelan's grin broadened, having the audacity to smile. "You act like you're afraid of me, and rightfully so. But maybe I can help you relax ... like you did last night while I hid under your bed, stroking my cock as you cried out my name."

What a fucking psycho, I thought, except there was a slight flip in my stomach at that, though. God, my thoughts were just as screwed up as his were. Now that he was impossibly close, I didn't want to utter a single word. His hand pulled at the hem of my shorts, and his fingers slid underneath, inching further, touching my wetness. Keelan only prodded gently at first, like he wanted to get a reaction out of me, but I wasn't about to give him one.

My body, however, didn't get the memo. It arched involuntarily against his fingers as Keelan slid inside of me.

Closing my eyes, I tried to go somewhere else as he fucked me with his fingers, his warm breath now caressing my ear, but I couldn't. It was *his* face that I saw as he moved in long, rough strokes that hit all the right places. I sunk my teeth into my lip, not wanting to make a single sound. My body had betrayed me enough already.

"How often do you do that?" he asked. "Fuck yourself while you think of me?"

I shook my head, not wanting to answer those questions. Hell, it was hard to focus on them in the first place with the way pleasure was spreading through me. I hated that *this,* as fucked up as it was, was still the thrill I sought.

"Last night, I came on your carpet while under your bed," he continued. "I thought about straddling you while you slept, jerking off again until I came all over your naked chest, but I convinced myself that would probably be a bad idea. Taking you by surprise and chasing you down the hall was much more fun." He leaned forward until his lips touched my ear. "Pulling the soiled condom from the trash and leaving you an earring with a little heart-shaped note on the mirror—painting the scene to make you paralyzed with fear."

My eyes widened. *Jesus Christ.*

His movements sped up, pumping me faster while my chest heaved. I tipped my head back as pleasure rippled through me. I tried desperately to keep the sensation at bay, but it was pointless. My body was betraying me in the vilest ways. Keelan was a killer. I shouldn't *want* this.

Damn him. The psycho knew *exactly* what I liked. Exactly what I craved. A shudder rolled through my body as my pussy continued to throb around his fingers, more intense with each passing second, until I could no longer hold back.

It wasn't long before my orgasm consumed me. My whole body trembled as I cried out, right as Keelan's hand squeezed my throat. It was just like in the past when we fucked, pinning me down and keeping me where he wanted to as he made me come.

"Fuck, Sadie," he cursed. "You're such a good girl. I practically came in my jeans just from your moans alone."

A sudden guilt wrapped around me, and my cheeks flushed, as if someone had poured a bucket of cold water over me when the realization of what had just happened settled. It was even more fucked up as Keelan pulled his hand out of my pants and proceeded to lick his fingers, *tasting* me.

"Now," he said as he stepped back, giving us a small amount of space, just enough for me to catch my breath and process what the fuck just happened, "tell me where I can find some rope."

His gaze was as intense as ever, drinking in the sight of me. It was like he was observing every inch of my body, but something about his expression changed as his gaze landed on my throat, illuminated by the soft light from the moon outside the front door window. Keelan trailed his finger over the side of my neck—weirdly soft compared to what he had just done.

"I'm pretty fucking good at choking that delicate neck of yours without leaving marks, Sadie." His eyes turned more darkly intense as he continued to stare at the bruises on my neck—the marks that Brian accidentally left me. "How the *fuck* did you get these?"

CHAPTER 11

Sadie

When I refused to answer, Keelan grabbed my wrists and dragged me across the room to the sofa. I dug my heels into the carpet, but it was to no avail.

"You're going to make this harder than it has to be, aren't you?" he said, his eyes briefly skating down to my throat again where the bruises were. As I debated covering my injuries with my hand, he shoved me onto the couch. There was an uncomfortable pause as his nostrils flared, and his eyes pierced into mine. "I have to tie you up, Sadie. *Rope*. Where is it?" His jaw tightened. My noncompliance was already irritating him, much to my satisfaction. I was positive that Mason had something like rope in the garage, but I wasn't about to share that.

I leaned back against the soft cushions, folding my arms over my waist.

"Really, Sadie? Are you going to make me drag you around this fucking house?" I pinched my brows together and lifted my chin.

I wasn't going to cooperate, and the bastard knew it.

"Fine," Keelan said. "Dragging you around, it is. Let's go." He reached down, seized my thin wrist in a vise grip, and lugged me to my feet. He dragged me through the house until we went into the garage. There, Keelan found a pack of zip ties in Mason's tool chest. "This will do."

He moved me back to the couch and sat me down on the floor, proceeding to zip tie and secure my ankles and wrists with them. He then took some blue ribbon he found in my crafting chest, weaving through the holes to secure me to the heavy coffee table. While the throw rug I sat on was soft, my lower back ached.

"Alright, I think you're secure enough. Do you want some water?" Our gazes locked, mine burning with fury, his cold and smug. Anxiety pulled at me relentlessly. I had no idea what he had planned, and the wait made it so much worse. At least if he was going to kill me, I could prepare myself. Waiting for the unknown was torture.

When I pressed my lips together and didn't answer, he ran his hand through his dark hair, clearly frustrated. He styled it differently now since the last time I saw him. One side of his head had been shaved close to the scalp, with the longer hair brushed over it. Before he went to prison, he let the wavy locks hang loose around his ears, concealing some of his piercings.

Now, the haircut accentuated all the tattoos on his neck. Shapes and shadows danced and clashed across the skin of his throat. From the looks of it, Keelan had gotten a few more pieces on his arms. Little of his tanned skin was visible under all that artwork, ink trailing from his knuckles along his muscular arms and shoulder and painting his entire torso down to his hips.

But Keelan kept his face unmarked; his beautiful, cold features didn't need any ink. He was alluring despite his tainted, evil heart.

"No, I'm fine," I finally answered. I didn't want Keelan to slip something into the water and drug me. While he had never hurt me physically in the past, that was before I betrayed him.

Keelan's eyes narrowed, and he kneeled on the floor beside me. He grabbed my tied wrists and leaned in. I watched as his Adam's apple bobbed while he re-examined the darkening bruises on my neck from Brian.

"He didn't mean to do that," I said, knowing exactly what he was thinking. "Brian cares about me, Keelan. He'd never do this on purpose—"

"And yet ... he did."

My brows furrowed as his blue eyes grew dark, nostrils flaring in ... anger. Was he angry about me being hurt?

"It was an accident. Those happen, you know?"

"Not when you're experienced and know what to do. Which, clearly, he doesn't." His tone grew bitter as he spoke. I knew better than to argue with him, so an awkward silence fell between us. "Are these too tight?" He rubbed his thumbs against my skin near the ties.

I shook my head, trying to ignore the smell of him near me. "No. It's fine."

Keelan inhaled sharply before standing up, moving to the reclining chair, and settling into the cushions.

"Are you expecting any visitors over the next few days?" Fear rattled me as I shook my head. Was he planning to torture me for that long before killing me?

Over the last twelve months, my social circle has been pretty pathetic. Sure, I had met a few women in town with whom I would meet for coffee or wine on the weekends. But it never expanded to visits to my house. Mason, who was like family, never came over unless there was a maintenance issue. Given my circumstances, I liked my privacy and space. Now I was alone ... and not even the neighbors would hear me scream.

"Good," he said, glancing at the wall clock behind me. "I'm going to hop in the shower, and then we're going to bed. It's past midnight, and"—he smiled widely—"we have a very long week ahead of us."

I squeezed my eyes shut and dropped my head. I didn't want to play whatever game he was concocting. If he was trying to drive me insane, he was doing a great job at it.

"I don't get it," I said. "You hunted me down, broke into my house, and tied me up. What do you want if not to kill me?"

The bastard shrugged. "Let's just say you're more valuable alive than dead. I'll explain more on the drive."

My head turned up. *Drive?*

"What do you mean 'drive?'" I asked cautiously. "Where are you taking me?"

"Home."

"Home?" I repeated. "Keelan, *this* is my home now. Besides, if you don't kill me, your family sure as hell will the minute I'm spotted in Los Angeles." I stopped, watching the smug grin on his face grow bigger. Temper flared in my head. "Did you really break out of prison, drive three thousand miles to find me, just to take me back to California?"

Keelan just kept looking at me with that damn beautiful smile.

"You do realize that you're a fugitive, right? Meaning that if a cop stops us and recognizes you, you're going right back to prison."

And I'll happily testify again to make sure you rot forever.

"Then we'll have to work extra hard not to get caught."

"There's no 'we' in your scheme. *You* thought it would be a good idea to kidnap someone and then force them on a cross-country drive back to where they imprisoned you in the first place instead of lying low. That's literally insane." Shaking my head, I scoffed. "How did you even escape, anyway?"

"The details aren't important."

Oh, great. "Did you kill people again?"

His lips turned up. "I didn't kill anyone."

Silence spread across the room. What that meant was Keelan may not have pulled the trigger; someone he hired or that his family hired did the killing. Not that it mattered. It was all the same to me.

Death by his hands.

His gaze intensified, forcing me to avert my eyes from his. Whenever he looked at me, his expression was always too intense. Of course, Keelan always acted inconvenienced by my presence unless I stripped off my clothes for him. For the sake of our families' business agreement, we tried to tolerate each other. There was no love and certainly no respect. If anything, we used each other's bodies to numb the situation our fathers tied us to so we didn't kill one another.

"Come on," he said, grabbing the scissors from the coffee table and heading toward me. I tried to wrench on the plastic ties to get them to break, but they just burned into my wrists. Keelan crouched down and cut the ribbon instead of slicing my throat. Then he held onto my wrists and lifted me to my feet.

"I'm going to trip up those stairs," I grumbled.

Keelan looked down and nodded before cutting my ankles free. "It's a good thing you have a whole stack of these ties. I'll re-tie new ones once I get you on the bed."

"I'm not going to lie in the same bed with you!" An angry growl escaped my lips. "Tie me up. I don't give a shit. But you're sleeping on the floor. That's the least you can do after putting me through all this."

A laugh escaped Keelan's lips, his grin growing into a playful smile. "Oh, you're still the little princess I remember. If you think, after months of sleeping on a prison bed, that I'll take the floor over that soft, plush mattress, you're out of your goddamned mind."

Once he had me on my feet, he pulled me to his chest and looked down, his tall, muscular six-foot-four body towering over mine.

I'd forgotten how tall he was over my five-foot-seven stature.

"Then *I'll* take the floor," I suggested, practically pleading now. "Tie me to the vent. I don't fucking care. I don't want to be anywhere near you."

"Princess, I'm not so sure about that. Your eager pussy seemed to enjoy my touch not too long ago when you came all over my fingers." Keelan smirked down at me. Before I could call him a fucked-up pervert or kick him in the shin, a tiny meow broke our stare down. Poe had jumped up to the back of the couch.

Regardless of my well-being, I knew deep down Keelan would never hurt Poe. Keelan was a lot of things, but he loved animals as much as I did. Especially cats. His violence was only ever toward humans, ever since we were kids. He was a vicious asshole who thrived on hurting people. But animals? Never.

"What's your cat's name?" he asked, still holding the zip ties with one hand and scratching Poe behind the ear with the other. By how Poe leaned into the scratching, it seemed he liked Keelan well enough—little furry traitor.

"That's Poe," I explained, my voice trembling slightly. "I found him as a stray in the forest while on a run last spring. Someone had dumped him there."

Keelan's blue eyes softened. "You always wanted a cat."

I nodded. Father was allergic and hated animals in general. No matter how many times I begged him for a cat growing up, he always said no.

"Does Poe sleep in the bed?" he asked, petting him along his back. The tuxedo purred even louder, and his green-yellow eyes closed in kitty bliss.

I shook my head. "He usually sleeps down here or the bedroom window perch. But if I keep the door shut, he won't beg."

Because Brian would randomly stop by to stay overnight, I had to keep my bed clean from cat hair. But I couldn't tell Keelan that; it would send him into a rage at just the thought of another man beside me while I slept.

Keelan nodded. "Alright, then. We'll keep the door shut. I need to know that if you try to run, you have a few barriers to slow you down."

I knew then that I wouldn't run. Not while Keelan was next to me, at least.

Once tied to the bed, I leaned back, watching Keelan slowly re-move his clothes before disappearing into the bathroom. Despite already being in good shape, it was obvious that he prioritized his workout routine during his time in prison. His body was much more chiseled and toned than I remembered. I let out a small ex-hale. Keelan and my personalities constantly clashed, but physical attraction was never absent from our time together. It annoyed me that was still the case. I felt fucked up in all kinds of ways. And that was precisely why I needed to find a way to get away from him.

After hearing the shower turn on, I immediately started work-ing on slipping my wrist through the zip ties. Keelan had kept them somewhat loose, so they didn't pinch my skin but not loose enough that I could slip my thumb through it without breaking the bone first.

I had another idea: slide the plastic up and down the metal headboard poles until it shaved off enough to snap it free.

It would take me hours.

I didn't have hours. My heart was hammering again; I had to get out of this.

After fifteen minutes of rubbing the inner part of the zip tie against the metal post, the shower turned off, and I stilled. "Shit." I was out of time.

When the doorknob turned, I sat upright, resting my back against the bed and straightening the blanket with my untied hand.

Keelan came out with a towel wrapped around his hips, water trickling down his torso over the raven tattoo that covered his belly.

My breath hitched as he bent down to pick up his pants, and the towel moved slightly. I swallowed and turned away, not wanting to watch when it fell to his feet.

"I need to throw these in your wash. Where is it?"

"Are you planning on making yourself at home?" I sneered. The bastard was acting like this was his place, too, and I hated it.

"Sadie," he said, my name like a warning of punishments to come if I didn't answer. "Where's the washer and dryer?" He wouldn't ask me again.

Despite the fear and something darker roiling in my stomach, I rolled my eyes and jerked my head to the bedroom door. Having Keelan away a little longer would give me a chance to focus on getting out of the restraints without being distracted by his chiseled, half-naked body.

"Down in the garage. There're detergent pods on the shelf above them."

"Alright," he said, eyeing my laundry basket by the closet, throwing his stuff on top, and then picking it up. "Stay put now." He walked past me with a broad smile and then had the audacity to wink at me as he left the room. With all the time I spent away from him, I forgot how much I hated that man.

The moment he stepped into the hall, I got to work, sliding the zip tie up and down and wincing every time the plastic bit into my skin. In my mind, a plan had already developed. With the washing machine being as old as it was, it usually took a little while to get started. I'd grab Poe and run to the nearest gas station. In my frantic head, that made perfect sense ... aside from one thing. I couldn't free my hands.

I might have to break my thumbs.

Shit! This wasn't working. I kept at it, sliding it up and down the headboard posts, watching the cheap paint chip off little by little.

After roughly ten minutes, I gave up, plopping back on the mattress and looking up at the ceiling fan, tears once again running down my face.

I'm dead. There was no way out of this. Right now, he was playing with me, but the moment I let my guard down or stopped being valuable to him, he was going to kill me for what I did to him.

Keelan walked back into the room and stopped at the edge of my bed. "Alright. I'll throw everything in the dryer in the morning. For now, it looks like I'll be sleeping naked."

"Absolutely not. Are you insane?" I barked out a nervous laugh, trying to move to the edge of the bed, but I winced as my chafed wrists rubbed against the zip ties. "Ow!"

Keelan slid underneath the covers before reaching over my shoulder, the mattress dipping beside me. As his arm crossed my vision, my eyes caught the sharp end of a kitchen knife. I gasped, trying to move further away, but his other arm wrapped around me and pulled me up against his chest. His hardened cock pressed up against my ass, and I stilled, a tinge of arousal hitting my core.

How can any of this be turning him on?

When I braced myself for the knife to press into my throat, he continued reaching before cutting off the ties. "You're hurting yourself, princess."

I tried to wrench from his bear hug, but he only squeezed harder, his cock once again pressing into my ass. "Why the hell do you care if I get hurt?"

He responded to me by pulling my hair tie, freeing my bun, and then burying his face in my damp hair, inhaling deeply.

This can't be happening. Is he sniffing me?

Anger burned the fear in my gut into ashes. *That bastard thinks he can do what he wants to me.*

"Keelan, I'm seeing someone else. He could call or come back at any moment. You need to stop this."

He didn't remove his irritatingly lovely face from my hair and neck, only chuckled a little before he touched my stomach. His fingers slid under the hem of my tank top and grazed the skin where the tattoos he gave me were.

"Do these marks make you think of me?"

What the hell? That's what he wants to talk about right now?

I swallowed. "Never," I lied. "I wish I could burn them off." In fact, briefly, after I escaped, I had planned to but didn't go through with it. For whatever damn reason, I couldn't.

He chuckled again, finally moving his head back and resting it on his pillow. "Good night, Sadie," he said. "If you try to run or get out of my hold while we sleep, I'll know."

Keelan was right. He was always a light sleeper. It was rare that I stayed the entire night with him during the times we hooked up when we were engaged, but when I did, it only took a shift on my pillow for his eyes to snap open.

"And if you run, I will catch you before your feet reach the hallway. I don't have to tell you what will happen to you once you're caught because I think you know. Am I clear?"

I nodded quickly, taking heed of that warning and biting back an insult. I would wait until morning when I knew for sure I could reach my car. Until then, I had to pretend he wasn't there so I could fall asleep.

But it was going to be impossible.

Not with an escaped convict keeping me caged against him.

CHAPTER 12

Sadie

The urgent need to pee stirred me awake, my eyes fluttering against the streams of sunlight coming through the open bedroom window. The warmth pressing against my back and legs reminded me of who was sleeping next to me. With Keelan's arms wrapped around me like a blanket, I began to sweat uncomfortably.

"Keelan," I murmured, looking over my shoulder. "I need to pee. Let go."

He squeezed my waist tightly before releasing me, allowing me to sit up and move free of the covers. I stretched my arms overhead, hearing the snaps and pops in my shoulders from being held in one position all night.

Quickly, I scurried into the bathroom, shut the door, and locked it. I pressed my hands against my eyes, releasing a shaky breath. I couldn't think clearly with Keelan in my space. My heart thudded as the dangerous situation took root. I *had* to figure out how to escape that monster in my bed and disappear. I'd likely never be

able to return to this life I'd built, but Poe and I could go somewhere else. The idea of starting over again made my throat tighten,
but I couldn't allow myself to become a prisoner again. I needed
to make a bulletproof plan—no sudden, irrational decisions. Sadie
Ryan must be smart about this.

If only I had the brains of my brother, God rest his soul.

After relieving myself, I went to the sink and washed my hands
before I took a good look at myself in the mirror.

I look like I wrestled with a bear.

The state of my red hair, tangled and mussed, and my bloodshot,
swollen eyes were a clear sign of how much I cried last night. I
grabbed a hairbrush and combed through the knots and snags.
Then, I splashed cold water over my face, alleviating the raw heat
in my eyes.

Think. There had to be something in the bathroom I could
use as a weapon. Small scissors, a razor, hairspray? How far was I
willing to go? Would I be able to kill Keelan if it came to that?

As I kneeled to open the bathroom cabinets under the sink,
Keelan knocked on the door sharply, startling me. "Sadie, I don't
like you having the door locked against me. I would hate to break
it off its hinges if you don't come out now."

Fuck off.

I swallowed, knowing he'd question any response I gave. "Keelan, I can't go anywhere. So, how about you let me wash my face
in peace?"

He sighed as if frustrated and stepped away, taking his shadow
under the door's crack with him. I took a deep breath to steady my
nerves and returned to my search.

For an added measure, I turned the faucet on again.

Looking into the cabinet, I moved things around as quietly as possible. I pulled out a plastic storage container and sifted through its contents. There were bottles and brushes, but then I spotted my eyebrow tweezer. This one had a sharper edge. It would do.

Do what exactly?

I didn't know yet, but having something sharp in my hand wouldn't hurt. I cursed myself for throwing away the hairspray last month.

With the tweezers safely nestled in the waistband of my shorts, I stood up and focused on taking slow, steady breaths to quiet my pounding heart. I unlocked the door and stepped out into the bedroom. Keelan had dressed in the same clothes he wore last night, now freshly laundered. As I walked into the room, I noticed he had not only taken my basket but also dumped all the clean clothes onto the bed, where he was now carefully laying them out to sort.

"What are you doing?" I asked, perplexed.

"Folding your laundry, princess," he turned to look at me, blue eyes shining with amusement. "Would you like to join me?"

I blinked. Seeing a unicorn jump roping would have been a more believable sight than this. "No, I don't want to join you."

Keelan's lips widened into a playful smile—the one he had given me dozens of times when my defiance amused him. "Well, if you don't fold your laundry, all your pretty clothes will wrinkle in your suitcase, sweetheart."

I snorted and crossed my arms over my chest. "Wrinkled clothes are the least of my concerns, Keelan. I'm not leaving my home. What part of that do you not understand?!"

I tried to level my best death glare at him, but that only made the asshole smile wider. "Here," he said, tossing me a pair of sweat-pants, as if he hadn't heard a damn word of what I had just said. "It's pretty cold today. Put those on."

Great. Now Keelan's dressing me like a damn doll.

Since arguing seemed futile, I glanced at the pants, bent my knee, and grabbed them. Before I slipped off my shorts, I stealthily took the tweezers out and bunched them up with the sweatpants he had thrown at me. As he turned to continue folding my clothes, I slipped off my shorts, pulled on the pants, and tucked the tweezers into the waistband.

"Sadie...." his voice trailed off as the sound of tires crunching on gravel came through the window. I stilled, hot ropes of panic seizing my stomach. "Don't—"

I bolted through the opened bedroom door, sprinting down the hall toward the stairs. If I could make it down, I could finally get help from whoever that was. Authorities would arrest Keelan again, and I'd be free. But when I reached the bottom of the stairs, the runner snagged on my right foot, sending me crashing to the floor. I opened my mouth to scream, but Keelan's rough hand wrapped around my mouth, smothering the sound. The total weight of his body pressed on me, his legs pinning my body. I grabbed onto his wrist and dug my nails into his skin, desperately trying to loosen his grip enough for me to yell. Keelan's lips grazed the shell of my ear, his breath warming my cheek.

"Shh, princess. Quiet, now," he purred before flipping me onto my back, breaking my hold on his wrists. He adjusted his grip over my mouth, legs pressed against my hips. "I don't want to remind you of what will happen if you don't behave. Blood is tough to scrub out of floorboards."

I sobbed against his palm, tears burning in my eyes. I slapped his wrist hard before letting my hands fall to my sides, brushing his knees.

Keelan exhaled softly. "Did you lie to me last night about not expecting company?" Irritation covered his every word, and I knew things rarely ended well when Keelan was irritated.

I shook my head against his hand. I wasn't expecting anyone to come by today. It was just my luck that my fugitive ex-fiancé was hiding in my house, and someone dropped by for a visit. Now, whoever was outside was in danger.

The knock at the door made us both look over, and I struggled harder under his grip.

"Stop," he hissed through his teeth, keeping his voice low. "Listen carefully. I'm going to remove my hand, and you won't do something fucking stupid, or else whoever is out there will meet a worse fate than being tweezed to death like you planned for me."

My stomach dropped. *Shit.*

"Hey, Tess?" a voice called out from the other side of the door. Oh my God. It was Mason.

I pulled on Keelan's wrist, shooting him a frantic look that I needed to talk. He eased the pressure on my mouth, allowing me to whisper.

"Who the fuck is that?" he asked, tensing his legs against my hips painfully.

"Ma ... Mason. He's my boss."

Keelan's brows furrowed. "Why is your boss at your home?"

His voice shifted into that terrifying tone I knew too well. If I said the wrong thing, Keelan would snap and hurt Mason. When we were "together," Keelan treated me like a possession. He deemed any man in my life as a threat to his prize.

"This house is his," I explained. "He's renting it to me. Mason helped me build a life when I had *nothing*. Keelan, please, he's sixty-eight years old. Old enough to be my grandfather. He doesn't deserve to be hurt. Please don't hurt him. Please."

It felt as if my pleading was futile.

Keelan looked down at me. "If he sees me, he'll be able to identify me to the cops once they realize you're missing. You know I can't let that happen."

I shook my head furiously. "Then I'll make him leave before he does. He won't come inside."

Keelan's Adam's apple bobbed, and then he nodded after a painful second.

Thank God.

Keelan climbed off of me and wrapped his hand around my upper arm, helping me stand. Before I could walk to the door, he increased the pressure on my arm to the point of pain and yanked me to him. He grabbed my chin to force my gaze on his face and leaned in close. "This is your only warning, Sadie. If you do anything that alerts him to my presence or that you're in trouble, I *will* slit his throat and make you watch his life spill out on the floor."

He would.

Keelan would be sadistic enough to kill another innocent man and make me watch. I'd seen it before, and that bastard held no remorse or guilt for his actions. That night, over a year ago, I saw the cold demon Keelan had become when our eyes locked in that warehouse. Blood soaked his white shirt, splattering his cheeks and chin. Fear had consumed me entirely then, making me sick to my stomach, yet those cold eyes never changed. It made me wonder if Keelan Blake was human at all.

I shuddered; even after all these years since we met, he was still a monster who relished in the pain of others by his hand. It was an image that I'd never been able to forget.

The thought of Keelan hurting Mason made my stomach roil so much I thought I would vomit right then and there. I had to be careful not to give anything away in my face or eyes.

"Okay," I said, nodding quickly. "I promise—I won't do anything."

Keelan led me to the front door, releasing my arm before stepping aside to lean against the wall. He nodded in agreement before I took hold of the handle and unlocked the deadbolt. The door swung open, and Mason's beaming face greeted me in the morning sunlight.

Don't cry. Just breathe. You have to protect him.

"Mason ... um, hey," I said, adding a rasp to my voice. "What are you doing here?"

Mason smiled, clearly happy to see me, as he always had been since that stormy night last fall. My mind raced with the thought that this wonderful man was in danger because of *me,* and something terrible would happen to him if I somehow made a mistake.

"Morning, Tess," he replied. "I tried calling you after your text last night about the power box going off again. I'm so sorry for the delay in fixing it. You know how busy things get at the store, and I haven't had a free moment. I'm here now, though."

"Oh, right," I said, shaking my head. "I forgot I sent you a message."

"Yeah, when I called back, it went straight to voicemail."

Because Keelan shut it off and hid my charger.

"When I went to bed last night, I let it die. It didn't even occur to me to charge it this morning. I'm sorry. I started feeling sick when I got home from the store last night. If I didn't feel better by this morning, I had planned to call you to take tomorrow off and recover."

Mason's brows wrinkled. "Sick?" he asked. "You do look a bit pale. Do you need anything?"

The fatherly tone of his questions nearly broke my heart in half, and tears pressed behind my eyes.

I shook my head slowly. "That's really sweet, Mason. I'll be okay, though. Brian dropped off some medicine before he left for New York. I honestly just need to sleep."

Mason smiled, but something in his eyes gave me pause. Concern? Worry? Was he deciding whether to stay and help with something else or go home?

Please, go home. Please.

"Look, the power box is on the side of the house," he said. "I won't have to come inside. You head back to bed, and I'll be in and out in fifteen minutes. All I need to do is change the troublesome fuses."

"Mason," I said, fighting to keep my voice steady. "You don't have to do that today. It can wait."

"I can't have the power going out on you while you're sick, Tess. It won't take long."

I swallowed hard. Mason couldn't see Keelan from the side of the house, especially outside.

"Um ... okay, sure," I said. "The stove keeps shorting out, and the garage did yesterday. Oh, and my bedroom lights."

There was a sharp pinch on my hip as I felt Keelan's fingers squeeze. Hard. He wasn't happy that I didn't send Mason away, but what choice did I have? If I vehemently denied help, Mason would suspect something. I had to let him work, and then he would leave. He would be safe.

"Okay, great," Mason said, pulling his small yellow tool bag over his shoulder. "You feel better soon, hun. Call me if you don't feel better by tomorrow or need anything."

I smiled warmly. "Thank you."

After shutting the door, I pressed my forehead against the wood and started sobbing.

"Well, that wasn't very smart of you," Keelan snarled.

"What the hell do you mean?" I asked through shaky breath, turning my furious, tear-soaked gaze to him. "He won't see you, and it's more believable to have him fix the fuses I've been asking him to do for the last month than if I just urged him away. You can wait fifteen minutes, Keelan."

Keelan's blue eyes were like chips of ice as he cocked his head. "Oh, princess. As much as I want to wait the fifteen minutes, there is one minor problem."

My eyes widened, and my stomach dipped.

"I hid my car near the carport on that side of the house. So, unless you suddenly drive a black Ford Edge, I will have to take care of the old man."

CHAPTER 13

Keelan

Sadie's green eyes widened, shimmering with tears as the reality of the situation crashed into her. I snatched her wrist and squeezed it hard enough that the bones creaked.

"We can figure something out. I can make up another lie about the car. Please," she begged, yanking against my grip.

She's going to fight me on this the entire time.

"Sorry, princess. You fucked up, and now I have to take care of this loose end."

"I didn't 'fuck up.' I did what you asked, you dick," she seethed through her teeth. "Don't hurt Mason, or I'll spend the rest of my life making yours a living hell!"

My eyebrows flew up in surprise. When did Sadie Ryan get so feisty? It didn't matter because we would do things my way, starting with the old man. I yanked her toward the stairs, where I had left my bag last night. As I clenched around her waist, I sifted through the bag with my other hand, eventually locating the syringe and pulling it out. "It'd be easier if you didn't flinch for this." She saw what I was holding, fear painting her face beautifully, and she started thrashing.

I twisted her arm behind her back, pressing my weight into her until her knees buckled and smacked the wood floor with a crack. Sadie let out a pained wail, but I released her wrist and slapped my hand over her mouth while removing the cap on the syringe with my thumb. I stuck the needle into the soft skin of her neck and pressed the plunger.

"You ... monster," she gasped, her eyes fluttering, and her writhing body slowed against me. "I ... will ... never forgive—"

Sadie's eyes closed, and she slipped into unconsciousness. From what Gavin told me, the sedative had a four-hour window, so I had plenty of time to kill Mason, hide the body, and get Sadie in the car. After checking her pulse, I scooped Sadie into my arms and carried her over to the couch. I laid her down and covered her with a bone-colored throw.

In the morning sun, I noticed that Sadie hadn't changed much in the last year. Her skin was slightly paler than I remembered. Her soft skin used to have a warm beige tone with cinnamon freckles sprinkled across her nose and cheeks, courtesy of the California sunshine. Now, it was more like porcelain and void of any touch of the sun.

Her red hair looked like copper, with strands of caramel gold hair peeking through. The only thing she didn't change was the tattoos I gave her on her abdomen. It felt like I was looking at a stranger. Sadie really did try to erase her old self to stay hidden.

She tried to erase *me*.

I reached out to stroke her cheek. The last time I looked into those peridot-green eyes, there was so much fear and disgust behind them. So much pain and hatred after seeing me take a life.

A life worth taking. I did what I had to do.

Yes, I had slit a man's throat, but it surprised me when she looked at me in horror, tears streaming down her face, and spoke her truth on the stand at my trial. I held that hateful gaze, making a promise that one day, I would break out of prison and find her.

No, I would never be the knight in shining armor Sadie dreamed of. This was no fairytale. I was a demon lurking in the shadows of her worst fucking nightmares.

"Alright, sit tight, princess. I'll be back."

I pivoted on my heel and went to my bag again, leaving through the back door leading into the garage. The garage was empty, with the metal side door swinging back and forth in the wind. I peered around the corner and saw the old man was outside by the power box, whistling a tune while fiddling with some circuits.

I stepped onto the gravel, letting the stones crunch loudly under my feet. Mason stilled at the noise and turned toward me. "Oh, did you—" he started before seeing me, his brows knitting together. "Who are you?" The old man took a tentative step back as he took in my appearance.

I stood much taller than Mason, and being tattooed from neck to knuckles was more than surprising. I would be a dime a dozen in Los Angeles, but here in this small, wholesome town, a man like Mason had likely formed an unfavorable opinion of me.

And he was right to do so.

Mason carefully kneeled and reached for his toolbox. I took another step toward him, hands raised. "Ah, ah. Take it easy, old man."

The fool didn't listen and fished out a hammer. He didn't lunge to attack me; he only gripped the tool as a warning.

"Are you a friend of the tenant?" Mason asked, his voice shaking a little. He was careful to avoid using names—he couldn't disclose that a woman was living here alone if I were a stranger off the street.

I moved closer. "I've been more than a friend to her," I replied. "So, you've been a stand-in father for Sadie, or 'Tess,' for the last year?" I watched as his body shifted slightly. "You can relax."

Mason's eyes narrowed. "Somehow, I don't believe you."

I offered a warm grin. But Mason knew. He knew a killer was waiting behind that smile.

"What do you want with her?" Mason asked brusquely, glancing behind me toward the garage door. "You didn't hurt Tess, did you?"

"Sadie," I corrected, "is just fine. You need to worry about yourself."

"I knew she was hiding something from her past. Now I see that it was *you.*"

I shrugged. "Everybody has a dark past. You'd be surprised by how much Sadie kept hidden from you in this cookie-cutter life she built for herself. Trust me, Pops. I'm not here to hurt her. I'm taking her *home*. But ... I can't have you calling the cops."

"Please," Mason begged. "As much as I should beg for my own life, I care more about ... Sadie's. I'm begging you to leave her alone. Whoever you are, she doesn't deserve anyone to hurt her."

I was less than two feet away from him now, and by how he straightened, I knew Mason would go down fighting to protect Sadie, no matter the cost. A feeling of admiration bloomed. Sadie had no one she considered family to fight for her before. This man, who only knew Tess, a lie, was still willing to go to his death to make sure she was safe. Mason figured out she was on the run and did everything he could to ensure her safety—the home, the job, and a family.

Like a protective father.

A protective father she never had.

When the screwdriver he'd been hiding behind his back came straight at my skull, I caught it, twisting it to the right until Mason's wrist bent, and he let out a piercing cry. He was a frail old man, and though I rarely gave a shit who I killed, the men I executed deserved it. They were at least on equal ground when it came to strength.

Sadie was right; I would be a monster to kill Mason, who had done absolutely nothing wrong. He was only trying to protect someone he saw as a daughter, and here I was, hurting him like some heartless bastard.

Guilt flooded me, and I was fucking pissed off about it.

I grabbed Mason's collar with my left hand, jerking his head toward me right before I gripped his shoulders and spun him around. As he tried to wrench free, I pulled out the other syringe that I slipped into my pocket and stuck it in the neck. His body crumpled in my arms as the sedative took effect, and I caught him before he hit the ground. After scooping him up, I brought him inside the house and placed him in the rocking chair. I pulled up the footrest to prevent him from falling, making his position in the chair nice and cozy.

"Alright," I said, turning to Sadie while she slept, "time to pack your shit and go."

It didn't take me long to find a large suitcase and a few empty duffel bags in the closet. When I opened the suitcase, I saw it was halfway packed with essentials, like Sadie was ready to make a run for it at a moment's notice. I tossed in a few more clothing items and toiletries before bringing the bags to the car. Poe watched me from the staircase with rapt interest when I returned inside. I smiled at the little tuxedo and scratched the back of his ear.

"I'm sorry, bud. You can't come with us on the road trip. But don't worry, I'll make sure you're taken care of for the time being, and maybe someday we'll come back for ya."

He blinked his gold eyes at me before heading back upstairs for a nap.

While exploring the rest of the house, I carefully scanned each room again, searching for any other items we might need to bring: water, snacks, or medicine. I topped off Poe's water bowl and poured a generous amount of dry food into a larger bowl, ensuring he would have enough to last for the next few days. I found some dried catnip and sprinkled it on the cat tree near the living room window.

An apology for taking his mom away.

The next part of my plan was going to be a little trickier. Mason was still sleeping in the chair, and though it could still take hours, I needed to get us on the road and as close to the state line as possible before he awoke. The moment he did, he was calling the cops.

I entered the kitchen, found a yellow pad of Post-it notes, and jotted down my message: *Take care of Poe.* Then, I stuck it to his forehead.

After I cradled Sadie in my arms, we made our way to the car, placing her in the passenger seat. She stirred a little, but the sedative was working. I zip-tied her right wrist to the seatbelt and adjusted it so it wouldn't cut off circulation.

Rushing back inside, I shut the garage doors, turned off the lights, and ensured the heater ran on a timer.

I think we're good.

After settling back in the car, I started the engine and gave Sadie's sleeping form one last glance before pulling out of the gravel driveway. I focused on the road ahead, leading us out of Vermont and back to California.

To the hell we were born in.

CHAPTER 14

Sadie

My cheeks warmed as the sun shone through the passenger-side window glass. A slight crack in the window let in the cool breeze. When I slowly came to, opening my eyes, the car spun, and nausea climbed to my throat.

At this point, I knew I was inside Keelan's car, but not where we were or where we were going. I had been slipping in and out of consciousness, tied to a seatbelt and listening to Keelan whistle his own tunes while the radio stayed silent. Beside me, my captor took me away from a home I had grown to love. A place, for the first time in my life, I felt safe in.

I slowly sat up straight and looked ahead of the road, feeling my stomach churn.

"Keelan, do you have anything I can puke in?" I asked, finally turning my head to look at him.

He reached into the driver's door slot and pulled out a bag. "Will this do?" he said, handing it off. His eyes flashed with a hint of concern, though I wasn't sure if it was genuine. I couldn't escape the reality that I was being held prisoner in a car with Keelan, a real-life demon in human skin, who held my life in his hands.

Taking the bag in one hand while my other clutched my stomach, I leaned forward, my dry mouth hovering over the paper bag's opening. But nothing came up.

"You slept longer than I thought you would. Nausea is normal, though. It'll pass—"

"Fuck off," I said, still waiting. All Keelan did was respond with a subtle and arrogant snicker under his breath while his eyes turned back to the road. My distress amused him, and as much as I didn't want to show how much his presence bothered me, it was clear as I scrunched up my face and flared my nostrils at him. "I hate you. Do you know that? I hate everything about you. Especially this."

Keelan turned to me, and this time, he didn't smile; his eyes only focused on mine, and something dark flashed in them. Speaking to Keelan the way I did was moronic, but at this point, dying would be a gift.

Once I realized nothing would come up, I placed the bag on my side of the door, just in case I was wrong.

My heart was pounding so hard in my throat that I was sure I was going to pass out again right as a thought hit me. "Mason! Poe!"

"They're fine, Sadie," Keelan said, but my mind raced at all the possibilities of what we left behind when he took me from my home. "I mean, they're probably fine. Mason should be waking any moment now, too, and the little Post-it note I left on his forehead instructed him to watch over your cat."

My mouth gaped.

"So, you can relax. I didn't kill your friend." He reached over, placed his hand on my thigh, and softly rubbed it as if he were comforting me over this news, like he wasn't the reason for all this happening in the first place.

He's crazy.

"You stuck a Post-it note to his forehead?"

His lip turned up. "I didn't want anything to happen to your cat. So ... yeah."

I blinked. "You ... you ..." Tears threatened to fall. I could see Keelan glance at me from my peripheral, his jaw muscle ticking.

"Come on, Sadie. He's a cat. He'll be fine."

The tears started falling, and I let out a hard sob, my breaths coming in gasps. I pulled my knees into my chest despite the restricting seatbelt and the damned zip-tie around my right wrist. I pressed my eyes into my sweatpants, desperately trying to anchor my thoughts before anxiety consumed me.

"What the hell is the matter now?" he asked, squeezing my thigh. I slapped it away with my free hand and whipped my head in his direction.

"Poe is my only friend in this fucked up world. The only one who kept me sane when I felt so lonely that it strangled me. He's not just any cat. He is *my* cat."

Keelan's eyes widened in shock at the ferocity of my voice, but his face remained blank. His eyes went back to the road. A few minutes passed while I cried quietly against my folded legs. Poe would be all alone if Mason didn't wake up, and Keelan forced me to leave him behind. A new spark of anger burned in my chest, and I furiously wiped away the tears.

"Keelan," I said softly. "You have to stop. Turn us around. You know that the moment Mason wakes up, he's calling the cops. There will be a massive manhunt by every police force in every city we pass. Your face will be on the news station. What is wrong with you?"

I'd always known Keelan to be unhinged and careless, but I never thought he'd go as far as escaping prison to commit yet another crime: kidnapping.

"What's your endgame here?" I asked. "What exactly do you want from me?"

Keelan gripped the steering wheel and kept his eyes on the road, his face taking on a more serious expression.

He cleared his throat. "You know your mom was the one who told me where to find you?" he said, causing my mouth to drop in surprise. I had been so terrified since I realized someone was in my home that it never even crossed my mind to wonder how he found me. But my mother? She wouldn't have done that.

"You're lying," I said. "She would never—"

"Sade, you've been in that family long enough to realize that no one, not even your goddamn mother, can be trusted," he said, cutting me off. "You've lived in this tiny bubble, thinking good people were bad and evil people were good. I think the only one you were ever sure about was your father. Your mother, though ... you trusted her way too easily. All it took was a little threat to ruin her body, and she crumbled and revealed all the secrets you thought she'd keep to protect you."

I swallowed, and tears burned my eyes. It was risky involving my mother to help me escape, but she had endured a lifetime of torture from my father. For once, I thought she loved me enough to ensure the monsters in our life never found me. I had hoped she would protect me from becoming like her, trapped in a life of crime, domestic violence, and exploitation. It wasn't my father she shared my location with, but the man she, at some point, was sure would kill me someday.

"Did you kill her?" I asked. "Because if you didn't, you know she'll go to the police and tell them where to look first. Let me also remind you who those same police officers *actually* work for. They won't arrest you, Keelan. They'll kill you."

Keelan smirked. "Oh yeah. Big ol' scary Finn. Your father is the least of my worries. I'm sure your mother is busy ensuring all the footage of her sneaking into your dad's office so that she could fuck the house chef is deleted. I think you're good for a while before the ones working for your father go hunting for me."

My mouth gaped open, and I turned away from him. My family was exactly the same as they were before I ran—no loyalty to anyone but themselves.

Self-serving assholes.

"Any more questions, princess?"

"Stop calling me a princess! I'm not Sadie anymore, Keelan. Sadie died before she left California. That spoiled little *princess* everyone thought I was is dead."

Keelan ignored my rant and turned on his blinker, pulling off the highway onto a ramp that did a full three hundred and sixty degrees to head northeast on another highway. My stomach heaved as the car's movements caused my head to spin.

"Okay, I need you to pull over, please."

"Use the fucking bag."

"Keelan!" That time, I shouted, puke involuntarily coming up, but I choked it back. This was going to be messy, and a small paper bag wouldn't cut it.

"Fuck ... alright."

Keelan veered off to the side of the road by a sign that named the city up ahead and put the car into park. I watched him reach into the glove box and pull out a switchblade, and my body stiffened. Instead of reaching over to me, he exited the driver's door and walked to my side, swinging the door open and reaching in.

"Don't move."

He slipped the blade under the zip tie and snapped it off, then he gripped my upper arm and pulled me out of the car.

When my chest hit his as he yanked me toward him, his face hardened. "You try to run, I'll chase after you. If I catch you, I fuck you, then I tie you down in the backseat with the luggage for the rest of the trip. Don't be stupid."

My stomach tightened at those words. I gave him a nod as more vomit reached my throat. Before I could step back, it all came up.

Unluckily, Keelan was able to move out of the way as I projectile vomited over the dead grass by the highway guardrail.

Immediately, I felt my hair pull back, and I kneeled, Keelan keeping my long red strands out of my face. Then, once I thought it couldn't get more bizarre that Keelan was ensuring my hair stayed clean of puke, his hand touched my back, and long strokes up and down my spine caused my body to still. With each caress, my body warmed and tingled, and my mind raced in confusion.

"I know what you're doing, Keelan," I said. "But I'd like you to move back."

He didn't stop. He continued to invade my space, and the powerful aroma of his cologne overwhelmed me. It was a familiar scent that I never forgot. "I'd rather not have my car smell like puke," he said. "I'll keep doing what I'm doing."

When I was sure I had thrown up everything in my stomach, I leaned back, feeling his hand lift from my shirt, as I plopped my ass on the gravel-covered ground.

Relief swept over me that he was no longer touching my back. I would no longer have to fight how his touch made me feel. Though the sour taste in my mouth made my stomach recoil again, I kept it down.

"You know," Keelan started, and I looked up to meet his eyes staring down into mine. "If your dad would have ever suspected your mom of knowing where you were, he would have done the opposite of what I did. Aisling shared your location with me, and I spared her little finger. Your dad would have cut it off despite her cracking under the pressure. Just for fucking kicks."

I gaped. "You threatened to cut off my mother's finger?" Of course, he did. "You're a psychopath, you sick fuck."

Keelan's lip turned up. "A psychopath would have killed your boss and slept like a baby that night. I may not give a shit about most people and what happens to them, but I'm capable of empathy."

Empathy? No one from my side or his ever showed me empathy. If he truly cared about me and how I felt, I'd be snuggled up on the couch with my cat right now and with a glass of white wine, watching reruns of *The Vampire Diaries.*

"What if she told you nothing? Would you have cut her finger off?"

I waited, hoping to see something shift in his eyes, but nothing did. "Yes," he said. "I knew Aisling helped you escape. So, yes. I would have cut her finger off for not telling me where you were."

My stomach dipped. Keelan was indeed the heartless bastard I knew he was.

"You're a lot different from how you used to be," Keelan said, cocking his head to the right. "Who knew my wife would care so much about the mother who did shit to protect her from a father who beat her until her skin turned purple?"

I winced at his words. "I am not your wife. I'm not your anything," I hissed. "You're just an escaped convict who broke in and kidnapped me. My family might be unworthy of my love, but they aren't the ones who abducted me from a life where I finally found peace."

"Life? Like what, with that *boyfriend* of yours? Maybe I should have confronted him before he left and showed him what happens when you touch another man's property. I guess it makes sense how you'd not think it was a big deal that the asshole put a bruise on your neck." The coldness in his voice sent a shiver down my spine.

I clenched my teeth. "Brian isn't my boyfriend. We're just dating."

I don't know why I felt the need to make that crystal clear, but perhaps it was because of the deadly tone in his voice. Either way, Brian was now a roadblock he had to eradicate.

Keelan narrowed his eyes at me, and his lips turned up. "Not your boyfriend, huh? Like you're not my wife? It sure seemed like a lot more than a fuck buddy who has been hanging around your house for the last two weeks."

I scrunched up my nose. "Brian is a hell of a lot better man than you. He actually cares about my well-being and only wants me to be happy. Something you know nothing about."

"The bruises on your neck tell me otherwise. It sounds to me like *Brian* doesn't care all that much if he did that."

I clapped my left hand over the bruises and glared at him with my puffy, red eyes. Suddenly, Keelan kneeled in front of me and reached his hand out, grabbing my wrist hard and yanking it away from my throat. The pain from his grip shot up my arm, and I hurled a series of insults while I cried out in agony. With his free hand, Keelan gently touched my neck where the markings were, gingerly gliding his finger down before stopping. His face, though, held no love or compassion. If anything, he was looking at me with disgust and horror.

He's going to do it here. I'm going to die right here on the side of the road.

"Just kill me now," I demanded, my voice trembling. Keelan's eyes ... did they soften a little? His blue eyes changed, and his thumb released from my neck and dropped to my chest, resting there as he pressed his lips firmly together.

What the hell is going on?

"Little princess," he said, "why the fuck would I kill you? You're mine, Sadie—my *wife*. As much as the arrangement between our parents brings fucking misery, you and I are bound, and I don't want to disappoint the family. Maybe I'll go back and kill that ... *fuck buddy* of yours. But, while I won't harm you nor kill you—despite your hysterics—I *will* kill anyone who touches you. I promise nothing but violence on that subject."

As we stared at each other for an uncomfortable amount of time, Keelan finally released his hand from me and walked over to his trunk, pulling out a water bottle and coming back to my side. I averted his gaze, grabbed the cool bottle, and twisted the cap off.

I quickly swished a mouthful of water around my mouth, hoping to rinse out the puke still coating my gums. After spitting out the water a few times onto the gravel, I swallowed the last bit, which helped quench my dry throat. "Thank you," I said. I hated being polite, but being hostile with Keelan wouldn't win him over.

At this point, I knew that whatever I did from here on out, I would have to earn his trust so that I could run the moment he let his guard down. Once back in the car, I leaned my head against the window and tried to watch the world roll by as we pulled off the side of the road and down the highway through Vermont. The intensity of what had just happened was frightening, but even beyond all that, he still pulled such sensations from the dark parts of me I was afraid of.

I shook the unspoken thoughts away and sunk deeper against the window. As we drove, I watched the endless sea of snow-covered trees roll by. Eventually, my eyes closed, and I drifted into a sleep filled with stars and butterflies.

CHAPTER 15

Keelan

We drove in silence for the rest of the day. As night fell, Sadie drifted into a fitful sleep with her head wedged between the car window and the passenger seat. She had looked way too uncomfortable, so I offered her a rolled-up sweatshirt as a pillow. Instead of taking it like a normal person, her stubborn ass told me to go fuck myself and leave her alone.

Once she finally fell asleep, I turned on some music, allowing Sleep Token to soothe my nerves. At least with Sadie sleeping, it gave me some time to think about my next move.

Before I left Burbank, I had planned the entire trip, mapping out the route, identifying specific gas stations, and even picking motels where we'd put our heads down each night. So far, everything had gone as smoothly as I needed it to.

I hated the risk of staying at motels, but thankfully, this next stop wasn't a motel at all. It would give us some seclusion. We were headed to a family-owned property an hour southwest of

Cleveland, about eight minutes off the highway. There was a car there, as well, so it would be easy to switch out this one.

Though the family lived and breathed the business, they wanted a place away from it all. We didn't use it much, maybe twice a year, mainly in the summer. Gavin reminded me that although the Ohio cabin was vacant, a cleaning crew came monthly to keep it in good shape. Those they hired also maintained the property, trimming trees and clearing the deck of leaves each week.

Right now, I could use some food, water, and clean towels for a shower. This place was perfect.

We still had several days of travel before reaching Los Angeles. After that, I could finally retrieve the box her brother, Patrick, had hidden before his death. Taking Sadie back home was the only way I knew how to protect her. Something dangerous was happening, and she was in the crosshairs of bloodshed. Before I could brood on it further, I shifted in my seat, and a sharp pain in my lower back derailed my thoughts. I groaned.

Fucking hell, I need to stretch my legs.

I squinted at the faded road signs on the highway, searching for our exit—Spring Valley Road—just a few miles away. I shifted again, trying to ease the pressure on my spine. Driving from California to Vermont had been fucking murder on my back, old injuries reminding me of their existence. Luckily, now that I had retrieved my prize, I could take more breaks from driving.

Right as I reached for the water bottle between Sadie and me, my phone rang, and I picked it up, holding it to my ear.

"Where you at, Kee?" Gavin asked, followed by a yawn.

"Hey, Gav. We aren't too far from the cabin. After Sadie's boss spotted this car, I'm hoping that old Camry is still running, so we can ditch this one and take the other."

"Fuck. How the hell did that happen?"

I sighed. "Just bad timing. Sadie's boss showed up the morning I grabbed her. He spotted the car while working on the power box. By now, the cops have probably been to her place, and he's already given them the description. You think the keys are inside the house?"

"Yeah, we never take them out of the junk drawer in the kitchen. Dad said that the car was used when they stayed there last June. So, it should still work and have gas." There was a slight pause before he added. "Oh, and don't forget to remove the license plates and replace them with the ones I gave you. Don't leave anything behind."

"Got it."

There was another long pause.

"Kee," Gavin started. "Has Sadie been giving you a hard time?"

I flipped my blinker on and exited the highway. We were almost there.

"That's an understatement of the fucking century. Sadie's been fighting me since we left the house. Very ungrateful, I must say."

"Ah, come on, Keelan. You did kidnap her from her hiding spot."

He wasn't wrong. I had taken Sadie from the only place she had ever truly felt safe, maybe the only sanctuary she'd ever known. But guilt wouldn't help me now—I had to swallow it down and keep with the plan.

"Have you told her yet?"

I frowned. "No, and I don't plan on it until we get closer to Burbank, and she has nowhere to go if she makes a run for it."

"Yeah, that makes sense. Alright, keep your guard up. Enemies are making moves. Don't get caught."

Shit.

"Yeah," I said. "I gotta get going, but I'll call you again at the next stop."

"Okay, good luck, Kee."

As I flipped on my blinker to turn left onto the next road leading to the property, Sadie began to stir, and I could tell she was getting stiff from sitting for so long.

Almost there, baby.

It took us about ten minutes to reach the property. It was so dark now that I had to flip on the high beams to see where the hell I was going. Once we reached the driveway, I turned off the car and stepped out. The only sounds were of nature itself. A gentle breeze rippled over the water on the lake, with the soft rustle of swaying trees around it. There was even the distant hoot of an owl and a few chirping frogs. I took a deep breath, allowing the clean, cool air to fill my lungs and shake some of the exhaustion out of me. I knew there were other homes surrounding the lake, but I didn't see any lights on. We were completely alone as the rest of the town slept.

I walked over to Sadie's side and opened the door. She'd be much more pleasant to scoop up and place right under the sheets, but I needed her help to carry the stuff to the house and then hide the Ford in the carport.

"Sadie, wake up," I said, giving her a poke in the shoulder. "I need you to walk."

"I'm awake," she said, turning to her side. "Please don't make me get out yet."

Jesus.

"We're here," I said, reaching inside the glove box and pulling out the pocketknife I usually carried on my belt strap.

I brought it to the plastic ring around her wrist. She flinched away, but I ignored her, pulling the zip tie up from her skin and cutting her free. The skin underneath was red as if it had been burned. Sadie must have been trying to cut the plastic for a few hours while she pretended to sleep to avoid speaking with me. Irritation boiled over as I grabbed her sore wrist gently so as not to press into her wounds.

"Listen carefully, princess. Don't attempt to pull a fast one on me while we're here. We may be in the middle of nowhere, but I'm a fast runner. Please don't do *anything* to draw attention to the neighboring homes around the lake, or I will make you regret it. Understand?"

I reached over, slid my arm in front of her stomach, and un-buckled her seatbelt. "What are you doing?" she asked frantically, slapping at my arm as I scooped her up. "Let me go!"

"Well," I said, grinding my teeth while she continued to slap at me. "If you don't walk on your own, I'm going to have to throw you over my shoulder until we're on the porch."

She stared at me, her jaw going slack, as if she couldn't believe I'd behave like a caveman.

I would.

"Fine! I'll walk," she said, giving me a light slap on the shoulder that I barely felt.

I smiled as I sat her down next to the car and looked into her eyes. She craned her head, her stubborn face scrunching up.

"What is this place?" Sadie asked, her gaze turned away from mine as she took in our surroundings. A massive lake stretched around the open space, the moon lighting up the rippling surface. Beside us, the family's wooden cabin was barely visible, with all the lights off.

Thick trees towered above the ground like silent sentinels, pines blocking any view of the outside world besides the lake. Even the main road had vanished from sight, leaving only the wilderness to welcome us.

"Byron bought this land when Gavin and I were kids," I said, glancing around the secluded area. "It's safe enough for us to crash here tonight, but there's something we need to take care of first."

"Like what?"

"Well, after your little stunt with Mason and him spotting this car, we gotta ditch it. There's another car parked on the property that we can take, so we need to get everything out of the Edge."

Sadie didn't respond, but I could see in her eyes that she wasn't listening. She was too preoccupied with contemplating an escape route.

Sneaky little thing.

"We're all alone out here, honey," I said, and her eyes, icy with rage, met mine again. I had to say, her sass was pretty adorable.

If it wasn't clear by now who was in charge, she just got herself a rude awakening when I crossed my arms tightly over my chest and said, "If you don't cooperate and do everything I ask, I'm going to throw you on this hard dirt road and fuck you from behind until you can no longer walk." Her jaw dropped again, and she looked at me in stunned silence. "No one will hear you scream."

After taking one step back, Sadie looked around again and swallowed. "Fine," she growled. "Psycho."

With a stubborn snarl, dramatic stomp of her feet, and door slamming, Sadie helped me gather all the bags and drop them by the porch steps. I made her get back into the car, and we drove around the cabin to the carport in the back.

Once we pulled under the expansive metal canopy, it took me about ten minutes to remove the license plates and gather the last few items from the trunk.

I put the plates inside my backpack and went to the Camry, covered in a green plastic tarp to repel the elements. I had Sadie help me remove the tarp and cover the Edge, securing it with the bungee cords. Even if someone came around and saw the car, they wouldn't know it was the same vehicle Mason reported to the cops. I made a mental note to toss the plates in the lake in the morning.

"Alright, that's taken care of," I said, wiping dust on my jeans.

I let out a breath of relief and looked over at her. She still had her eyes on the tarp, shivering from the cold. "What ... what now?" she asked, turning to me.

"Now," I said, looking over my shoulder at the cabin, "let's get inside."

CHAPTER 16

Keelan

Thankfully, the moon offered us enough light to find our way through the backyard without falling into unseen holes or twisting an ankle. Aside from a few homes around the lake, the cabin was in a secluded plot of land with endless grassy fields and distant trees. When we reached the bottom of the stairs, we grabbed the bags and walked up to the door, dropping them on the wraparound porch. I noticed Sadie in the corner of my eye. Her gaze darted around, most likely searching for a house nearby to run to.

"Stop trying to look for an escape route," I said, taking a step toward her. "The houses are too far apart for anyone to hear you scream for help. And even if you tried to run, I'll have you hogtied before you make it three feet."

Sadie flipped me off and sat on a metal deck chair, folding her arms around her waist. Her copper-gold hair blew slightly in the breeze.

"Come on, stop pouting, and let's go inside. I just need to find the key," I said. It was almost two in the morning, and every inch of me screamed for sleep. My back felt like hot knives had been buried in my muscles.

I kneeled and lifted the dusty welcome mat. *Fuck. No key.* My gaze swept over the porch, searching for any spot where Byron might have hidden it.

There was an overturned terracotta flowerpot under one of the windows.

"If the key isn't here, I'm going to have to break a window," I said, heading to the flowerpot. I lifted it up and saw a bronze key underneath. My raw nerves started to settle.

"We can sit out here for a moment. It's nice out," she said, looking up. Her demeanor had noticeably changed. Maybe she only needed to get out of the car because it made her stir crazy.

Or was Sadie afraid to be alone with me again in a dark cabin deep in the woods?

Having a fully furnished porch that encircled the house was a nice touch. The cabin had a warm-brown wood exterior, multiple bay windows to let in the natural light, and spacious rooms that we used to stay in for a couple of weeks at a time. The isolation was perfect for reading, drawing, or scavenging for treasures in the fields. Sometimes, even mafia families needed to get away from it all. We stopped going after Mia started high school; now, we hardly use it except for Gavin's side of the family.

"It's not that nice out, princess," I said, placing the key in the lock and turning the knob. "I'm fucking cold and know damn well you are, too."

"I'd rather go home," she muttered, so quietly that I almost missed it.

I scoffed. "Knock it off; that's getting old." I marched toward her and grabbed her arm, attempting to pull her up, my fingers digging into her skin, and Sadie hissed in pain. "We've been on the road for almost ten hours. I'm exhausted. So how about you stop being a whiny brat so we can get warm and sleep?"

Sadie's eyes sparkled in the darkness with unshed tears, and something yanked at my gut. As much as her betrayal enraged me, and how much I wanted to punish her for it, her fear caused me to feel something other than rage.

I felt ...

I shook my head. Now was not the time for interpersonal perspectives. I needed a shower and rest. "Come on," I said.

Once I finally got her on her feet and moving toward the door, I shoved it open. Immediately, I felt the warmth of the heater that the cleaners had left on when we walked inside.

"Set the bags behind the couch," I ordered. "Let's explore a bit, and then we can carry them to the bedroom. I need some water. You?"

When I was met with silence, I turned around and watched Sadie slowly step back toward the door that was still wide open.

"What the hell are you doing, Sadie? Get over here."

She still didn't respond, keeping her eyes locked on mine as she continued to walk backward.

She's gonna run.

Sadie turned on her heel and bolted for the open door. She didn't get far before her foot caught on the hallway runner, and she fell forward, her stomach and left hip hitting the door frame.

I lunged for her, seizing her ankle, but she was army-crawling halfway out the door.

Oh, come on.

"Let me go!" she screamed and reached out, attempting to claw herself free.

I was already on her, straddling her back and reaching for her outstretched arm. Before I could get a hold of her wrist, she slightly twisted her body, the terracotta pot in her hand slamming against the side of my head. Bursts of light filled my vision as I fell to the ground, warm blood trickling from my temple.

She had already slipped out from beneath my body, and darkness threatened to claim me. The sound of her shoes hitting the deck made my blood boil, and I dug my nails into the mangled floor runner to keep myself steady. Shards of the pot and dirt trickled onto the rug, along with drops of blood.

Slowly, I lifted my head and saw Sadie's red tank top disappear into the dark and around the corner of the cabin.

Oh, Sadie, that was a mistake.

Anger burned against the pain, and the world stopped spinning enough for me to pull myself upright. I straightened and kicked the shattered remains of the flowerpot before touching my head. Feeling sticky blood and jagged flesh, I smiled with icy rage in my teeth.

"My little *fucking* princess," I whispered into the dark fury consuming my brain. "There is nowhere you can run to where I can't find you."

The pain was intense, but I cracked my neck and sprinted after her. This game of cat and mouse was making my dick grow hard under my jeans, and I grinned as I ran toward where she disappeared.

I heard rustling grass as I rounded the building, which led to an open field bordering a small grove of pine trees. Wild excitement took over my mind, and I laughed, racing toward my frightened, cornered little deer. Sadie tried to sprint away, but her weakened, hungry body couldn't find the energy to push on. I quickly gained on her. She glanced over her shoulder and screamed when she saw me.

"Help! Someone, help me!" Her cries filled the empty field. Even if someone did hear her screams, no one would come to save her in time. We were all alone.

"What the hell were you thinking?" I growled as I cornered her at a fence behind the property. "Stop running from me." She looked around with panic in her eyes, regretting running in the wrong direction.

I could practically smell the terror rolling off her skin now, and my cock hardened in response. Her face was wet with tears glistening under the moonlight, and as I stretched my hand to grab her shirt, she screamed again. "Leave me alone, you monster!"

"Never, princess."

I gripped the red fabric, feeling it tear under my fingers, and yanked her hard. Sadie's body twisted with the force of the pull, and she fell hard against me, sending us tumbling to the dirt. Sharp sticks and rocks gouged my arms as we dropped, sending another bolt of pain flashing in my skull. She scrambled to get out from underneath me, but I was faster, grabbing her arms and flipping her painfully onto her back, her hands pinned beneath her body. I slammed my knees into her thighs and wrapped my hands around her throat, cutting her air off completely.

"I mean, I *did* warn you earlier what would happen if you tried to run. What a big fucking mistake this was to do what you did," I grunted.

Sadie arched against me, thrashing to free a hand to fight me off. My cock pressed painfully against the fabric as I pushed my weight into her hips and throat. Her face reddened, and I noticed something else happening while she struggled to breathe.

She's getting turned on by this even as I'm choking the life out of her. Her nipples are hard as fucking rocks.

The realization tempered my anger, and I lessened my grip on her, allowing Sadie to draw in a thin stream of air. "Get ... off of ... me, Keelan," she gasped. With her arms pinned and her legs spread between my knees, I had her completely immobilized. Keeping one hand firmly on her throat, I trailed the other down her ribs until my fingers slid under her sweatpants. Her slick desire betrayed her. My fingers lingered between her folds for a moment, as if to emphasize that I *knew* she wanted this. No matter what she was saying. I pulled my hand free and met her hateful gaze.

"How about, 'get me off, Keelan,' instead?" I grinned, licking her sweet taste off my fingers. "I know you say you don't want me to touch you, but why lie to me, sweet wife?"

"Stop calling me that!" she shouted, tears streaming down her cheeks as she looked away. "You're going to break my bones, asshole! You're acting just like my fucking father. He never gave a damn about how much pain he put me or my mother through."

I blinked in shock at the pain in her voice, and guilt reared its ugly head in my chest. *God fucking dammit.*

"I'm nothing like your father, princess," I repeated, reaching to cup her cheek and returning her eyes to mine. "I won't hurt you tonight. Instead, I'll make you come so hard you will have no fight left in that tiny body until morning."

Sadie stared at me as her eyes grew wide with terror. Even her struggle had subsided at that moment.

"All this struggling has put me in a slightly better mood. I'm not even tired anymore. Now, will you please shut those pretty lips of yours, so I can fuck you?" Sadie narrowed her eyes and flared her nostrils. A small squirm followed, but it was meaningless below my weight. "Open your legs for me. I'm not in the mood to play fucking games."

Slowly, she did what I said. And that was all I needed.

"That's my girl."

I leaned down and let my lips brush against her collarbone before pulling up her torn shirt and kissing her tattooed abdomen. She jerked against my mouth, and I nipped her hard. It was a warning and a claim made at the same time.

"Don't squirm so much, or I might make you bleed. Now, how about I play with that pretty pink pussy?"

I unzipped my jeans and pulled my cock free. Sadie's eyes may have been full of hatred, but I saw the desire there, like a dark secret rising. This was just like when we first got together. The taste of fear, anger, and lust was a delicious cocktail that fueled us every time we fucked.

I grabbed her sweatpants and slid them down past her knees, revealing her soaked underwear.

"You're so fucked up," she spoke again, her voice trembling. One of her hands dug into my biceps, nails trying to scratch me, but I grabbed both her arms, pinning them against the ground by her wrists. Using my cock to push aside her panties, I found her ready and eager for me, even though she would never admit it aloud. Her hips twitched against me, urging me to plunge deep inside. I raised my eyes and locked in with hers.

"Even when you fight me, your body tells me a completely different story, babe. A year is a long fucking wait since the last time I filled you up. The moment I touched you in the house and your pussy drenched my fingers, it was pretty fucking clear you missed this just as much as I did."

Even in the shadows, her cheeks flushed. It was as if she hesitated, but when I felt her trembling legs squeeze against my hips, she'd made her decision.

Without another word, I slammed myself inside of her pussy. She cried out as her back arched and her hips bucked into mine, driving my dick deeper. I groaned, freeing my hands from her wrists, and used my left arm to lift her ass off the dirt—the intensity of her warmth and how sensitive I had become almost overwhelmed me.

Fuck, it's been such a long time since I had her little pussy wrapped around me like this.

Sadie tilted her head back, silently urging me to choke her again as I fucked her. I knew I wouldn't last long, so I squeezed her with my right hand hard and fucked fast. Every thrust I gave her was more violent than the last, reaching the depths within her I *knew* only I could. Only *I* could have her perfect body reacting like this.

"Oh ... God," she managed to whimper, her eyes closing as she arched below me. With my hands all over her body and my cock inside her, Sadie was *mine* again, in every sense of that word. Her inner muscles continued to throb and tighten around me like she wouldn't last much longer. And neither would I.

"You take my cock just as good as I remember, baby," I groaned, watching pleasure flood her face.

The delicate veins in Sadie's neck swelled under my grip, and her eyes rolled back as her release built into a fever pitch. Her slick walls tightened further around my cock, and like before, I couldn't last any longer. An orgasm tore through me as I filled her pussy with my cum, emptying every single drop I had. Sadie opened her mouth in a silent scream, and her release quickly followed. Her pussy pulsated so tightly that she nearly pushed me out right there, but somehow, I managed to keep myself buried in her. The throbbing madness drained me entirely, and I had to brace myself before I fell on top of her. After a few minutes of catching our breath, I eased myself out of her and leaned back, grinning.

"There, that wasn't so bad, was it?" I quipped. *"Now* we can go inside and get some sleep."

Once back in the house, I shut and bolted the door, so she didn't try that shit again. For added measure, I dragged a chair from the dining table to jam under the doorknob. Then, I went into the supply closet and grabbed a broom to clean up the broken pottery and dirt.

"The Sandersons own this property," I said as I turned around to dump the debris in the trash. "There are no landlines, and everyone nearby is asleep, so don't expect rescuers to come here. You're stuck, so deal with it. Your attempt to flee has failed."

Sadie's jaw tightened, and she lowered her head, avoiding my gaze. Instead, she occupied herself with the bags, picking up the black one and slinging it over her shoulder.

"The bedroom is that way," I said, pointing to the hallway across the living room.

Gavin informed me that they kept the utilities on for potential last-minute family visits and to allow the cleaning crew access for property maintenance.

There was a plug-in diffuser somewhere because the smell of artificial pine was hanging in the air, and my nose started to itch. Sadie smirked in my peripheral as she passed me, but I focused more on a hot shower and bed. My head ached considerably, and I needed to rinse the dirt off my wound before bandaging it up.

When I reached the hallway leading to three bedrooms, I said, "Keep moving. It's the bedroom to the right, across from the bathroom. Let's unpack and get ready to sleep."

I didn't even know what she said, but she mumbled something under her breath. Before Sadie entered the bedroom, I grabbed her arm and spun her around. "Act like a brat all you want. But you are *mine,* and I will do everything I can to keep you. You may not like this, but I have my reasons for taking you back." My right hand trailed down her raised arm, and my finger played over the peak of her left breast.

"Knock it off, Keelan," Sadie hissed. "You got what you wanted from me earlier. Now, let me go so I can shower."

I sniffed the air. "Great idea. We smell of sex and potting soil."

"What is wrong with you?"

Snickering, I opened the bedroom door and turned on the lights. It was a spacious room with wood paneling and some of Aunt Serena's landscape sketches adorning the walls. There was a queen-sized bed with deep-blue covers, and the bathroom to that room was to the right.

"Well, it looks like we're cuddling up again." I pushed her inside and locked the door. "Now, strip and get in the shower. I'll be there in a minute."

She crossed her arms and snapped, "So, I have to shower with you now?"

I exhaled and dropped my bags at the foot of the bed. "The shower is too small for two people, first of all. Second, I'll watch you so you don't get another stupid idea and try to bolt. Get in there, I want to go to bed. Now that my dick isn't inside you, I'm wiped out."

Sadie frowned before storming into the bathroom, ripping off the torn tank top and the rest of her clothes. She cranked on the water and stepped inside. I followed after her and sat on the toilet. Sadie reached for the sliding glass door, but I grabbed her wrist and wagged a finger at her.

"It stays open, Sade," I murmured.

She gave me a defiant look but didn't argue, keeping the door open as she reached for the soap.

As the soap lathered and slid down her stomach, I found my gaze drawn to the stars tattooed on her abdomen—the ones I had marked her with. The stars held a meaning for Sadie, but they also had a meaning for me; she just didn't know it yet.

CHAPTER 17

Sadie

The aroma of freshly brewed coffee and the warm, golden glow of sunlight filtering through the window onto my cheeks gently coaxed me awake.

God, I need that coffee.

I wasn't sure when Keelan slipped out of bed, but waking up alone was a pleasant surprise. It was the first time Keelan had given me space since he had taken me. Stretching my arms wide with a yawn, I looked at the clock on my nightstand. It was eight a.m. My biceps and chest were killing me from trying to crawl out the door after I slammed on my hips. I was sure there would be a bruise there. Not to mention my pussy ached from how hard he fucked me.

I still can't believe we did that.

Throwing my legs over the mattress, I sat up, my eyes looking down at my bags. I jumped off the bed and rummaged through my duffel bag, finding some socks to keep my feet warm. It was freezing in this cabin.

Once I entered the kitchen, I spotted Keelan with his back to me. He was shirtless, with black sweatpants hanging low on his waist. My stomach did that annoying flip when he turned around, his tattoos and chiseled stomach on display.

He smiled when he saw me and headed to the dining table. "Something to eat before we hit the road," Keelan said, placing a plate of warm pancakes beside a mug of freshly brewed coffee. That sweet scent filled my nose again. God, I was so hungry. I hadn't eaten since we stopped for gas yesterday morning.

"I don't want to eat next to you," I said stubbornly. The cozy couch by the fireplace looked way more inviting.

"Sadie," he said, irritation crossing his features, "sit your ass down and eat." He dropped to his chair with a smirk before cutting into his pancakes. He was clearly ignoring my death glare.

Instead of complying, I walked up to the coffee and picked it up, stepping back a few feet and feeling the warmth seep through the mug into my hand. "I'm not hungry, then," I replied, taking a small sip and tucking my left hand under my armpit while assuming a defiant posture. "This will do."

Keelan's blue eyes flashed as he wiped his mouth carefully, set the napkin on the table, and leaned back into the wooden chair. He folded his arms just like I did, mocking me. "Let me remind you that everything I have ever done in my life, I've done with a purpose. You can hate me all you want, pretend to be disgusted by my cock inside of you ..." My mouth gaped open. "But the sooner we return home to Los Angeles, the better I can protect you."

I sighed, placing my coffee back on the table, and relaxed my arms, letting them fall loosely at my sides. "What exactly are you protecting me from, Keelan? My testimony put you away for murder. Your family wants me dead because of that, and my *own* family has abandoned me. Who or what are you protecting me from, if not the entire Blake family? I'm just waiting for you to snap and kill me yourself."

Keelan's eyes never left mine, but I involuntarily squirmed when he licked the small golden bead of maple syrup from his upper lip. My pussy ached with the memory of the primal, rough sex we had last night, and the traitor ached even more with a desire for that tongue to slip inside me. Keelan was unbothered by my rant, but he enjoyed my discomfort.

"I can understand why you feel this way. But have I killed you yet?"

I pulled my brows together, trying to find the proper snarky remark, but all I said was, "Well, no, but—"

"Then shut your mouth before I shove something between those lips to keep you quiet."

As vile as that sounded, my traitorous pussy clenched at the thought, and I pulled my thighs together, looking over at the plate of food that was now getting cold.

"Still not hungry, princess?" he asked with a knowing smirk. "Last chance to sit at the table with me, or I'm going to eat your pancakes, too."

I grabbed the mug again, taking a slow sip. "Still not hungry."

Silence filled the space between us as I drank my coffee, and Keelan dove back into his breakfast. I held steadfast in my denial that I would join him in eating, moving over to the couch instead and feeling the pleasant warmth of the fireplace. Yes, I was starving, but now I had dug a hole that my stubbornness would not let me out of.

I want those damn pancakes so fucking bad, but I like the fact that I can deny him something he wants and get away with it.

Once he finished his meal ... and mine, Keelan walked over to a drawer on the island and pulled out a set of car keys. "Gavin mentioned some fuel might already be in the car to get us to the next gas station. We'll have to stop at some point."

I gave him a slight nod and then headed into the bedroom to change, put on fresh deodorant, and brush my teeth. I heard the sink faucet come on and Keelan washing the plates and mugs.

These were very domestic tasks for a murderer and kidnapper. The thought brought an involuntary smile to my face. I shook my head and hurried out of the bathroom to change and pack my ruined clothes. I dressed in a pair of leggings and a long-sleeve black shirt that offered far more warmth than my outfit from yesterday.

After Keelan finished tidying up and packed his own things, he grabbed the Camry's keys and replaced them with the Ford's. "After you, princess," he said with a lopsided grin, gesturing to the door as I slung my bag over my shoulder.

Another day on the road as his captive.

When we exited the cabin, the air felt crisp, and for once, the wind was gentle, not biting into my skin like last night. I waited as he opened the trunk and loaded our bags and a few items from the house that we could use on the road: dry snacks, drinks, and a first-aid kit we found in the linen closet that he had used to help tend his head wound.

Once I put on my seatbelt, he walked over to my side. For once, he didn't zip-tie my wrist, and for that, I was grateful.

"I don't like that the zip ties are hurting you. So—" Keelan's body filled the space between us as he leaned toward me. "I'm trusting you not to run," he said. "But if you pull the same shit as you did last night, I'll not wait for permission to slide my cock inside of you. I will take you while you scream and sleep like a baby afterward." Keelan came closer, his lip barely brushing my ear. "I'm going to ruin your body for Brian and every other loser you try to replace me with each time I claim you because this, right here—" He placed his hands on me, cupping between my legs. Heat flooded my face, and I closed my eyes, focusing on breathing. "This right here belongs to me, whether or not you want it to. Do not fucking test me today, Sadie."

The tension was so heavy I couldn't breathe. Growing up with Keelan, I saw every side of his personality. His cruelty toward me and others since we were children. I watched him slit a man's throat and look damn proud of his handiwork. This possessive side, along with the promise of violence, was what scared me most about him. Keelan wanted to own me, body and soul.

I nodded, but his hand remained between my legs, rubbing the sensitive part with the pad of his thumb. Wetness began to seep, a betrayal to my mind, which denied this intrusion.

"Are you sure you're not hungry? 'Cause I still might be." The heat of his gaze burned a trail from my face to the part that—despite my fear—ached for more of his touch. "I think you're forgetting who's in charge right now. If I tell you to spread your legs for me or even eat some fucking pancakes, you will; you defying me is pissing me off."

I nodded once more, feeling my racing heart climb to my throat. "Are you seriously that upset about the damn pancakes?"

The tattoos on Keelan's neck bulged as he swallowed, his Adam's apple bobbing as he took in my wary expression.

His thumb began to circle faster against my clit through the fabric, and suddenly, the topic of pancakes was no longer relevant.

"Keelan," I moaned, and my head fell back, resting on the seat.

"Does your boyfriend fuck you as hard as I do?" he asked. "Does he make you this fucking wet when he touches your body, even when you're pissed off and acting stubborn as hell?"

"That's ..." I closed my eyes, trying to picture myself somewhere else, but it was futile. "That's none of your damn business."

Keelan slid his hand away from between my legs and up to the hem of my shirt. He eagerly gathered the fabric and lifted it from my stomach, revealing my tattoo. His other hand touched the various constellations, the marks he left on my body. It was the stars that tied us together, his claim over me.

No matter how hard I tried to erase his existence after the trial, the tattoo was the constant reminder that my father sold me to a violent man who took my body as his possession, a body he then branded—becoming a relentless addiction that burned me alive. Keelan was teasing me now, tracing the star lines from my stomach to the waistband of my pants ... and I let him. But I didn't dare move. Perhaps some part of me didn't want to either, despite the fear devouring my veins.

"Is that so? Well, I would disagree with that. Everything about you is my business." Slowly, his hand slid beneath my leggings and panties, probing at the wetness that gave me away. His lips curved into a wicked grin, as if it thrilled him that I still reacted to his touch like that. "I'll tell you what I think, Sadie. I bet every time he fucked you, you pictured me ramming myself into your wet, eager pussy instead."

Although I wanted to close my eyes and surrender to his touch, my gaze stubbornly remained on his, refusing to betray the rush that spread through me as his fingers found my entrance.

He lightly prodded three of his fingers against my heat, though my tightness resisted his entry. His eyes locked onto mine.

"Cat got your tongue?" Keelan taunted me when I didn't respond, but instead, I gripped the seat, my body slumping forward slightly. His other hand reached for my thigh, spreading it open to give him easier access to my aching core. Everything inside me was racing, aching for more of the bliss that only he could bring out of me. I sunk my teeth into my bottom lip, trying to keep my breathing steady. "Mm, no need to speak. This pussy of yours tells me everything I need to know."

His fingers slid into me, stretching me out. This time, I couldn't hold back the moan in my throat. Faced with the fact that he was staring at me with a smug smile, clearly pleased with himself, I shut my eyes. My lips parted, and I allowed my hips to grind against his hand, more and more eager to reach that blissful point. I couldn't even sit up straight anymore, pressing my palm against the side of the driver's seat as he pumped his finger inside me. Harder. Faster.

As his fingers threatened to unravel me, his ringtone cut between us, and a growl rumbled from his chest.

He continued to pump his fingers in and out of me, my release imminent. But then he pulled his phone from his pocket and set it on my trembling thighs. To my horror, he put the call on speaker as I climaxed.

A moan escaped me as Gavin called Keelan's name. He reached over and covered my mouth with his other hand to silence me as

I cried out. My legs clenched together as I moaned into his palm, the sound muffled.

Holy shit.

"Hey, Gav," Keelan said with an arrogant grin while he pulled out his hand and licked his fingers. "Give me just a second."

Keelan picked up his phone and turned off the speaker. I was finally coming down from my orgasm, and heat flushed my cheeks.

No way Gavin didn't hear that.

"We're leaving the cabin now," he said as he placed the phone to his ear. "We just had to take care of a few things in the new car." He turned to me and winked. "What's going on?" Keelan adjusted the hard bulge in his jeans and smirked as he caught my eyes, watching him push it down. I fought the urge to roll my eyes and adjusted my clothes back to normal.

Though I couldn't hear what his cousin was saying, the urgency in his voice was clear.

"I don't care. Finn can go fuck himself and die," Keelan fumed, and my eyes went wide.

"Keelan," I started, but he threw up a hand to silence me.

"I'll call you once we get to the next stop. Don't tell my dad we stayed at the cabin. The less the family knows, the easier it'll be to return to LA. Also, Gavin, you need to get Mia out of the tattoo shop. This shit is about to go down, and they won't care who's in the way. The shop will be their first stop, and they'll target her and drill her until she spills our secrets. She's too young to handle that shit."

They exchanged a few more words before saying goodbye, and Keelan put the phone back in his pocket. He closed my car door before going around and climbing into the driver's seat. I turned my body slightly toward him, my heart pounding.

"What's happened to Mia? Keelan, she—"

"She isn't involved in any of this," Keelan assured me, but my gut told me that something far more sinister was happening back home that involved my father.

"What's happened, then, with my father?"

"After your testimony at my trial, the feds opened an investigation into both our families' businesses. They're focusing on your father's government dealings and my dad's tattoo parlors around the city. They even have agencies in Vegas keeping an eye on the art galleries."

That didn't surprise me. Our families had been involved in corruption since I could barely walk. They had nearly every goddamn police officer, politician, and official covering my family's tracks. My father, now the mayor, facilitated multiple coverups and buried scandals.

After Keelan went to prison, I thought the Blakes would bury the business and go into hiding until the heat died.

"Keelan. What happened?"

Keelan slowly looked up and met my eyes, an unrecognizable look in them. "Your dad is back in town and found out about my escape. Though your mom had turned off the cameras in the hallways to sneak the chef in, she didn't have access to the grounds. When security said that I had been inside his house and killed one of their men, Aisling met the end of his fist."

"Oh my God!" I cried out, gripping my chest. "Keelan, did he—"

He reached out and took my hand in his. "Gavin says that she's alive, but she's in the hospital with a fractured eye socket and a broken arm."

Anger replaced horror and boiled my blood. As much as I wanted to get away from Keelan and go back to Vermont, right then, I wanted to kill my father. He hurt my mother because of *me*.

Because of me *and* Keelan.

"You could have avoided all of this if you stayed in fucking prison, like you were supposed to, and left me alone. You put my mother in danger, and now Mia ... You're dragging everyone around you into a hell they don't deserve."

Keelan's nostrils flared, and his eyes fluttered closed briefly, as if absorbing my accusation. He knew Mia was too good and innocent for this corrupt life and was very protective of her. This new information was likely eating away at him.

"What now?" I asked. "What shitshow are you dragging me into, Keelan?"

"Not important."

And his mask is back up.

"Bull-fucking-shit. Could you give me something? Anything. Or else I'll fight you every step of the way. You can't leave me with *nothing.*"

Keelan seemed to consider my request as his eyebrows pulled together.

"What do you need from me, if not to take revenge for what I did to you?" I was pressing him, but I didn't care.

Keelan put his hands on the steering wheel and leaned against the seat. His eyes found mine. "There's a lockbox I need to find before your father does. And I'm not sharing anything more than that ... for your safety, of course," he said with a smile, showing all his teeth. "So, as much as you'd like me to let you go, I can't yet. This little adventure is so much more fun with you by my side. Just trust me that killing you isn't on my agenda ... for now."

Though I was happy that Keelan was divulging some of his plans, it wasn't enough. What was I supposed to do with that information? That night in the warehouse, he destroyed what little trust we had. Now Keelan wanted me to sit quietly in a car with him for five days while he went on a treasure hunt for some lockbox.

"What's in this box?" I pressed.

"Yeah, that's something I can't tell you."

I huffed. "Of course, you can't." Leaning my shoulder against the car door, I turned my attention to look out the window. "Until you do, I can't give you any trust. So, maybe go fuck yourself until you decide not to be so vague."

Keelan ignored my rant and started the car. He uttered a small curse as we pulled out of the dirt driveway and onto the main road.

"Great," he muttered, brushing me off. "Gavin underestimated how much gas was probably in this car. We need to stop at the next exit. You're going to come inside with me, and you're going to behave like the perfect little hostage."

Or else.

Of course, the terrified part of my brain told me this was the perfect opportunity to seek help. They could overpower Keelan and save me if I could somehow signal a good Samaritan. But that other part of my brain, the more rational part, told me he would kill anyone who tried, and I wasn't stupid enough to put someone else at risk. I had to be smart about it.

Last night, I failed to escape.

The next time I ran ... I wouldn't.

CHAPTER 18

Sadie

Ten minutes later, we pulled into a small gas station two miles off the highway along a wide stretch of empty farmland. Gray clouds covered the sun, casting a gloom over the land. The atmosphere felt heavy—but no snow had fallen onto the cracked asphalt.

As grateful as I was for Keelan not zip-tying my wrists again, the red chafed stripes on my skin itched and throbbed incessantly. If he were to bind me again, I'd bleed.

Just find some damn handcuffs or soft rope already.

After parking, we exited the car, and I stretched my sore legs. Keelan reached out and rolled my sleeves down, so the marks on my wrists wouldn't be visible.

"Listen, Sade," Keelan said, holding out his hand to me. "We're going inside to get a few more snacks that we didn't see inside the cabin, maybe some cold, fresh food. Once I pay for the gas, we leave. Don't speak to anyone. Understood?"

I nodded, taking his rough, warm hand in mine, and followed close behind him. I tried my best not to give anything away with my posture or eyes. It had to go smoothly, or Keelan was going to kill someone because of me.

As we entered, the bell above the door chimed, and I looked around the station. It was pretty small and cramped, with only one guy who looked like maybe a trucker, wearing a red plaid shirt with dark jeans and a ball cap with an American flag stitched on it. The man moved slowly toward the back, searching through the racks of beer in the cooler. He tipped his cap back to scratch his forehead, and I could see his head buzzed close to the scalp. There were also several scars, tattoos, and welts marking his sun-tanned skin. The man couldn't have been that much older than us, but it seemed like his life had thrown a few curveballs at him along the way.

The cashier was a young man, probably in his late teens or early twenties, with a pale complexion and dark freckles adorning his cheeks and nose. He wore a blue polo shirt with the company logo embroidered on the left breast and black khaki shorts. He had dark brown hair and round glasses perched high on his nose. When the bell chimed, the clerk stealthily slid his phone out of view as we walked past. A small TV was on in the background, broadcasting some local news.

We stood out, especially Keelan, a tall man covered in tattoos, walking in with a woman who likely looked meek and terrified despite my best efforts. I tried to school my face into a mask of interest at the rows of candies and other junk food. I felt a little dizzy, and my stomach growled, reminding me I should have eaten those goddamn pancakes.

After grabbing his drink, the plaid-shirt man made his way up the chip aisle on the other side from where we stood. He was carrying two water bottles and a bag of chips, flashing me a warm smile as he moved to another aisle a few rows away.

"Anything you want to eat, honey?" Keelan asked, squeezing my hand hard in a warning. He was already reading my body language, the intensity of his temper filling the air around us. I offered my best, sweetest smile.

"An iced tea and a turkey sandwich would be great ... *dear.*"

Keelan smirked at me before pulling me down the aisle toward the coolers. While he gathered my iced tea and an energy drink for himself, I went over to the deli stand a few feet away and grabbed the cold turkey sandwich.

After we gathered everything we needed, Keelan handed me the chilled glass bottle and a few additional snacks he had picked for me to carry.

When we reached the front, I spotted the cashier kneeling next to the shelves of cigarettes, putting away cartons. "Be right with you guys."

Keelan leaned against the edge of the counter and glared at me. "Princess?" he purred.

"Psycho?" I chirped back with false cheer, giving him a mocking grin.

Keelan tilted his head at me, eyebrows raised at my audacity. Defiantly, I met his gaze, shifting my weight so my left hip was cocked in a stubborn posture.

"Thanks for your patience," the cashier said, scanning our items and putting them into a bag. "Is that everything?"

"Thirty-five on pump six," Keelan responded.

After the employee added the fuel to our total, Keelan handed him the money. When we stepped away from the counter, he turned to me.

"I want you to wait over there," he said, pointing to a small kiosk four feet from the counter. "Can you be a good girl and manage that?"

I pressed my lips together, resisting the urge to scream for help. The fact Keelan was getting away with this was infuriating. I had help right here, ten feet away from me. All the cashier had to do was call the cops, and I'd be free.

"Sure," I said, biting back the response I wanted to tell him.

Keelan subtly nodded before moving past me toward the magazine rack on the other side of the store, and I walked to the kiosk where the medicine was. I watched him while a few more customers entered the store, my back pressed against a rack. The trucker was in my peripheral, now heading to the counter to pay for his items.

Anxiety gripped me then, feeling like my lungs were collapsing, like I couldn't suck in enough air.

Keelan isn't even looking at me anymore. It's like he's trusting me to be an obedient dog and stay.

My mind raced with possible routes I could take to run out and find help. But what if that got everyone in here killed? It would be my fault.

The room went silent, a faint ringing in my head as panic and indecision gripped me. Escape was right through that door, but the fear kept my legs rooted. I didn't know what to do.

What do I do?

A tap on my shoulder broke apart the echoing tunnel of my thoughts, and I looked from Keelan's back to the smiling face of the maybe-trucker.

Oh, God.

"Sorry, miss. I'm checking out, but I need to grab some medicine, and you're blocking them." His tone was polite, low, and gravelly, but my heart started pounding. Keelan couldn't see him talking to me.

I blinked, struggling to process his words and move out of the way.

"Can you move a little?" he asked, voice still kind.

"Oh, yes, sorry. Long morning." My voice was barely above a whisper. I shifted away from the stand to the right when the man reached out and skated his fingers along my belly.

It was intentional.

The fuck?

Immediately, I tensed and took a wider step back, my shoulder hitting the corner of the rack and causing a bottle of meds to fall. Panic surged through me, and I instinctively reached out to catch it. The bottle of iced tea fell from my grip and crashed to the linoleum floor, shattering into shards of glass.

"Shit!" I cursed, kneeling to clean up the glass, but the trucker held steady on my shoulder to guide me away from the mess.

"It's okay, baby cakes. I got it. You're gonna cut your pretty self." The trucker's grip on my shoulder was firm as he pulled me back, but his hand still lingered on my skin. He then released me to grab the remaining items in my arms. "Let me help you with those."

"No!" I snapped, my pulse pounding in my ears, each beat a desperate reminder that I was fucked.

Of course, I didn't want the man touching me, but mostly, I knew Keelan would rearrange the bald man's face if he didn't back off.

"It's okay," I blurted. "I've got it."

My hands were trembling as Keelan's familiar presence loomed over me.

"Excuse me," Keelan said, his voice more controlled than usual, "but did she ask you to place your hands on her?"

The man looked up, meeting Keelan's stony gaze, and my shoulders stiffened.

Shit. Shit. Shit.

"He was just helping me ... babe," I said calmly, trying to tame the beast that was Keelan Blake.

Was the man a creep? Of course, he was. But if Keelan caused a scene, the cops would swarm this place within minutes.

But then again, that was what I wanted ... right?

A low growl came from Keelan's chest, and I reached out, placing my hand on his cheek. "Let it go, Keelan. We can leave."

"Hey, dude. What's your deal?" the man asked, backing up a step. "I was just tryin' to help, like she said."

Keelan's eyes left the man's and looked down at mine. There was a brief pause before Keelan nodded. "Alright, fine," he said, and I released my breath.

"Great," I said, looking down at the broken drink. "Um, I need to get a broom or something."

"It's okay, miss," the clerk called from the counter. "I'll take care of it."

Keelan nodded to the cashier and grabbed my elbow, marching us out the door and leaving the mess behind.

"You're hurting me, Keelan. Let go."

He didn't let go. In fact, the pressure on my arm only increased.

Why the hell is he acting like I'm the one who did something wrong?

My heart pounded as we made our way back to the car. He shoved me against the driver's side door, ordering me to stay put. While Keelan filled the tank, my anxiety grew.

"What is wrong with you?" I asked before I saw the creepy man walking out, a small plastic bag in his left hand. He headed across the parking lot toward a lifted blue Dodge pickup truck parked parallel to us.

Keelan looked around, eyeing the corners of the canopy roof above the gas pumps.

"What are you doing?" I asked.

Keelan didn't look at me when he answered. "Looking for the cameras."

A knot formed in my stomach as he stormed toward the man's truck.

I know that look. Fuck ...

"Keelan!" I shouted and ran after him.

There was no way he was about to kill a man for simply touching me, intentionally or not.

"What the hell is wrong with you? Stop!" I shouted, but it was too late.

Keelan strode up to the man, cuffing the top of his head to knock off the baseball cap before he seized the back of the man's neck and pulled him back. Then he slammed his face against the window. There was a sickening crunch before the man wailed and tried to grab his broken nose, but Keelan slammed his face into the glass again. The man swore loudly, swinging his arms in an attempt to fight Keelan off.

"Oh my God!" I cried out, rushing over, but Keelan held up one hand to stop me, while his other hand held the man's throat. There was blood all over the man's driver-side door, more blood oozing down his nose and over his lips.

Before I could protest again, Keelan's hand tightened, and he lifted the man's chin to reveal his tattoos right below his jaw and along his neck. The ones I had seen in the store. It looked like a couple of letters and a symbol I didn't recognize.

"You wanna tell her what those mean?" Keelan asked, and I stilled. "Yeah, I was gonna let it slide for you touching her without her consent. In fact, it took a lot of fucking control not to snap your neck the second I saw you place your greasy hands on her. I thought, naw, you weren't worth my time. But then ... then I saw your prison tattoos. I'm feeling extra annoyed today, and I need something to help ease that frustration."

"Fuck you, man," the bald man shouted and spit right in Keelan's face.

Okay. Now he's a dead man.

Keelan wiped the bloody saliva from his face with his left sleeve before his knee came up and slammed into the guy's groin. "Being proud of your repulsive crimes, so much as to wear it on your neck, makes you expendable. No one likes a rapist and a woman beater, you fucker!"

The man tried to scream, but only a hoarse wheeze came out. Despite the pain, he once again tried to wrench free from Keelan's hold, but there was no point. Keelan was all height and muscle.

"I'd kill you, you worthless fuck, but your days are already numbered with tattoos like that." Keelan released his grip on the man's throat right before he grabbed the back of his neck again and slammed his face so hard into the doorframe that the skin on his bottom lip ripped open and more blood sprayed out. The bald man's eyes rolled back in his head, and he slumped to the ground. Keelan released his hold on him and let the man hit the asphalt.

My instinct was to bolt, but the moment I stepped back, Keelan's eyes looked down and met mine. "Don't even think about it, babe. Get your ass back in the car. Now!"

He didn't have to warn me twice. I wasn't a fool. The look in Keelan's eyes was venomous and deadly, and I wasn't about to stoke that fire and burn myself alive.

CHAPTER 19

Keelan

"You know," Sadie started. "As cruel as you were to me when we were kids, I never thought you'd turn out to be the most sadistic one in your family." She kept her gaze on mine, and the slight lift in her chin added to the bravado in her voice. "I was wrong about you."

This was the first time she had spoken to me in the nine hours we had been driving since we left the gas station. By then, it was almost six-thirty, and the sun had dipped below the horizon. Sadie's judgmental eyes turned away from me as I drove into a motel parking lot. She ran her hand over her mouth, clearly frustrated and angry.

I tried to hide my smile, but her ridiculous behavior was too funny. "I never claimed to be a good man, princess," I replied, pulling the car into a spot close to the motel door. "You just hoped I would be, so it would ease your guilt when you let me fuck you."

Her head whipped back toward me, and her mouth gaped. I teasingly slid my tongue over my lips, watching her squirm in her seat. Her brows furrowed, and her expression shifted into disgust.

"Well, it was a mistake that will never happen again. I regret all of it."

"Is that right?" I purred as my hand made its way to her inner thigh.

Her weak spot.

Sadie stiffened under my touch but resisted pushing my hand away—still determined to prove a point. But that pouting, stubborn look on her only made my dick grow hard. "Because, how I see it, you haven't regretted any time I was inside you. Not then or now. Come to think of it, I think you kinda liked it." I lightly squeezed her thigh. "You probably enjoyed it when I chased you last night, too."

"Oh ... you goddamn asshole, Keelan. Like I have a choice now, with you holding me hostage. And two years ago, long before you slit a man's throat, I was taken as property by a monster who hated me. What the hell did you expect me to do? Cry every day and live in complete misery after I said, 'I do?' I hoped that if you felt anything for me at all, you'd change."

"Change?" I raised my dark eyebrow at the word. My lips curled into a wide grin as my hand slid up her thigh before pulling it away. "There is no changing me, Sadie. Arthur Blake raised me, for fuck's sake. He taught me and my brothers everything we needed to know to survive in our business. That includes killing anyone who got in our way and not batting a damn eye when we did it. I am who I am, and you would be smart to remember that. I took you as a *gift*, nothing else. You should have known your place when our fathers gave you to me, as you will now."

As soon as I said those words, I saw the impact they had on her. Her jaw dropped, tears welling in her eyes. The defiance was gone, and only hurt and despair remained. If we wanted to get to Los Angeles in one piece and open the lockbox, Sadie needed to be obedient. I couldn't let her think I had gone soft. It'd be easier if she feared me.

I cocked my head as I drove the nail home. "What's the matter, Sadie? Did you think we would *ever* have a meaningful relationship back then? Did you think I came to collect you because I *wanted* you? Don't be naïve."

Sadie's nostrils flared, and she turned away from me, staring out the car window. "Go fuck yourself—"

The muffled sound of a phone vibrated behind us. Sadie's phone was ringing in my bag. *Fuck, I forgot I turned it back on to snoop through her text messages.*

Luckily, she had a burner phone with the GPS feature turned off, preventing anyone from tracing her location.

Sadie's eyes widened, and she spun around to reach toward the backseat. I grabbed her wrist and yanked it back, squeezing it until she winced. "Don't," I warned, gritting my teeth. I released her wrist and grabbed the duffel bag, unzipping the front pocket. I reached inside and pulled the cell phone out. There was an incoming call from Brian Danon.

Motherfucker.

"Looks like the little prick you pretend isn't your boyfriend is calling you." Sadie's eyes widened as I handed her the phone. "Go ahead, sweetheart. Answer it."

She shook her head, but I shoved the phone closer to her face.

"Answer the fucking phone!"

Sadie hesitated but nodded and took the phone. As she looked down, I noticed he'd sent several text messages, and she had about ten missed calls from him.

Yeah, that looks like he's a lot more than some guy she fucks.

"Okay, okay," she quickly said as she pressed the call button and held the phone to her ear.

"Ah, ah. Speaker," I said under my breath.

Sadie nodded, pulling the phone from her ear and pressing the speaker button.

"Hey, Brian," she said, her voice hoarse from holding back a sob.

"Tessie, what the hell? I've been trying to call since last night. Are you okay?"

Tessie? Why did that nickname irritate me so badly? Tess isn't even her real fucking name.

Sadie sighed and leaned back against the seat. Her hands trembled, and something told me she was debating doing something very stupid.

Reaching into my holster, I drew my gun and pressed the barrel against her side, hidden from view in the parking lot. Sadie's breath stopped as the hard metal pushed into her hip. My eyes locked with hers, daring her to do it, but it seemed that the gun was enough persuasion to keep her mouth shut.

"Oh, God, I'm so sorry. I lost my charger last night, and my phone died. Then I woke up sick."

"Sick? Do you need me to call someone?" His annoying voice irked me further. I pressed the gun harder into her side.

"No, Mason came by and dropped off some stuff. I still have a fever, but I'll be okay. Honestly, I just need to go back to bed. I miss you, babe."

What the fuck?

My jaw clenched, and my nostrils flared. I dug the barrel of the gun into her side again until she flinched.

Her expression was pretty terrified; Sadie knew she had made a mistake.

"I'll call you tomorrow, Brian. Is that all right?"

There was a moment of silence on the other end until he replied, "Yeah, of course. I'll text you in the morning. Get some rest, baby. I miss you, too."

Brian ended the call without saying goodbye, and Sadie dropped the phone in her lap, her body shaking now.

"I did what you asked." She covered her mouth to muffle the sobs. "Take the phone, and get that goddamn gun away from me."

"Gladly." I grabbed the phone, placed it back into the bag, and removed the gun from her side. I leaned in, gently grasping the back of her head, running my fingers through her long, red hair, and drawing her closer, my breath brushing against her skin. "Be very careful how much you push me from here on out, *Sadie*. Do you understand?" She only answered with a nod before I released her. "Alright. I'm going to zip-tie you for the time being while I get us checked into the motel. Can you be a good girl while I do?"

Sadie nodded as her eyes glistened, and she looked away. While she kept her eyes toward the passenger window, I pulled out the zip ties, re-securing her to the seatbelt. Tears were running down her cheeks and dripping onto her lap, but she made no move to wipe them. Something ugly burned my heart, but I ignored it and continued tying her.

Once I was certain she was securely bound, I grabbed a T-shirt from my bag to hang from the window and used the sun visor to cover the front glass. "Give me ten minutes."

A young woman with light-beige skin, long black hair, and an hourglass frame stood behind the desk. When she saw me approaching, she adjusted her red blazer and stood a little straighter.

"Welcome in, sir. How may I help you?"

I greeted her with a warm smile, pulled out my fake ID, and slid it across the desk. "Just one night for me and my wife, please. One king or queen bed will do."

"Look at you all prepared," she beamed, picking up my ID and typing into her computer. "Makes my job easy. I just need a credit card on file." She typed a few words into the computer before smiling back. "How's your day going?"

"It's going," I said, pulling out my wallet and asking, "Do you guys accept cash?"

She nodded. "With tax, you're looking at eighty-six dollars and fifty-six cents. You'll have to pre-pay with cash."

I pulled out eighty-seven dollars even, and she offered up the change, handing me the room card and directions to the room.

While she wrote the room number down on the room key card slot, I leaned back a little, peering out the lobby window to the car.

No sign of my princess escaping.

"Thank you, Mr. Wilson," she said as I returned my attention to her. "Enjoy your stay."

I picked up the keycard and returned to the car.

When I opened the passenger door, Sadie turned her head away from me as I cut the ties and pulled her out. After grabbing our bags, we went inside the motel and took the elevator to the second floor.

The small room smelled of lemon, vanilla, and grapefruit, which, luckily, didn't irritate my sinuses. It was spotless for an off-the-highway motel. One bed stood against the center wall, and a small table sat next to a bronze metal floor lamp in the corner. A couple of cream and gold abstract paintings complemented the hunter-green wallpaper.

I locked the door and secured the top latch before tossing our bags onto the floor. "I'll order us some food in a bit. You're not refusing a real meal this time. You can't possibly be functioning on chips, water, and that half-eaten turkey sandwich."

Sadie averted her eyes from me and looked around the room. "Sure." But she wouldn't meet my hardened gaze.

She can't behave like this forever.

I walked toward her. Only then did Sadie glance over her shoulder to look at me while trying to move away. Clearly, she wasn't going to make any of this easy for me. I wasn't in the mood to deal with her theatrics. We were running out of time and closer to being cornered by the damned cops.

"Sadie," I growled, grabbing her arm and pulling her against my chest. The back of her head bumped against my collarbone as I held her tight, snaking my arm around her thin waist. She struggled to break free, but I only squeezed tighter. I wanted her to know this wasn't a fucking game. That I was the only one in control here. Most of all, I wanted to fuck this damn attitude out of her. But not now. I had to hold off on that. "This trip will be much more pleasant if you stop being such a spoiled, entitled brat."

Sadie attempted to dig her fingernails into my thigh, but I held her still, trapping her body. I pressed my weight into her until she was slightly bent underneath me.

"I can't breathe, you bastard," she said as I crushed her in my arms, reminding her I could take her whenever I wanted. "Let go!"

I chuckled as I pressed my lips into her hair, breathing in her scent.

Damn. Sadie smelled so fucking delicious. I could never get over how my body reacted to her intoxicating, alluring scent. Even after all these months, that feeling never faded. My instinct wanted to ram myself inside her and coat my body in her scent as she moaned beneath me. But we'd been traveling all day, so she likely wanted to shower. Which would make that delicious smell disappear.

I don't want it to disappear.

Finally, I released her, and Sadie hurried away, keeping her body turned toward me so I was no longer behind her. Her eyes burned with fury—the kind that warned me she would scratch my eyes out if I came too close.

The thought of her struggling made my cock thicken and twitch. "Go take a shower," I ordered. "I have some phone calls to make, so you'll have a little alone time for now. Then we eat."

Sadie didn't argue, but she pointed to the blue duffel bag I brought in. "What's in this one?"

"I didn't want to lug all the bags up from the car, so I grabbed this one with your shower stuff and pajamas," I said, giving her the bag. "Keep the water running after you finish. I need to clean up, too."

Sadie snatched the bag and rushed into the bathroom, locking the door behind her.

As if that flimsy lock would keep me out.

After I heard the water turn on, I pulled my phone out of my pocket and dialed Gavin's number.

It rang twice before Gavin's voice came on the line.

"Hey, man! Where you guys at now?" Gavin's cheery voice came through the receiver.

"A hotel about ten miles from Davenport. Sadie's in the bathroom cleaning up. We're crashing in a cheap motel for the night. What's going on right now?"

Gavin sighed heavily. "The shop got raided this morning, and they took some paintings off the back wall. Detective Harris fucking Bridges is working this investigation."

Goddammit.

"He's been a thorn in my dad's side for ten fucking years."

My cousin cleared his throat in agreement. "Yeah, and he's determined to take us down. In case things go sideways, I'm sending you the software to the laptop now. It'll be inside the secured drive I set up before you left. Once you're able, send over the key through the software, and I'll try to process it from my end with help from someone on her side of the family. Unless you tell her everything and get her to do it for you."

I groaned. "Yeah, that won't be happening anytime soon. God, Patrick would have been so much better at this. I just tattooed the designs. I don't do all that techy shit."

Gavin cleared his throat. "Are you sure there's a box of files?"

"Yeah, I'm positive. Patrick didn't die for all this to go to shit. He trusted me to see this through."

"Have you told her anything yet?"

"God no, I can't even get her to eat a fucking pancake, and that's her favorite breakfast."

Gavin laughed. "Well, you might not have a choice as to when to clue her in."

"I'm not ready for her to kill me yet. We're having too much fun playing cat and mouse."

Gavin snorted. "I'm surprised you're not already dead. She's not the easiest to control."

Leaning against the bed, I ran my hand over my face. "I'd rather get her across state lines and back in LA without more fighting. Once we get closer to home, I'll tell her. Maybe when we get to Vegas."

"Alright, good deal. Just don't get pulled over by the cops. The closer you get to the California border, the more likely you'll hit a checkpoint."

"Noted. Keep me posted on any developments with the feds."

"Will do," he said. "I'll text you in the morning."

"Alright, I'll talk to you later, then. Thanks, Gav."

I threw my phone on the bed and looked at the bathroom door, but the shower was still running.

Slowly, I walked up to the door and leaned against it, closing my eyes. Fuck, Sadie was so close, naked, soap dripping down her body. She'd fucking lose it if I came in, though. I stressed her out enough by holding her at gunpoint.

Fuck it.

I placed my hand on my doorknob, ready to slam my foot against it to break it down, but the water turned off.

After a few seconds, I heard her rummaging through her bag, and she whispered, "Fucker," which made me chuckle.

I stepped back as she stormed out, wearing nothing but one of her silky black nightgowns with thin straps, which reached only a few inches above her knees. It was practically lingerie.

"I want the other bag that has my clean underwear and pjs that cover me more than this. All you put in this bag is the sleepwear that barely covers my ass."

I shrugged and bit my bottom lip, taking a few more steps back before my shoulders hit the wall, and I sized her up. The nightgown hugged her in all the right places, offering me easy access to the spot I craved the most. Sadie had been giving me an attitude all damn day, and it only made me want to devour her right here, right now.

"Mm," I hummed. "You look fucking good in it, though."

She scrunched up her face. "I want one of your T-shirts, Keelan."

I threw my head back and laughed. "Do you need my scent on you? I mean, I can give that to you without the shirt ... in *other* ways. I'd like you to loosen up."

"Don't be gross," she sneered, that defiance back on display. Nothing got me more excited than seeing my princess squirm under my gaze. "You're such an asshole." Her insult was mumbled as she tried to move past me, but I swept my arm around her waist and tossed her onto the bed.

Sadie immediately tried to jump off, but my hand was already grabbing her throat when her feet hit the floor. She tensed underneath me, but the defeated look in her eyes told me she had submitted.

Or at least, that's what I told myself.

Whether she wanted to admit it, Sadie needed this just as much as I did.

"Not so fast, baby girl. What's the rush?" I asked, lowering her back onto the bed, my legs caging her in.

Her sweet, luscious aroma hit me as I got closer. It was a mix of the scent of Sadie and lavender soap, and a growl rumbled deep in my chest. My eyes watched her breasts move up and down as she inhaled sharply. "Keelan, I can't—"

"Shh, of course you can. Just relax. You've been way too tense since I abducted you, and I need you to cooperate tomorrow on the road."

"Fucking hell. Can you blame me for being this tense? This isn't going to help me cooperate," she retorted.

I smiled at her little lie before my firm hands glided up both her thighs while my knee moved between hers, spreading them apart. "I mean, you slept like a little angel last night after I wrecked that pussy of yours in the dirt. This is exactly what you need."

Sadie pressed her lips together and let out a slow, long exhale.

God, I have to taste her. Right. Fucking. Now.

CHAPTER 20

Sadie

My heart raced as Keelan's hands glided up my legs, and when they reached my hips, I tried to shift to escape. But he quickly gripped them, pinning me down on the bed. Whether or not I wanted to admit it, Keelan Blake had all the power in that moment—a power I *wanted* to surrender to.

Wanted to but shouldn't.

"Take it easy, princess," he purred. "This will be a hell of a lot more fun if you stay still."

Will it, though?

He leaned over me and placed his knees on the bed, the left one on the outside of my right leg, the other pushing my thighs apart. His hands gripped the black silk of the nightgown and shifted it up to my waist. I was bared for him.

Oh my God, even his hands on my hips are making me wet. What the fuck is wrong with me?

I escaped him because he murdered a man in cold blood, and I didn't want to live with such monstrous violence—forced to exist alongside a man who killed so easily, so gleefully. I had lived through enough in my life. Just yesterday, I watched him bash a man's face into his truck until he broke his nose. Sure, according to Keelan, the guy was a sick bastard, but still, he didn't even flinch. He didn't even hesitate.

Brian, I quickly thought. Brian ... he was who I wanted. No, he was what I *needed*. Brian would have protected me from that man and quickly got us the hell out of that gas station. He was an attorney. Brian would have hoped that someday justice would be served to a man like the one who placed his hands on me, letting the law do its job ... or karma.

Brian would never, ever show that level of violence. It wasn't in his nature.

I closed my eyes and tried to imagine the kind, handsome, gracious man Brian was, but the image wasn't there. Instead, it was Keelan's intense, beautiful blue eyes, his tattooed, chiseled body, and his full, wet lips that offered so much pleasure for me to touch ... and taste. To *take* me.

Keelan's devilishly handsome face never left my mind since that day in the courtroom. The look he gave me as the officer led him out would haunt my dreams for twelve long months. It was a promise and a threat that this was not over. *We* were not over. He wouldn't rest until he found me, even if it was the last thing he ever did.

I could run again, but I would never be able to hide.

That burning blue fire in his eyes trapped me right at that moment. Keelan Blake was a dangerous animal hellbent on leaving his mark of ownership on my body and soul. He would make sure that no other man made me feel the way he did.

No man would touch me the same way as he did.

"Keelan, stop. How many times do I have to tell you I'm with someone else? This is wrong."

"Sweetheart, if this were wrong, your body wouldn't be begging for me like this," he murmured, his voice laced with smug certainty. There was truth behind those words, a truth that I hated. I gasped quietly as his hand skated across my belly, the tips of his nails tracing over the stubble above my wet heat. "Besides ... I thought he *wasn't* your boyfriend."

"Keelan," I repeated, "Brian, he's—"

My voice trailed off as he looked at me with hooded eyes. There was fury behind them, and my muscles locked up. I fucked up by saying Brian's name again. Keelan lifted his hand from my stomach and grabbed my throat.

"If your pretty lips mention that asshole's name again, I'll take a picture of me fucking you from behind and send it to him."

He squeezed my throat, but it wasn't hard enough to cut off air or hurt me. It was the same grip he used during sex, the kind that he knew I liked ... the kind that reminded me of who I belonged to.

And it was never Brian.

"I promise, Sadie, that man won't have anything to do with you after I tell him about all the dirty things we've been doing on this trip and plan to do."

My breath hitched, and my fingers dug into the blankets beneath me. The pressure on my throat was too alluring, and I didn't resist as he pushed my legs farther apart. What was it about Keelan holding me down like this that made me drip with desire? A single thought drowned out the logical ones tucked in my mind. I wanted him to slide inside of my pussy and fuck me until only *his* name left my lips.

"Mmm, that's what I thought, baby."

Keelan released my neck and roughly slid both hands down my body, causing goosebumps to skate the back of my legs. He wrapped his hands around my hips and lifted them as he bent down, pressing his hot lips against my folds, teasing me.

I cried out against the sensation and twisted the fabric of the blankets in my hands. Fuck, I was going to come just from his heated breath. He inhaled, taking in the scent of my arousal, the betrayal of my sensibilities. My body was begging for him to taste me.

The bastard knew it, too.

"You can say whatever you want, Sadie, but this sweet little cunt is desperate for my touch. I know you. I know your needs in a way he never could. I know exactly how you like to be fucked." His eyes met mine again, dark and possessive. "Like you're my fucking property."

Keelan's mouth found my heated core once more, but this time, there was no teasing. He dove in, devouring me without mercy. His tongue flicked over my clit relentlessly, sending waves of sharp pleasure that made my body lose control. All my defenses crumbled at that moment, and I completely gave myself to him.

I lifted my hips, grinding into his mouth. He groaned and applied more pressure to my clit. I had no control over the whimper leaving my mouth, my body swirling with pleasure and need.

"Keelan," I cried, biting my bottom lip. "Don't stop. Oh, God, don't stop." My voice came out breathy and pathetic, and I hated myself for it. I should stop. I *needed* him to stop. Yet neither of us was willing to pull back. He pressed his tongue against me, sucking that tender spot as his finger slid inside. I gasped more loudly now. My head fell back, my hips arching into his mouth.

"Fuck, Sadie," Keelan said while keeping his mouth against my opening, his tongue now replacing his finger. He pumped his tongue in and out of me, fucking me with his mouth. His finger stimulated my clit, keeping both sensitive spots occupied at all times. My legs were shaking against his head already, and I was hanging on by a thread.

I was so close already, and I hated that he could draw yet another orgasm out of me so easily. I tried to fight it, at one point making a feeble attempt to withdraw my hips just to make it all last a little longer, but Keelan caught me with ease, keeping me in my place. Right where he wanted me. There was no escaping him.

"Oh, fuck ... oh, fuck!" I swore as I shook against him, the pleasure building at the base of my spine. Keelan fucked me harder with his tongue, showing no intention of stopping. He *wanted* me to drown in the pleasure. Keelan wanted me to know he owned me now as much as he did back then. And he was fucking right.

It wasn't long before my orgasm hit me. I had very little control over the way my body responded to his touch. Trembling. Pulsing. Quivering. I struggled to catch my breath as pleasure rippled through me, consuming every inch of my body. Yet Keelan kept going, using his tongue and fingers to make a point.

I was his.

When he finally pulled back, his eyes were dark as they looked at me. A hard bulge was prominent in his jeans as he stood up, sliding down his zipper. Still struggling to regain my composure, I *tried* to keep my eyes on his face as his cock sprang free from his pants.

"Come here," he demanded. Still breathless, I swallowed. "Put it in your mouth."

"Fuck you."

The corners of his lips curved up like my words amused him. Then he suddenly grabbed me by my legs, yanking me down and sliding me across the mattress. I let out a slight squeal before he dragged me off the bed to my knees right in front of him. His hand wove through the strands of my hair, close to the scalp, his cock right in front of my face.

"All of this will be far simpler if you stop fighting me, sweetheart," he said. His cock was right in front of me, ready to be taken. A part of me wanted to make him suffer in whatever way I could find. But at the same time, I wanted him to lose himself to pleasure like I did—to show that I still held power over his body the way he did mine.

My gaze remained locked on his as I allowed him to guide my head forward, opening my lips to take his cock into my mouth. Right away, he filled me up with his shaft, hitting the back of my throat. There was nothing gentle about the way Keelan fucked my mouth. There was nothing gentle about the way I took him.

My tongue roughly rubbed up against his cock, stimulating him from all the angles. Tears filled my eyes as I gagged on his length, but I refused to pull away. My teeth scraped his skin to draw out the pain that he liked. Keelan's grip tightened in my hair, holding me in place ... controlling every breath I took. Saliva dripped down my chin from the force of his thrusts, and I loved every single second of it—the way his body tensed above mine. He was on the edge. I could feel it.

"Fuck, Sadie. Your soft lips feel so fucking good around me," he groaned, his head tipping back for a moment. His thrusts grew more erratic as he had barely any control left. I could feel his tip at the back of my throat as I bobbed my head back and forth, each movement accompanied by a soft gagging noise that seemed to push him closer to the edge.

He was almost there.

Keelan's pleasure was mine, even after all these years, because the urge to reach for my aching pussy was overwhelming. But before I could touch myself, he suddenly pulled back, sliding himself out of my mouth. I gasped, startled, as he gave his cock two firm strokes and spilled all over my chest.

For a moment, I was frozen in shock as he moaned through his release. The expression he made as he climaxed was nothing short of beautiful, but it did nothing to calm the irritating fact that I needed to shower *again.*

I shoved him backward and scrambled to my feet. As I did, my angry gaze locked on his satisfied one.

"Is this the part where you call me a fucking asshole?" he asked, the annoying smirk returning. "Where you pretend that I forced you to do something that your pretty little pussy and mouth had been dying for again since we left the cabin?"

My mouth parted. "You *are* a fucking asshole, Keelan. That has always been a fact." He was such a goddamn smug prick. Yet the cooling claim on me was present all the same. I moved to pass him, intending to go into the bathroom, but he grabbed my arm.

"Where do you think you're going?"

I glared at him, yanking my arm against his grip. "What the hell does it look like I'm doing? I'm going to clean up."

His eyes darkened as they moved from my face to my chest. He smiled wickedly. I already knew he was planning yet another thing to humiliate me. That's what psychos like him did. "No, I don't think I'll let you do that." Keelan reached up and began to rub the cum on my chest and neck all over my skin, coating me with *him*. "I like you like *this*. Claimed by me," he said. "The way it always should be."

Keelan wrapped his other hand around my head and leaned close, his mouth claiming mine in a possessive, desperate kiss. His tongue danced around mine. I leaned in, surrendering to that gentle part of him that would vanish by morning.

When Keelan broke the kiss, he stepped away, pointing behind me. "Get in bed."

Defeated and exhausted, I nodded and crawled into the bed but didn't lie down. Instead, I leaned against the wall and pulled the sheets up to my chest to cover the sticky mess. Keelan walked to the other side of the bed and picked up his phone from the pillow it landed on.

"I talked to Gavin while you were in the shower earlier." His tone was calm and casual, as if he hadn't just rubbed my chest with his bodily fluids moments ago.

Shocked, I blinked at the news. "Oh yeah? What were you two talking about? Or am I not privy to that?" I asked, hoping that he'd finally give me some answers about what the hell was going on.

"I—" he started before looking down at his phone. "That lockbox I told you about ...?"

"What about it?"

Keelan cleared his throat. "Patrick is the one who left it for me. He hid it somewhere. There was something big going down with our families, and he knew it was the only way to protect you. To protect *all* of us."

My eyes widened, and I dug my nails into the sheets.

"Gavin is keeping an eye on things with our families until I get it. So, maybe, for once, you trust that there's something more happening than me 'taking revenge' for your betrayal. You may not want to hear it, but you don't have a choice. You never did."

My brows furrowed in a bitter mix of confusion and anger. A prickling numbness, like icy needles, spread across my skin, and I felt detached and cold. Patrick? My dead brother is behind this goddamn nightmare? As much as I hated Patrick for mistreating me growing up, I grieved his death for months. Something about hearing Keelan talk about him set my gut on edge.

What the hell is going on?

CHAPTER 21

Sadie

That night, I slept like garbage. While Keelan had made my body feel incredible, the mere mention of Patrick dug a thorn of unease and sadness into my heart. He had been dead for well over a year, and while I had moved on from grief, his name still twisted me. He was an awful bully toward me when we were kids, but that was primarily because of my father. Patrick wanted to have Dad's approval when it came to software coding. He tried everything to keep the praise solely on him, which resulted in him tormenting me. Our father's desire for the perfect copy of himself left a lasting scar on my brother. Even as adults, Patrick and I had a cordial relationship at best.

I wanted to love my older brother, but the rift was too great.

Growing up, I often had intense, vivid dreams that woke me from nightmares in a cold sweat. I was absolutely certain that something was watching me from the closet. Those dreams kept me up for hours, and my mother, bless her damaged heart, didn't know how to console me. Dad would scream at me to go back to sleep and stop embarrassing him in front of the household staff.

I often wondered if my mind was trying to process the reality of being a part of a fucked-up criminal family, where the father beat his children and wife at every slight or imagined transgression against his image. But instead of escaping to someplace safe, the dreams would only drag me into a deeper hell. When I turned twenty-one and Keelan and I started hooking up, the dreams seemed to subside, and I could finally sleep through the night.

But tonight was different. I wasn't dreaming of something dark and frightening that I didn't recognize. It was a memory, something I had long forgotten about—an unpleasant one.

"Why did you invite him, Patrick?" my ten-year-old self snapped. "Keelan hates me!"

Patrick smirked, his brown eyes glittering with mischief. "Everyone hates you."

My mouth gaped.

Jerk!

I walked over to the oldest tree in the Ironwood Cemetery and plopped down on the browning grass. I crossed my arms and glared as my brother's best friend walked through the front gate and headed toward us. Keelan Blake was Patrick's age, just months away from turning thirteen. He wore a blue T-shirt, black shorts, and checkered sneakers for our adventure.

"Hey," Keelan said, but I wouldn't look at him. Instead, I picked up a nearby stick and started drawing shapes in the soil. But ants were nearby, so I dropped the stick and jumped up, brushing the bottom of my jeans.

Patrick smiled and started rooting around the dark gray back-pack, pulling out an old instant camera. "This was all I could find in the house. I think it's our mom's, but she won't notice it's gone."

Keelan turned his head to look at me and grinned, showing all his teeth. "Are you scared, Sade?" he asked, gesturing to the gloomy cemetery grounds. "I heard a ghost come out just now. We can catch it with that camera."

I scrunched my nose at him and stuck my tongue out. He was trying to scare me, but it wouldn't work. It was just after sunset, and the wind shook the nearby palm trees. It was a creepy place, but nothing as scary as my house.

"Is Gavin coming?" I asked. Even though Gavin was Keelan's cousin, he didn't pick on me like Keelan and his brothers did. His presence would be welcome while I was with these two assholes.

"Naw," Keelan replied, picking up my discarded stick. "He's out of town with his family for the weekend. Looks like you don't have your little savior tonight."

Was he threatening me?

Of course, he was. He was Keelan Blake.

"Alright, let's go," Patrick said. "We can snap some photos over by the older crypts. But we gotta be fast since the cemetery's security will show up soon."

We started walking north toward some of the larger crypts and mausoleums. It was darker now, and despite the nearby roads, it was eerily quiet. My skin prickled.

"Boo!" Keelan shouted, startling me. I immediately punched him hard in the arm, which hurt me more than him.

"You asshole," I cursed. Patrick snickered from up ahead.

Keelan grinned and wagged his finger at me. "Careful, Sade, or you'll get in trouble with your mommy. Since when does the precious Sadie Ryan cuss?"

I wanted to go home already.

Ignoring Keelan's teasing, I pushed past the boys, pretending that none of this bothered me. After a few minutes, we reached the area with the most crypts and mausoleums. "This looks like a good place to take a photo," I said, pointing to a tombstone ten feet ahead. I noticed a new grave dug just one row down, with a pile of dirt beside it. We moved closer and read the name on the newly carved headstone.

"Randall J. Plumperdink," Keelan read, and the three of us snickered.

"Man, his parents must have hated him." Patrick laughed before snapping a photo of the tombstone. He wandered away to look at the plaques adorning a marble crypt nearby.

"I dare you to jump in the hole, Sadie," Keelan challenged.

I quickly shook my head. "You're crazy, Kee," I said, glancing down the hole. It was pretty deep, and if I went in, I wouldn't be able to climb back out.

"Come on. I'll help pull you back out. Don't be chicken," Keelan teased as he moved to stand next to the dead man's headstone. I walked closer to the dates on the stone. Randall was thirty-five years old and died two weeks ago.

Man, that's gotta suck.

Keelan went over to the grave next to the empty hole and started sorting through the bouquet of flowers someone had left in the small plastic holder. Despite the urge to scold him, I decided it was better to ignore him. Instead, I went to the back of the headstone, leaned against the cool stone, folded my arms on top, and put my chin on my wrist.

I stared out at the dark cemetery, wondering when Keelan would head back over to me.

"Here," he said. I looked to my left, and Keelan was holding out a single flower in his hand. Even in the gloom, I could see distinctive heart-shaped blossoms in a shade of pink that I loved.

"A bleeding heart flower," I marveled. "Did you take this from someone's grave? Won't that make their ghost haunt you?"

Keelan shrugged. "Patrick told me that you guys were dealing with some bullshit this past week with your parents. Thought you'd like this since pink is your favorite color."

I was stunned. Since when had Keelan ever been this nice to me? My current tally was ... zero. Despite that, I reached out and took the flower, appreciating its simple but beautiful shape. I snuck a look at Keelan's face, expecting him to make some kind of snide remark or insult me again. But he just looked at me with an almost uncomfortable expression.

"Hey guys, look at me and smile," Patrick said. We both looked up and smiled while holding peace signs. The flash left spots in my eyes, and I rubbed them to clear them away. When I looked back at Keelan, the strange expression was gone, and he was back, grinning like a cat that had caught a mouse.

"Come on. Jump into the hole, you chicken," Keelan prodded again.

I turned and sneered at him. "Jump in yourself, dick," I said, but my quip didn't hold much weight. Keelan was already five-foot-ten and bigger than the other kids. Climbing out of the grave would be easy for him. "I don't trust you two to help me if I can't get out. You'll just leave me in there."

Already annoyed with being so close to him, I marched away from Keelan, but he reached out to grab me, and I flinched away.

"That's right, Sadie. Run away, you big scaredy-cat. We don't want a dumb, worthless girl like you here, anyway."

My body froze in anger, and tears stung the back of my eyes. I clenched my fists and turned around to look at Keelan. His handsome face lit up with malice, and he grinned wickedly. He had never called me "worthless" before, and that hurt more than I thought it would.

"Damn, Keelan, that was harsh," Patrick said while laughing.

My nostrils flared at the two boys, but I kept staring at Keelan. "Why are you always so mean to me?" I asked. "Actually, never mind. Your dad is Arthur Blake. You're all a bunch of psychos."

"Jesus, Sadie!" Patrick shouted. His expression was a clear warning to shut the hell up.

Good thing our father wasn't here. I wouldn't be able to walk for a week.

Keelan stormed over to me and grabbed my arm, squeezing so tight that his nails dug into my skin. "Watch your mouth, you little brat. God, you're such a fucking princess, aren't you? No wonder you don't have any friends. Go home, Sadie. Find someone else who actually wants you around, although I doubt anyone does. Even your own family doesn't want you."

The tears came then, staining my cheeks. I wanted to punch him in his stupid face, but my father wouldn't like that. He would punish me worse than Keelan ever could. Instead, I yanked my arm free and walked away from the grave.

"Fine!" I yelled, throwing the bleeding heart flower that he had given me on the ground. "But fuck you, Keelan." I turned to my brother, who had a weird look on his face. "And fuck you, too!"

CHAPTER 22

Keelan

We were out before noon, allowing us to sleep in for once instead of getting up at the ass crack of dawn to hit the road. Since it was such a late start, I decided to stop once we crossed the Nebraska border, unless we had to use the bathroom or needed gas.

This time, the tension between us was less hostile. After yet another vague conversation about the lockbox, we spent the night wrapped up in each other's arms, our bodies sweating against the sheets. I wouldn't go as far as thinking she was enjoying my presence now, but we weren't fighting, and she wasn't trying to run away. So, that was a start.

We drove across state lines, exchanging only a few words, which was fine. Sadie was curled up in a ball, her pretty little head resting on the pillow we stole from the motel. The afternoon exhaustion hit her hard, and within minutes of us leaving a gas station, she was asleep. As Sadie snoozed, I snuck a glance at her sleeping form.

Last night, once I mentioned Patrick, something shifted in her. One moment, we were making some progress by her surrendering her body to me completely, and then the next, the sound of her deceased brother's name from my lips pulled her back into a shell of cold anger. I thought she would try to pry more information out of me about the lockbox, but she didn't. Instead, it seemed like bringing up her brother's name bothered her even more.

Patrick was worse of a dick to her than I was, who delighted in his little sister's torment. He made her life as a child a living hell, thanks to that fucking bastard father of theirs. I was his best friend, but even I would never stoop to bullying Mia the way Patrick tormented Sadie.

I would rather cut my hand off. Growing up, I tried to divert his attention from hurting her as best I could, but it wasn't enough. When he died, I saw the relief written all over her face, even though she grieved over him. If Patrick were still alive, I would've ...

"Keelan?" Sadie's voice broke through my dark thoughts, and I glanced at her, noticing her eyes looking glossy from sleepiness.

"What is it?" I asked, keeping my tone neutral.

Sadie looked toward the road as we merged onto I-180 South toward Lincoln, Nebraska.

"This is where you said we're stopping for food, right?" she asked. "And to sleep?"

I nodded. "I figured we could shower first. Does that work?"

Options. I was giving her fucking options.

The look she gave me made it clear she was as surprised as I was that she had a choice in the matter.

Sadie pulled her brows together. "Not so bossy anymore, are you?" she asked distastefully, but I could have sworn there was the ghost of a smile on those soft pink lips. A different tightness coiled low in my belly.

"Watch the attitude, Sadie. Or I'll replace that look with my cock shoved down your throat again. And trust me, when you're gagging on my cum, you'll have no choice but to obey and swallow it down."

Her jaw dropped with a hint of blush touching her lips, and she turned away, crossing her arms over her chest. But I saw her thighs subtly press together. Wicked thoughts crossed my mind, but quickly, hunger overruled what my dick wanted to do.

The road we took across the country wasn't unfamiliar to me; my father made sure to drag me and my brothers, Logan and Aiden, along with him when making business contacts. That's why I was able to plan this so carefully. I knew this route well. Mia was left at home with her mother—my stepmother, Lily. Those trips always included the Ryan family. Finn and Arthur did their business deals best when working together.

The last time we were in Lincoln, Nebraska, Sadie had barely entered middle school. All she wanted to do was study hard so she could leave her family someday and head off to college, but when the time came, her father refused to let her go.

It wasn't that he didn't want her to have an education; he just wanted to have control over it. He had enrolled her in a private local college, having his security team constantly following her everywhere she went. Finn couldn't have an uncontrolled teen living on her own for the first time and embarrassing him on the local news. Everyone knew him in the political circle ... so they'd know her, too.

As a child, he'd drag her on these trips, forcing me, Patrick, and my brothers to babysit her while Arthur and Finn did business. One of those trips was in Lincoln. The family he took on board lived here in the city, and their sons ran a restaurant near our exit.

Memories washed over me that I had long buried. I wasn't sure if she'd remember.

I pulled out my phone, quickly searched the restaurant website, and made a reservation for two hours from now. The highway sign reminded me of a small motel not too far from the restaurant's exit. Glancing at Sadie again, she didn't seem to notice the sign or the location.

Perfect.

Thirty minutes later, we checked into the small and rather sketchy-looking motel. Unfortunately, this one didn't accept cash. But I knew everyone had a price. The clerk, a tall and skinny man, skeptically eyed both of us when I handed him an additional three hundred to pocket for himself. Of course, the bastard took it without hesitation and nodded in agreement. The look I gave him then warned him he would do whatever I needed of him, or he'd meet the other end of my knife.

Once inside the room, I tossed our bags onto the ground. "Dinner's in an hour, princess. Shower and put on a dress tonight. It's in the suitcase."

Sadie regarded me with suspicion. "Where *are* we going?"

I waved off her question. "Take a shower, and put on a dress, Sadie ... unless you wanna go naked."

"God, you're such a weird pervert sometimes," she bit out before stomping into the bathroom and slamming the door.

She's going to make me end up punishing her later.

I waited until she turned on the water and went to the suitcase. After unzipping it, I rifled around until I found the package I had folded into a pair of my jeans so Sadie wouldn't notice. While she showered, I slipped out of the room and went to the car, hiding the package under the driver's seat. I hurried back inside and sat on the bed as Sadie emerged, wrapped in a white towel. My cock twitched at the sight of her wet, naked body, and I thought about tearing that towel off and fucking her senseless against the paper-thin wall. But I had a plan and needed to follow through.

"Shower's all yours, psycho. The water pressure is garbage, though," Sadie said. She went over to the second suitcase and sorted through the clothes. "Well, it's nice that it's not all nightgowns like my other bag." She reached inside and pulled out a black dress. "You packed one of my dresses? Why would you do that?"

Shaking my head, I stood up and walked past her. "You're not wearing that tonight. I bought you an outfit before I reached Vermont. So, put the damn thing on. It's in the white box. Don't worry; I remembered your measurements, so everything should fit."

"Keelan, I don't want—" she started, but I headed to the shower, keeping the door ajar so I could eye the exit if she were to run out of our room. After turning on the water, I patiently waited for steam to fill the cramped space before stepping into the shower. The hot water burned deliciously against my inked skin as I lathered myself in soap.

Sadie's right. The water pressure is shit.

The suds trailed down my back and thighs, covering the intricate designs in thick foam. As I scrubbed, I thought about all the details

I had discussed with Gavin. Everything had to go as planned, and I hoped to God Sadie would give me even just an ounce of that trust.

Though she didn't know it yet, she was essential to finding that lockbox and taking down her family. She was in danger, and I'd be damned if I let someone take away what was mine. Sadie would have the rest of our lives to get over being mad at me if everything went according to plan.

After a few minutes, I rinsed off and stepped out of the shower. I looked at myself in the mirror, my body covered in whorls of black and gray.

A tattooed demon with a princess in my claws.

Chuckling, I dried my hair and wrapped the towel around my waist, leaving it low for my wife's gaze. I stepped out of the bathroom, and Sadie was already dressed in the outfit I bought her. My mouth gaped open as I drank her in.

Fuck.

The satin black had small blue and red roses printed along the slightly flared skirt's hemline. The fabric hugged perfectly around her slim waist, and the neckline was a halter. Sadie swept up her wet hair into a simple high bun, and she sat on the edge of the bed, adjusting the black stiletto heels I bought her as well.

"I don't get why I have to dress up for a burger joint, Keelan. This is a bizarre power move, even for you," she remarked as she stood. Her eyes immediately fell on my dangerously low towel, and another deep blush painted her cheeks before she looked away. Sadie looked breathtaking, even with the scowl on her face.

I closed my mouth and smirked at her. "Come on, babe. You know that everything I do has meaning. Now, don't be a brat for one night. We leave in twenty minutes."

I pulled the towel away and let my cock get some fresh air. Sadie made a slight choking sound as I moved to grab my clothes from the suitcase. She scooted away from me and stared out the window. Part of me wanted to grab her by the hair and yank her onto the bed, shoving that skirt up and fucking her relentlessly all night. But I wanted us to reach neutral ground again so my plans would remain intact.

Playtime can wait until after dinner.

Twenty minutes later, we pulled into the restaurant parking lot. Sadie looked over at the building, her eyes narrowing in concentration. I knew then that a vague memory was resurfacing.

"Wait .... That door looks familiar," she started, leaning into the passenger window. The name of the building was out of view. "We've been here before, haven't we?" She turned to look at me. "I've been here before, with my dad. This is the restaurant with the gold filigree butterflies."

I smiled and nodded. "We came here once when you and I were kids. You were about to go into middle school."

"This was the restaurant where Dad treated me with decency. We even talked like a father and daughter should. That was rare for him, which makes this so familiar."

"Do you remember the name, Sade?" I asked, putting my hand on her knee and tracing circles with my thumb.

Sadie glimpsed at the pink sign that glowed just out of sight. Her eyes lit up as the last bit of memory snapped into place. "Oh my God. This ... this is the Luna Butterfly. Wow, this—"

"Was where our fathers made the first deal to unite our families. We were too busy sneaking shots in the back alley to know a whole lot of what our dads were doing inside."

Sadie smiled. "This restaurant is why I love butterflies so much."

Her mouth twisted at the memory. It was the first of many meetings over the years before the one that ended with Sadie and me engaged. It was here, in this very place, that I saw Sadie for who she truly was and why I made that vow to protect her, and only her, as a young boy.

Sadie's peridot eyes sparkled as she took in the restaurant, and the memories of that one single happy moment in her life twinkled within them.

"I wonder if they still serve that strawberry crème brûlée?" she said, but it was more to herself. "God, I actually remember that."

I pulled the car into the parking spot and cut the engine before grinning at her. "There's only one way to find out," I said as I exited the car. I carefully tucked the package under my sports jacket and went to open the passenger door for her. I took her hand in mine and gently helped her out. The light from the lamps painted her body gold, and I felt my heart tighten. She really was a beautiful little thing—a lovely, breakable princess.

Once inside, we gave the host our reservations, and we were seated immediately in a booth tucked away from the other patrons. The restaurant hadn't changed in the last decade. It was as if time couldn't touch this place, and it would stay this way forever.

The server—a middle-aged woman with medium-brown skin, brown eyes, and graying hair tied up with a thick pink ribbon to complete her uniform—approached us to take our drink orders. Sadie ordered an espresso martini, and I ordered a scotch.

"Excuse me," I said. "Could you bring a bottle of champagne as well? It's a special occasion."

The server smiled. "Right away."

After she left, Sadie stared at me. "Why would you order champagne, Keelan?"

"Like I said, it's a special occasion, princess. It was your birthday this week."

Sadie's face became confused. "Birthday? No, Keelan. My birthday isn't until February."

"True," I said, "but that's what you have listed on your fake ID." I gave her a small smile. "We'll celebrate both. Happy twenty-third."

The server returned with our cocktails, an ice bucket containing a bottle of champagne, and two crystal flutes.

"Are you ready to order any appetizers or entrees?" the woman asked.

"Yes, this may sound odd, but could you bring one of every appetizer on the menu?" I said, offering a charming smile to the server. Sadie cocked an eyebrow at me, her lips pressed against a smile.

Ah, she remembers doing that as a kid. Finn would get pretty annoyed, but since Arthur paid for the bill most of the time, he didn't say shit.

"Of course. Anything else?" she asked.

"Yeah, do you still serve the strawberry crème brûlée?" she added.

"We do, actually," the server replied. "It's the owner's mother's own recipe, so I don't think they'll be getting rid of it anytime soon."

Sadie responded with an excited smile and said, "Cool. We'll split that, too."

The server smiled and wrote the request down on her pad. "No problem; we'll have all of that out shortly."

The woman returned to the kitchen, and a quiet bubble settled over our booth. Sadie was still looking at me with a confused expression. "I don't understand. Why are you doing all this?" she asked, twisting her fingers in her lap. "You've never been this kind to me. Like, ever."

"I already told you, it's a special occasion. Here," I said, reaching behind and pulling the brown paper package from my waistband. "This was supposed to be your birthday *and* engagement present last year. But as we both know, we didn't quite get to that date to exchange gifts."

Sadie shifted uncomfortably. That night, she had a magazine she posed in all for me, but instead, she watched me kill a man, dropping her gesture into a puddle of water in a rundown warehouse.

I slid the package across the table, and Sadie took it carefully, tearing the top of the paper. I watched in anticipation as she reached inside. Sadie gasped as she pulled a black leather-bound book from the package. The twenty-two-karat gold accents gleamed in the darkness of the restaurant.

"It's a first edition of Mary Shelley's *Frankenstein*," Sadie exclaimed. She turned the book carefully in her hands, examining the gilded edges of the paper, and her fingers played on the soft leather bindings. Her eyes sparkled with unshed tears as she looked up at me. "How did you know I wanted this?"

I lifted my shoulder in a shrug. "Shortly after we got engaged, you told me about some of your interests and mentioned that you wanted to start collecting rare books, starting with the woman who created the sci-fi genre."

Sadie looked back at the book and carefully wiped away a tear that threatened to splash on the leather. "I didn't think you cared about anything I was interested in. I was just somebody you got tied to."

She raised her head back to look at me, and for the first time since I'd taken her, she smiled—a radiant, warm, beautiful smile that promised so many unspoken things that a monster like me never deserved.

"Thank you, Kee. I love it."

That long-forgotten nickname. My heart seized on that word, and a crack started to form—a crack in the shape of her.

Yes, I'd been a dick to her since we met, and even now. But my reasons had always been simple. I spent my life protecting her from the cruelty of her brother, her family, and the world. She never deserved any of them. Never deserved any of the shit from this fucked-up world. Sadie Ryan was the blood in my veins, the breath in my lungs, and the kindest glimmer my blackened soul ever had. I would break the world apart if it meant she smiled like that for me forever. No man would *ever* lay a finger on what was mine again. I'd kill them all before they took her away from me.

My heart squeezed so hard I thought it was going to burst into my chest cavity. I looked into those sparkling peridot eyes that were happy because of *me* and smiled back. Though I wanted to profess that to her, the only words that left my lips were, "It was nothin'."

CHAPTER 23

Sadie

The sound of Keelan's yawn jolted me awake as he shifted beside me in bed. I looked through the open shades of the window as Keelan climbed off the mattress, seeing the sun right above the building across the parking lot. We slept in again.

After dinner last night, I told Keelan he could sleep on the floor. Wouldn't you know, the bastard snuck into bed when I fell asleep at three a.m. The pressure of his arm around my chest startled me awake. I tried elbowing him away, but he only gripped harder.

As frustrating as it was that he couldn't give me space, there were times when we slept that I felt his erection press against my ass. If I was being honest, the thought of him forcefully pinning me down and having his way with me caused a knot in my stomach.

God, I'm so pathetic, and I'm starting to not even care.

Was I more frustrated with him ... or myself?

When Keelan got out of bed and went into the bathroom with his change of clothes, I sat up, stretching my arms and relishing in the cracks and pops of my spine. I climbed out of bed and padded over to the suitcase. I shifted through the clothes until I found my black T-shirt and a pair of black leggings. Not wanting to be undressed in front of Keelan again, I quickly threw on the clothes and worked on brushing out the knots in my hair.

As I combed through my faded red hair, my thoughts wandered back to last night. Keelan gave me a gift that had meaning and thought behind it. He *actually* listened to me when I told him about my ambitions to build a rare book collection. I would have never thought he paid attention to anything I said, just wanting to fuck me and forget I existed afterward. When I thanked him, Keelan had a strange look on his face, but then he shrugged like it was nothing. It was infuriating trying to read him. We'd been around each other for years, but he was still a damn enigma—a monstrous one who killed without remorse.

The bathroom door opened, and Keelan walked out, dressed in jeans and a tight blue T-shirt that made his sapphire eyes stand out. Without realizing it, I was drinking in the sight of him. Keelan Blake was a beautiful man, and those tattoos only enhanced that beauty. Whenever we were having sex, I would take moments to memorize the tattoos and the intricate lines that made the art meld to his body. Despite the bullshit contract engagement, I really did want to try to understand my future husband better.

Suddenly, the memory of the man Keelan killed in the warehouse flooded my mind. The gurgling scream, the exposed bones and larynx of Richard Wertz's throat as the knife severed them in half. And the blood, the endless black-crimson blood.

Nothing about that night made sense. *Why would he kill my dad's employee like that?*

Keelan noticed me watching him and smiled, making me feel uneasy. I turned away, quickly finished brushing, and then braided my hair into a simple plait.

"Are you ready to hit the road?" Keelan asked as he packed away the clothes lying on the floor.

I nodded, went to the rickety nightstand, and picked up the *Frankenstein* novel. My fingers traced over the gold designs again, and my heart grew full, even with the horrible memory still in my head.

"Maybe we can buy a small tote or something to protect that book for now," Keelan suggested, breaking my train of thought. I turned to find him watching me with a gentle smile, and a blush crept up to my cheeks.

"Yeah," I said, grabbing my bag. "That's a great idea. I'd be sick if something happened to this book."

Within ten minutes, we packed up and walked out to the car. Keelan had slipped the desk clerk another hundred-dollar bill with the unspoken threat of "Talk, and I'll come back and cut you open."

It was a beautiful morning. While I knew I was still an unwilling passenger on a car ride from hell, the fresh air and blue skies felt good. I closed my eyes and took a few breaths, taking in the smell of flowers and pine trees.

I miss Mason's property. I miss the open air.

"Alright, get in, princess. We gotta get going." Keelan now sounded annoyed. He was completely different now from how he was at the restaurant. It was as if he had seen his own vulnerability through his kindness and the gift and was attempting to bounce back to the dick he always was. "We aren't stopping again unless we sleep, eat, or fill up gas. We got about seventeen more hours to Vegas. We may have to crash in Colorado, but we'll get up early enough not to lose any time on the road. Our next stop after that is the Strip."

Kind Keelan was an act. "How about you just give me a minute, so I can appreciate a nice day without the escaped convict getting on my ass?" I muttered, closing the door and putting on my seat-belt.

"Don't start, Sadie. We have a lot of ground to cover today," Keelan said as he started the car. "We can appreciate the nice weather when we get to Nevada."

I pressed my lips into a tight line, glancing out the window as Keelan drove us out of the lot and onto the highway heading west. As much as I wanted to protest, I decided to let it go.

"City boys never appreciate a beautiful fall day like this one," I whispered to the window, but it wasn't loud enough for him to hear.

Dad had always warned me about putting my feet on the dash. A head-on collision or even a fender bender could snap my legs or drive them into my face ... or something like that.

Today, I didn't care about that warning. A calm had settled between Keelan and me, and we were actually talking. In fact, we laughed and made jokes. We told stories about our time together as kids, and I reminded him how much of a bully he was. Keelan, of course, never apologized and laughed even more.

He had a nice laugh.

With my hair now tied into a messy bun, feet propped on the dash, and the window slightly cracked open, I leaned back in the seat and breathed in the crisp, Colorado air. It was freezing near the mountains, but I wanted to feel that icy wind on my skin. Looking out at the mountain peaks, I watched as the sun slowly set behind them, painting the sky in so many different colors.

Those mountains are beautiful.

As we rolled down the endless curves of I-70, Keelan mentioned that we were almost to our destination. But almost to where? I knew we were about to meet his brothers in Vegas and, from there, Burbank. But as to what we were doing when we arrived, I still didn't know. Every time I asked, he refused, reminding me that I am not privy to any information unless he deigns to tell me.

I am his prisoner, after all.

Keelan kept one hand on the steering wheel, his tattoos tinted orange by the sunset, and the other tapped rhythmically against his thigh. He seemed so ... relaxed, as if this was another road trip rather than a kidnapping plot involving a dangerous escaped convict.

"Sade, remember this song?" Keelan asked, breaking my gaze away from the rocky cliffs. He smiled as he turned up the volume on the radio. The familiar notes of "Suffocate" by Bad Omens flowed from the car speakers. When Keelan was tattooing my constellations, this song blasted through the shop while he worked. I loved it so much that I made him play it on repeat for two hours.

"No, not at all," I lied, but my lips curled, teasing him. He knew about how obsessed I became with that song.

Keelan's eyes darted to me before returning to the road. "Aren't you happy I talked you out of that butterfly tattoo?"

"I really did want that butterfly."

"Yeah, but everyone has a butterfly tattoo."

I shrugged. "Yeah, so? My idea would have been unique, and with your skills, it could have been pretty cool. Butterflies all start confined within cocoons, but once they break free, they can spread their wings and escape. To show the world their beautiful colors, no longer bound by what nature had forced them into." I turned to look at him. "To be away from everything that makes them feel so afraid."

Keelan didn't say anything, nor would he meet my gaze. Instead, he continued tapping on the wheel and turned up the music to drown out the possibility of this conversation going any further. I rolled my eyes before pulling the lever on the side of the seat to raise me upright, my legs slipping back to the floor. Reaching out, I lowered the volume so I could talk.

"Clearly, this doesn't matter to you," I said, cocking a brow at him. "When we get back to California, I'll just ask Gavin to give me one."

I mentally smirked. That would earn me a stern glance.

"Are you trying to provoke me?" he asked, almost teasing. But I knew there was an edge beneath the light tone. A coded reminder of what kind of punishment he would give me later for suggesting another man touch my skin.

God, it's so hard to get him to open up.

"How upset were you when your dad told you that you'd have to marry me?" I asked, changing the subject. "Be honest."

Keelan swallowed, and the muscles in his jaw tightened. "I wasn't upset," he said, glancing at me momentarily.

I laughed. "Yeah, right. According to Logan, you threw your dad's favorite whiskey decanter against the wall, sending glass shards all over the kitchen floor."

Keelan snorted, his lips forming a smirk. He remembered. "That wasn't why I threw it," he replied. "Arthur caught me at a bad time."

My eyes narrowed, and I sat back in the seat.

That was *not* the story that made its way through the families. Logan told me that Keelan was so angry about the engagement that he broke a few other items in the house. He hated me that much.

"We got into a bullshit argument about how I handled a client earlier that day. I was fuming and ready to leave when Dad threw in that tidbit of information. My hand was on the doorknob when he casually said, 'Oh, and don't make plans to leave town this weekend. You have your engagement party tomorrow night. You can't disappoint your *blushing* bride.'"

He turned to me and met my eyes for a brief second before turning back to the road, and my stomach tightened a little. I wasn't sure why this new information made me feel uneasy. Perhaps it was because he was trying to explain away this illusion I apparently had regarding the forced engagement, though he was probably lying.

"I wasn't angry that they gave you to me. That's just the nature of things when you're bound to this life. It irritated me that they were forcing *you* against your will. While I may have earned the spot in Arthur and Finn's agenda, you didn't. You weren't meant to be trapped in their world."

And yet, he trapped me in *his*.

Keelan didn't look at me again. My insides twisted into knots. That wasn't how I remembered it. He never gave a shit about how I felt about any of it. The engagement party was such a negative experience I tried to forget. But I remember that night clearly. Mom had made me wear a blush-pink dress covered in tiny white pearls. I wore matching pearl earrings and a necklace that felt like a noose around my neck. Dad didn't say much. He only smiled for the guests and, when no one was watching, warned me to, "fucking behave," before heading into the dining room.

We all sat at the table, every member of our families attending—even Patrick, who mocked my outfit and commented to Keelan about how I would finally be of use. There was a meal and multiple toasts with champagne. Keelan and I were forced to sit together, fake smiles plastered on our faces, but only anger and disgust were beneath the veneer. My future had been decided for me. That's when I started filling my glass with the bubbly liquid that would numb me.

After five glasses, I was drunk off my ass. I managed to sneak off to the bathroom without anyone noticing. After peeing and crying, I emerged to see Keelan waiting for me. He grabbed my wrist and led me upstairs to his bedroom. I was too hammered to protest, so instead, I threw myself at him. Keelan had drank almost as much champagne as I did, so it wasn't as though he was taking advantage of me. Before we knew it, we were kissing and tearing each other's clothes off.

That night, Keelan took my virginity.

The sex was frenzied and *rough,* with Keelan slamming me onto the bed and fucking me from behind. There was no foreplay from either of us, and the intrusion of his cock was painful but felt *so* good. For the first time since being told I was engaged to the violent Keelan Blake, I felt alive. The next day, my pussy was swollen and raw to the touch. I had bled on his bedsheets, too. After I went home, I wondered if sex was always that chaotic or if Keelan was some kind of unhinged animal. Either way, I soon realized that I was his new toy to play with whenever he wanted.

Most women would rightly be afraid. To me, it was a secret thrill that warred with my shame over it.

There was a chuckle in my ear, and my thoughts scattered, pulling me back to reality.

"What?"

"You."

"What about me?"

"I can always tell when you're daydreaming," he quipped while smiling. "You were thinking about the party, weren't you?"

No way I'm telling him that.

"The party? Ugh, no. I try my best to forget that night."

Keelan turned the music down, and I braced for some smart-ass comment or insult. But he didn't say anything. We both knew the truth about that night. We abandoned our mutual hatred and found comfort in the one thing we could give away without any regret—our bodies.

Silence suddenly filled the space between us, heavy with everything left unsaid all these years.

The tension seemed to grow in the moments that followed as we continued down the dark road. I turned to look out the window again, the clouds moving against the starry night, trying to focus on anything but this conversation.

"Sadie? Why did you do it?" Keelan's voice was quieter now, almost fragile. I couldn't look at him. "Why did you testify against me?"

He can't be serious.

"You know I didn't have a choice," I replied, keeping my eyes on the towering peaks of the Colorado mountains. "If I didn't, you would have killed me."

Keelan laughed. The fucker dared to laugh at my fear. Our families disposed of "witnesses" all the time. How could I not have assumed that would have been my fate, too?

"What is so goddamn funny about that?" I snapped, turning to him. "It was you in prison or me dead, Keelan. If you didn't slit my throat, your father or brothers sure as fuck would. Testifying gave me protection from the families. I was *done* with all that bullshit. Including you." My words were as sharp as glass, and I aimed right for the jugular. "You killed a man, Keelan. For no reason. What did you want me to do? Lie? I didn't love you, and I was tired of being property written in a damn contract. If anything, it gave me an out. I no longer had to marry a man who would kill me in my sleep on a whim. I wouldn't have to share a bed with someone who didn't see me as a human being, just a transaction."

The bitterness in my voice tasted like venom, and I hoped it burned his soul.

Keelan swallowed, jaw tight. "Well," he said. "Your little escapade didn't last long, did it? Don't think that you freed yourself from anything, Sadie. You're still mine—my ... transaction. You have no say in the matter, even now."

My jaw dropped, and despite myself, tears stung my eyes. I knew it. I fucking knew that Keelan didn't give a shit about me or my well-being. I was a fool to believe he had even one speck of decency when he gifted me that book. Keelan was still the same—my tormentor.

"I wish you had just left me alone."

Suppressed anger clawed at my gut, warring with a thousand other emotions I didn't have names for. The air inside the car became suffocating. I had to crack the window farther to let in more ice-tipped wind. The sharp cold was a desperate attempt to feel something other than the rawness in my heart.

To feel anything else.

I turned away but saw him glance at me from my peripheral. For a moment, he looked like the boy I had grown up with, who I fought with over stupid shit. Who gave me a flower to cheer me up. Something in my heart ached. That boy was gone, replaced by this cold-hearted man who killed and hurt for his own satisfaction—an escaped convict who kidnapped me from my home for selfish desires.

My gaze drifted from the jagged rocks to the highway. The sun was behind the mountains now, and a halo of gold and pink light framed the horizon. It was a beautiful Colorado evening sky. But something else drew my attention, something twinkling in the distance.

Those are flashing police lights ... shit!

My heart lurched, and adrenaline poured into my veins. It was a roadblock.

"Fuck!" Keelan swore loudly and took his foot off the gas.

We were far enough from the checkpoint that Keelan could turn off the headlights and maneuver the car behind some shrubbery on the side of the highway.

"Get out," he ordered, the words sharp. "You're driving."

"What?" I stared at him, panic crawling up my throat. "No!"

The look he gave me set my heart racing in terror, and I nodded. The intensity in those icy eyes was enough to make me obey. I ran a shaking hand through my hair before I opened the car door.

When he came to the passenger side, Keelan grabbed my wrist, squeezing it hard. "Do not say a goddamn thing unless you want a cop's death on your hands." He paused, and for a split second, I saw something akin to fear in his eyes. "Please, Sadie. Don't make me hurt anyone."

My throat dried as I nodded again, my heart slamming so hard against my ribs it hurt. The world seemed to close around me, and the thin air throttled my lungs.

"If that roadblock is for you ... they'll recognize you, Keelan. I won't be able to—"

"Most likely, it's just a standard checkpoint, and they'll wave you through once you identify yourself. I'll be hidden in the trunk with the gun. You'll figure it out. Because if you don't ... if you do anything to signal you're in trouble, I'll shoot those cops right between the fucking eyes. I didn't go through all this to be caught. Do you understand?"

The lump in my throat damn near strangled me as I swallowed, tears stinging behind my eyes. "I understand."

Keelan waited until I slid behind the wheel. He went to the back of the car and climbed into the trunk. The latch clicked, and I glanced at the rearview mirror. I wasn't stupid enough to believe he didn't have a way out of there.

Looking out at the dark, empty highway, I inhaled deeply and shifted the car into drive. My clammy hands squeezed the steering wheel hard as we drove toward the flashing lights. My entire body screamed to turn around, drive the car into a ditch, and run into the woods. But I didn't. I couldn't.

The police lights were blinding as I pulled up, and the officers waved me forward. Their expressions were neutral, but their eyes were honed on my face. I forced a smile—at least they couldn't hear my thundering heartbeat.

"Evening, ma'am," the officer who waved me forward said, leaning down to peer into the car. I saw his eyes scanning the passenger and back seats to ensure I was alone. "Mind telling me where you're headed?"

"Um, sure, yeah. Las Vegas," I replied, my voice too high, too thin. "It's my friend Kristen's bachelorette party. I've never been there."

The officer smiled, the corners of his dark eyes creasing, and gave me a quick nod. He scanned the car again. "Everything alright?"

Shit.

I didn't think I looked that nervous, but considering the stress I'd been under, maybe my face showed more than I thought.

Offering a tired-sounding laugh, I said, "Oh, yeah. I'm just exhausted. I've been driving for hours."

The officer studied for a moment before taking a step back from the car. "May I see your license, please?"

Was that allowed? I had no idea what the law was regarding checkpoints or roadblocks. Not wanting to appear suspicious, I reached into the bag where my wallet with the fake ID was. I slipped out the card and handed it to him.

Please, God, don't let him look in the trunk.

The officer read the name on the card. "Tess Larson from Tucson, Arizona," he said before smiling and handing it back. "Hope you win big this weekend. Congrats to your friend."

Relief washed over me, leaving my insides trembling and cold. I smiled back cheerfully. "I'll do my best. Thank you, sir."

He waved me on, and I carefully drove past the lights and traffic cones back onto the highway. I checked the rearview several times to ensure I wasn't being followed. It felt like my heart was going to explode.

I drove down the highway for several miles before my heart stopped thudding in my ears. My hands were shaking so badly that gripping the wheel until my knuckles turned bone white was the only thing to stop the tremors. My mind was screaming at me to keep driving, to find the nearest town and go to the police.

As I looked for any road signs, I heard a thud behind the passenger seat. Before I could scream, Keelan's hand wrapped around my throat from behind, and the cold steel of the gun pressed against my temple. I lurched, swerving the car almost into the other lane.

Oh my God. The bastard climbed out from the trunk through the backseats.

"Sadie, pull the goddamn car over." His voice was so cold, so lethal. Acid boiled in my gut, and my body went numb. Wordlessly, I pulled the car onto the dirt shoulder near a grove of aspen trees. I didn't dare breathe, not with that metal promise of death against my head.

"Thought you could pull a fast one on me?" he whispered, lowering the gun from my head.

"N ... no," I croaked, my throat thick. My chest tightened with pain and terror. "I was trying to find a place to pull over."

"Little liar. I know exactly what you were trying to do, princess." Keelan squeezed my throat. Another threat. "Just remember, you have no freedom. Run all you want. Scream, plot, pray—I've already outmaneuvered you. I've strategically planned this for over a year, princess. No one's coming to save you."

CHAPTER 24

Sadie

According to the last road sign I had seen since we passed the checkpoint, we were less than two hours from Grand Junction. I still felt on edge after being questioned by that cop. Even though I wanted my freedom, I was more afraid that they'd find Keelan because I knew exactly what would have happened if they did.

Keelan, noticing how tense I was during that next hour, suggested we do something other than stop for gas or snacks.

"Alright, listen," Keelan started after shutting off the engine. He reached out and placed his hand on my knees, gingerly caressing my leg. The hairs on the back of my neck stood on end as I waited for whatever threat or warning he was about to give me. Despite the rising tension, he squeezed my thigh before pulling away.

What was that? Was he comforting me?

Keelan pulled his T-shirt over his belt, concealing his gun on his hip. "I don't like seeing you this intense and shut down, so maybe a drink and a decent meal will help. I'm sure you're dying to stretch your legs."

All I did was nod quickly, hoping everything would go as smoothly as I had imagined. It would eat away at my soul if Keelan hurt someone else.

Just like the checkpoint, I wasn't going to run. I wasn't going to tell anyone I was a prisoner.

Keelan got out first, came to my side, and opened the door for me, reaching out and taking my hand. He ran his thumb gingerly over my skin before wrapping his fingers around mine and leading me to the front door. "Behave, princess."

The laughs and memories today were now forgotten, and we were back to this.

You got it, psycho.

The place looked like the typical dive bar we had seen on the road trip so far. Motorcycles lined up along the front curb, and old country music played from the jukebox, blaring out each time the door opened.

There were a few shops on the other side of the road that were now closed, but other than that, there weren't many places I could escape to, anyway. This bar seemed to be out in the middle of nowhere, and the streetlight barely illuminated the road. I would get lost within minutes due to how dark and secluded this town was.

Once we stepped inside, a few heads turned, looking at us. The small crowd consisted of heavily tattooed bikers with beautiful women in their arms, groups of people shooting pool, and a couple of men taking shots and laughing.

Keelan would fit right in, but I stuck out like a sore thumb.

We reached the bar, and Keelan gestured for me to sit. He ordered a beer for himself and a cranberry cocktail for me.

He remembered what I liked.

"Okay, Sadie," he said, facing me once the bartender placed his beer on the counter. He had a playful smile adorning his lips, as if he wasn't an unhinged kidnapper carrying a gun on him that he planned to use if I got out of hand. "Truth or dare."

I let out a small, breathy laugh. "I'm not twelve, Keelan. Give me a break."

This wasn't the first time we'd played this juvenile game. When Keelan was seven and I was five, our families started forcing us to spend time together, so he and my brother often hung out. During that time, I watched them play this game. I was never invited—not until I turned eight. My brother and his friends introduced me to the game, which quickly became a source of torture for me. It gave Keelan an excuse to humiliate me—and he always did.

"Come on," he said. "We spent the last few hours talking and sharing stories. I thought we were making progress today."

"Progress? You made me lie to a cop while you hid in the trunk with that gun. All I could think about was that if I fucked up, you'd kill him. You also held the goddamn gun to my head. My nerves haven't settled one bit, you absolute fuckwad."

"You laughed this morning, didn't you?" he said with a playful smile. "We've done nothing but fight or fuck on this trip, and now you're all tense again."

I slowly turned to him and glared despite the involuntary flip my stomach did when he brought up fucking.

"So, how about you have a drink and play a game with me? Then we can start over?"

"You want to start over?" I said. "Keelan, I'm a captive, being dragged across the country to help you find some fucking box that my *dead* brother left behind that has nothing to do with me. Not only that, but you decided to be *kind* to me last night at dinner. I'm guessing that was some manipulation tactic to get you on my good side? Now you want to play some game that we did as kids where you always picked me to confess something I didn't want to or do some stupid shit to embarrass me. I'd rather pick a song on the jukebox and join that couple by the dartboard."

I wasn't exactly sure where to go when I hopped off the chair and grabbed my drink, but I dramatically marched away from him. I didn't get far before Keelan grabbed the back of my neck and yanked, causing me to fall a little and splash my drink over my black shirt.

Dick!

Frustration built inside me as the sticky, sugary liquid soaked through my shirt and, most likely, all over my beige bra.

That is going to stain.

Keelan pulled me back to the bar, grabbed my drink, and put it down. "Sit your ass back down, Sadie. Before you make me cause a scene."

I bit my bottom lip out of anger but obeyed, hopping back up on the tall barstool. This time, I wouldn't turn to look at him. Instead, I grabbed my drink, pressed the glass to my lips, and knocked down the entire cocktail in one long chug.

I set the glass down and immediately felt the alcohol loosen the tension in my body and dull the edge of my thoughts. I sighed and leaned back against the chair. Keelan placed his hand again on my leg like he did in the car, but this time, he ran his hand up my thigh and between my legs. I stiffened as his thumb pressed over my clit through my thin leggings. "Truth or dare ... wife?"

I closed my eyes as he began to rub circles, and I squeezed my thighs together, taking a slow and steady breath. The sensation was irritatingly wonderful, and part of me wanted to slap his hand away. The other part was holding me back.

"Would you like another?" the bartender said, and I looked up. My cheeks flushed pink. Despite his complete disregard for public displays of perversion, Keelan surprised me by lifting his fingers from that sensitive spot, though he kept his hand on the inner thigh so close to it. Once the bartender placed her hands on the edge and met my eyes, he removed his hand completely from between my legs and grabbed his beer, taking another sip.

The asshole was smiling.

"Yes, please," I said, swallowing down my nerves. I knew the only way I'd get through this evening was to get completely obliterated. I thought about that, being vulnerable around him. Though Keelan was an unapologetic criminal, a small part of my brain somehow trusted that he wouldn't do anything to me in that state.

A very, very small part of my brain.

"Truth," I said, thinking this might be the safest of the two options.

Keelan smirked, and his eyes raked over me.

I'm not going to like this question.

The bartender placed my drink in front of me, and I picked it up, taking a slower sip of my cranberry vodka this time. The ice-cold burn anchored my spiraling thoughts, easing the anxiety from my shoulders and legs.

"Despite your fear and complete hatred for me, did you think of me when Brian fucked you?"

I choked on my drink, almost spitting all over him.

The audacity of this man. "No," I said curtly.

"Liar."

My nostrils flared, and though I didn't want to give him that satisfaction, I suddenly felt a little brave. "Okay, fine. Yes. I mean … sometimes." I looked away. "Brian's … different. That's not always a bad thing, Kee."

I knew that would earn me a glare.

Good. Seethe about it.

"I see…." he said, leaning back in his chair while taking a swig of his beer, his eyes never leaving mine.

Despite how much I knew that probably burned a hole in his chest, it was the truth. I cared for Brian. *Wait, I still care for him.* Except, what we had was different. Brian was sweet, intelligent, charming, and had his shit together. Just because sex wasn't wild and animalistic like mine and Keelan's was, Brian didn't kill people. Brian respected me, unlike Keelan, who only wanted my body—a pretty little object he could use. Though, his confession in the car had me second guessing that detail.

But Brian doesn't make me feel alive when I come.

Something in Keelan's eyes shifted then, a subtle yet dangerous edge in his eyes that caused my stomach to tighten. Particularly when he slowly grabbed the napkin his beer had been resting on and crumpled it with his hands.

Great.

"Truth or dare?" I asked, hoping to pull him out of whatever crazy thoughts were going through his head from that comment.

Keelan's eyes softened then, and he smirked.

Thank God.

This time, he raised his brow, as if he were genuinely curious about what I would ask him to do. I was never this bold, so I had to show him I wasn't afraid. I also knew Keelan would do absolutely anything I asked him to. He was always a loose cannon and feared nothing like he had to prove a point.

"Dare," he said, and my brows shot up. This was too easy.

"Okay," I said. I couldn't think of anything crazy, so I just spoke the first idea that came to mind. "I dare you to let me hold your gun until we leave the bar."

Alright, maybe that was a little crazy.

Keelan's lips parted, and he flashed his teeth when he grinned, cocking his head slightly to the right like he was thinking about it. It was ballsy, and most likely, he'd laugh and tell me no. It didn't hurt to try.

He leaned back in his chair and adjusted himself, reaching over to the holster on his hip and pulling out his gun. Okay, that surprised me. When he hesitated, I let out a small giggle. "I was always better at this game than you."

Keelan's playful laugh actually made me smile, and I wasn't sure why. It was rare how often he'd laugh like that, like some schoolboy who had just had his first kiss. That "nothing bothered me" look and the way he licked his bottom lip seductively, though I don't think he was intending to look sexy as hell doing it.

He grabbed the bottom of the gun, pulled out the magazine, and emptied the chamber before putting it on my lap. "Here," he said. "I don't trust you won't shoot me with it."

"You're cheating."

"You said gun, sweetheart. You never specified if it had to be loaded."

I wrapped my hands around the gun and sighed. The weapon's weight was imposing, though I had handled firearms like this growing up. My dad always made sure my brother and I knew how to defend ourselves, even though he wanted us to use them for intimidation, not safety. I just had to find a way to get those bullets back from Keelan, and I could leave.

Maybe I can club him with the damn thing.

"Truth or dare?" he asked, taking a few more gulps of his beer to finish it off. He waved his hand for the bartender to come over and ordered another. It had been a while since I had seen Keelan drink, but if he kept this up, I wouldn't be sure we'd be able to drive out of here, which could also be to my advantage.

"Dare," I said, knowing I would regret this one. Maybe it was the vodka numbing my brain, but I felt braver and braver by the minute.

I also didn't want him to ask me any more questions about Brian.

Keelan smiled and leaned so close to my ear that his warm breath brushed against my cheek. "I dare you to follow me to the bathroom and suck me off until I cum all over your pretty mouth."

At those words, a rush of excitement surged right through my core. But I also knew this was my opportunity if I was ever going to have one again.

Keelan can't kill anyone if I have his gun.

"Okay," I said way too quickly, watching his brows shoot up in surprise. He was probably thinking I'd put up a fight or argument.

Keelan leaned back and pulled his shirt up again to unhook the gun holster. He then pulled my shirt up and placed it on the inner part of my leggings, securing it over the strap. Once done, he gestured with his head to the gun, and I slipped it into the holster.

"Let's go," he said, reaching out his hand.

While he placed the magazine in his pocket, I downed the rest of my drink and put it back on the bar. I took a glance around the room. The patrons paid us no mind as we rose from the stools and headed toward the hallway in the back. Keelan grabbed my hand and escorted me to the ladies' room. Once inside, he began to unbuckle his jeans.

"There isn't a lock on the door, Keelan," I said. "Someone can walk in."

"Then you need to hurry," he said.

I swallowed and moved to him, kneeling on the hard tile bathroom floor. I watched him pull his cock free, and it was already hard and ready, the veins bulging along his shaft. Despite myself, I could feel the pulse of arousal in my core.

"To be honest, Sade, I didn't take you for a girl who runs for the first dick who said hello to you. How did you meet him, anyway?"

"Really?" I said, looking up. "You ask for a blowjob, and now you want to know about ... him?"

"I'm entitled to know about the asswipe who thought he could touch my wife."

"Jesus Christ," I groaned, leaning back on my heels. "We met in town. He and I ran into each other a few times before he asked me out at the shop. Happy, you weirdo?"

"I'll be happy when I break his jaw, and you're filled with my cock again. Speakin' of which ..." Leaning back against the sink counter, he reached out and tightly tangled his fingers in my hair.

"Put it in your mouth," he ordered.

I wrapped my lips around his cock, having to stretch my mouth to fit his girth, and began to suck. Keelan sighed and moved his hips, his thrusts going deeper until I almost gagged. He wasn't slow or tender but aggressively pushing himself into me as I used my tongue to caress his hard length.

It was pretty clear that this was my punishment for responding how I did when he asked about Brian.

"Take it like a good girl, Sadie. I *dare* you." The corners of his mouth turned up into a wicked grin.

I closed my eyes as I sucked, using my hands to grip his muscular thighs. Keelan moaned, his hips bucking again, harder and faster.

"I'm already close."

How is that even possible?

When I looked up, his expression was pure pleasure, and his head fell back. "Fuck," he cried out. "This is just another reminder of who you belong to." He closed his eyes, and his jaw tensed. "Forget it. I'm not coming on your lips. I want you to swallow, baby. All of it."

Another thrill bounced in my stomach. Keelan was the only guy I had ever done that to, and I'd be lying if I told myself I didn't fucking love it. The taste of *him*.

With a few more thrusts, he let out a moan, his warm liquid filling my mouth. I swallowed the slightly salty fluid down until he pulled out and then used the inside of my shirt collar to wipe the remaining cum off my lips. Keelan was still dripping from his cock when I stood, but he moved past me, heading to the towels to clean himself up. Slowly, I stepped back until my hand touched the handle.

And then I bolted out the door.

All eyes looked at me as I maneuvered around the tables. I couldn't stop, though. I had to get as far away from Keelan as possible.

Once outside, I looked around. It was so dark, and though a few men and one woman were hopping onto their bikes, I kept running. It would take too many precious seconds to explain that I was being held captive and needed to escape. Keelan would catch up, and who knew what would happen then?

Behind the bar was another parking lot facing a forest that was too pitch black to see through, only a barbed wire fence that gleamed slightly from the moon.

Up ahead, I heard laughter and a few bottles hitting the fence.

I didn't want to scream to draw attention to myself, so I ran to where the voices were. There was a black Chevy Malibu with a man sitting on the hood chugging a beer. His friend was on the other side of the car, taking a piss into some bushes.

"Help," I said, but I kept my voice low, watching the man zip up his pants and come back around the side of the car, both staring at me. "I need to use your phone. Please."

The men exchanged glances, and what followed sent chills up my neck.

They ... *smiled.*

"I gotta say, we don't see women like you at this place," the man on the hood said, biting his bottom lip. "Fuckin' beautiful." When the other guy smiled widely, he flashed his crooked canine, which happened to be one of the few surviving teeth in his gums. The men reeked of booze, even from ten feet away.

"Never mind," I said, placing my hand on the holster where the gun hid under my shirt. Of course, it wasn't loaded, but they didn't know that. "I'm going to leave."

The man on the hood jumped off and placed his hand on his crotch, grabbing himself and moving it in circles suggestively. "Come here," he said before spitting onto the gravel.

I didn't wait before I pulled out the unloaded gun and aimed. "Back the fuck up!" I warned, hoping they overlooked the missing parts with the dim light around us—the two sneered, clearly unphased by the weapon.

The darkness of the parking lot was too much. Even with the faint light of the utility pole nearby, I couldn't see shit. Suddenly, the pissing man ran toward me and slammed his fist down onto my wrists, which caused me to drop the gun.

Fuck!

He shoved me toward his friend, who caught me by the arms in a tight grip. I screamed this time, slamming my heel onto his foot and attempting to head-butt him, but he was too strong. The man started dragging me to his car, the both of them hooting with joy at the pretty bitch they caught.

Everything after that became a blur. The man slammed my face against the hood of his car, keeping me pinned on my stomach while he zipped down his pants, lining himself up with my ass. He gripped the back of my leggings and tugged, attempting to pull them down. As I tried to kick at his knees, I went to scream again when warm liquid splashed over my cheek and onto the car.

My eyes grew in horror as the man collapsed beside me, a shining, dark wound at the center of his throat, and I moved my hand to my cheek to see what it was: blood. I turned slowly to see Keelan standing there with a bloodied knife.

Behind him was the guy who had grabbed me, lying on the ground with a massive knife wound on his eye. Keelan's expression was fierce and feral. I didn't want to look down, but I did. The man who tried to rape me lay lifeless, his eyes wide and his throat brutally slashed, the crimson liquid dripping from the hood onto the gravel.

"Are you okay?" he asked, his nostrils flaring as he reached out. I was trembling so badly that I couldn't answer. Once he wrapped his hand over the back of my neck, he pulled me close to his chest, hugging me so tightly that I could barely breathe. "You're safe. Fuck, Sade, you're safe."

Safe? I wasn't safe.

"We need to go before anyone at the bar sees these men," he said. "Come on."

This time, I didn't fight him or try to run. Instead, I took his hand and let him lead me past the bloody men. I should have been terrified that Keelan killed them, or at least mortified by how easily he had done it. I had seen him do it before. But this was different. Instead of terror and panic at the murder, what I felt was relief. Though the man who held my hand had kidnapped me, all I wanted was to be by his side, away from the dead monsters who only wanted to hurt me.

CHAPTER 25

Sadie

When I was twelve, Dad had come home drunk with one of his buddies. I hated it when he was drinking because it always made his violence so much worse. I would run and hide in my bedroom, pulling my knees to my chest and swaying back and forth until my mother's screaming would stop. She protected me from him by allowing herself to take on his wrath alone.

One night was different, though. This friend and colleague of his had put his hands on my mother. She tried to fight him off, but he was too strong, and my father was in the other room. He was too drunk to even know what was happening before it was too late.

When silence fell in our home, I walked out of that closet and crept downstairs. My father had a gun pointed at his friend, whose pants were down around his ankles, and my mother was crying, her dress torn. She trembled on the couch, angry red marks on her forearms. It happened so fast that I felt like, for the longest time, I had blanked out the memory.

Blood was everywhere: on the walls, the couch, and my mother's face. I watched from the stairs as she leaped into my father's arms. For once, he was tender, wrapping his arms around her for comfort and telling her everything would be okay. We had people for that ... people who could get rid of the body and clean up the mess so we could continue to hide our family's sins.

Even monsters had their limits, I guess, especially when others intruded on their territory.

To my mother, he was her savior then. He was the husband who had given out justice to a much more evil man. My dad cut back on his drinking after that.

Last night, behind the bar, something broke inside me. I didn't want to see Keelan like that. Keelan protected me from that same fate, but all it did was remind me of his capacity for violence. That moment didn't change my father. Would it change Keelan?

Keelan had never raised a hand to my cheek or bruised me like my father did to me and my mother. He saved me last night. Only he had put me right back into his prison. Instead of letting me breathe and clear my head, I had to pretend it didn't happen while being shoved back into a car with a man who had taken my freedom away.

"Keelan, I need to get out of this car. Please," I said, turning to him. My eyes were swollen from crying most of the night.

We slept until eight a.m. by the roadside, and then we continued the trip. We only stopped once to wash the blood off our bodies and discard the clothes in a small creek beside the road before swapping the Camry for a Honda Accord we had stolen. Then we continued on to cross from Utah into Nevada. It was a long stretch from Grand Junction, Colorado, though, after the bar. I was exhausted, and my nerves were frayed to the point of snapping.

"I'd like to reach Vegas by three," he said, looking at me in his peripheral. "We'll stop when we're there."

"If you'd like me not to turn into a bitch, then I suggest you stop this fucking car," I hissed. "See." I pointed to a sign before the next exit. "There's a rest stop right ahead. Stop the car and let me out."

Keelan's brows shot up like my outburst had caught him by surprise. I thought he'd soften a little and cave, but instead, he just replied, "No."

"Why are you being a dick about this?" I asked, fully turning to look at him. "I'm not suggesting going someplace public where someone can see you and call the cops. Clearly, no one cared about your fugitive status at Luna Butterfly or that bar, so you must not be a hot topic."

"It's not up for discussion, princ—"

"Stop calling me *princess!*" I screamed, my nerves and resolve shredding. "I'm not spoiled or entitled. My life has been fucking miserable! I've been beaten, tortured, kidnapped, and sold by people who were supposed to give a shit about me. Not to mention almost ..." I couldn't finish that awful sentence. Tears streamed down my face as frustration built in my chest. "All I wanted was to live in Vermont, work quietly in a bookshop, and watch TV with my cat. But no, you had to come and fuck it all up because of what? You were lonely and needed someone to keep you entertained while you went looking for some lockbox my brother left you? Or because you wanted your little prize back, that was gifted to you by our parents? Sadie Ryan is dead. I want to go home to my fucking cat! I'm done with all this shit."

Keelan's eyes darkened to slabs of bluestone, and his lips twisted into a scowl. His hands tightened on the steering wheel to the point his knuckles went white. "Sadie, you are my wife. *Mine.* And if I want you to be by my side during this road trip, you will do as I ask and be fucking grateful I haven't killed you already."

It was as if I had forgotten a murderer was sitting beside me, just waiting for the right moment to punish me. Without thinking, I pulled my elbow back and swung forward, punching Keelan in the jaw and causing him to swerve on the highway. His head whipped back to me, and a look of pure rage replaced his icy demeanor. He quickly pulled the car off the highway onto a small frontage road. I expected to feel terror at what I had done and begin pleading with him. But no, instead, I felt nothing but my anger—cold and brutally numb. The car stopped, and Keelan stepped out and stormed to my side. He wrenched the door open, leaned in to unbuckle me, and grabbed my arm. With a forceful yank, he sent me tumbling onto the asphalt, the sharp pain of scrapes shooting through my elbow and palm and the cold wind biting at my exposed skin.

Keelan reached down, grabbed me by my hair, and dragged me around to the back of the car. I kicked and thrashed, calling him every name I could think of.

"Let go of me!" I screamed, hoping that someone nearby would hear me and help. But there were only woods and roads to swallow my screams. Keelan dropped me on the ground as he popped open the trunk. I attempted to jump to my feet, but his foot slammed down on my shoulder, pinning me.

"You fuck!" I screamed. "What the hell are you doing?"

He's getting a weapon.

I closed my eyes, fear taking over the rage, and waited. Waited for the darkness of death.

Instead, I felt his hands wrap around my body and lift me. I opened my eyes and looked down. The trunk was open and empty.

The fuck! Is he going to shove me in the trunk like a suitcase?

As I thrashed in the iron vice of his arms, Keelan reached up and ran his fingers through my tangled hair, then glanced at the dirt on my arms from the fall. Slowly, he brushed off the debris and then gingerly ran his thumb over one of the scrapes like he was trying to heal it with his touch.

"I've tried being patient with you, Sadie. I thought we had reached a fucking understanding the other night. But it would seem you need to cool off a little longer. So, I'm gonna enjoy some goddamn peace while we drive. And you can finally get that alone time you've been begging for."

No. No. No.

He shoved me inside and easily dodged my feet as I kicked at his stomach. Once I was in the trunk, Keelan looked down at my furious, tear-streaked face, grim and angry.

"Try to calm down, princess. It'll make for an easier trip."

"Keelan!" I screamed as he closed the lid. I tried kicking it and screaming, but he ignored me, put the car into drive, and headed back onto the highway.

It was dark inside the trunk, and only a tiny crack of light leaked in. As my eyes adjusted, I tried to push on the lid. It refused to budge. Even the backseats wouldn't push down so I could do what he had done in the last car. I remembered a safety tip about knocking out the taillights and sticking your arm out to wave. I shifted my body to where my feet were angled to kick the back of the lights. Slamming my foot repeatedly, I expected a little give on the taillights, but nothing happened.

"I'm going to kill you, Keelan Blake!" I screamed again, kicking the wall of the trunk. I took a few breaths to slow my racing heart and tried to look around. The air inside the trunk was uncomfortably warm but not suffocating.

As I pulled my knees to my chest, my left leg brushed against something solid. I wriggled my arm down, and my fingers brushed against a metal pipe. Tire jack? Keelan must have forgotten to take it out, as it seemed to have rolled to the very back of the trunk. I wrapped my hand around the pipe and pulled it close to my chest. It was the length of my forearm, something easily concealed. The metal kept me grounded against the claustrophobia that lay in wait in my mind. The hum of the road was soothing despite the cramped space, and I decided to close my eyes and wait. When Keelan finally stopped the car and let me out, I was going to knock him out cold.

CHAPTER 26

Keelan

Goddammit. The situation had gotten completely fucked up. Guilt weighed heavily in my chest since I put Sadie in the trunk, knowing that it was my fault she hit me in the face to begin with. Not only that, but she cut her hand and arm on the asphalt when I dragged her out of the car. Hearing her terrified, angry screams during the first thirty minutes fucking ate away at me. All I wanted to do was bandage her scrapes and let her sleep as I drove to Las Vegas. I rubbed the sore area on my jaw, and frustration boiled in my veins. Her constant fighting and arguing left me with little to no choice.

Yeah, you always had a choice, you asshole, I berated myself further. *I should have fucking listened to her, given her space to breathe. She was almost raped, for fuck's sake.*

Though it wasn't nearly as hot as it would be if I stuffed her in there during the summer heat, regret and shame burned a hole in my chest.

God, I was acting just like my old man, like *her* old man. That fucker would have taken one step further and broken her leg so that she couldn't run. The idea made my stomach clench. I could never do that to Sadie, no matter how pissed off I was.

Yet I still hurt her.

After an hour or so, Sadie fell silent, but I could still hear her shifting occasionally, so I thought she was okay. I waited until I saw the road signs for St. George before deciding to let her out. It would be the best place to fill up on gas and stretch before the last hour to Vegas.

Hopefully, by now, she'd learned her lesson about pushing back. I wanted her to calm the fuck down before we reached the hotel.

Not that I blamed her. She did witness me slashing through two men's throats.

I pulled the car onto the offramp and turned right toward a gas station. The neighborhood nearby was quiet and backed into what looked to be red mountainous plateaus. I parked the car and climbed out, looking around to see how many people were there. Luckily, I was the only one at the pumps. But the silence made my insides churn. Sadie wasn't moving around at all anymore.

Fuck. I let my temper cloud my judgment.

I couldn't open the trunk here, not in a public space like this, with cameras everywhere. I looked around again, taking in the details of the neighborhood just up the street. The best spot to get Sadie out would be in a secluded spot near those mountains. I looked around once more before hurrying inside to hand the cashier money for the gas. After that, I filled the tank and hopped back in the car. I pulled out of the station and drove to the adjacent neighborhood.

Almost there, princess. Please be okay.

After a few minutes of driving past the rows of houses and small parks, I noticed a few areas with trails leading into the mountains. There weren't enough trees for cover, but the sun was high in the sky, and I wasn't sure how quickly the heat would rise in the trunk.

Luckily, I found an empty playground and parked the car along the sidewalk. I got out and hurried to the back of the car, using my keys to pop the trunk. When I looked down, Sadie was curled into a fetal position, her eyes closed, and her clothes drenched in sweat.

"Oh fuck, oh fuck," I whispered, leaning down and scanning her over. Was she breathing? The angle of her body was so that I couldn't see her chest moving.

"Sadie?!" I called out in a panic, my heart pounding against my throat, choking me with fear. Just as I went to scoop her out of the trunk, a long metal pipe came out from underneath her and cracked against my skull as Sadie swung with all her strength. Blood gushed from my forehead and dripped into my eye, temporarily blinding me.

Staggering back, I watched Sadie leap from the trunk, and I tried to grab her waist. But she shoved me away, and with my disorientation, I fell back, and my head hit the curb. More blood filled my mouth as my teeth bit into my tongue. I spat out onto the street and wiped the blood from my eyes. Staggering back to my feet, I turned and saw Sadie vanish between two houses across the street.

A growl rumbled deep in my chest, anger numbing the searing agony that rattled my brain.

That's three times now she's run from me.

I sprinted after her, going between the houses she just passed. After crossing the fences, I came onto another street. From a distance, I saw Sadie running from house to house, banging on the front door. Shit, I had to hurry, or someone was bound to answer. I bolted down the street, gaining enough ground for her to whip her head around and see me on her tail.

She jumped off the front steps of the last house that didn't answer and ran around the side to the front fence. Close behind, I heard her opening a gate, and when I got close, Sadie tried to slam the door in my face. But I grabbed it and shoved it back open, making her stumble slightly.

"Someone, help—" she started to scream, but I lunged, covering her mouth with my bloody palm and seizing her neck with my other hand.

"Hitting me in the head and running off again. Are you serious, Sade—"

Her knee drove into my fucking groin....

"Fuck!" I swore as she tore from my grip, instinct driving me to grab my injured balls.

Sadie ran into the backyard, and I glanced up to see her going for a brick wall bordering the mountains' open space. She jumped to try and grab the very edge of the wall. I regained my composure and started after her. Sadie couldn't quite hold the lip of the wall, so her fingers slipped off.

She looked behind and saw me approaching around the backyard pool right before she spun on her heel and ran again, but I grabbed her by the elbow. Sadie kicked at my shins and dug her nails into my arms. I slammed her body into the brick wall, my cock twitching.

She had no idea what her little fight against me was doing to my body.

"Get your goddamn hands off of me, you sick fuck!" she shrieked.

"Alright," I ground through my teeth. "I guess I had you bashing my head with a pipe coming, but that doesn't mean I won't still punish you for it."

Sadie's eyes grew wide, but I didn't give her enough time to react before my mouth crashed against hers. My hand slid from her arm to her sweat-coated hair, grabbing a fistful. Blood soaked into her reddish-gold strands as I gripped tight. Fuck, even with a pounding headache and blood still dripping down my neck, my cock was hardening even more with her struggling.

But Sadie seemed feistier than expected because she sank her teeth into my bottom lip, tearing the soft flesh to the point of breaking the skin.

I cried out, releasing the kiss. Sadie's swollen mouth glistened as she licked my blood off her lips, a look of satisfaction on her features.

Jesus.

My gaze went down her body, and my heart twisted at the sight of her scraped arms and hands.

As she took a heavy breath, I pulled her into a hug, gentle not to touch her wounds, as I smoothed her tangled hair. Once her body melted into mine, I drew her into another kiss. This time, her tongue slipped into mine, and I moaned as she kissed me back. "God, Sadie," I said as I broke the kiss. "I thought I had killed you by putting you in that trunk. I'm sorry, okay? I was wrong. I should have given you that peace after what happened."

Sadie swallowed, and her brows pinched together like she was debating if I was sincere or how completely unhinged I really was for kissing her after all that. "It scared me, Keelan. I could have died in there."

My lips curled into a smile. "But you didn't." I pressed closer, letting my dick dig into her thigh. Her breath turned ragged, and desire burned beneath all that anger and rage in her pretty green eyes. It only made my cock swell painfully.

At this point, any chance for her to believe my apology was gone. I grabbed her shoulders and lifted her from the wall.

"Well, let me at least cool you off," I said playfully before launching her tiny frame into the pool behind us. Swirls of steam rose from the churning water.

When she emerged, I hopped in after her, grabbing her shirt before she could swim toward the steps on the other side. "Not so fast, Sadie," I warned.

Wasting no time, I yanked her shirt over her head and tossed it onto the patio. My lips claimed hers again. Once again, Sadie kissed me back, her tongue sliding against mine. The water was at our throats as we kissed, concealing us from prying eyes, if there were any.

God, why was I so turned on when she fought back? It was clear that her mind wanted to hate me, loathe my existence, but her body craved my touch. Every time I touched her, I broke her resistance a little more. Because she was mine. Sadie could deny all she wanted but couldn't escape that truth.

Her legs wrapped around mine as I pulled her shorts down, slipping them off and tossing them with the wet shirt. I fiddled with my pants for a moment before I pulled my aching dick out and slammed it into her. Her head fell back and pressed against the pool's edge, moaning at the fullness of me. She looked beautiful when I fucked her like this, claiming every single inch of her tight pussy.

"That's it, sweetheart. I know this is exactly what you need," I hummed against her lips. She had been bratty for too fucking long, and that attitude of hers needed to be fucked right out of her. Her pussy throbbed around me, begging for more with each thrust of my hips against her. Sadie gripped my shoulders, her eyes closed as I held her close. Her lips were parted—she'd been so lost in her trance that she was soundless.

Her tight pussy massaged me from all angles, showing just how much she enjoyed having my cock inside her. One of my hands knotted in her wet hair, yanking her backward roughly.

"If you did what you were told, this would be so much easier. I don't know how often I must drive that point home." Sadie's eyes fluttered open then, her eyes pleading for more, begging for more. She squeezed my waist with her thighs, keeping me close as I rammed my cock harder and deeper into her. "But you had to be a *brat*, didn't you? You enjoy getting a rise out of me. It's almost as if you do it, so I'll punish you in the way you fucking like it ...."

Still no response, only pleasure-filled breaths and splashing water.

"What's the matter, baby? You're awfully quiet now," I continued. Another bolt of ecstasy shot from my cock, flooding my body with violent shudders with every thrust. "I hope you don't think you'll go unpunished for what you did today."

I pulled her head up to me and kissed her harder, my tongue grazing her lips. Breaking the kiss, I smirked at her.

"Hold your breath, princess."

"What—"

With those words, I tightened my grip around her hair, pulled her from the edge of the pool, and then dunked her head back and underwater. She suddenly squirmed against me—from shock—but I kept her close and continued ramming myself into her. Harder. Faster. As mercilessly as ever.

A second passed, and then two, and then a few more, before I finally dragged her head back up. She gasped for air, barely having the time to open her eyes before my lips collided with hers. My kiss was demanding, barely leaving any chance for her to breathe. The panic that coursed through her, visible on her face, only fucking aroused me more. I wanted to bury myself in her like this forever.

"You'd be smart to remember one thing, Sadie," I said after releasing her mouth. "Every breath you take, it's because I allow it." Sadie tried to protest—to beg me not to do it, but in a heartbeat, her head was underwater again. I wouldn't do anything to harm her—not really—but I needed her to know I wouldn't tolerate fucking around any longer. I only kept her under the water for a few seconds before I pulled her back up, still thrusting wildly. This time, I gave her a chance to gasp for air.

"You asshole!" She coughed before I shut her up with another kiss and shifted her backside against the edge. I had her completely pinned to the pool wall again, my body keeping those legs open for me. It was too much now, and we couldn't hold back. Every inch of my body needed her like I needed air. Reaching down with my right hand, I slid my fingers along her thigh until I found her clit. I pressed on the bud and rubbed it in slow circles. She cried out.

"So fucking eager for my cock, aren't you?" My left hand grabbed her throat and squeezed, restricting her airflow.

And she fucking loved it. I saw it in the way her face scrunched with pleasure, her eyes rolling back into her skull as she shook violently against me.

"That's my good fucking girl," I praised her. At those words, I felt her orgasm ripple through her and her pussy tightening around my dick. More broken moans blended with breathless gasps as she came, squeezing my cock so fucking tight I needed to pause my thrusts for a moment. Her inner muscles were pulsing, now charged with a sensitivity that I really fucking enjoyed—especially when she came without my permission.

Quickly, I pulled myself out of her, spinning her around so she was now facing the wall, and I shoved myself back into her tender pussy from behind.

"Keelan! God, I can't—I can't take it," she cried out, but I quickly covered her mouth, blocking her breathing once more. Despite her words, I knew she *could* take it. Her little cunt was sensitive, but that would only make the second orgasm hit her more intensely. She melted back against me, breathing heavily as my pace grew faster. My lips pressed against the back of her neck.

"God, Sadie. You'll be the fucking death of me," was all I managed to say before I reached my point of no return. With one last thrust, I came deep inside that pulsing cunt, her orgasm chasing mine immediately as it squeezed me with delicious intensity. She whimpered against my palm, and I finally released her mouth.

"Oh, God," she panted before I kissed her gently this time. My touch was softer now as I ran my hands down her naked body, conveying one message—I didn't ever want to hurt her. "That was ... *fuck.*"

After a final peck, I managed to pry myself away from her. But as I moved away, the sound of a sliding door alerted me. I looked to see what I assumed was the homeowner staring at us, mouth gaping as an older woman took in the scene in her pool with shock and horror.

I grabbed Sadie's hand. "Come on," I told her, grinning wildly. "We need to go."

CHAPTER 27

Sadie

It was late afternoon when we reached the infamous Las Vegas Strip. By then, the tension between Keelan and I had subsided. I couldn't say that what happened in St. George wasn't intense, but for once, I didn't resist when he took my hand in his on the center console. Fucking in that stranger's pool while the woman watched in horror stirred something dark and wild within me. Keelan didn't care that we had been caught. He didn't care that the woman would call the police about what she saw, creating a more dangerous situation of being caught before we reached Vegas. All he cared about was making me feel so goddamn alive.

And he did.

Keelan wanted me, not just as his possession after our fathers gifted me to be his wife. Maybe it started off that way, an obsession he didn't want to let go of. But something changed along the way. When he apologized, something had fundamentally shifted in his eyes. Keelan *cared* about what happened to me. I knew that now.

Even right before I tried to cave his skull in, the look on his face when he thought I had died in the trunk was real.

The thought of losing me scared him deeply.

But it also confused me. Keelan had never cared for anyone other than Mia before. He wasn't capable of it.

Maybe I was too broken to mind that someone who killed indiscriminately wanted me alive and safe.

I guess we can be broken together.

Together like a mosaic of jagged shards of colored glass fitted into a beautiful abstract of our souls.

Keelan placed his hand on the bandage we placed over his wound before we left St. George and winced.

"Are you okay?" I asked, but it was a ridiculous question. That was twice now I had split his head open with a hard object.

"It won't be my first scar," he said with a gentle smirk. "It'll match perfectly with the terracotta pot one. A memory of our time together." I laughed at that, our first inside joke. He smiled at me with a warmth that pulled at my heart. "Alright, I need you to come in with me to check in," Keelan said as he pulled into the Bellagio's entrance. When we reached the valet's stand, he reached behind, grabbed a black baseball cap from his duffel bag, and put it on, covering the dressing. Even with the hat and the green zip-up hoodie that hid the tattoos, Keelan still looked sexy as hell.

He climbed out of the car and walked to the other side before the valet could open my door.

"Move," he said, giving the young man a look that had him retreating a step. He opened the door and held out his hand. "Mrs. Blake."

I scoffed and shook my head. "Ms. Ryan," I reminded him for the thousandth time.

Keelan gave me an amused grin as I climbed out of the car. He tossed the keys to the valet before grabbing our bags from the backseat. After handing the man some cash, he was given a ticket, and we headed for the doors.

A rushing sound drew my attention, and I turned around to see that the iconic fountain had begun a show. "How much cash did Gavin give you before you came to get me?" I asked. "This place is expensive, and knowing how you are in Vegas, you wouldn't have booked the cheapest room."

Keelan paused and gave me a playful smirk. "I do like to make a statement, especially after what we did in St. George. I'd be surprised if we make it a night before police track us here. It was quite a show."

I blushed, pressing my lips to keep the smile away.

"Aiden and Logan booked the room for us under an alias. This place doesn't accept cash, anyway."

Fair point.

"When did you have time to call them and tell them we were coming?"

"While you were in the trunk." He said it so nonchalantly that I couldn't help but laugh.

We entered the lobby, and I took a moment to admire the décor of the Bellagio. I hadn't been here for almost three years, and it was just as beautiful as I remembered. I made a mental note to ask Keelan to take me to the Botanical Garden later.

He led me away from the doors, past the front desk, and toward a set of stairs leading to the casino. A short man with a bald head and dark goatee awaited us. He and Keelan shook hands, and I saw a small yellow envelope pass between them. The bald man glanced at me, nodded once, and brushed past me to head out the door.

Keelan tucked the envelope under his armpit and retook my hand. "We're already checked in. Let's head on up."

"What was that about?" I asked. When he didn't answer immediately, I pressed my heels into the patterned carpet.

"Kee."

Realizing I wouldn't take silence as an answer anymore, he said, "More cash, fake passports and IDs, and the keys to the hotel room. My brothers want us to join them for a business meeting, and then we can go to The Bank tonight."

My brows pinched together as I cocked my head to the right, studying him. "Is that all?"

He nodded.

"How long are we here for?" I asked.

Keelan reached up and tucked my long hair behind my ear. "Until we hear the police sirens outside."

The Blake brothers didn't book us the penthouse our families used to stay in during previous business trips, which was a clever move because that would be where the cops would start searching. This was a simple room on the second floor. It was easier to access the stairs and get the hell out of there if we needed to.

When we walked inside the room, a chill ran down my arms. Despite it being November, the hotel liked to keep their rooms at a frosty sixty-five degrees year round. My California blood hated being cold. Keelan set down the bags and closed the door, snapping the deadbolt in place.

Before I could reach for the suitcase with my sweater inside, Keelan wrapped his strong, tatted arms around my waist and pulled me in, bear-hugging me from behind. He had already pulled off his sweatshirt, so the heat of his skin pressed into me, causing a wake of goosebumps down my back and legs.

I leaned into his touch and closed my eyes, leaning my head against his chest. We had fucked an hour ago, but I wanted more. My God, I couldn't get enough of his hands on me.

I *needed* more.

"Keelan," I moaned, tilting my head back and parting my lips. He slipped his left index finger inside my mouth, his thumb holding my jaw into a hard grip. I sucked on his finger, tasting him with my swirling tongue, picturing his cock in my mouth. My breath grew heavy when Keelan's other hand skated up my side and cupped my right breast.

"When are we meeting your brothers?" I asked, pulling my mouth away from his damp finger, my voice barely over a whisper.

"A little over an hour, but I have to call them in about fifteen minutes to discuss plans."

"Fifteen minutes, huh?" I said, biting my bottom lip. "What can you do to me in fifteen minutes?"

He loosened his grip on my chin and turned me around, my body still flush with his. "Well," he started. "I kind of want to punish you properly for running away from me. The pool was just a warm-up."

I felt the thick ridge of his cock twitch against my stomach as he pressed into me. Apparently, the notion of punishing me was turning him on. My breath hitched as I looked at him. Keelan was so tall I had to crane my neck to peer into those burning blue eyes.

The mere mention of punishment elicited a thrill in my belly, and he knew from my peaked nipples that his threat turned me on, too. His deliciously wicked smile lit up, and he slowly walked me back to where the bed was. My mind began to play out the fantasy I had been having about him for the last year. A twisted fantasy that I only allowed when the lights turned off and fear no longer dominated my mind.

It was just like the dark romance books I liked to read. I would picture Keelan coming for me, taking me hard and mercilessly against my will for being a bad girl and testifying against him. I would surrender to him, screaming for him to stop, when deep down, I didn't want him to. When he touched me for the first time in the house, that dark part of me relished in the pleasure.

It was only fantasy, though. I knew Keelan would never hurt me like that, not after seeing the flashes of kindness and care in his eyes. Just like the books I read, if I wanted it to stop, I would shut the pages.

With Keelan, I had my safe word.

That one word gave me control, but right now, I wanted him to own and devour me. Taste and abuse my body until the marks of his soul burned into mine, branding me. The tattoo was only skin-deep. I wanted ... no, I *needed* more.

I needed Keelan Blake to hurt me.

"Lay down, baby girl," he ordered, nudging me down with his finger.

I climbed onto the mattress, lying back fully. When my head hit the bed, Keelan moved over me, caging me with his thighs. He removed his T-shirt, displaying the canvas of tattoos covering his perfectly toned body from his hips to right below his chin.

He was a fucking beautiful, dark god.

Keelan leaned down, kissing my bare shoulder gently. The press of his lips was tender—too afraid to break me. Frustration coiled in my spine.

Break me, goddammit.

"Why did you hit me with that pipe and run away from me, Sade?" he asked, his tone shifting to something else. There was another threat behind his voice—soft, slow, and deadly.

"What can I say?" I whispered. "I needed some fresh air."

He laughed, the sound like dark honey to my senses. Keelan's finger touched the center of my chest, where the moon phases were, then slowly glided down until it reached my exposed belly, resting on the constellation tattoo. He then moved his eyes from my shoulder to the tattoo before leaning forward, kissing it gingerly, and running his tongue over it, lower … lower.

Oh God, there was no way we'd be done in fifteen minutes.

As I watched him kiss my stomach, he paused, lifting his head and staring at me with hooded eyes. Something in his features changed, and my body stiffened. I knew that predatory look.

"You know," he started, "before I left Gavin's shop, I grabbed a couple of things."

I swallowed, unsure of what he was getting at.

"Do you remember the safe word, Sadie?" he asked, and my stomach did an anxious flutter.

Keelan knew my fantasies of wanting to say "no" while he forced himself on me, taking me ruthlessly while I attempted to wrench away from his tight grip. So, we came up with a safe word when we were engaged and trying to heal our frustrations from being forced into a marriage we both didn't want. The word made it clear to him that I truly wanted him to stop, no matter how many times I said "no" or "stop" before that.

"Butterfly," I answered, and he smiled.

"Don't move."

Keelan swung his leg over me and dismounted from the bed. Frigid air replaced his warmth, and I shivered against the AC, which bit into my skin. I pushed up on my elbows and watched him walk to where our bags lay.

What is he doing?

Keelan kneeled to unzip his duffel back and started sifting through the clothes. He pulled out a large black pouch and a Ziplock bag with what looked like a few folded paper towels and walked back to me. He put the pouch on the bed and pulled it open. My eyes widened when I realized what it was.

I sat up so I could bolt, but he grabbed my hips and flipped me onto my stomach, his knees pressing me into the mattress. I thrashed and squirmed, but the weight of him was too much.

"Princess. Don't fucking move," he warned. There was something so deadly in those words that my nerves turned to ice.

I obeyed as the thrill of the unknown tingled in my core. Keelan placed two colors of ink on the blanket and started to prep and wrap the tattoo gun he kept in that bag, then slid the waistband of my leggings down slightly, exposing the top curves of my ass.

"What are you doing?" I asked, my voice trembling. From excitement or anxiety, I couldn't tell.

"Branding you, of course," he replied calmly, as if he heard my thoughts before. "This will only take fifteen minutes. Stay still."

While finishing wrapping the gun, he sprayed my skin with a small bottle of sanitizer and wiped it clean with a towel.

I felt myself already dripping between my legs with anticipation. His other hand, which wasn't holding the gun, slowly glided down my ass, using his fingers to spread my cheeks apart. His middle finger trailed down the center, lower and lower, until he reached my pussy. Slowly, he slid it inside and began to pump his finger in and out while the needle touched the skin below my left hip.

I didn't know how the fuck he was able to keep his hand so steady as he ruthlessly and mercilessly thrust his finger so hard that it hurt.

"Fuck, Keelan. It hurts. Please stop!"

"Shut your fucking mouth, or I'll make you bleed," he warned.

He was already biting my skin with the tattoo gun. The needle hit my nerves, and I had to bite down on the pillow. I gripped the bedcover and tried to arch my hips into his fingers, but he used his elbow to press me back down. "Easy, Sade, or you'll mess this up."

Fuck. I wanted to move so badly, but I knew I had to stay still.

At some point, the pain blended with pleasure, coursing through my body like a raging storm. Small, muffled moans left my lips as I completely surrendered to the new sensation. It was an odd mix—a sharp sting of the tattoo gun on my skin and his fingers buried deep inside my pussy.

"Keelan ..." I whimpered, feeling myself rise to that point of no return. Surely, I wouldn't be able to maintain my composure.

Almost as if he could read my mind, he said, "Don't move, or I'll find another punishment that isn't as fun."

I wanted to tell him I couldn't hold back, not anymore, but before I even had the chance to do so, my orgasm rippled through me. Hard and fast. All I could do was try to stay still as I trembled from the sweet release, moaning into the mattress.

"That's a good girl," he said, though his fingers continued to move along with the strokes of the tattoo gun. The dangerous combination threatened to tip me over the edge, but as I felt myself getting to that bliss again, he finally pulled the gun back. Though I was afraid, the eagerness to see what he had drawn elicited a thrill in my core.

Nothing he created was short of perfection. So, even though he said he was branding me, I knew I would love it, regardless.

"Done," he said, pulling back fully. "But don't get up yet."

I obeyed, wondering what was next.

Keelan returned with another towel and wiped the tattoo clean. I winced a little right before he placed some ointment that he had retrieved from the bag over it. Then, he put a small strip of plastic wrap over the skin with thin layers of tape.

Just as I was about to get up to head to the mirror so I could see what he drew, I heard his shuffling as he removed his pants.

Looking over my shoulder, my gaze locked on his. The intense look in his eyes and the devious smile touching his beautiful lips sent a chill down my spine.

"Sadie ..." he said, using his hand to press into my waist and shoving me back on the mattress. Another small whimper escaped my lips when my breasts pressed into the covers, and he positioned himself between my legs. "You never fucking listen, do you?" He used his hands to pry my legs apart. Arousal pooled between them, but I'd be damned if I let it show. He wasn't going to take me without a fight. My fingers attempted to dig into his knees that were caging me in, determined to make him wince, even though he would overpower me every time.

In one quick motion, he grasped both my wrists, pinning them above my head, while his hand held me open as he rammed himself into me.

Pain shot through me with that first thrust, drawing out a loud cry.

"Stop!" I demanded, squirming beneath him as I desperately tried to withdraw my hips from his ... even if that was, truthfully, the last thing I wanted. My entire body shuddered from the roughness of his touch. The dominance. The possession. This was what we did, what we knew. What we *liked*. "I said stop!"

I attempted to scream again, but he used one hand to hold both wrists while the other moved to cover my mouth, muffling my voice. "No one is going to save you, princess."

A screech tore through my throat, but of course, he was right. No one would hear me now.

I wanted to do it again—shout at him, fight back, force him to take me rougher—but before I had the chance, his hand moved from my mouth and wrapped around my throat while he pressed his chest into my back. He was so heavy on me that I could barely breathe.

"I warned you, Sadie," he murmured, now fucking me harder as I whimpered beneath him. Pleasure and pain and his tight grip on my throat consumed me. "Now you'll get the privilege of breathing when I decide so."

His cock rammed in and out of me, hitting me deeper and deeper every time and stretching me out. The lack of oxygen made my mind swirl, even more so when I got to that point where my reflexes kicked in, demanding to breathe. I squirmed and kicked my heels against his thighs from beneath him, struggling to get air.

Right at that moment, pleasure hit me all at once. My orgasm spread through me so violently that I thought I might pass out, both from its intensity and the lack of oxygen. Keelan finally released my mouth, only to slam himself wildly into my pussy two more times before he came, too. Our moans echoed deep through the room until they dispersed into slow, heavy breaths.

After Keelan was spent, he collapsed over my back, adjusting his enormous frame to the right so he wasn't resting on me anymore and pressing into my newly drawn tattoo.

"Alright, princess," he said with a small, barely noticeable smile, running his thumb along my spine in a gentle caress. "Take a look, and then clean yourself up."

I carefully eased off the bed, feeling his cum drip down my inner thigh. My pussy was aching from how hard he slammed into me, and my tattoo felt so swollen and tender that I took my time walking over to the mirror. I turned around to see what Keelan had done to me.

Oh my God. My mind raced as I looked at the text he had tattooed on me.

"You are mine, Sadie Ryan," Keelan said, still lying on the bed. "You belong to me. That will be your reminder for the rest of our lives. If you ever leave me or if Brian or any other man touches you again, they will see *that*. It will not only remind you of who you belong to, but you'll think about how much you dripped for me while you got it. You can't remove that mark without causing a scar. My name will be the only one on your lips, my taste on your tongue, my hands on your skin, and my cock in your pussy. No matter what, you will be marked."

The lines were beautiful, sharp, and clean. Each cursive stroke ran horizontally, about three inches wide. The design was flawless and placed perfectly on the skin, like it was made for me.

Though beautiful, the black and pink text caused a feeling of shock and horror as I re-read the name he branded right above my left buttock: Keelan Blake.

As fucked up as it was that Keelan tattooed his name on me, there was a flutter of emotion that bounced in my chest, and wetness pooled between my legs all over again.

I was his.

CHAPTER 28

Sadie

"Sadie?" Keelan called out through the bathroom door, giving it a light tap. "We gotta leave soon. You dressed yet?"

"Just give me a second," I said, fixing my freshly curled hair in the mirror and grabbing a tube of lipstick from my new makeup bag. I applied the light pink-nude shade to my lips and pressed them together. After spraying some perfume I knew wouldn't trigger Kee's allergies, I took a second to admire the dress I picked out in the boutique on the Strip.

It was a deep-rose two-piece dress with long straps woven around my upper arms and neck into an elaborate halter. Although the neckline was a sweetheart design, accentuating my cleavage, it wasn't low enough that I couldn't move without my breasts spilling out. The top was above my belly button, and the skirt hung low on my hips, showing off the detailed lower half of my constellation tattoo. The dress also had gold-plated butterfly fasteners that flashed when I walked.

The outfit was gorgeous and very different from what I would typically wear. I was never allowed to stand out, and after I escaped, I tried even harder to be invisible. Giving myself another once over, I smiled at my reflection.

Tonight, I get to live a little.

With that, I opened the bathroom door and stepped out. Keelan had his phone pressed to his ear, and when he turned, his voice cut off mid-sentence. His sapphire eyes widened as he took in my appearance. I smirked and spun in a circle, showing off my curves and exposed skin. A wicked smile formed on those full lips, and my core pulsed. Keelan wore black pants, a black leather belt, and a cerulean blue button-down shirt that accentuated his lean body to mouthwatering perfection. His tattoos peeked out from his neck and hands, but he covered the rest.

He was dark *and* beautiful.

"Yeah?" Keelan said to whoever he was talking to on the phone. "No, I'm listening. Sorry, Aiden. We'll be down in a few minutes," Keelan said into the phone, eyes still on me.

He tapped the END button and put the phone in his pocket.

"Wow," he breathed. "You ... you're breathtaking. I've never seen that shade of pink on you before. It ... it suits you."

I bit my bottom lip nervously, his compliment taking me aback. "Thank you," I said, swallowing. Why was I feeling so nervous right now? "Um ... so, this meeting. Do I have to sit and be silent, or do you need me to listen and contribute?"

The odd look on Keelan's face left no doubt that my question had bothered him, but it was the truth. My dad rarely involved me in the business trade.

Most of the time, he'd order my mother to serve the men drinks if we hosted at our house or entertain the men's wives while the men did business. For me, I was always told to stay silent and watch—learn—because a woman had to know her place unless she was doing something useful. What my father didn't know was that I was a hell of a lot smarter than he gave me credit for. When he didn't think I was paying attention … I was.

"Well, I'd prefer it if you weren't involved at all. But just listen and learn. It's been a while since you were involved in the coding stuff, right?"

"I haven't tried to learn anything more since I was sixteen," I replied, the bitterness of those lessons burning my tongue. My father would belittle me if I made any mistakes when working with the graphics in the software program and often compared me to Patrick during his criticism. When I was sixteen, Patrick stepped in and told Dad that since I was such a failure, it wasn't worth teaching me anything and that he should focus on *only* Patrick's skills.

What they didn't realize, though, was that I never stopped learning, just in case I would have to use it to earn my freedom from my family someday.

"Don't worry about it, princess," Keelan said, taking my hand. "Maybe we'll both learn something tonight."

The elevator opened to the casino's main floor, crowded with patrons, dealers, and drink servers. Keelan had to lean close to talk to me as we weaved through the throngs of people.

"The private room is just across the floor where my brothers are waiting inside. Don't let what they say bother you. Behave."

I answered with a nod.

The room was away from the main gambling floor, with a gold plaque that read "Red Ivy Suite – Private" attached to a solid, dark oak door.

Keelan opened the door and ushered me inside. The other Blake men were seated at a small, round table, flanking an older, paunchy man with a receding hairline. The man looked nervous, and I didn't appreciate his lecherous stare once I was in the room. Keelan's oldest brother, Aiden, smiled and stood, coming over to hug me. He looked so much like his mother, Evelyn. Same nose and brown, cat-like eyes. Unlike Keelan's black hair, Aiden's was lighter like his father's, a chestnut brown with natural highlights. He had a larger build, and I could see he had put on more muscle since I last saw him.

"Sade! It's so good to see you. You look beautiful, by the way," he chirped. Logan had also stood, waiting to pull me into a hug, as well. Although Logan was ten years older than Keelan, they shared striking similarities in their jet-black hair, facial features, and build. The only real difference was that Logan inherited their mother's dark eyes like Aiden had. Logan's personality was more lethal than any of his siblings. If he felt he was being slighted, his attitude would flip on a dime. He would go from cheerful and charismatic to ice-cold and ruthless. He didn't hesitate to unleash violence on anyone, even his own sister. Keelan told me once that he broke

Logan's left hand after he punched Mia on the arm for merely being in his space. He couldn't work on his paintings, and Arthur was furious.

The two were much older than Keelan by over a decade. Keelan was considered the "surprise baby." Sadly, Evelyn was killed in a car accident when Keelan was two years old. Arthur, not wanting to raise his sons alone, married Lily when Keelan was five. Two years later, Mia was born.

Keelan's brothers were assholes just like their father, but they always treated me somewhat kindly growing up, even when they took part in bullying me.

"Oh, by the way, Sadie," Aiden exclaimed, reaching into his coat pocket. "Logan and I got you a present."

He pulled out a flat black box and handed it to me. Keelan's nostrils flared, and I could see the veins in his neck twitching beneath his skin.

"It's not from them," Keelan said. The possessive anger rolled off him like thick smoke.

Aiden's dark eyes started to twinkle. "Okay, fine. We did all the work, though."

I narrowed my eyes at the box and noticed the company logo with the capital letter "B."

Goddammit.

"Are you serious?" I asked, whipping around.

"I have to know where you are at all times, just in case you decide to impale my head and run off again."

"Consider it a wedding present," Aiden said.

Shooting a look at Keelan, I opened the box. Inside, on some white foam, was a delicate silver bracelet. The chain was so polished that the metal looked almost white in the light. Attached was a silver charm in the shape of the letter "B." Small white gems were encrusted inside the charm.

The family business wasn't all codes and art. The men treasured their women like they treasured jewels. They had to know when and where they were ... for their protection. At least, that's what the men told us. The little charm worked as a tracking mechanism. Only the device's app could release it once it was snapped on.

I handed Keelan the box and held out my wrist. "Fine, put on the beautiful thing," I said with a fake smirk. It was pointless arguing. Keelan would force it on me if I protested, and I really didn't want to make a scene in the suite.

Both brothers exchanged a glance and chuckled quietly.

"Keelan, you better be taking good care of your wife. Now that you finally got her back, and she's not running from you anymore," Logan said with a playful smirk while clapping his brother on the back. "Or I'll steal her right out from under you."

"Shut the fuck up, or I'll break your goddamn teeth on this table," Keelan growled, snapping the chain together and meeting my eyes. "Sorry, babe."

"I think you've forgotten who runs this family now, Kee," Logan said, interrupting us. "You may have been locked up for the last twelve months, but one anonymous call to the feds, and we'll take your little lady with us while they drag you back to the big house. Trust me, they won't make whatever fucking mistake they did again that caused you to break free."

"Well, this family reunion just got a lot less exciting," I said, no longer wanting to be near them. "I'll just sit over here."

I shuffled away from the two ice storm brothers and sat on the small red-gold loveseat, nervously fluffing out my skirt. Aiden noticed the movement and turned to the man seated at the table, who looked even more uncomfortable. He smiled and gestured for everyone to take a seat.

"Gentlemen," he said, "Let's get down to business. We shouldn't keep Mr. Larkspur."

The brothers nodded and took their seats. The meeting lasted about an hour, during which they taught their client how to manage the software, where to input the key, the location of assets, and other matters related to Larkspur's racketeering business. My stomach roiled during the conversation. Too many memories of my dad's meetings and lessons were rising to the surface.

"Alright, I watched the initial coding map live, so I didn't have to leave my paperwork with Roberts. This is what you did with it, huh?"

Sam Roberts was my second cousin on my dad's side. He and Patrick used similar tactics and styles for the graphics they created to help embed the code before they passed it on to an artist.

Aiden reached behind him and pulled out a large brown paper package. He handed it to Mr. Larkspur, who looked it over quizzically. "This is it?"

"That's it. Take a look for yourself."

Mr. Larkspur tore the top of the package off and pulled out a framed oil painting. He looked it over and let out a low whistle.

"You wanted an oil painting, so we gave you a replica of Di Paolo's *A Tuscan Moonlit Night*. It's in the patterns of the stars, Larkspur. Right there."

Logan ran his index finger over the details in the sky. It was beautiful. By looking at it, you'd never guess a hidden message was concealed inside.

"Let's wrap this up," he continued. "You can either take it with you now after we receive the remaining deposit or have us ship it to you. You can then hang your dirty little secrets on the mantle for your guests and family to admire."

I looked a little closer at the landscape of the Tuscan countryside at the end of twilight, the moon's glow filling the sky with hints of stars peeking over the green hills. I gasped at the swirls of color and the masterful execution of brush strokes in the piece. Even Keelan was shocked at the level of skill in the painting.

"Where's the key phrase?" Mr. Larkspur asked.

Logan pointed to the stars in the painting. "All the key phrases are done in Morse code within the design. The rest you can't see."

Mr. Larkspur leaned forward and squinted his eyes at the painting. "Got it," he said, but his tone was rife with doubt. "Are you sure?"

Logan let out a breath of annoyance and leaned forward, placing his elbows on the desk. "It's in plain sight, Mr. Larkspur. After our associates from the Ryan family have compiled the information into the image, it's sent to one of our studios or the tattoo shop. After that, we convert it into priceless works of art. Which you are now an owner of." He pointed to the painting again. "Upload a photo of this into the software, enter the key, and your secrets and those you want to blackmail someday will be right before your eyes."

"Aiden, you've gotten better," I said, keeping my eye on the painting.

Keelan and his brothers were all equally gifted, but they still took on their own style. While Keelan and Gavin were tattoo artists, Aiden and Logan specialized in paintings or murals.

Sometimes, the secrets in the artwork were out in the open, in someone's hallway, home, or business. The world never knew they carried the person's deepest, darkest sins.

"Still not as good as my little brother. Right, Kee? Those tattoos you create are next level," Aiden said.

"So, where is the code? I still don't see anything in the stars," Larkspur said. "This Morse code, you say."

Aiden's jaw tightened, and I could tell this old man was pissing him off. "Right there," he said coolly. "The dashes and the dots. It's the phrase you gave us over the secured line. Unless someone is looking for it, they won't notice. The rest of it is called steganography. A series of small symbols embed the code into the medium, imperceptible to the naked eye."

"It's secure, Mr. Larkspur," Logan jumped in. "There is no doubt in the Ryan family's or mine's work. Which you would be wise to never fucking talk about if you want to keep making your fortune."

As if sensing the threat in Logan's tone, the man smartly shut up about the painting. Twisting the fabric of my skirt in my fingers, my eyes stayed glued to the picture.

Once the men had exchanged paperwork, I stood and walked up to the painting. "May I?" I asked, and Mr. Larkspur nodded.

I leaned forward and looked at the details. It has been a while since I had seen Keelan's brothers' work. My eyes found the stars, and right before me was the Morse code, the only thing the naked eye could see from the image. The lines were clean, mixed in the sky's dark blue, oranges, and reds. The man's key phrase.

When our family started the business with the Blakes, Patrick suggested putting the key into the actual image just in case the client forgot it and wanted to keep that, too, a secret. But as I stared into the drawing, looking at the stars, dashes, and dots that connected them, my stomach tightened a little.

"So, Keelan," Mr. Larkspur said, breaking my concentration. "You provide concealment in the form of tattooing. Tell me, how lucrative is that monetarily for your shop? That must be difficult, not only transferring an encoded design made by the Ryan family, but then detailing it onto someone's skin."

Keelan grinned, showing all his teeth—clearly showing a barely leashed temper. "Well, seeing how our shop is the most highly sought-after tattoo studio in Los Angeles, I'd say, quite *lucrative*. The design process is similar to my brothers' work. I use the tattoo concept to conceal information, whether in the shading, colors, highlights, or even the line work itself. It's the same 'hide in plain sight' concept that my family specializes in. My cousin and I hide them on the skin. People pay a lot of money to hide their crimes. If they're ready to die with them, they can burn their own fucking body."

As Keelan continued to explain his art, my gaze turned from the stars on the painting and dropped to my dress, where some of my constellation tattoos peeked out from the skirt's waistband. As much as I hated the circumstances, I really did love this tattoo. It molded to my body so perfectly that you'd think I was born with it on my skin. But as my eyes found the constellations, I stilled. Something I hadn't noticed before until I had focused intently on it as I did with the painting. It was similar in the strokes of the lines and the points under each star. When the connection clicked, my heart stopped, and shock gripped me.

No. No, Keelan wouldn't have. No way. There, right into the lines of the stars and the blended colors that connected them, was a design similar to the painting before me.

There was Morse code on my body.

My vision tunneled, and my heart pounded against my ribcage. Keelan tattooed a code onto my body, concealed within the stars. I stepped back until my heel hit the chair, and I sat back down, careful not to draw Keelan's attention.

I looked again.

Jesus. What the fuck is going on?

"Sadie, is everything alright?" Keelan's voice cut through my thoughts, and I lifted my head. His face was calm, but I could see concern and confusion in his eyes. I schooled my panic and smiled at him.

"Of course. I was just lost in thought. Sorry," I replied, hoping my calm tone was convincing enough.

Now is not the time to lose your shit, Sadie. Wait until after the meeting and when his brothers leave. Then force the truth out of him.

Another thirty minutes passed before the meeting finally concluded. Mr. Larkspur handed Aiden a small suitcase, which I assumed contained payment for the canvas. They exchanged handshakes, and Mr. Larkspur departed with his priceless artwork tucked under his arm.

By the time we left the room and made our way to the gambling area of the casino, my hands were shaking. It felt like all the air in my lungs was a vortex of ice and fire, crushing me with every step.

"Well, another crooked soul in our clutches. Eh, boys?" Logan said. "Aiden and I have to call Dad and report him on the transaction. Do you two want to meet for dinner in two hours? I know a fantastic steakhouse a few blocks up the Strip. I always crave a bloody steak after I take a pound of flesh."

Keelan, still eyeing me suspiciously, nodded. "Ya, just shoot me a text when it's time to go. Sadie and I'll grab a drink and then hang out in the room for a bit."

The brothers nodded and disappeared into the crowd. Keelan's hand wrapped around my arm and yanked me behind a nearby pillar, concealing us.

"You wanna explain what your deal is, princess?" he asked.

"My deal? *My* fucking deal," I hissed, anger and betrayal in every word before I poked my belly right over one of the stars. "Morse code? Really? You *branded* me with a goddamn code? I made quite an effort not to stare too long at this design after I escaped to Vermont. If I had looked at it long enough, I would have recognized the pattern." I shook my head. "This entire time? God, I'm such a fool not to have thought you would have done something like this. This entire time!" I took a step toward him, closing the gap between us. "Is this why you wanted me to come along for a ride?"

My words came out cold with outrage, terror, and betrayal. Keelan's irritation melted into shock and what looked like guilt. He reached for me, but I slapped his hand away.

"How could you do something like this to me?" I asked, tears forcing themselves into my eyes. "Does this have to do with the lockbox? You said that Patrick left something behind, and you needed to find it, right? I don't understand. Why is this on me?"

"Sadie, I had planned to tell you once we arrived—" When Keelan reached for me again, I slapped him across the face as hard as I could.

Fuck, that stung.

"Don't touch me," I said, stepping back. "I need a goddamn drink."

I spun on my heel and charged onto the gambling floor, my skirt billowing behind me as I walked. Several men ogled me as I walked by, and one hollered for my asking rate. I lifted my hand, flipped the man the bird, and kept walking.

Fucking pigs.

When I reached the packed bar area, a woman with black hair and dressed in a simple tuxedo approached me. "What can I get for you, Pretty in Pink?" she said.

Despite my heated temper, I smiled at the nickname. "One shot of tequila, please. Top shelf."

"Do you have a room number, or would you like to pay here?"

"Please bill to 255."

"Coming right up, sweetie," the woman said, disappearing down to the bar's end and pulling out a step stool. As she fetched my drink, my mind played out everything since Keelan kidnapped me from Vermont. The vague hints, the lockbox, Patrick's death, and why we had to return to Los Angeles with me on his arm. I clenched my hands into fists, and a heat crawled up my neck.

It's all within this tattoo. It's been under my nose, literally, for over a year.

"Here you go, hun. Enjoy," the bartender said, sliding a shot glass of golden liquid toward me. I picked up the ice-cold glass and lifted it to my lips. It was smooth at first, before the slow burn went down my throat and to my stomach. Despite the warmth, a small shudder ran through me. The alcohol dulled my anger a little, allowing me to think rationally.

I was so determined to move away from my family name that I barely acknowledged anything connected to it. After everything that had happened over the last year, I didn't *want* to see the tattoo as anything more than a soured memory. "I have been a goddamn fool for too long," I murmured, my voice lost in the din of people around me.

Keelan will never be the good man I hoped he would become. His being all sweet this last week was just a glimmer in black ink. He will lie, steal, and kill as he sees fit. This tattoo was put on me for a reason. That son of a bitch is going to tell me why.

Clearly, it had something to do with this lockbox. What else could it be?

I pushed off the bar and walked back to where I left Keelan. He was leaning against the same pillar, one hand in his pocket, the other rubbing the bridge of his nose.

Even through all the anger coursing through my blood, I could never deny how beautiful that man was.

Ignoring my pang of conflicting emotions, I grabbed his arm and yanked him toward me. Feeling reckless, I grabbed his jaw with my other hand and forced him to look me in the eye. "You are going to explain everything to me, Keelan Blake. Right. Now."

CHAPTER 29

Sadie

Keelan took my wrist and led me away from the casino floor, where the noise of people and slot machines was less deafening. We found an alcove with a cushioned bench and hardly anyone around to eavesdrop. He gently sat me down and then stepped back until his back hit the wall.

"Please understand that everything I've kept from you was for your protection," he said, running a hand through his black hair. "I didn't want to lie to you, but I swore to Patrick to keep those secrets on your body—secrets that could take everyone down in both our families."

I looked at the floor and swallowed. "How? What is this code, Keelan? And Patrick? Really?" I said. "You involved my brother?"

It was clear Keelan was biting the inside of his cheek. "No, Sadie. Patrick involved me ... *and* you. He stole crucial files from your father and hid them. Patrick knew that once those files were discovered missing, it would only be a matter of time before the people in those documents came for him. It was the only way to ensure no one found it except us."

I blinked as the realization hit me before he even said it.

"The code is the coordinate to where the lockbox is. He created the code and told me how to place it in the design we did for you. Patrick made sure that when the time was right, the two of us could get that box together."

All the air I had been holding in released from my lungs.

I was a fucking map.

"You could have said no or put the code on your own goddamn body, Keelan!"

Keelan smirked. "Where would I put it, honey?" he retorted, holding his arms wide. I covered my eyes and hung my head. He was right. Keelan's *entire* body was covered in tattoos.

"So ... you don't even know where the box is? He didn't tell you anything?" I asked. No more games. Before my brother died, he instructed Keelan to put a code on my body to where he'd hidden secret files. I needed answers. I *deserved* them. "What's in those files, Keelan? Did he tell you that, at least?"

"Before he died, Patrick began gathering files to blackmail your father and his associates. He wanted out, and he wanted to take you with him to protect you. During his search, though, he found something. It was something that scared him so badly that he took those files and came to me. This was darker and more sinister than anything our families had done before. That's all he told me; it was enough for me to do what he asked. Patrick was my best friend, and I had *never* seen him so frantic before."

I dragged my hand from my eyes and cupped my cheek, pressing my lips into my palm. Patrick had so many secrets he kept close to the vest. Despite our extremely strained relationship, my brother *did* try to help me. I knew that deep in my heart. His bullying persona mostly had been an act to spare me from our father's fists as often as possible. Although, I knew part of the bullying was to cope with the immense pressure that he was under. He constantly pushed me away from the business so the corruption wouldn't taint me or result in getting swept up in a raid if the feds came for us. Patrick didn't want the sins of our family to take me down with them.

So instead, he hid them on my body—the ditzy, naïve daughter that no one paid attention to.

"From what he told me before his death," Keelan continued, "he secured three files' worth of documents containing enough information to take down the entire Ryan and Blake empire, company and all. The lockbox has everything. Every dirty cop, politician, lawyer, and everyone else involved with your father and mine would go down in flames. He was waiting for the right time to hand over the documents to the FBI since it was too risky with so many people in your dad's pocket. Then he died with only the code leading to where they're hidden."

Shock and horror hit me all at once. We were so fucked.

"Patrick loved the wealth the business gave him, but he cared more about your safety. This was the only way to save you," he continued. "He knew that his death was imminent, so he was desperate to hide the documents. These files had to be protected, and he knew I would guard you with my life. Putting the code for the map onto you was our best option."

It was so hard to wrap my mind around all of this. There was a code hidden on my skin this entire time. While I knew I wasn't as skilled as my brother—and never would be—I couldn't fathom that I hadn't noticed until now.

Because the last year left you so traumatized that looking at the tattoo was too difficult. Before then, you were too selfishly wrapped up in fucking Keelan to notice.

"Sadie, even if I could read that Morse code, I don't know how to use the program to decrypt the image. I just tattooed the key to the hiding place. My father protected our side of the family by ensuring we didn't learn anything beyond that. It was too fucking risky with so many enemies. When it was safe to do so, Patrick expected *you* to do it."

I stood, the skirts of my dress swishing around my legs as I paced the hall. "The program is like riding a bike. It's been a while since I used the software, but if I can get through the access point, it should be straightforward."

"And the key phrase?" he asked.

"That's simple Morse code, Kee. That's the easy part. Though I don't need an online translator to help me, it will take some time to read the letters. If I don't type in the phrase exactly how it's entered, it won't work, and the program is designed to lock us out. I basically get one chance before it would prompt the administrator of a breach in the system. And, well, the admin is dead, so ..."

Keelan smiled. "You won't mess up," he said reassuringly. "You've let your bastard of a father's criticism make you believe you can't do it. But you're just as skilled as Patrick. I've watched you, Sadie. Since we were little, I've seen you learn and memorize every detail of what your brother and cousins did, even when your dad stopped teaching you. You've got this."

My eyes welled with tears. No one ever told me I was smart, valuable, or needed. Patrick did what he could, but Dad was determined to drive us apart. For a long time, I believed my brother hated me. But he didn't. He wanted to destroy our father and save me.

Taking a breath, I looked down at my exposed midriff and pulled up the hem of my top to expose more of the constellations.

"So, did you intend for it to be written upside down?" I asked.

Keelan looked around, checking to see if anyone was nearby. The hall by the alcove was empty, save for a couple of college kids who were on their phones. He then took my hand and leaned in, as if to kiss my cheek. "We can't talk anymore about this here," he whispered directly into my ear. "Let's take a picture of the entire piece back in the room and read it together. Once we find out where Patrick hid that lockbox, we'll pack up and get to Los Angeles."

My heart ached from being kept in the dark for so damn long. But I understood why Keelan did what he did by not telling me. Patrick had a reason for doing this: placing the code with me. I wouldn't let that reckless idiot have died in vain by doubting the one person he could trust with these secrets.

"Alright. Let's do it."

Keelan nodded, and we headed toward the elevators. Once we were alone inside the cab, he turned to me. "Gavin sent me the software to a laptop he gave me before I left Burbank. It's installed in a secured folder, and any data will be wiped when I press the kill switch so no one else can see the information. Once we read it, I'll call Gavin, and we'll have to leave. Are you ready for this?"

The nagging, dark voice in my mind told me this wouldn't be easy and that I was not good enough. I shoved that doubt aside and squared my shoulders, keeping my eyes on Keelan as I answered, "Yes."

Once back in our hotel room, I stripped off my top and skirt, letting the beautiful pink fabric pool at my feet. Keelan's eyes flared, but he pulled out his cell phone and snapped a photo of my entire torso. I changed into leggings and a white T-shirt, and we sat down at the small table to examine the photo. I took the picture and brightened the image as far as possible, altering the contrast until the dark was sharp and stark against my skin. Using a notepad and pen, I examined different sections of the image in detail.

"Okay, so obviously, this right here is Morse code, but there are so many stars in this design that I need to make sure I know exactly what is part of the code and what isn't," I said. "Before putting it into the stars, did he show you anything?"

Keelan shook his head. "I just remember the code starting here," he said, pointing to the blended shades of black at the top of the first constellation. "It's so tiny, but you can see how some of the lines are broken up into dashes and where the dots start."

I narrowed my eyes at the design, hoping it began where my finger pointed. "One dash, two lower dots." I turned to him. "Write that down."

Keelan began jotting down the short dashes and dots and looked at the design with me.

"The code's design is a series of what we call dits and dahs interspersed throughout. The way Patrick designed it is all within the stars and the colors that connected them. It looks like it continues until it gets to the upside-down crescent moon." I pointed to the tattoo. "Dark," I said. "Write that down. The first word is 'Dark.'"

We kept working as I gave him more dots and dashes to jot down.

"Shit. The way this looks, I can't tell if it's a dash or a dot," I said. "It's blending too much with the darker colors."

Keelan leaned forward to look at the image with me. "Looks like a line ... er, dash. I'm pretty clean with my work, Sade. That's definitely a dash."

I squinted my eyes at the small speck that irked me. After a moment, I saw the tapered ends of a line, so I nodded. After directing him to write down several dashes, dots, and a sideways dash, I gave him the next set of words. "I think this section means 'Skies Kiss.'"

Fuck. I think.

"Are you sure?"

"No, Keelan. I'm not sure. Even if we put it into some Morse code translation website, if I mess up the sequence, it won't work. One mistake and it can spell out an entirely different phrase."

Keelan reached out and placed his hand over mine. "You got this, Sade."

I grinned. "Let me see the pad." I took the notepad from him and jotted down the last of the dits and dahs. "Alright, I think I have it."

"What does it say?"

Holding up the pad, I read, "Dark Skies Kiss Stars Good Night." I turned to him. "Pull up the program."

Keelan walked over to his duffle bag and pulled out a silver laptop. He powered it up and double-clicked on a yellow folder on his desktop. Immediately, a pop-up came, and he typed in a few numbers Gavin had sent him. "Okay, we're in." He turned to me. "You're up."

I nodded, pulled the laptop in front of me, and spotted the program hidden in a subfolder. It took about ten minutes to get the program up and running.

It had been years since I used the system my family created, but the moment it showed up on the screen, everything I had learned came flooding back. With the login prompt on the screen, I entered the specific sequence of numbers and symbols Patrick had me memorize as a kid to access the data. The screen flashed blue, and then it turned white.

"Did Gavin give you a USB cable or Bluetooth?" I asked.

"Oh, right. Give me a second."

Keelan rushed to his bag, pulled out a short black cord, and grabbed his phone. He plugged the two together, and another small pop-up window appeared, asking if I wanted to upload images. I clicked a few buttons, and the photo transferred into the program directly.

Another prompt appeared, asking for the six-word phrase to unlock Patrick's map.

"Well, we're about to find out if I wrote it down correctly."

I typed in the words *Dark Skies Kiss Stars Good Night*.

Then, I clicked "Enter."

Please work. Please work.

When the system scanned the image without locking us out of the program, we knew we did it, and my shoulders relaxed.

Thank God.

"What are we looking at?" Keelan asked. "Is that it?"

"It's pulling up the location through something similar to Google Maps. Look," I said, pointing to the GPS coordinates.

"Well, will you look at that," Keelan said.

I turned on satellite imaging and zoomed in on the spot with the mouse pad. "It's the Los Angeles subway, but this is an old tunnel we used to explore as kids. See the red symbol? It's been closed off for twenty years. That would make for a good hiding space if you think about it."

Keelan saw the look on my face, and his eyes softened. "Are you okay? I mean, I—"

"I'm okay, but Keelan ... I need to call my mom. If Patrick left such catastrophic information for me to find, she's in danger, too."

I stood and ran my hands through my hair. My body felt like wires were zapping my skin and bones, making me shake. "I know Aisling was a shitty mother to Patrick and me, but she's still as much of a victim of my dad's monstrous behavior. She helped me escape. It's now my turn to save her."

Keelan placed his hand on my arm as he nodded. "I understand. Let me make a quick phone call, and we'll start packing. I'll type the coordinates in my phone since mine is encrypted. We'll have to wipe the computer with the killswitch and shred the notepad."

He then turned and walked to the hotel door, and that's when I took a moment to breathe.

I did it. *We* did it.

As he stepped out, I went over to our bags and started packing, taking a few more breaths to calm my nerves. As I folded one of Keelan's shirts and placed it inside, I noticed something folded on the bottom, another shirt wrapped around it. I pulled the shirt free and unwrapped it. My brows furrowed as I saw something I wasn't expecting ... and my breath caught.

It was the magazine I had posed for. I knew it was the same one from that night Keelan killed Richard because I had accidentally torn the bottom right corner of the cover when I pulled it from my bag.

I opened the magazine, seeing dark, reddish-brown fingerprints on the cover. Every muscle of mine locked tight as if bound by invisible chains. Keelan's hands were covered in blood in the warehouse. This was Richard Wertz's blood.

Oh, my fucking God.

The edges of the pages were also wrinkled from water damage after I dropped the magazine in a puddle. My vision tunneled, and there wasn't enough air in my lungs. I stood and stumbled back.

It had been over a year since I stopped having panic attacks like these over what happened. Back in Vermont, they would happen late at night when memories of the murder would resurface. Why would Keelan keep this? Not just keep it, but bring it on the trip. Was this a trophy of his last kill before being locked up?

Fear and anger overwhelmed me, but I tried to push them back. I didn't want to feel like this anymore. I accepted the fact that Keelan was a murderer, a cold-blooded killer, but seeing this again after all these years made my body feel like it had fallen into icy waters. Suddenly, I couldn't breathe.

I need fresh air.

I was spiraling.

Having no idea where I would run off to, I walked to the hotel door and opened it. Keelan was standing in the hall talking to someone on the phone. He turned and saw that I was moving away from him.

I'll be back. I just need air.

The words were lodged in my throat; I couldn't speak. My lips were tingling and numb, my hands aching with sharp, electric pulses. The attack had me firmly in its grasp.

"Sadie?" Keelan said, his eyes examining my face before going down to my hands. Words, so many screaming words, died in my throat. I could only take a few steps before I bolted for the elevator.

I wasn't running away. I just had to get away from him *then*. To breathe. To breathe outside these hotel walls.

My finger jammed the elevator button as I heard Keelan running after me. The world seemed to blur around me as the doors slid open. Luckily, there was no one else in there. But once I was inside and the doors started to close, Keelan's hand caught them, causing them to re-open. He stepped inside, reaching for me. I backed up until my back smacked into the metal railing.

"Sadie, breathe," Keelan said, putting his hands on mine. I felt a sharp tug and realized he had taken the magazine from me. In my panic, I didn't even know I was still holding it.

"Please," I begged. "Please get it away from me." I wrapped my arms around my chest in a hug, hunched over, closed my eyes, and tried to control my breathing.

"Hey, it's gone. Okay?" he said. I opened my eyes a little to see him fold the magazine and tuck it into his waistband before pulling his shirt over it. "It's gone." He cupped my face. "Fuck. Baby, take a breath."

The elevator doors slid shut but didn't move since I hadn't pressed a button. I shook my head. "Why would you keep this? I testified against you because you killed a man in cold blood and then smiled about it—so fucking happy with your handiwork while he bled out. Now I'm here, reliving that awful nightmare. Why? Why did you do it, Keelan? Why did you ruin everything?"

Keelan stepped closer, and the smell of his cologne hit my nose. I felt my shoulders start to relax.

"I should have burned that magazine, but I couldn't. It was all I had left of you. I had no idea if I would ever see you again, so I had Gavin keep it safe. I just—" He ran his hand through his hair. "I don't regret what I did to Richard. He deserved to die, and I will never be sorry for taking his life."

I looked up, and my eyes went wide. "Why? Why does death and violence give you so much pleasure?"

He shook his head. "It doesn't. But you wouldn't be standing here with me right now if I didn't do what I did. I would have lost you."

I blinked. "I don't ... I don't understand."

"Sadie ..." My name trailed off his tongue, and he swallowed as if his throat had tightened. "Richard was going to hurt you."

The pain in his voice was so raw that I snapped my head up to look at him. My mouth gaped at those words. "Wha—what?"

"Richard Wertz worked for your father as a software engineer. But Finn had also tasked him with following you. Patrick found out about it and came to tell me. He wasn't sure why Finn would do that, and that bastard only told him to 'trust the process.' That was when Patrick knew something sinister was at play and started collecting information. But then, Patrick died, and I saw Finn slip Wertz an envelope at the cemetery. After the funeral, I followed

Richard back to his house and broke in after he left. I searched his office until I found the envelope."

"What was in it?" I asked, terrified of the answer.

Keelan sighed. "There was cash and a contract to have Patrick killed."

My body felt frozen, but I wasn't in shock that my father would have a hand in this. Tears filled my eyes and dripped down my cheeks. My father arranged to have Patrick, his golden child and the future of his company, murdered. I wanted to scream and rage and curse the man. But I couldn't yet. I needed to hear the rest.

"Go on."

"I was fucking furious. That asshole had the audacity to look upset at Patrick's funeral. I decided to return later that night and find out more information before I made plans to kill him. When I returned to Richard's office, I saw the magazine on his desk, opened to your picture and your tattoo on display. I didn't know you had done the photoshoot as a gift for me. Patrick's cell phone wasn't found by his body, so once we realized it wasn't suicide, it was pretty clear that whoever killed him took the phone."

"He had his phone?"

Keelan nodded. "It was on the desk where the magazine was, and a secured text exchange I had with Patrick was open. Richard used some kind of backdoor to hack into the phone, bypassing the lock and other security measures. He read all the messages. Richard *knew* what that tattoo was. There was a magnifying glass right beside it."

My mouth gaped.

"He was obviously looking for those missing documents. I don't believe he told your father about it, though. If he did, your father would have come for you months ago. Richard had been working for your family for years. You never crossed paths with him because he was assigned to Patrick as a mentor. He was the one who taught Patrick how to utilize Morse code in the designs before sending them to my family. It wouldn't take much for him to figure out what we had done."

Keelan's words hit me like a wave, pulling me under. *Richard.* A name that meant nothing, yet somehow, this man had single-handedly destroyed everything I loved. This stranger took everything from me.

"There were a few other messages on Patrick's phone. One was a text exchange between Patrick and Richard. He was trying to recruit him to help blackmail your dad a few weeks after Finn hired him to track down the files. When Patrick refused to help him, Richard shot him in the chest and then collected the payment from Finn."

I pressed my hand to my chest. "Oh, God."

Richard Wertz's business ventures were mentioned during the trial, and my father looked furious at the news. It made sense now. Richard had planned on screwing him over after he had paid him to kill his son. The police never found out who killed my brother, not that they investigated all that much. The official ruling was suicide, but Mom and I knew that wasn't true.

"So, why was my dad having this man follow *me?*" I said while shaking my head.

"My guess is to make sure that you were behaving appropriately, especially after our engagement. It's likely that he discovered you went to that photoshoot, too, and took a copy once it was published to try to decode it. The business ties between Finn and my father needed to stay intact if they were going to expand their fortunes. But Sadie, your father beat you and your mother your entire fucking lives until he handed you over to me. There is no depth of depravity that rat bastard won't go to."

Keelan was right, but I didn't want to admit it. I didn't want to think that my father would go so far as to have a man follow me for something other than protection. Or that he would hire someone to kill his own son.

"After Patrick told me he was going to expose the families and that he had been working on taking them down for months, he had finally figured out how to do it. He refused to disclose the files' contents but had a graphic ready with the key phrase and code embedded in the image. He knew I would protect you with my fucking life if I had to. I never, ever thought someone would see that tattoo."

More tears flowed down my face. "But then I messed up and posed naked, showing the entire world where our family's biggest and darkest secrets lie."

Keelan shook his head. "Don't blame yourself; you didn't know."

He dropped his hands from my cheeks and wrapped his arms around me as my breathing picked up. "Easy, baby. It's okay. Richard would have taken you from me, decoded the message, and then killed you to tie up loose ends."

My legs buckled beneath me, but Keelan caught me by the waist to keep me from falling.

"Sade, look at me," he said softly, and I looked up. "Yeah, I killed someone for you. I would do it again and again if it meant keeping you safe and keeping you from being hurt by someone, just like

I did with those men behind that bar. And I'll sleep well at night every time I do it, knowing no one can touch you."

"But ... why? You have always been cruel to me."

Keelan shook his head. "You saw what you *wanted* to see, but that is so far from what I felt—so far from the truth."

"Then tell me, Keelan." I slammed my fist against his chest. "What is the truth? Why would you kill anyone to protect *me?!*"

"Because I'm in love with you!" His voice rose as he spoke. "Because I fucking love you, Sadie. I didn't realize what it was to love a person so much until this trip. I've always had this desire to protect you since we were kids. The night in the cemetery, when I said those awful things to you that made you ignore me for months, was only to get you to run out of that cemetery. Patrick wanted to throw you into that open grave and leave you there for hours as a prank. I knew you wouldn't believe me, so I did whatever I could to get you to leave. I even broke Jeffrey Stevens's leg on the football team my senior year because those guys had a bet on who could take your virginity first."

I blinked, but a small smile reached my lips. "You did that?" I chuckled at the memory. "Jeffrey said he fell down the stairs, but his story kept changing."

"I can't get you out of my fucking mind. I can't even think straight half the time." His eyes began to glisten. "You're the first face I see when I wake up and the last thought before I fall asleep. The idea of you becoming my wife, not because our parents forced us to but because you want me just as much as I want you, feels as natural as it is to breathe ... like you have always been a part of me—that missing piece to my fucking sanity. Losing you would destroy me, Sade."

As those words left his lips, the elevator moved, taking us up to the fourteenth floor. Keelan quickly moved to the side as a couple with a small child entered the elevator and pressed the button to the lobby. My mind was racing now, unable to grasp his confession.

Keelan loves me, I repeated in my thoughts. I wasn't just a possession to him. *He loves me.*

He saved my life.

CHAPTER 30

Keelan

I had to get Sadie back into the hotel room. She was exposed, and being around a chaotic casino and drunk assholes was the last thing she needed. As soon as the elevator stopped to let out that intruding family, I pressed the button to take us back to our floor. Sadie hadn't spoken since I confessed my heart to her. It was starting to scare the shit out of me.

When we reached the room, I led her inside first and shut the door behind us, giving her a moment to breathe before finally turning to face her. Her silence filled my stomach with knots. When I did turn around, Sadie was already walking over to the bed and then sat down on the mattress, an expression of disbelief as she stared at the TV across from the bed.

Did I completely freak her out?

Fuck.

Carefully, I pulled the magazine from my waistband and lowered it into my opened bag. Seeing the blood on those pages scared

Sadie so badly she had a panic attack. I was so fucking stupid; I should have burned the damned thing back at the shop.

She had been through more than most. Of course, some of it had been my fault, but I regretted nothing. I wanted her to fear me in that courtroom, so she would hide until I could escape and protect her myself. But even three thousand miles away, she wasn't safe. Sadie would never be safe. Not until this fucking nightmare was over for good.

And my current admission in the elevator had likely been the last straw to the rest of her fears.

I approached her with a slow step. For once, I didn't want to play cat and mouse or engage in this push-and-pull dance we had been doing the past week.

"Sadie," I called gently, but she didn't budge. She didn't even bother to look over at me. Her chest moved up and down rapidly, like she was hyperventilating.

I slowly crouched in front of her, kneeling on the carpet before capturing her chin between my fingers. My other hand rested on her chest, feeling the crazy drumming of her heart. If this continued, I worried she'd end up passing out.

"Breathe," I told her gently, her chest rising slowly against my palm. I lifted her head slightly with the tip of my finger from my other hand, forcing her to look at me. Her eyes finally met mine, but they were blank. She was emotionless—I had shattered something inside her. Sadie repeated the motion, breathing in deeply again. "Fuck, are you okay?"

Finally, she let out the smallest scoff, quickly followed by a sniffle, as I gently dropped my hand from her chest. "Keelan, I have literally never been *less* okay than I am right now. Except maybe when I saw you kill that guy."

There's my girl.

I fought the small smile threatening to curve my lips, trailing my thumb down her jaw. More tears welled in her eyes as she stared at me.

"You know you're fucked up, right?" she told me. It was a truth as plain as day—one I desperately wanted to change but would never do. In a world like ours, I *had* to be fucked up to protect her. If that were the price that I needed to pay to keep her safe, I'd gladly do it again and again and again.

"I might be," I responded, "but it doesn't change the fact that I *love* you."

She blinked once, as if she still didn't believe the words that had just left my lips. They felt foreign on my tongue, even if—on some level—I had been aware of them for the longest time. I had loved her for as long as I could remember.

"I love you," I repeated, wanting the words to sink in.

"Stop saying that. That's not—that's not what we have. That's not what we do." Sadie shook her head. "You're incapable of love. You—" Her words cut off. I dragged my hand back from her face. Perhaps, on some level, she had been right. What I showed her this far had not been love in the way she *needed* to be loved. I had always been possessive, merciless, incapable of saying the words that felt so odd to say aloud. Yet, now that I had spoken them, I realized perhaps I was more capable of loving her differently than I had thought.

Without thinking, I leaned in, pressing my lips against hers. Carefully, I pushed on her shoulders so Sadie's back was against the mattress. I climbed onto the bed, my knees on both sides of her thighs. My body curved over her, not as a cage, but as a shield. A shield from the fucking cruelty of the outside world.

The kiss was soft and gentle. For the first time, I didn't ferociously claim her lips or battle her for dominance. Instead, all I wanted was to savor her taste. Enjoy the moment.

I expected her to pull back, but she didn't. Instead, with a moment of hesitation, Sadie surrendered to the kiss. My hand found the side of her neck, lingering there but not applying any pressure. It didn't take her long to break free from whatever chains had bound her mind in a haze of panic and resistance. Sadie's hands grabbed the front of my shirt, pulling me closer.

Oh, thank fucking God.

The movement was urgent and rough, but my free hand lingered on top of hers, preventing her from rushing this.

I don't want to rush it.

Finally, when I pulled back, that desire lingered in Sadie's gaze, threatening to burn me alive. Her pink lips remained parted, her eyes locked on mine as if wondering what I'd do next. I needed to have her—I needed her more than air, but not in the usual way we fucked. I wanted her to know that I was capable of *loving* her—to *know* those words were true.

Leaning back, I grabbed the bottom of my shirt and pulled it over my head, tossing it on the floor beside us. Before I moved closer to her, I grabbed the hem of her top. My mouth met hers in yet another kiss, but it was brief before I pulled back to remove her shirt. I needed the heat of her skin against mine. My hands then drifted down her body, caressing her gently, before I reached her pants, tugging them down her legs. She lifted her hips, helping me take them off, along with her underwear, before she was bare for me, and my lips met the skin of her stomach. Slowly and gently drifting upward. Inch by inch. My eyes locked on hers, drinking in those beautiful green eyes that bewitched me years ago.

I watched her wince a little as she shifted further up on the mattress.

"What's wrong?" I asked, pausing.

"Oh, um, my ass hurts a little from rubbing against the plastic you put over the tattoo," she said. "I can handle *that*, though."

My lips curled while my hand drifted lower, fiddling with my pants to take them off. Before I could, she sat up and gripped the sheets.

"Butterfly, butterfly," Sadie said quickly. It was as if a bucket of icy water had been tossed over me as I froze. *Her safe word.* One she had never used before, even when I took her for the first time behind the family cabin.

"What?" I questioned.

"Butterfly," she repeated, swallowing a little.

Was she serious? Using it ... now?

"Sadie, what's going on? I'm not going to hurt you. Is it your tattoo? Is it me? We've literally just had sex hours ago."

"We did," she confirmed with a slight nod. "We *fucked*, Keelan. But this ... whatever you're doing now, it feels different. It's not ... fucking. We haven't done this before."

My pants pooled at my ankles as I moved on top of her. "You said I'm incapable of loving you. I want to show you I'm not," I told her. The heat of her body was already radiating into mine, pleading for me to come closer, but I refrained. I wouldn't force her if she didn't want to do this. "Do you trust me?"

A small, nervous laugh escaped her lips. "Don't ask me that."

I reached out and cupped her cheek. "Do you trust me enough to give me one chance to show you I meant what I said?"

Being rough with her was all I ever knew. It worked for us, but right *now*, I wanted it to just be her and me. I didn't want her to hurt, even if it brought out those sexual fantasies and pleasures we both always needed and escaped to.

Sadie searched my eyes and then slowly nodded. My head dipped lower, my lips finding hers again. Our kiss lasted for a long time, drawing out small and muffled moans as I positioned myself against her pussy.

Then, in one slow movement, I slid myself inside.

Fuck.

I was a man of many weaknesses, but she was, so far, the best one. I'd easily sell my soul for one taste of her—to sacrifice everything to have Sadie by my side.

Her inner muscles clenched around me, welcoming me with throbbing and pulsing as I thrust my hips back and forth. Slowly. Deliberately. Her entire body was already shuddering beneath me, whimpers leaving her lips as I rocked myself into her.

At last, our kiss broke, and she tipped her head back. "Keelan. Oh, God!" she moaned. One of my hands grasped her thigh, holding it open further, while the other rested against the mattress, supporting my weight so I could *watch* her. Every time her lips parted, every moan, every heavy sigh ... I wanted to see all of it.

Her breasts bounced with each thrust, pressed up against my bare chest, the sound of her wetness accompanying my movements. Sadie's hands ran up my sides until her fingers dug into my back muscles, holding me close. The slight sting of her long, elegant nails set my skin ablaze. I moaned as she truly *held* me.

"You feel so good, baby. A fucking goddess," I told her, meaning every word. We were made to connect like this. Two fucked up souls that could only find peace by each other's side. Her eyes fluttered shut with pleasure as she ran her tongue over her bottom lip. It was a glorious fucking sight to watch, enough to tip me over the edge as I made love to her.

Made *love*.

For once, I couldn't call it fucking.

Nor did I want to.

"God, Keelan. Oh, God," she cried out again as I moved at that angle she liked, hitting that spot deep inside her. Just seeing her bare for me like this was enough to make me come on the spot, but somehow, I refrained, wanting to make this last.

Gently, I guided one of her legs over my shoulder while the other remained open, my body now entirely pressed against her, feeling her everywhere at once.

"Keelan, I'm so—oh, God, I'm so close," she moaned, each word dragging out with pleasure as her body shuddered against mine.

No games, I reminded myself.

"Come for me," I urged her gently, wanting to feel her come all over my cock. I wanted to be drenched in her arousal, marked as hers, until the end of time. Then her orgasm hit. Hard and fast. Sadie's hands gripped the sheets, and her back arched from the bed. Her eyes rolled back into her skull, lips parting as she gasped for air, and her body shook.

Her inner walls tightened around my cock to where I could no longer hold back either, and in a heartbeat, I joined her in that release. The ecstasy that washed over me consumed every inch of my being. All of it belonged to her—all of me. I came deep inside her with a heavy moan, buckling on top of her tiny frame as my lips desperately found hers. Telling her everything she needed to know with that kiss.

Sadie had to know that, at that moment, I deeply loved her. It wasn't just an obsession that I couldn't free myself from. Though I knew I could never let her go, could never breathe without knowing she was mine, my desire for her went so far above that fucking marriage agreement our parents made.

Fuck the contract. I wanted her to *choose* to be mine.

Because I chose her.

The pleasure seemed to drag on forever, leaving us both breathless and entangled in each other, and the bliss that followed was equally satisfying. Slowly, I forced myself to pull back, rolling onto the bed beside her. While we lay there silently, I reached out and drew her into my arms.

Her back pressed against my chest, my chin resting on top of her head. The heat of her felt like coming home after being lost in a snowstorm. A sense of peace fell over us. For once, there was no fighting, no lingering annoyance between us. It was another feeling entirely.

One that made me wonder if something like this could become an everyday routine for us. A future that I never thought would be possible. I made a mental promise that once all this bullshit was done, we would start our lives together. I would dedicate my life to making her happy.

Happy and *safe*.

I listened to Sadie's quiet breaths, wondering if she had already fallen asleep before she gave me an answer to that question.

"Keelan?" her voice was soft, like the sweet taste of honey.

"Mm?" I tightened my grip around her, holding her close as the peaceful warmth of her body seeped into mine.

"I ... I love you, too."

CHAPTER 31

Sadie

After lying in each other's arms for a while, we rolled out of bed and took a long shower together. Keelan helped me clean my tattoo, and it soon led to me to my palms pressed against the wet tile for support as he fucked me until my pussy was raw. I honestly wasn't sure if I could take any more, at least tonight. After finally drying off and putting a tiny amount of ointment on my tattoo, we dressed for bed and climbed under the covers.

Keelan called Aiden and told him that we were staying in for the night and that he would talk to him and Logan tomorrow. Then we ordered room service—pancakes and fruit—while I made him watch an episode of *The Vampire Diaries*. Begrudgingly, Keelan admitted to liking the show and said he could relate to Damon. That made me giggle so much that Keelan started laughing with me. It felt so *normal*, watching TV with the man I loved.

"Before I forget," Keelan said, yawning and reaching into the drawer of the nightstand. "Here's your phone back."

I blinked in surprise. Honestly, I didn't think he'd ever give it back. "Thank you," I said. "Um ... am I allowed to call whoever I want?"

Keelan's expression hardened. "Depends on who you want to call."

Okay, so my newfound freedom still had conditions. It wasn't Brian or the cops I wanted to call, so hopefully, he'd loosen the ropes a bit.

"I still need to call my mom. I don't even know if she's been released from the hospital," I said, awaiting his response. When he gave me a slight nod, I powered the phone on and quickly dialed her cell. It rang several times before the automatic voicemail message started playing. "Shit. She's not answering."

"She might already be in bed. You can try calling her in the morning," Keelan replied, gently tugging my arm. "Come on. You've got to be exhausted. Let's get some sleep."

"Okay."

I turned the volume up on the phone so that if Mom called, I would hear it even in the dead of sleep. Placing the phone on my nightstand, I slid under the covers. Keelan's warm hands found my waist and pulled me into his chest. His lips pressed against my hair and neck, sending delicious shivers down my spine. Within minutes, my eyes grew heavy, and I soon slipped into my first peaceful sleep in over a year.

I wasn't sure how long I'd been sleeping before a sawing noise startled me awake, and I sat up in bed. I looked around for the noise source before I noticed it was next to me. Keelan.

Oh my God, Keelan's snoring.

I had never seen Keelan in a deep sleep. He was such a light sleeper that even the slightest movement would wake him. I never stayed overnight with him, either. After we'd fuck in the past, I'd slip out of his bed and head home. Slumber parties were a little too intimate for us. But even before I'd leave his room, I never, ever heard him snore.

After a few minutes of listening to his breathing and watching his chest rise and fall, I reached over and gently nudged his shoulder. "Kee?" I whispered, but no sound other than soft snores answered. He looked so peaceful like that, a tatted angel carved from darkness.

A few hours ago, Keelan Blake confessed his heart to me, and after we made love, I told him I loved him, too, which was the truth. I loved that tattooed bastard; I just never allowed that pure feeling to take root and grow. Keelan was always so cold and aloof with me that I felt I couldn't try until last year. When I did the photoshoot, it was meant to be a gesture of not only building a bridge of companionship but also a way to show my willingness to work toward loving him, cruel marks and all.

It took a while for the love to emerge from its ice-cold cocoon.

Rubbing my thumb on his skin, I reached for the phone with my other hand. I clicked the screen on and saw that it was just past two a.m. There were several missed calls that I hadn't cleared from my notifications and a few text messages from Brian. The missed calls were from an unknown number, though, and they had called over twenty times, mainly during the hours that Keelan and I were *occupied*.

What the hell?

Thinking it was my mom reaching out on a private number, I selected the number and hit send. My heart plummeted into ice as it rang.

"Sadie?" an unfamiliar male voice said on the other end of the call.

I was silent at first, knowing I had to keep my voice quiet so as not to wake Keelan. "Who is this?"

"Your mom is safe for now. But I need you to meet one of my associates at the Henderson Executive Airport in thirty minutes, or we put a bullet in her head. Just you, Miss Ryan. We've got surveillance. If you bring Keelan, you'll watch your mother bleed out."

Before I could demand proof of life from the sick fuck who was calling me, I heard my mother scream in the distance. Instantly, tears filled my eyes, and I covered my mouth to muffle a hard sob. "If you hurt—"

They hung up.

Growing up as the daughter of a mafia boss, I knew how this played out. Since I could walk, my father instilled in me the belief that this world was filled with monsters worse than him. If ever I were to face one, I had to be smart and do everything I could to stay alive. The message was clear. Come alone.

I can't just leave Keelan. Can I?

Keelan had already warned me that dangerous men were out there trying to find me. Someone else besides Richard Wertz, the man Keelan killed, must know about the code. I couldn't leave my mother to die because of me. I had to go.

Quietly slipping out of bed, I padded over to the bags and pulled out leggings, a blue T-shirt, and my black sneakers. I glanced back at Keelan, who looked so serene in his slumber. My heart cracked. He was going to be so scared and angry when he woke up.

Should I leave a note?

I looked for the notepad on the table but remembered where it went. Shit. Keelan had shredded it completely and flushed the pieces down the toilet. I ran my hand through my hair. I couldn't leave my phone behind if those bastards needed to call me again.

In the darkness, something glimmered in my mind, and I smiled.

Yup, that'll work.

Once dressed, I went to the small dresser and grabbed the fake ID and some money from the envelope Keelan got from the man in the lobby. Once he sees the items missing, he'll assume right away that I left for good. After grabbing the phone and slipping it into my pocket, I took one more look at Keelan.

No matter what happens, I will survive this. Keelan will find me; whoever has my mother will pay dearly for it.

"I'm not running away, Kee," I whispered. "I promise. Come find me when you wake up, okay?"

With that, I turned on my heel and left the hotel room, leaving my dark angel in his slumber.

Twenty minutes later, the cab driver who allowed me to pay in cash pulled up to the private airport. Only one plane was waiting on the landing strip, and the pit in my stomach told me it was for me. I paid the driver and stepped out, looking around for anyone waiting at the entrance. The desert night wind brushed its chilling claws over my bare arms, and I shivered. A movement caught my eyes, and I turned to look.

A Black man in a navy blue business suit and an "all business" look walked out of the airport and headed toward me. My heart pounded, but I kept my face calm. I would not panic or plead. My mom needed me to help her like she did for me last year.

"Miss Ryan. We've been expecting you," the man said with a gentle smile. "Please come with me."

My eyes narrowed on his belt, and confusion hit me. The man was wearing a federal agent's badge.

What the hell is happening?

For a moment, I thought maybe the police were working with the FBI to use me to get to Keelan and arrest him, but kidnapping my mother is one fucked up way to do it. This was something far more than just catching a fugitive.

He took my arm and led me away from the airport's main entrance toward an open gate on the landing strip, where that single plane was waiting. The jet was small—a Gulfstream G5—and a short flight of stairs led to the open cabin door. As we walked closer, the man escorting me lifted a walkie-talkie to his mouth.

"Sadie's here."

We reached the stairs, and another man stepped out from the cabin wearing a sleek black suit that had a few buttons opened at the top and a gun strapped at his waistline in clear view. My body felt like it had fallen into icy waters.

Oh my God.

"Brian?" My jaw dropped, and my entire body became numb. "I don't understand. You're … you're supposed to be in New York. How—" I swallowed. The space around me felt suffocating as the feeling of trepidation gripped my throat. "Where's my mother? Why aren't you in New York? What the *fuck* is going on?"

"Hey, Tessie," he said, smiling at my stunned face. "Oh, I'm sorry. It's Sadie. I'm glad you got here in time. We almost left without you."

"I don't understand," I said, my lips barely able to form words. "How ... what are you—"

"Easy answer, babe," Brian cut me off. "I'm here to take you home and to your mother. Get in the fucking plane."

I flinched at those words and the sudden shift in the man I cared about. Brian didn't talk to me like this. The man holding my arm shoved me forward. Not wanting to risk my mother's safety, I climbed the stairs, coming face to face with Brian. He ran his hand down my arm and clamped his fingers around my wrist.

"I've missed you," he murmured. "We have a lot to catch up on. Come on." He pulled me inside the plane, where two other men I didn't recognize were seated near the front. After speaking with the others and locking the cabin doors, the pilot started the jet and directed it down the runway. Brian led me to the back of the plane and pushed me down into a seat. He took out metal handcuffs and chained me to the armrests before sitting across from me. The cuffs dug deep into my skin, cutting off much of my circulation.

The pain in my wrists gave me enough clarity to snap out of my shock. "What the fuck are you doing, Brian? Why are you involved in this?"

"I've always been involved. I'm an FBI agent from the Los Angeles field office. Your dad hired me to follow you to Vermont last year when he realized you were planning to run. When it came time to take you back to LA, that tattooed prison fuck had beaten me to it. So, I was forced to track you until we could get your mother, and you decode that message on your pretty skin for us." A smile reached his lips. "Thank God Keelan took your phone with you; I've had a tracker on it since we met."

My stomach pulled into a hard knot. *This can't be happening.*

"I overheard you two lovebirds arguing in the casino about the code Patrick had Keelan hide in your tattoo. God, Sadie, I've been doing this job for many years, and this entire time, we all thought Patrick and Keelan had given you the files themselves. But no, instead, Patrick hid them himself and then made Keelan put the map to find them on your naked body. I gotta say, those guys did a hell of a good job hiding it." He straightened his suit and leaned back into the chair. "When we get to your mother's location, you'll tell me the key phrase."

I stared at him. "I don't know how to read Morse code. Patrick was the genius, not me."

"Bullshit," Brian said, placing his elbows on his knees. "You're a pretty smart girl, Sadie. You were taught the same techniques. I'm sure you can figure it out when your mother's life is in your hands."

The plane increased its speed, and within seconds, we were airborne. As calm as I tried to make myself feel, the terror of being separated from Keelan was starting to leach in.

Once we were at cruising altitude, Brian rose from his seat and walked up to the front of the plane, rifling through a black backpack before taking out a small device. He returned to my seat and switched it on, a small crackle of static echoing.

"You know," he started. "One thing I've learned while my agency and I investigated the Ryan and Blake families over these last ten years is how much those men love to protect their women. If it's not hiring security to follow them around, it's creating pretty jewelry with tracking devices on them, so they can find them if they ever try to escape."

Fuck. The bracelet. That was the only chance for Keelan to find me.

"Finn understands how important it is that I get you back to him safely. Logan and Aiden were quite cooperative in assisting me tonight. Their idea was brilliant. Make it seem like it was Keelan's idea to place that tracker around your wrist ... but not for his sake. For mine. Finn wants Keelan arrested again. If Keelan tracks you, I'll be able to deliver him to your father, too."

Traitors.

Brian held the device next to my wrist, but he was way, way too close for my comfort. When the black box hovered over my wrist, a high-pitched whine emitted, and several green lights flashed. While he leaned into me, he inhaled my scent so close to my neck. When he grinned lasciviously, I debated head-butting him.

Brian seized my wrists, forcing a hiss of pain from between my teeth. He turned my left arm, and the silver bracelet glimmered in the overhead light. Then he clicked his tongue and lifted the device, pressing a button. The metal bit into my skin as he squeezed it before it finally released.

"Ow! Asshole!"

He held up the bracelet. "This little trinket will help us when we get to California. Once we land, I'll reconnect the chain, and the tracker device's signal will reactivate. Then we wait for Keelan to follow us into the trap."

"You're a lunatic," I said, risking the chance that he would strike me. My eyes narrowed at Brian's smug expression, and I kicked him in the shin. "You lied to me for months, made me feel safe and cared for, treated me with kindness. Put a fucking tracker on me? We slept in the same bed, you creep. Why?"

His cheeks reddened in anger, raising a hand as if to grab me, but he quickly composed himself and sat back down. "Why did I seduce and lie to you? It was my job, Sadie. Finn told me that the best way to save myself from going to prison was to monitor your every move and find the files. He's also paying me a lot of money to deliver you to his doorstep. Getting to fuck you was just a perk of the job, and I took it very seriously."

I let out a derisive snort. "Sure, bud. If that's what you call fucking."

I turned my body as far away from him as I could and stared out the window, watching the twinkling lights of Vegas fade out of view. Despite the anxiety and horror of the situation, exhaustion settled deep into my bones, and I pressed my head against the window, praying that Keelan would wake up soon and notice me gone.

Please find me, you psycho.

The plane landed with a jolt, snapping me out of my thoughts as I straightened up to peer out the window. From what I could see in the darkness, we were on the private landing strip in LAX. My body felt so stiff, and my hands were close to numb due to the handcuffs. Brian watched me as I rolled my shoulders and cracked my neck. I met his gaze and sneered at him.

"Whatever my dad paid, it will never be enough when Keelan gets his hands on you," I warned. "You'll wish you just left me alone."

He didn't respond. Instead, he proceeded to unlock one of the cuffs, pulled me to my feet, and shoved me down the aisle to the exit. One of the waiting men took my arm and directed me down the stairs to a windowless van.

"Good grief, could you be more of a stereotypical villain?" I muttered as they shoved me into the back. Brian climbed in after me and secured the handcuff to a bar welded to the floor. I tried to flex my fingers, but they were so stiff from the cuffs that they hurt too much. Soon, the van was driving down an unknown road.

"Brian, could you at least loosen the cuffs? I can't feel my fingers," I said.

"Can't handle some handcuffs?" he scoffed. "I thought you liked it rough?"

I rolled my eyes. "It's only fun when you know how to do it right. Which you *clearly* don't. God, the number of times I had to fake it with you is embarrassing now that I think about it."

"I'm going to miss that smart mouth of yours. In more ways than one," Brian said, his eyes softening, almost pleading. "I need you to cooperate, Sadie. Finn will kill me if you don't tell me what's on that tattoo. Then he'll send someone else to do the job. Someone who will be far worse than me. They'll torture you, cut off your fingers, and much worse."

"Oh, so scary," I mocked. "I don't know where the files are or even know how to read this goddamn tattoo, so save your breath."

There was a sigh. "I'm sorry about this, then."

The next thing I knew, Brian's hand grabbed my throat, and my head was slammed into the wall of the van. Stars filled my vision, and sharp, terrible pain ripped through my skull. Before I could react, he stuck a needle into my neck, and darkness pulled me into its depths.

CHAPTER 32

Keelan

The sun's rays shone through the hotel window, stirring me awake. I smiled against the soft pillow beneath my head. That was the best sleep I've had in, frankly, years. I turned over to Sadie's side of the bed, needing to wrap her warm, naked body in my arms. But when my hand hit the bed, there was only a cool pillow and crumpled sheets to greet me. Ice coated my heart.

"Sadie?" I called out, sitting up. Silence answered, and I leaped out of bed, running to the bathroom. When I opened the door, it was empty. "Fuck!" My eyes searched the room before running both hands through my hair.

Where did you go, princess?

So many thoughts raced through my head as I hurried to my bag and pulled on a pair of boxers. The dark part of my brain told me that Sadie had run away. But how could she do that after what happened last night, after I finally admitted to her after all these years? She wouldn't have left after that.

Maybe she's downstairs getting coffee. Except she knew not to go down there without me. She wasn't allowed.

Unless she's being a brat and testing me.

After quickly dressing, I went to the nightstand and picked up my phone. Logan had left a message saying he and Aiden would be in meetings all morning and would meet us when Sadie and I were ready for the day. I needed to call Gavin, but before I did, I scanned the room again for anything unusual. That's when I spotted that the yellow envelope that Jeremy gave me had been torn open and left sitting on the dresser.

I walked over to the dresser and emptied the contents. Half of the cash and Sadie's fake ID were missing.

Fuck!

A knot of fiery anger boiled in my chest, and I crushed the envelope in my hand. Sadie had no idea how badly she fucked up. Leaving me again? After I poured my heart out to her? I closed my eyes and pressed my fists against my forehead. A mix of emotions played war in my heart—anger, bitterness, betrayal ... heartache. Could I really blame her for this? I kidnapped her and dragged her away from the safe life she made for herself. While it was for a good reason, maybe she couldn't come to terms with that. Maybe Sadie realized last night that she couldn't let a monster like me into her heart.

But ... she told me she loved me, too.

I opened my eyes and looked down at my phone, opening the GPS app linked to the bracelet. Did she really think I wouldn't check that?

I tapped the passcode in and waited for the map and coordinates to load. When they did, my eyes narrowed on the flashing icon.

"What the ..."

I zoomed in on the map and checked the log history. It showed that Sadie arrived in California around four a.m. at a private landing strip at the Los Angeles airport and had traveled to a storage building a few miles north. The signal stopped there.

Something felt very wrong about this. Why would she run if she knew I could track her?

Unless Sadie wanted me to follow her.

Where are you going, baby?

Sadie's phone was gone, too. I tried calling it, but it went straight to voicemail. I dialed Gavin next.

Pick up, Gav. Pick up.

He answered on the second ring. "Holy shit. Kee, I was just about to call you."

My stomach dropped at the urgency in his voice. "What happened?"

"It's Aisling, man. Finn just called your dad and told him someone broke into their house last night. Some masked men held Finn at gunpoint while they kidnapped her. No one knows where they took her. You and Sadie need to come home *now.*"

"Sadie's gone, too." There was a tremble in my throat as I spoke. "It's safe to assume that whoever has Aisling now has them both."

"Oh fuck. What do you need?"

A notification pinged in my ear, and I pulled the phone away to see that the GPS app had been updated. "Hold on," I said, putting the phone on speaker. "The bracelet I gave her was offline for hours, but it just picked back up again."

"Where is it?" he asked as I zoomed in closer.

"Somewhere outside of Burbank. Gav, I need a car waiting for me at LAX. I'll be there as soon as I can."

"I'll meet you at the airport, then. If more than one person kidnapped them, you'll need backup. Should you call your brothers?"

"I don't have a choice; I need their private jet," I said. "Driving would take too goddamn long, and this fake ID won't cut it at the airport. My face is most likely plastered on every television, and if I'm caught, the feds will be waiting for me at the terminal."

"Alright. Get the hell out of there. I'll see you soon."

I hung up the phone and texted Logan before sliding my phone into my back pocket. I hurried around the room, gathering our clothes and tossing them into the suitcases and bags. My hand brushed against the pink silky fabric of the new dress Sadie wore last night. She looked so stunning with those golden butterflies that I almost fell to my knees before her. Sadie Ryan held my heart in her hand for so long that I no longer needed it in my chest. I needed her to live, not to be lost in the darkness that was my life. She was mine. No one would take her away from me again.

Holstering my pistol under my shirt, I grabbed the bags and rushed out of the room.

Hang on, Sade. I'm coming for you.

CHAPTER 33

Sadie

I don't know how long I was unconscious, but when my eyes fluttered open, I was no longer in the van. My head was pounding, and a warm, sticky substance was on the side of my face. Blood. Carefully, I looked around.

It seemed like they'd moved me from the van into a poorly lit storage building with pallets and crates along the walls, rafters above, and a chest-height metal table roughly five feet from us. Near the table lay a large, black rucksack bag and some water bottles leaning up against it.

When I tried to move, I realized that my legs and arms were bound with ropes, and I was in a chair that was bolted to the floor. No one else was in the building.

"Sadie?" a raspy voice spoke behind me. I whipped my head around, ignoring the vicious thumping in my skull.

"Oh my God. Mom! Mom, you're alive," I said, my throat tight with relief.

My mom was strapped to another chair just behind me. Her silver-streaked blonde hair, normally styled to perfection, hung limp around her face. I could feel the rough plaster of her cast brushing the back of my arm. Her face bore dark bruises, and a nasty gash cut across her heart-shaped lips. I couldn't see her green eyes through the swelling.

Anger coursed through my veins. "Was that all from Dad?"

She nodded. "When your father returned from his business trip a few days ago, he saw security footage from when Keelan broke into the mansion. I couldn't hide the fact that I spoke with him. He knows, Sadie. Your father knows everything."

My stomach leaped, and bile rose to my throat, a reminder that my father did that because of me.

I bit my bottom lip as anger coursed through my veins. Keelan had told me what my father did, but I hadn't expected it to be *that* bad.

"There's a lot you don't know, Sade. Your father learned that I've known where you were hiding this entire time and that it was me who helped you escape."

I let my head hang. "Jesus, I still can't wrap my mind around all of this, let alone the fact that the man I've been sleeping with for the last eight months was using me as part of his job description. He was one of *them* this entire time."

"Finn told me that Brian Danon had been following you since the moment you left that courtroom. He was an agent on his payroll who he had a lot of damning information on. Brian would have done anything to keep those secrets hidden."

I turned and looked over my shoulder. "Patrick found out, though. Brian's dirty laundry is in the files they're after."

She nodded. "I wish Patrick had told me. I could have helped."

I shook my head. "You know the men in the family always leave out the smarter ones."

My attempt to smile was futile.

"What I don't understand," I continued, "is why wouldn't Dad just take me himself to get that information? If he's known where I've been hiding, why not fly to Vermont and come get me himself? It's not like he's afraid to raise a hand against me. Torturing me for the file location would have been fun for him."

"If he couldn't hide you behind the walls of our home, surrounded by security, then having you hiding out in another state with a federal agent watching over you was the best outcome, all while having the agent search for those files in your home. Your father figured that someday, he would get that information. He might be a monster, but he wouldn't kill you. Yet there are men in this city whose files are in those boxes who would. Running away under a new identity was the best thing for him, too. He just didn't like the fact that I hid it from him."

My father was never going to change. He hired a man to kill his son, so why wouldn't he do the same to me if I didn't give him what he wanted? Mom may have thought Dad would hold back, but I knew better.

Patrick not only gathered incriminating information about everyone on both sides of the family and their clients, but he found something else. He entrusted Keelan with hiding the location, knowing the risk if anyone found out. Patrick died to make sure no one could get their hands on those secrets—except for me and Keelan.

"Where is he now?" I asked. "Did Brian say what his next move was?"

She shook her head. "Brian hasn't said anything I haven't already told you. Your father's plans changed when he discovered Keelan had escaped and was coming after you. Brian, who had been monitoring your movements, reported that you had been taken and that he had been tracking you both. If Brian couldn't get that information from you—this code you have—then he was hoping you and Keelan would lead us to the files. He worked with Arthur to set up a trap in Vegas, using Keelan's brothers to make sure the two of you separated and you got on that plane with Brian. It wasn't until I was dragged out of the house and thrown into an unmarked car that I realized that the kidnapping was all set up by your father. Of course, I knew he had to pretend to be shocked that someone broke into the house for the security cameras, putting on a show for the police when they showed up."

Tears were now threatening to fall. Yes, I ran because it wasn't safe for me in Los Angeles anymore, but at what cost? My own mother's life was now in danger, and I couldn't protect her.

"I won't let your father or Brian hurt you, Sadie. I'm so tired of living with death," she said. "After Patrick died, I continued to exist in this selfish cycle, this haze of alcohol, to numb my pain when you were suffering so much. I knew there was a risk in sending Keelan to get to you first, but I couldn't take being a coward anymore. I told Keelan where you were because, in my gut, I knew he was the only one who'd truly protect you. He might have been a bully in your eyes growing up, but I know a man in love when I see it. That kind of love your father could never give me. But Keelan would with *you*."

I flinched in surprise. My own mother saw the real Keelan before I ever did.

"Mom—" I started, but the sound of a metal door opening cut me off.

It was Brian.

He closed the door behind him and sauntered over to where we were, carrying the burgundy briefcase he always had on him.

"Sorry for the accommodations, ladies," he said. "I would have gotten you some cushions, but time's running out. Sadie?" Brian walked over to the metal table and set the briefcase on it, flipping up the latches and pulling out a laptop. After Brian powered the computer on, he connected his phone to it, glancing at the screen while he typed in everything to pull up the software.

Shit. Dad must have cloned the program.

"Finn expects me to get the location within the next thirty minutes," Brian said. "He set us up here in one of the warehouses Arthur owns, so if we don't do this quickly, he and his men will head this way. And, trust me, they'll be a lot less friendly."

That means we're right back in Burbank.

"Finn already walked me through the steps. Now I just need you." He pulled up the prompt for the key phrase and then turned to me. "I took a photo of the tattoo while you slept. Read to me the key phrase. Now."

"Go fuck yourself, Brian," I cheerfully replied.

Brian let out a heavy sigh, pinched the bridge of his nose, then pulled out a handgun from his waistband and walked toward us. My blood turned to chips of ice as he leveled it at my mother's head. "Do not make me blow your mother's brains out, Sadie. Read it to me. Now."

"Jesus, okay!" I shouted. "Lift my shirt, and I'll try to decode the tattoo. I'm rusty, so it might take some time."

Brian pulled the gun away from Aisling's face and slipped it back into his holster. He went over to me and grabbed the hem of my shirt. But as he lifted the hem, his fingers brushed my skin in a gentle caress. "You know," he murmured, looking up to meet my eyes, "I really do care about you. I don't want your dad to hurt you. Please cooperate, and this whole fucking mess can be done with."

I looked down at Brian and stared into those blue eyes that had once made me feel safe. Where affection and care once lived in my heart, they were replaced by disgust and betrayal. This man lied to me for months, spying on me just so my dad could get the files Patrick had stolen. Those pretty blue eyes were the eyes of a liar.

Lies for a lie, Brian.

Saying nothing, I took the hem of my shirt in my teeth and bent as much as the ropes allowed me to look down at the tattoo. I knew I couldn't tell him the actual location of the documents, so I had to think fast.

"Okay," I said around the cloth, swallowing down my nerves. "It says 'Shadows in Silence.'" Brian stepped back, his eyes narrowed, and I released the shirt from my teeth.

I was banking on the fact that Brian hadn't a clue how long it would take to read Morse Code, hoping he'd believe me.

"Type that into that prompt, and the location will appear on a map."

Brian gave me a quick nod and walked back over to the laptop, typing in the phrase.

My hands were fidgeting against the ropes, and my breaths became shallow.

"What the fuck?!" Brian cursed, slamming his fist against the laptop keyboard. I watched with delight as a series of error codes flashed across the screen and locked him out. Then the desktop blinked once with the blue screen of death and shut off.

"Shoot," I said flatly. "I must have gotten it wrong. Well, it's too late now." My lips curved into a smile just before Brian came marching over, gun raised again, only this time it was aimed at *my* head.

"You think I'm an idiot?" he asked, rage burning in his eyes. "No fucking way you'd do that on purpose if you didn't already have the location. Where the fuck are the files?"

I shook my head. *I can't tell him. I won't.*

Closing my eyes, I turned away. *Think dammit.* I knew I had to tell him something. It wasn't my life I cared to save at that moment. It was my mother's.

Where could I lead them that would buy time for Keelan to arrive without being killed or taken away?

At least I grew up in Los Angeles County.

I needed somewhere that was obscure enough that it would take them an hour of searching before coming up empty-handed, so I wracked my brain. Then an old memory bloomed in my mind.

"Sadie?" Brian asked, his voice rife with impatience. "Tell me where the files are. Last chance."

"Fine!" I snapped, turning back to him. "Elysian Park. The map pinpointed where they grow non-native trees and shit. You'll have to explore the Chavez Ravine Arboretum, near the playground. A note in the program stated they're buried under a painted red stone used as a memorial on the grounds. Exactly fifteen inches down.

That's all that popped up on the screen when Keelan and I looked it up in the hotel room. Patrick hid them there."

Brian glanced at me before stepping back to retrieve his phone from his pocket. He dialed a number, set the phone on speaker, and instructed the man on the other end to search the location for any red memorial stones.

There was a muffled reply before Brian ended the call. I closed my eyes and leaned my head back, the throbbing in my head easing into a dull thud. Patrick and I went to Elysian Park once as kids with our nanny. It was one of the rare times that we played as siblings without fighting. It was a treasured memory of my dead brother.

It's also a real bitch to get to, regardless of the time of day. So, hopefully, I had bought Mom and me thirty minutes to an hour before they knew I was lying. Brian sat on a nearby box and leaned back, exasperated and stressed.

"For your sake, I hope you're not lying," he warned.

"For your sake, you should let my mom and I go before you get killed. The money you made from this bullshit will *not* protect you from Keelan Blake. You may think you'll catch him using me and that tracker as bait, but you don't know what he's capable of when it comes to me. That man will fucking kill you."

Two hours later, my ass was burning from the damn chair. Brian didn't say much as he sat in the chair beside the table. Then his cell phone rang. Brian sprang up and walked away from us, the receiver pressed to his ear. A few seconds passed.

"Fuck!" he cursed, slamming his heel into the chair beside him and sending it flying ten feet across the room.

Well, here we go.

"Sadie," my mom whispered frantically. "Did you—?"

"Yup," I replied quickly. "I'm not letting Patrick die in vain. They're never getting that location."

"Sadie!" Brian shouted, storming over to me. He grabbed the front of my T-shirt, tearing the fabric around the collar. My wrists and ankles screamed as the ropes cut and burned into my skin. Despite my restraint, I hissed in pain.

"Tell me what the code *actually* says." The look in Brian's eyes broke me. This wasn't the man I knew. "I don't want to hurt you, but I will have no choice." He let go of my shirt and took one step back. "Sorry that I have to do this."

Brian's left hand cracked across my face, sending a lightning bolt of pain through the cut in my scalp. My head rocked to the side, and my mom screamed. Blood filled my mouth when my lip split, and I spat a mouthful onto the concrete, splashing Brian's brown loafers. I looked up at him, the man I once trusted, who had just assaulted me again.

"Typical man," I seethed. "Can't keep his fucking hands to himself."

"Shut up!" Brian shouted, and my body froze, not in fear. I wasn't afraid anymore. I was furious.

"You hit like a little bitch," I added and waited for another slap, but it never came. Instead, his eyes darted over to the cut on my lip.

"Fuck," Brian said, his brows pulling together. "I don't want to do this to you. Believe me when I say I did care about you. It wasn't just business. I mean—" He ran his hand through his disheveled hair. "It was at first, but—"

"I don't give a shit," I said. "My lies about who I am were only to protect myself from being killed. You, though ... you did it to deceive me and protect yourself from going to prison. You're nothing but a selfish dick. Please don't force me to share what my brother died to protect. Let me and my mother go."

Once he took a few steps toward me, a voice came through on a walkie-talkie he had connected to his belt.

"Brian," a man called out. "We have a problem. The security cameras picked up movement down the east hallway by the back alley. They're already inside."

Brian's lip curled up, and he turned back to me, meeting my eyes. "Lucky for you, I won't have to force you to talk. Once Keelan sees that I have your life in my hands, he'll do whatever the fuck I ask."

CHAPTER 34

Keelan

As I yanked the metal door leading into the storage building, a cacophony of alarms started blaring, rattling my eardrums. The fuckers must have rigged the entrances. They knew I was coming. Gavin and I ducked into a dark office, so I could take out my phone.

"Goddamn, that's loud," I said, looking at Gavin. "We'll have to hurry so they can't pin us down."

"Which way do we go? There're so many fucking hallways in this place," he said, looking down at the GPS on my phone.

"Now that we're close, the bracelet's tracker narrows the location a little more. It looks like she's down this hallway about twenty feet and through that door." I pointed to the black double doors on the other side.

"You know this is a trap, right?" Gavin said.

A wide smile grew on my lips. "Makes this so much more fun, doesn't it?"

Gavin pulled back the slide chamber of his Glock and flashed me a feral smile that told me he was ready for this. He was prepared to fuck someone up.

Two wolves ready to take on a pack of lowly scum.

I withdrew my gun and clicked the safety off before adjusting it into a two-handed grip. Keeping the barrel pointed at the door, we moved down the hall. I grabbed the doorknob and turned, slowly cracking the door open. Carefully, we stepped inside the dimly lit room. Gavin quickly moved to the right to cover the area there. I looked toward the middle of the floor, where two figures were strapped to chairs.

Sadie!

"Keelan, watch out!" Sadie screamed from the gloom as a baseball bat flew toward the left side of my head. I spun on my heel and caught the bat with my left hand, stopping it mere inches from cracking my skull. I raised my right leg and kicked the attacker hard in the gut, sending him sprawling across the concrete floor before hitting his head on a post. As I took a couple of steps toward the downed man, my eyes found Sadie, whose bloodied, terrified face shattered my fucking heart. Sadie and her mother had been bound by rope to two metal chairs backing each other. Red-hot rage tinged the edges of my vision when I watched her struggle to free herself the moment her eyes met mine.

I'm going to kill them all.

The fucker I had kicked slowly clambered to his feet, chuckling like an asshole under his breath. "Damn, Keelan, all that time in the prison yard made you strong. That was a hell of a kick," he said, stepping into the light. With a smug grin, he leisurely ran his hands through his dirty-blond hair, straightening out the mess. He cleared his throat and brushed off the dust from his suit nonchalantly, behaving like I hadn't just sent his body flying across the room.

"You motherfucker," I seethed as I recognized him.

"Who the fuck is this guy?" Gavin asked, coming to my side with his gun pointed at the man's chest.

"That's a dead man," I growled, pointing my gun right at him, but Brian raised his hands in surrender.

"Relax, Keelan. How about we talk about this?"

"There's nothing to talk about," I spat, raising the gun higher to aim at the center of his forehead. "You took Sadie from me, so unless your next move is to untie her, I'm going to fucking kill you."

Brian stepped back, closer to Sadie, and rolled his eyes to her. "Go on, baby. Tell him."

My brows furrowed, and my right eyelid twitched. *Baby? He's dead.*

Sadie swallowed, tears running down her cheeks. "My father hired Brian to track me. They now know the tattoo would lead them to those files Patrick collected. My dad has known this entire time. I didn't tell him shit, though. This cut on my mouth is proof," she said, turning her head to glare at him. "Baby, feel free to shoot the worthless bastard in the knee."

Surprised at the ruthless princess in the chair, I was more than happy to oblige her request.

Before I could pull the trigger, the crack of a gun went off in the dark warehouse somewhere to our right. Sadie and Aisling screamed. Gavin cursed and collapsed on the ground next to me. I grabbed his arm and pulled him behind a stack of wooden crates.

"I'm good, I'm good," he said with a low grunt. "The shooter only grazed my shoulder a little. Kill that smug prick." Gavin stood, grunting again. "I'll find the asshole who shot me. Go."

I nodded and bolted around the boxes. Before I could raise my gun, Brian was already barreling toward me, slamming his body into my gut and knocking me to the ground. The gun fell from my hand and skidded a few feet away from me.

Sadie screamed my name as my back slammed into the concrete, and Brian's fist collided with my jaw. The iron tang of blood filled my mouth, which only pissed me off even more. I wrapped my legs around Brian's midsection and grabbed his throat with both hands. Rocking my body, I tried throwing him off of me, but I couldn't get the right angle.

Gavin ran past us to the right, firing shots toward the rafters above. From over Brian's shoulder, I saw an armed man partially hidden behind a metal railing, aiming for my head. Gavin fired another shot, this time striking him in the throat. The man toppled over the railing and landed on the warehouse floor in a heap of broken bones and blood. Gavin grabbed the fallen baseball bat and charged at us, swinging it down onto Brian's head with a sickening thud. He slumped over me, and I was finally able to throw him off. Then Gavin reached down to grab my hand and help me up.

"I'm not sure if that guy was the one who shot me, so we'll need to hurry in case there are others."

There was a shuffling noise behind me, and I turned to see Brian up and moving to Sadie. I scooped my gun off the ground, aimed at his right shoulder, and pulled the trigger without waiting a beat. Blood splashed on the ground as the bullet sliced across the thick meat of his arm, and he fell before he could reach her.

Sadie shrieked again at the blood splatter, and Aisling tried to grab her hand to comfort her. Her body shuddered against the ropes, and her eyes were wide with terror. My chest tightened.

It didn't matter if Sadie wanted me only to slow Brian down, but once there was blood, her response broke something in me—like the warehouse—like the men behind the bar. Once again, I subjected her to blood, gore, and violence.

"Sade," I cried out, running to her. Gavin followed behind, keeping his gun trained on Brian's moaning body. "It's okay, baby, I'm here." I pulled my knife from its sheath and slid it under the ropes. I sawed until they snapped, freeing her and Aisling.

Immediately, Sadie jumped from the chair, throwing her arms around me. She buried her head in my chest and sobbed. I hugged her back, wanting to hold her forever, to kiss away the wounds and pain inflicted on her, but when Brian groaned on the ground behind us, I pushed her behind me.

Gavin still had his gun pointed at Brian's bleeding head. When he looked at me for instructions, I nodded once.

"Close your eyes, baby."

"Wait, wait," Brian shouted. "I can help you! Killing me won't stop anything. Even after they get what they want, they won't stop until they kill her and you!"

I held up my hand for Gavin to stop.

"You'll never escape this city without my help, Keelan. The dirty cops on Finn's payroll already know I'm delivering Sadie to her father."

My eyes narrowed to slits as I glared at him. The fucker was more concerned about himself than hurting Sadie.

"Listen to me. Finn isn't the only player in all this. If you kill me, you might as well deliver Sadie yourself and slap those handcuffs back on."

I stepped toward him. "What's Finn's next step?"

Brian shifted and sat up, placing his hand over his wounded shoulder. "He's expecting me to deliver her and the files within forty-eight hours. If I help him, he'll destroy the files that he has on me. That was the deal. Keelan, I never meant to hurt Sadie. I was desperate. I had a job to do, and I fucked it all up. Luring you here was my second assignment. Finn wants you dead or back in prison. This entire city will be swarmed with police and roadblocks if everything doesn't go exactly as he planned it to. The best thing you can do now is get Sadie out of here and someplace safe. If I don't report to Finn with an update, he will come here, and you're all fucking dead."

"Go wait with your mom," I whispered to Sadie, and I moved closer to Brian. She ran to her mother, wrapped her arms around her waist, and the two stepped back.

I holstered my gun and looked down at Brian. "Why are you telling us this? Getting me here was part of the plan, too, so why warn us now?"

Brian's eyes went to Sadie, softening into something sad, which irked me. "First, I'm not ready to die." He winced again, gripping his shoulder as blood seeped through his fingers. The motherfucker was going to pass out before I even had a chance to kill him. "Also ..." He kept looking at my wife with such disgusting longing. "I care about her, too. I know what I've done is fucked up, but it's too late now. Find the files before Finn finds another way to get his hands on her. You want to protect her? That's how. Get the files and bring him down. There is no way in hell you're leaving this city alive otherwise. But if you get my name out of those documents, I'll help you two disappear."

I barked out a laugh, resting my hand on the butt of my gun. "Yeah, right. You tracked my fiancée for almost a year, *fucked* her, lured her away from me, intending to hand her over to her dad, and now you want to save her?"

Brian shook his head. "When I took the assignment, I only cared about those documents. Finn was using them to keep me in line. You and I both know he's going to kill or hide her away once he gets what he wants. He doesn't know the code is in the tattoo, but he knows she has it. Even from the beginning, Richard only reported to Finn that Patrick handed the *files* to her. He completely misinterpreted the communication you and Patrick had before he died. He's convinced that's one of the reasons why she fled. He will torture his own daughter for that information, and you know it."

"And now?" I asked.

"After I overheard part of the conversation you and Sadie had in the casino, I reported to Finn that the code to where the files were was on her body. It's too late now. She's their target."

As much as I didn't want to believe this asshole, he was right. Finn only cared about his wealth and power. As mayor of Los Angeles, he had too much to lose, so he would need to destroy evidence incriminating him, including his children.

He already did it with Patrick.

I slid my gun out. "How do I know you won't go against your word once you have that file or turn me in to the police after we leave?"

Taking another glance at Sadie, he pressed his lips together. "You don't," he said. "But you don't have a choice, not when Finn knows you're both here."

Gavin looked at me, brows raised. "He could run out here and betray us, Kee."

I smiled and said, "True, but it would be really painful for him to walk, let alone run," right before I aimed at Brian's foot and pulled the trigger. "We'll be in touch, pretty boy."

Brian's screams pierced my ears as I holstered my gun again and went to Sadie. "Let's go, baby." I ran a finger gingerly near the gash in her head and down to the cut in her lip. The wounds Brian gave her. "I want to kill him," I told her. *Fuck, I needed to kill him.*

Sadie cupped my cheek in her palm. "I know, but please don't. For me, don't kill him."

Seeing her shining green eyes looking at me, feeling her warmth on my skin, made my heart soar. I didn't care who was watching or that Brian was wailing in the background. I grabbed the back of her neck and pulled her close, our bodies pressed together. Our lips met in a gentle, lingering kiss, her mouth warm and wet against mine. Fuck, I needed to care for her, worship her, love her, and make her feel safe again.

Make her *mine* again.

CHAPTER 35

Sadie

M y body ached from the pounding in my head down to the rope burns on my ankles. I placed my fingers over the wound on my lip, where the skin split when Brian hit me. With my eyes closed, I tried to escape into my thoughts—anything else to distract myself from what had just happened.

I didn't want to think about how the one man I thought I was safe with, after escaping my family, would hurt me the way he did. Brian betrayed me in the worst possible way. He manipulated my trust and made me believe I was with someone decent, only to shatter it with the ultimate deception. Yes, Keelan hid so much from me, but he never hid *who* he was. He was always honest about how far he'd go with brutal violence to survive. I knew from the beginning what he was. After all that, there was one thing I was certain about.... Keelan would never hurt *me*. Not like that. He would never strike me out of anger. He would never mark my body with such hateful wounds.

But there was something that surprised me: Keelan was willing to work with Brian despite how much I knew he wanted to kill him. If it meant protecting me, he would bury that part of him. That was, *if* Brian was telling the truth. If he betrayed us again, Keelan and I would be ripped apart, with Keelan either in prison or in a body bag.

"Sadie." My mother's soft voice broke me from my thoughts, and I looked up. Reaching out her hand to me, she softly wrapped her fingers around mine, giving them a light squeeze. Her left arm was in a makeshift sling, the cast cracked and dirty. Mom would need to have it repaired. "Gavin's taking me someplace safe for now. You'll stay with Keelan until the meeting. Okay?"

I shook my head, tears stinging my eyes. "I don't want you to go," I said. "Just stay here with us until all of this is over. Please."

My mother shook her head back. "You know I can't. Your father was so close to killing me a few nights ago, Sadie. If he finds out I'm helping you now, I'm dead."

She was right. There would be no mercy if Dad realized she escaped and helped us. Right now, with me back in town, he would do everything he could to silence the both of us. We were the only ones who could dismantle his entire empire and bury him in the rubble.

Those files were the one thing standing in his way of complete dominance. Once he had what he wanted, I was disposable.

"What happens after this?" I asked. "Even if they arrest Dad, you're not protected here. There are too many players in all this."

Aisling removed her hand from mine and placed it on my cheek. "I'll find somewhere to hide, too. For now, you and I will have to leave each other. We won't be able to make contact for a while. But someday, I will find out where you are. I will leave a code for you that no one else can read. Patrick was smart, Sadie. I have to believe that he knew that all of this would disappear someday. The only two people he ensured to survive were us. I'll leave the code with Gavin. Okay?" She rubbed her thumb over my skin, wiping away tears. "When that day comes, he'll send it your way, and I'll meet you on some beach on a remote island. We'll put our feet in the sand and drink cranberry cocktails. Deal?"

I smiled weakly and gave her a subtle nod before she dropped her hand. "Deal."

Gavin walked to the door, touching my mom's shoulder. "Alright, Aisling. There's another car waiting for you at our meeting spot. Time to go."

"I love you, Mom," I said quickly as she went to turn. We never said those words in our family.

Her smile was faint when she looked over her shoulder. "I love you, too. You'll make it out of this. You're protected by the one man I trust for *you.*"

She was right. I trusted Keelan with my whole heart now. But there was still the worry that one wrong move and I'd lose him all over again. This time, it would leave a hole burned into my heart that would never heal.

After Mom climbed into the car, I watched Gavin pull a black bag from the trunk and hand it to Keelan. They exchanged a few words I couldn't hear, and Gavin walked to the driver's seat to take my mother somewhere no one could find her. Keelan waited to come inside until they had driven down the road.

"Come on, Sade. Let's get inside."

The house we had arrived at belonged to neither of the families. It was a beautiful white Victorian-style house with black shutters and a white picket fence in Angelino Heights. It was the kind of home I had dreamed of living in someday. The only thing missing was a wrap-around porch where I could relax while reading a book.

Gavin wouldn't tell us who owned it, but he assured us we'd be safe there. Even Gavin had to keep his secrets to protect everyone involved.

Once inside, we placed our bags down, and I looked around. The furniture looked outdated yet clean, with walls covered in light purple-textured wallpaper and gray sheer curtains covering the windows.

Keelan wrapped his arms around my waist before I took another step into the hallway. The feeling of his warmth and security was everything I needed then. We were away from the danger for now, and as I took in the surroundings, I felt a fleeting sense of relief wash over me. We were out of that storage building; I was no longer being hurt.

No one knows where we are.

"Do you want to wash up?" he asked, and I silently nodded. "We have to clean your tattoo again."

He reached out and took me upstairs, finding the bathroom at the end of the hall.

The bathroom was smaller than I expected, given how massive the rest of the interior was, but there was a tub. It was vintage cast iron, white, and had bronze legs on each side designed like lion's paws. It was positioned under a round window, giving us the perfect view of the sky. There was also a narrow glass shower with a rainfall showerhead and bronze fixtures. Keelan opened a cabinet to the left and found fresh towels for us. He grabbed a thick navy blue one and placed it on the hook connected to the glass shower wall.

He turned on the water, checked the temperature, and returned to me. Immediately, I lifted my arms so he could pull my shirt off, one article of clothing at a time, carefully avoiding my bruised body. I hadn't realized there was more damage to my body than what Brian had done to my head and face. Bruises appeared up and down my arm from when Brian and one of his men grabbed me. More were along my ribs and back from what I could only assume was when I was unconscious in the van. The rope had chafed my wrists, leaving them covered in swollen red marks. On top of that, there were small sprays of blood from when Keelan shot Brian in the shoulder. I hadn't even realized how much had gotten on me and soaked through my shirt and onto my skin until right now.

"Here," he said, grabbing a bottle of antibacterial soap from his toiletry bag. "You'll need to clean the tattoo. Gently, Sade." I nodded as he leaned in and kissed me softly on the forehead. "I'll place our bags in the bedroom, bring you some clean clothes, and check the kitchen for something to drink."

After he left me alone in the bathroom, I turned and watched the steam forming on the glass. I ran my hands carefully over my arms, reassuring myself that the nightmare was almost over. Keelan, Gavin, Mom, and I were alive.

Taking a deep breath, I stepped inside, relishing the hot water. Slowly, I turned to face the stream, relaxing as the water rinsed all the dirt and grime away. Then I gradually leaned back and let the water run through my hair, washing the dried blood from the cut. It sent another bolt of pain through my skull, but it quickly dissipated. After gently shampooing and conditioning my hair until no blood remained, I picked up the antibacterial soap. Softly slathering it over my body, I was careful not to press too hard on Keelan's name tattooed on my ass. It was nice to get a thorough cleaning after Brian's abduction.

I was there for about ten minutes before Keelan walked inside and placed a glass of red wine and water on the counter. "You might want those when you step out," he said. "Make sure you dab the tattoo gently with this clean towel and then use this ointment once it's fully dry. Don't use too much of it. We'll have to arrange for some warm food to be delivered, but the homeowners left a few things in the pantry for us."

"At least they had wine," I said with a smile through the foggy, beaded glass. "Thank you."

I thought Keelan would leave me then, but instead, he disrobed, walked over to the shower, and came inside. Though I had already washed my body, he squeezed a small amount of soap in his hands and rubbed them together. "My turn."

I turned around, so he could rub the soap all over my back, pulling my wet hair to the side and over my shoulder. Not only was he gentle over the tattoo, but he was careful to avoid any pressure over the bruises. I closed my eyes, relishing in the feeling of his hands on me as he tended to my wounded body.

"I don't think you truly understand how hard it was to let Brian walk out of that warehouse," he said. "The rage I'm feeling now, seeing you like—"

"I know," I said, turning around to place my hands on his shoulders, "but I'm glad you didn't. These bruises will heal, Keelan."

He paused momentarily, his expression looking stern, as if trying to calm himself from reacting. I moved my hand to his cheek and smiled.

"My turn," I said, grabbing the soap and caressing his skin with a soft touch while I cleaned every inch of him.

There was something so sensual about what we were doing. It wasn't about sexual gratification but about intimacy in its purest form. Being touched and loved by someone who would kill for you—*die* for you.

"After we rest a bit, we need to get to that subway and find the files. Brian mentioned that my father will be hosting a party at our house on Friday night. There'll be clients and potential buyers there. It's the only way to assure our dads won't do anything stupid. Not everyone coming to the gala is part of our other business. They're legitimate buyers for the art."

I nodded, rinsing the soap from my hands. "What's going to happen to my dad?" I asked.

"If all goes as planned, he and Arthur will rot in a prison cell. Then you and I will disappear."

We had no choice. Keelan killed people and then broke out of prison. Regardless of his reasoning, he would have to do time. Keelan had to disappear, and I was going with him.

A million thoughts raced through my mind, but they settled on one thing. I hoped Gavin and Keelan thought about everything that could possibly go wrong.

We crashed just after seven p.m. and slept until noon the next day. It had been a while since I had slept more than five hours, and by how refreshed I felt when we awoke, I needed it. Even my body didn't ache as badly when I climbed out of bed.

Keelan and I got ready, had some coffee, and then went into the garage for the motorcycle Gavin left us last night. The keys were hidden under the front mat.

Gavin had swapped out the license plate and repainted the red along the base with black. He had to ensure the feds, likely tracking him to lead them to Keelan, wouldn't recognize it.

Keelan put my helmet on for me, so I wouldn't risk reopening the cut on my head while we both zipped up the leather jackets Gavin had bought and climbed on the bike. I hadn't ridden on one of these in years, but the times I did, I fucking loved it. I wrapped my arms around Keelan and tightly squeezed him, letting him know I was ready.

Reaching the subway outside downtown Los Angeles took us only about twenty minutes. This railway had run for years before it shut down. When we were kids, we'd often sneak in here before it was boarded up. It gave us something to do when our parents would leave us for days to take care of business. It happened often, which made sense to me as to why Patrick would hide something here—it was familiar to the three of us.

"God, so many memories are coming back," I said, looking over at Keelan, who placed his helmet on the bike handle. "We used to explore in here before the city closed it off, and Gav and Patrick would sneak off to smoke pot."

Keelan smirked at the memory. "Yeah, that shit always set off my allergies, so you and I would go exploring."

"By exploring, you mean leaving me in the dark and scaring me?"

"Same thing, princess."

That made me laugh. "Okay, let's go, you psycho."

Luckily, the area we parked was toward the back of the highway, away from passing traffic. Some security cameras were trained in the area, but Gavin's sources confirmed that they hadn't worked for years.

The city built an expansive brick wall near the entrance, now covered in red and black graffiti, and tall, thick weeds grew from the cracks in the concrete. Next to it was a closed gate secured with a padlocked chain to prevent it from being opened. We expected it would take more than casually walking inside to reach it. Keelan opened our bag and pulled out two hammers and a pair of pliers. "Let's get to work."

Keelan slammed his hammer into the lock, working on forcing the metal to snap. I kept watch while he worked, the bike and my body obscuring Keelan from anyone coming by. There was evidence of a homeless camp, but from the look of it, they had cleared out a while ago. Finally, Keelan used the pliers to pull at one corner of the lock, just enough to slam the hammer once more to break it free.

Once he opened the gate, we dropped our tools back into his backpack and walked inside. The space around us echoed as cars drove over the bridge connecting the subway. It was dank and dark, and I feared a dirty rat would run over my foot at any moment.

"I used to be braver than this," I said. "What was Patrick thinking?"

Keelan let out a soft laugh. "He was thinking how funny it would be for his little princess of a sister to get her hands dirty taking down his family."

"Ha ha," I said sarcastically, looking around again.

At the far end of the abandoned subway, we spotted the booth where they sold the tickets. It was right on the side of the first opening, where the train would have traveled to go under the bridge.

"Fuck," Keelan said, pinching his brows together in frustration. "I know we couldn't write it down anywhere, but maybe we should have before we went under here. The reception is shit."

"Here," I said, reaching out to grab his phone. "I'll head back to the entrance and see if I can pull it up."

"You're not leaving my side. Just give me a minute."

He messed with the phone some more, and then his lips curled up. "There we go. Right over that way, I think."

I grabbed the phone and turned it toward the railroad tracks, the flashing blue dot pointing south.

"Stay close, Sade," Keelan ordered, and we continued walking down the dank, musty tunnel.

We had to jump onto the railroad tracks and go underneath the bridge, using my phone's flashlight to see where we were walking. "Right here," I said. "If this is correct, it's hidden somewhere within ten feet of here."

"I don't think Patrick would have buried the files in the ground," Keelan said. "There's concrete under all this dirt, and if there were any flooding, it would be swept away or damaged. Let's check the walls first."

We shone our flashlights around the nearby walls and old al-coves, looking for any sign of recent activity. After a few minutes, Keelan spotted an area on the wall near an old utility box that showed signs of tampering. Upon closer inspection, I noticed that someone had broken off some of the old bricks and used metal plating to cover the damage. The metal was newer; only a thin layer of dust coated the surface.

"Here, hold your phone closer," he said, and I lifted it, focusing on that spot. He wedged a small crowbar from the backpack into the metal, and with a hard jerk, he pried the plate from the brick. Only a few nails held it up, so Keelan also removed those. Inside the hole in the wall was a narrow, rectangular plastic container no longer than my forearm. After pulling it out, he laid the box on the side of the tracks and looked up at me. "These aren't the files."

"What?" I said, kneeling next to him. My heart sank at the sight of the small box. "All this, and he didn't leave the one thing he said he would?"

Keelan attempted to open the lid, but it remained glued shut. He lifted it to his ear and gently shook it. "Fuck. Something is obviously in here."

"Do you think he'd put everything on a thumb drive? That doesn't sound like Patrick."

"No, I don't think so." Keelan cocked his head slightly to the right, narrowing his eyes at the container. "Back up," he said. He gripped the container, and I stepped back to give him some room. Keelan then threw the box at the wall as hard as he could. The box cracked in half upon impact, and the broken pieces hit the crumbled rocks.

I rushed over and used my light to shine on what fell out, and a smile reached my lips. "Fucking Patrick."

We both looked at the Polaroid photo taken thirteen years ago of Keelan and me posing in front of the tombstone and the open grave. "Randall J. Plumperdink," Keelan said, his voice tinged with laughter as he picked it up, reading the name on the tombstone.

"He wouldn't have," I said, knowing he absolutely would have dug into that grave and buried the files inside. "Okay, fine. That does sound like Patrick."

We had finally found it, but we had another stop to make.

I moved back against the side of the tracks and folded my arms, my mind returning to that day. "I really thought you hated me when you said what you said back then."

Keelan was silent, holding the photo in his hands.

"Come to find out, you already had a crush on me," I teased. Keelan slowly walked up to me and placed the photo in his pocket.

"Yeah. I mean, I still thought you were a spoiled little brat, but I thought you were cute." He reached out and tucked a strand of hair behind my ear. "Knowing you kept that bleeding heart flower in your little treasure chest that you had hidden in your closet, you did, too."

I smiled and placed my hand on his cheek. "Hey, you shouldn't be going through my shit," I berated teasingly. "I don't know. Maybe that's why Patrick hid the files at the cemetery. Maybe he knew that was the moment we were destined to be fucked up together."

Keelan laughed this time. "Unless he's sending us on a scavenger hunt for kicks, and it's not even there."

"Yeah, that also sounds like Patrick," I said, rolling my eyes. "I guess we're about to find out.

CHAPTER 36

Keelan

B rian kept his word and met me on the north side of Ironwood Cemetery at eleven p.m. Thanks to his connections, we were able to disable the security cameras along the fence. We had two hours to get to the grave and dig up the files.

If we were right and they're actually in there.

As he approached, I saw the distinct limp in his left leg, and sinister delight trickled down my spine. The fucker deserved so much worse, but I promised Sadie I wouldn't kill him. Instead, I made him walk from the entrance to this side of the cemetery.

"You're three minutes late," I said, making no effort to hide the snark in my voice. I smelled his cologne when he got closer, and my neck started to itch.

Everything about this man makes me want to kill him.

As if he could see the irritation in my eyes, Brian's mouth twisted into a grimace. "I would have gotten here faster if someone didn't shoot my fucking toe off my foot. Not to mention the fifteen stitches in my left shoulder. That was the most pleasant part of the experience."

"You deserve worse, asshole," I snarled. "Did you bring the tools?"

"Two shovels and a crowbar if we need to open the casket." Brian held up a burlap bag. "Where's the headstone?"

Taking out a small flashlight, I waved for him to follow me, and we headed toward the mausoleum. I was tempted to bash Brian over the head and dump him in an available open pit, but again, Sadie wouldn't be happy. So, I decided to behave for her sake. After a few minutes of scanning headstones, I found Randall.

Since the headstone had been installed over a decade earlier, a fair amount of dirt and grime had built up on the white marble, slightly obscuring the name. But I recognized the engraving and dates instantly. I shone my flashlight on the ground, where they laid Randall to rest.

I gestured to the overgrown and dried out grass around the headstone. "This is it."

Brian slung the bag from his uninjured shoulder and dropped it. He kneeled to unzip the bag, and when he reached for the first shovel, I grabbed his forearm.

"No funny business, *Brian,*" I said, speaking his name like it was bitter acid on my tongue. "We have a deal to keep us both out of prison. Once we dig up the files, you'll take any evidence linked to you, and that's it. The rest will go to the agents who aren't in Finn's pocket. After that, we're done. *You* are done with Sadie. Understand me? The only reason you breathe is because of that woman's kindness."

Brian looked at me with sadness and understanding in his eyes. Not that I gave a fuck about his feelings. "Agreed," he replied.

I took the shovel from him, walked over to the grave, holding the blade over the grass, and drove it deep into the earth. "Dig."

Over an hour later, we had dug at least four feet into the ground when Brian's shovel hit something hollow. We glanced at each other and started digging faster. Soon, we spotted a three-foot-long box peaking out. Brian set the shovel down and carefully climbed into the hole while I trained my light on the spot. He brushed aside the clumps of mud and pulled the box free. It was a short gray storage bin often used to store documents and other valuables from the elements.

"Thank God," Brian sighed. "I didn't want to have to crack open a coffin and get the files from a dead guy."

Despite my burning hatred of the guy, I laughed a little. I didn't need Randall's ghost following me around after all this shit. So, he got to stay undisturbed.

I reached down and grabbed the box, hoisted it over the hole's edge, and set it down next to the headstone. Brian scrambled out and limped to my side. I looked at him and grinned, showing all my teeth. "Alright," I gestured at the dirt-caked bin, "open it and get your files out. We're running out of time."

Brian snapped the locks free from the lid and pulled the bin open. My jaw dropped at the sight of three thick stacks of folders inside. Patrick had collected *everything* about our families. Brian started flipping through the labels until his name came up. It was a blue folder with an "employee" tag on the cover. Brian opened the folder and started sorting through the documents and photos, his face growing pale under my flashlight.

"So, tell me, what does Finn have on you that makes you his loyal pet?" I asked. "You must have done something awful to earn a folder here."

"Yeah, I did." Brian's jaw ticked as he met my eyes. "Do you remember the news about the CEO of EnviTel dying in that car fire five years ago?"

I nodded hesitantly. "Yeah, they ruled it an accident...." My voice trailed off.

"Well, it wasn't."

Oh shit.

"The company sold to Finn after the accident," I replied. "He acquired a fuckton of clients because of that merger."

"Yeah, he sure did. I killed a lot of Finn's competitors in the eight years since I joined the Bureau and his employ. Finn said he would commission your dad to hide my crimes in a painting. But he lied. Instead, he kept all the documents and photos as a way to blackmail me into compliance before Patrick stole them. Once I retrieved his daughter, he would destroy them."

Everyone in the Blake family speculated Patrick was gathering evidence to use against his father, so he wouldn't be forced to do business with him any longer. But that was only scratching the surface. Patrick was fucking fed up. I had no idea it went this deep. I honestly expected maybe a packet of files on a few big players, but not this.

"Good thing we got to these, then," I said. I pulled out an orange lighter from my jeans and tossed it to Brian. "Burn your files, and let's get the fuck out of here."

Brian nodded, flicking the lighter until a small gold-yellow flame danced to life. He held the folder over the fire until the paper started to smoke. He dropped the smoldering folder on the ground, turning it into a ball of bright light as the embers destroyed all of Brian's sins. Within minutes, the folder was a pile of ashes. Brian kicked them into the hole and picked up his shovel.

"Let's bury this poor bastard, and I'll call my colleague at the Bureau to meet me at the gate to pick up the files."

"You're sure that they can be trusted?" I eyed him, gripping the shovel.

"Yeah, his name is Shawn Daniels. He's a rookie, so Finn hasn't gotten his claws into him. One of the perks of being dirty is knowing who the other rats are. This kid is clean."

"For Sadie's sake, I hope so. She's been through enough bullshit because of that demon father of hers. And because of you."

Brian looked up, one eyebrow raised, but he wisely kept his mouth shut. We finished burying Randall's grave—to which I mentally apologized for the intrusion—and headed back toward the entrance. Brian called to have the rookie meet him, and I took the bag of tools with me before he arrived.

I hid behind the concrete barriers near the main building, my hidden pistol now in my hand. If Brian betrayed us, I'd kill both of them and take the files myself.

"You sure about this, Danon?" the rookie asked, his brown eyes narrowing. The man was young, at least in his early twenties, with rich brown skin and a slim, athletic build. His entire demeanor was honest to a fault. He was kneeling by the box, sorting through the papers.

"As I mentioned," he told Daniels, "I got a tip about Finnegan Ryan's illegal doings, and files detailing those crimes were hidden in a crypt. They're legitimate. Look." Brian pointed to a page Daniels had opened. "This is a contract to have Jerimiah Larson blackmailed for sexual exploitation to secure funding for that IT company. We've been trying to nail that fucker for months."

"Holy shit," Daniels said, putting the folder back and closing the box. He picked it up and stared at Brian. "Finn Ryan is the mayor of Los Angeles. This will be a huge break in many cold cases in town."

Brian tucked his hands into his pockets. "Yup, he's as dirty as they come. You need to get this back to HQ *tonight*. The sooner we take them down, the better."

Daniels already had his phone pressed against his ear. "By the way," he said. "Why the fuck are you limping so badly? What happened?"

Brian shrugged. "It's so fucking dark in that cemetery. I stepped into a divot and twisted my ankle. I'm going to have to get it splinted tomorrow. It hurts like a bitch."

Daniels nodded. "Alright, I'm connected to Cavalli back at base. I'll debrief him on what we found and bring these files into the office."

My heart was pounding against my ribs. The files were in FBI custody now, and whether Brian followed through with ensuring the families' secrets were revealed had remained to be seen.

Brian and Daniels exchanged more words, demanding that no one make a move until tomorrow night. Daniels promised to call him as soon as he had orders. They shook hands, and Daniels drove off, taking the death of my family name with him.

Good. I'm ready to burn the world if it protects my wife.

CHAPTER 37

Sadie

After Keelan returned to the house, we made love and fell asleep in each other's arms. The following morning, I awoke with a feeling of peace despite the impending confrontation with my father at the party. The only thing that helped me relax was Keelan's warm body, clinging to me like it was our last night in each other's arms.

It could very well be if this goes south and Keelan gets taken away.

A cold, sick feeling danced in my chest as I sat up from the pile of pillows. Keelan was still sound asleep beside me, his face the image of perfection. Smiling, I leaned down and planted a kiss on his lips, savoring that warm softness.

"Keelan," I whispered. His eyes fluttered open, and his hand trailed up my arm.

"Hey, baby," he murmured, pieces of his disheveled black hair sticking straight in the air. It was too adorable.

I dragged my right hand up his neck, pressing my fingers into the skin. He shuddered under my hand, and I grinned wickedly before biting my bottom lip. I loved the effect I had on him.

Then I scooted closer, pressing my lips against his jawline.

"Mm, your lips feel nice, baby," he purred.

Smiling, I continued to give him soft kisses straight down to his bare collarbone. "It's been so hectic these last few days. I need to touch you."

Not that he didn't want to be physical, but I could see the resistance every time we were close, and I would involuntarily flinch from his touch because of my wounded body. Though I hadn't fully healed, I needed him like I needed air.

I didn't care anymore if I was still tender; only he could make me feel like myself again.

"Your obedient hostage hasn't been taken roughly in a few days," I said, taunting him. "You haven't even ordered her around. I think she needs it."

The fire in my gut ignited a raw, untamed lust, and I knew by the look in his eyes it awakened something inside him, too. I needed to touch him and for him to reclaim my body as his in return.

Suddenly, he reached over and wrapped his hand over my throat, gripping and restricting my breath slightly.

It looks like he's ready to play.

Keelan quickly moved forward, hovering over me now and squeezing his thighs over my hips as he caged me in. I moaned and slipped my fingers under his boxers, my nails brushing against his straining cock. His eyes rolled in the back of his head as my fingers ran over the tip, probing further down.

"You never got it re-pierced," I stated in a low and husky voice, my fingers touching his warm shaft.

"You know, that takes a bit to heal. I couldn't risk not being able to fuck you when I was ready," he bit out right before lowering his mouth to my shoulder and nipping at my skin.

I readjusted my fingers around his cock, slowly stroking again.

Even with the angle that my arm was in, I was able to grip him fully, gliding my fist up and down his entire length.

As I stroked him, Keelan reached down with his other hand and slipped it inside my pants, finding my soaking wet pussy, and stuck two fingers inside in one violent thrust. Heat tore through my body, igniting in my head and coiling low in my stomach.

While he touched me, my hand began moving up and down again, rougher this time, pulling on his thin skin. I swallowed a moan as he leaned against me, urging me to move faster as he ran circles with his thumb over my clit.

God, I am so fucking wet.

"Keelan," I moaned, his fingers sliding in and out of me at a faster pace. "Oh, God. I ... I'm—!"

Keelan's head fell forward as I pumped his cock two more times right before he spilled his heat into my hands. Thick ropes of cum splashed against my fingers and his boxers, leaving us both breathless and lightheaded as my orgasm soon followed.

"Fuck," he panted.

My thighs squeezed against his hips, and I smiled, settling myself back on my pillow while wiping my hand against the blanket to clean it. Keelan's fingers were still in my pussy, wet and ready for him again. He knew *exactly* what I wanted. His fingers pulled out and started prodding at my entrance, teasing me. My entire body tensed. I moaned as he began pumping in and out, his thumb rubbing circles over my clit.

Slowly, I spread my legs a little wider for him, making my point. One he clearly didn't miss. "She wants a kiss."

A wild smile stretched across Keelan's face as he pulled his fingers away. He placed one kiss on the side of my jaw, and then he crawled under the blanket, nestling between my legs. I felt his mouth trail across my skin, teasing me before he settled right above my pussy, which was already aching for him.

"Oh, fuck ..." I murmured, sliding my hands beneath the blanket to grip his hair. I *needed* to make sure he wouldn't pull back.

Slowly, he found my bundle of nerves and began to suck, his tongue trailing across the sensitive spot to stimulate me further.

"Yes," I breathed, my body curving as I held onto his hair, arching my hips upward to grind myself against his face. He knew all the right places—all the ways to pleasure me and fill the cravings that continuously roamed through my body. "Right there. Please, yes ..." The words tumbled out of my lips, one after another, though I had very little control over any aspects of myself.

His tongue snaked inside me, prodding deeper, no matter the resistance I gave in return. There was so much pressure now, and I bit my bottom lip, feeling a wave of flutters spread through me. Keelan pushed his tongue deeper inside somehow, reaching all the tender spots.

Jesus.

I spread my legs further apart while one of his hands slid up my right thigh, grabbing my unmarked ass cheek. He squeezed my hips, pulling me up and adjusting my position. Keelan's movements were urgent, as if he desperately needed me as close as I needed him. The desire to be pressed against each other overcame everything else, to the point where I was practically grinding against his face, smothering him with my need.

Positioned like this, his lips brushed against my clit while his tongue continued to thrust in and out of me wildly. Keelan moaned, the pleasure humming in his throat. The sound vibrated through me, sending more tingles that only got me closer to my peak. I barely had any control over my body as I trembled against him, lost in the waves of sheer ecstasy that had me whimpering and quivering. Fuck, whenever he touched me, my body would surrender to him. Every time he took me, that claim became clearer.

It was nothing short of ownership. I. Was. His.

"Jesus, Sade. You taste so fucking good," he purred, the heat of his breath moving over my skin. I gripped harder on his hair as I rolled my hips into his mouth. I was so damn close to rising to that bliss, drowned in endless euphoria with every flick of his tongue.

"I'm coming," I said, my breath heavy. I *tried* to warn him, but the words barely made it past my lips before my orgasm struck me. Hard and fast.

"Keelan!" I practically shouted his name as I dripped all over his tongue. The sudden wave had me flinching backward, but he held me tightly in my place. He continued in a sweeping motion with his tongue to draw out my orgasm. My back arched, and my head pressed deeper into the pillow, his name repeating on my lips as I gasped.

It took a while for me to wind down and finally catch my breath. When I did, he flung the sheets back and moved over me, his mouth claiming mine as we shared my taste in a passionate kiss.

"I love you," I said after he pulled back, his palm resting on my cheek. A small smile curved his lips, and his eyes lit up.

"I love you, too. So fucking much."

Keelan placed his head on the pillow and looked into my eyes. His smile made my cheeks flush. I had never seen him look so happy before.

"Well," he said, his smile now reaching his eyes. "That was a nice little treat for the morning."

Keelan placed his hand on my arm and rubbed it gently with the back of his fingers.

"I don't know. That was more of a treat for me," I said with a teasing wink.

"Oh, I'm not complaining," he said before leaning in and gently kissing me again.

"I'm gonna wash my hands and then head downstairs to make some coffee in that fancy kitchen down there," I said. "Do you want a cup?"

Keelan nodded and sat back up, scratching his neck and back. "Yeah, with a generous amount of milk, please." He reached out and tucked a loose strand of hair behind my left ear. "I need to shower first, though. I've got cum all over my thigh."

"Poor baby," I smirked.

I kissed him again and slid from beneath the soft red covers of the king-sized bed we slept in. I quickly washed my hands and threw on a T-shirt and pajama shorts before heading out the door and down the stairs.

The kitchen was way bigger than mine back in Vermont. It had dark cherry wood cabinets, cool gray granite countertops, and, luckily, a coffee maker next to the gas stove. After a few minutes of searching for coffee grounds and two mugs, I pulled out the milk we had delivered yesterday from the fridge and began brewing the desperately needed liquid of life. The coffee tasted heavenly on my tongue as I took a sip.

My ears picked up the sound of the shower turning on. As I debated joining him, there was a noise by the front door. I stood up slowly and entered the entryway leading into the living room but flushed my body against the wall, keeping out of view from the window.

When I peeked around the corner, I saw the movement of two silhouettes behind the door's frosted glass window. Armed with only a piping hot mug of coffee, I waited.

"Sadie! Kee! Open the door!" Gavin's muffled voice called out, and my shoulders instantly relaxed. I hurried to the door, unlocked it, and stepped aside to allow him to enter.

"Gav! You scared the shit out of me," I scolded, setting my mug on an end table. "I almost doused you in coffee. I didn't want to make that sacrifice."

Gavin laughed as he placed two black duffle bags by the door. "Sorry. I texted Keelan five minutes ago that I was almost here, but he didn't reply."

Yeah, he was busy getting jacked off and eating me out.

"My brother was always notorious for ignoring my text messages when you were around, Sade," a cheerful, feminine voice chimed from over Gavin's shoulder.

"Oh my God!" I cried out. "Mia!"

Keelan's sister pushed past Gavin and ran into my arms, her thick blonde hair brushing against my face. Her hair, now cut and styled into a chic bob, framed her oval face perfectly and had a couple of bright pink streaks along the front. She had even added several floral tattoos on her chest. It must have been a recent addition. The last time I saw Mia, she was only seventeen.

She's so tall now, at least five-foot-nine.

Mia Blake was Keelan's younger half-sister and the favorite of his siblings. I loved her like she was my little sister, and we used to spend hours playing together. The last time I saw her was during the trial when she looked over at me from the benches with hurt and confusion in her eyes. Back then, I felt so distraught and guilty that I ignored her. Given how tight she hugged me, I didn't think she hated me for what I did.

"What are you doing here?" I asked when I released her. "I thought we were all supposed to meet at the party."

She straightened out her green V-neck graphic T-shirt that complemented her sapphire-blue eyes and black jean shorts. "I have to help Keelan cover the tattoos, and I brought you a dress. The doormen won't let you in if you're not dressed appropriately."

I nodded because that made more sense than the plan I had in my head and flashed her a smile. "God, Mia, it's crazy how much you've grown in just a year."

Mia nodded as I grabbed my coffee, and we walked into the kitchen. "Yeah, I started working as an apprentice at the tattoo shop about six months ago. Gav says that I'll get to work on my first client soon. The tattoo on my calf is one I designed myself."

She turned to show me the back of her leg. There on her light beige skin was a colorful peacock feather that looked like it had been snatched up in a breeze. The colors were vibrant, and the detail was near-perfect. My heart filled with pride. Mia was going to be an accomplished artist, just like her brother.

"Mia," Keelan called from the stairs and entered the kitchen. His wet hair shone under the lights, and he looked damn delicious in his black tank top and jeans. "What the hell are you doing here?"

"Keelan," I said. "Come on."

Keelan's eyes softened, but he still looked pissed. "Gavin, why is my sister here?"

"Relax, Keelan," Mia said, laughing. "Were you honestly going to march into the mansion looking like that? I'm here to help you get ready for Dad's party tonight. Gav told me everything, and I want to help you. I brought all of my cosmetics and a fake mustache that I bought from a friend who does costume makeup in Hollywood. I'll go grab it."

Before Keelan could speak, Mia left the kitchen to grab one of Gavin's bags. I bit my cheek to keep back the laughter in my throat and took another sip of coffee.

Keelan glared at Gavin before grabbing the mug of coffee I made him. "Brian called when I got out of the shower. He'll be here tonight at five to go over the next phase of this shitstorm," Keelan said. "His 'clean' superiors have received the files and are reviewing them today. Once that's done, they'll get a warrant to arrest Finn. The best we can do now is hang low at the house until we hear more."

"Does this shitstorm include Dad?" Mia asked him when she returned with her bag. Despite her serious expression, there was also a flicker of relief in her eyes, a sign that she was okay with the fact he'd be locked up.

Keelan walked over to her and slung his arm around her shoulder. "Yeah, Dad's going to prison after all this. His association with

Finn over the years will drag him down, along with Aiden and Logan."

"Fuck those two," Mia said. "They're the reason Sadie got kidnapped and hurt. Besides, those fucking bullies never accepted the fact that Arthur married my mom and had another kid. As far as I'm concerned, you and Sadie are my family."

"I've missed you, too, Mia," I murmured, sitting at the kitchen table and leaning back in my chair. "I feel guilty for leaving, but I did what I had to do to survive."

"Yeah, I was kind of pissed when you testified against my brother, but I was naive," she said. "If Gavin hadn't pulled me away from the family and helped me see things from another perspective, I wouldn't be here. I'd probably view my father in a completely new way." She folded her arms and leaned slightly into the doorframe. "Well, in any event, I'm glad you're home now."

"Yeah, me too," I said, and for the first time, I meant it.

When five o'clock came, Brian was on the front porch. Gavin answered the door, which was the wise choice because I wasn't sure Keelan wouldn't try to kill him on the spot. Brian walked into the kitchen, carrying a black bag. He avoided eye contact with me as he set it down and started unpacking the contents. Gavin stood in the doorway, watching to ensure Brian didn't do something stupid while Mia worked on concealing Keelan's tattoos on his hands and upper neck. It was the only part of his skin that would be showing once his suit was on.

While I sat at the dining room table, savoring more wine and the pizza we had ordered, I asked, "So, the pink color corrector cancels out black ink?"

Mia nodded as she dabbed a large makeup brush into the pot of pink makeup. "Yeah, a neat trick I picked up while doing my friends' makeup in high school. Watch this."

After applying the rest of the corrector, she took a concealer as close to Keelan's skin tone as possible, which I found funny since there wasn't much skin tone that wasn't ink. She started applying and blending it into the tattoos, letting it dry down. Next, she used another brush to apply a thick, waterproof foundation before setting it with translucent powder. I was floored when she finished covering the last part of his neck.

"I would have no clue you even had any tattoos under that makeup," I said. "I almost forgot what you looked like under all that. The last time I saw you without ink was in high school."

The way Mia blended the makeup over his hands and neck, you would have to get extremely close to see any hint of black ink on his flesh.

"There! Now I need you to sit still while the foundation dries," she explained. "If it oxidizes in a darker shade, I'll have to add some brightening concealer. Once that's set, Sadie, I'm doing your hair and makeup next."

Nodding, I turned slightly toward the kitchen, where Brian and Gavin were setting out tonight's supplies. I watched Brian shuffling around the kitchen, doing all he could not to look over at me.

Keelan must have threatened to end him if he did.

As I watched him, though, there was a tiny twinge of pain in my heart. This man spent eight months lying to me, making me believe he was an ordinary guy who cared. As much as I wanted to hate him, I didn't have it in me. But I knew I needed something from him.

"Keelan, I need to talk to Brian for a minute," I said, setting down my wineglass and standing up. Keelan's hand immediately wrapped around my wrist and pulled me back onto the seat.

"Sit your ass down," he growled. "You're not going anywhere near him unless I'm right beside you."

I huffed and leaned toward him. "Look, Brian lied and deceived me on my father's behalf. I understand why he did it. But I *need* to talk to him; I need closure on this." Keelan's eyes searched mine, his anger dampening. "What exactly do you think he's going to do inside this house with you glaring at him with your deadly, psychotic eyes from across the dining room, threatening violence?"

Though Keelan was right about keeping me away from him, I needed to close this chapter of my life if we were ever to move on with a clean slate. He rubbed his thumb over my wrist before letting go, and Mia smiled reassuringly at her brother.

"She'll be fine, bro," she said, interrupting us. "Sadie's got this."

Smiling, I rose and headed to the kitchen, swiping Keelan's hand away as he tried to reach out and grab me again. Gavin and Brian looked up as I entered, and Brian's eyes widened.

"Don't worry. Keelan said it's fine." I watched as his shoulders relaxed. "Gavin, can you give Brian and me a minute?" I asked.

Gavin hesitantly looked over my shoulder at Keelan, who must have given him the okay. He nodded and walked out of the kitchen. I went to the island and pressed my hands over the cold granite.

"We need to talk," I said, my throat tightening.

Brian set down a black radio and leaned against the counter, his bloodshot blue eyes finally meeting mine. He had brushed his hair into its usual style, but the confidence that once radiated from him was gone.

Brian nodded but said nothing. So, I did.

"For eight months, you lied to my face about everything—your job, your past—and you faked feelings for me so I'd trust you. Against my better judgment, I let you into my life, my home. Maybe it was because I craved someone so normal that could help me leave my old life behind. But that wasn't the case; my old life was sleeping in the bed next to me. God knows what you did in that house while I was at work, going through all my personal shit, trying to find files that weren't there. Then, when you took me hostage, you *hurt* me. You assaulted me when I didn't give you what you wanted."

Brian's cheeks burned red with shame, his eyes downcast. "If you only knew the shame I felt over what I did to you in that building—"

"Bullshit. You knew what you were doing."

"Yeah, and I'm sorry. Nothing I do or say will ever clean my hands of the awful shit I did to you. Though it was my job, I fell for you. I didn't find pleasure in lying, Sadie. I thought what I felt was real. Trust me, though, it hurts like hell. Keelan shooting me was justified, and I don't blame him for a second."

I narrowed my eyes at him and crossed my arms over my chest. "That sounds like a pathetic apology to me, and that's okay. I don't need to forgive you because you don't deserve it. I just had to speak my piece, I guess. You chose money and protection over decency."

He leaned forward and rested his arms on the counter, his glassy red eyes rising to my face.

"You and I are done," I said. "After tonight, we will never speak again. You will honor your agreement with Keelan and me by helping us escape. It's the least you can do."

Brian flinched at the coldness of my words.

"I hope one day you can become the sincere man I met in the bookshop and do something good with your life."

With that, I turned on my heel and returned to Keelan in the dining room, slamming the door on my relationship with Brian Danon forever.

Mia had finished and gone upstairs to get dressed. When she came down, she was wearing a long purple gown and fastened a silver bejeweled clip shaped like a flower in her hair. "Alright, Sadie, you're up next. Go grab the dress out of my bag. It's in your favorite color, of course." She grinned at me. "Then, we gotta head out. My dad expects me to greet the guests, and I have to be able to sneak Keelan in through the back door."

Keelan walked over and held something fuzzy in his hand.

"Oh, right. Let me do this first, and then I'll do your makeup and hair at the table," Mia said. "The bathroom upstairs is way too small to work." She grabbed the false mustache before facing Keelan and lining it up above his lip to check the best placement. She used some spirit gum to adhere the hair to his upper lip and a moist towelette to clean the excess glue.

"Note to yourself, Keelan. Never grow a mustache. You look creepy, but Dad probably won't recognize you from afar."

"Where will everyone be?" I asked Gavin, who leaned back against the island and folded his arms lazily across his chest.

"While Mia keeps most of the guests occupied, I'll take Keelan to the main living quarters to prevent Arthur from approaching him and introducing himself to the unfamiliar guest."

I nodded and looked back at Keelan, noting how ridiculous he looked, and she hadn't even put his wig on yet. Despite the urge to laugh at the fucked up situation, my hands were shaking.

"I'm scared," I said, and he nodded subtly. As I climbed the stairs, clutching the pink dress, I kept my eye on the two men lingering near the door.

"Brian," Keelan said, turning to him. "If you don't protect her, I'll not just blow off that remaining big toe of yours, I'll put a bullet through your skull. Do you understand?"

Brian swallowed and nodded quickly. "Yeah, I believe it." He started to walk to the living room.

"Oh, and Brian. One more thing."

Brian turned around again to face Keelan.

"Listen, I need you to do me another favor."

Brian folded his arms. "Sure. What's up?"

"Do you remember the name Andrew Wright? He was put behind bars for the death of Director Luis Rodrigo."

Brian nodded almost immediately. "I didn't know him, but I'm familiar with the case. It was out of my jurisdiction."

"I need you to look into it. He didn't do that shit, and I think by now, you know how easy it is within the Bureau to make things go away."

Brian grimaced but nodded in agreement. "Alright," he said. "I can't promise anything, Keelan, but I'll see what I can do."

"See that you do, or I'll shoot off the nine toes you have left."

CHAPTER 38

Sadie

B rian gently clasped my forearm, but I pulled back, my feet pressed into the grass of the Blake's front yard. When we left the house, I was calm, ready to face my father, but now, the nerves were hitting me hard. Yes, I knew this nightmare of violence had to end, but what if the plan failed? Everything starting now would have to go smoothly, as we discussed.

"I'm going to mess this up," I said. "What if I mess this up?"

Brian turned to me, brows wrinkled. "I've been doing this for a long time, Sadie. I promise you'll do great. Just breathe. Most of what you're telling them is the truth. Up until Keelan and I making that deal."

Sure, trying to get my dad to confess to murder and then walk out alive will be a fucking cakewalk.

Taking a deep breath to settle my pounding heart, I nodded.

"I have the warrant and recorder in my pocket. I'll turn it on when you ask him about Patrick."

I nodded again. "Okay, just to be sure, please go over everything again."

"Just corroborate my story. As far as my department knows, Finn contacted me to find you, and I did. Unfortunately, a mole within the Bureau leaked that information to Keelan. He escaped prison and got to you while I was out on another case. Now, I'll get reprimanded for taking a case outside of my jurisdiction, but the evidence in those files I burned last night will be gone forever. I may lose my badge, but I'll stay out of prison."

"Logan and Aiden saw me and Keelan together. It's safe to say they reported it to Arthur and my dad."

He nodded. "That's what we're basing all this on. If you act as if you're afraid of Keelan, they won't believe you. Right now, we need Finn to confess to hiring Richard to kill Patrick. My superiors have the files regarding blackmail, extortion, and other financial crimes. This murder-for-hire was the only one missing. If you want to put your father away for life, this is the only way to do it. He won't be able to use his connections or money to get away with murder."

"What if he suspects you're working with Keelan, and this backfires? You're delivering me to my abuser." Brian reached out and tucked a strand of hair behind my ear, a gesture of comfort. "Keelan will kill you if he finds out you touched me like that," I said with a small smile.

He retracted his hand quickly. "Yeah, you're right. I'd like to keep breathing, and I'm already missing a digit."

As I allowed myself to laugh under my breath, I pressed my hand against my chest, feeling my heart race. "Okay, I'm ready."

We walked up the steps to Arthur's front door. It had been so long since I'd been inside that house, and nostalgia warmed my heart a little. Despite the awful things I had to deal with, it wasn't all bad growing up alongside this family.

Keelan and I found each other this way.

We entered the slightly crowded foyer after Brian handed our invitations to the security guard at the door, and immediately, the icy bite of the air conditioning greeted us.

"Come on, we need to go down the hall to the office," Brian whispered. As we crossed the foyer, I looked over my shoulder at the main living room. Most of the guests had gathered in the main room, where lively music played, and servers carried drinks and hors d'oeuvres on silver trays. I scanned the crowd of California elites for my people. Gavin, Keelan, and Mia were there, waiting for Brian to signal for them on another device Keelan held on to if we ran into trouble. If I played my role correctly, we would get that confession. Then Brian would escort me to the restroom, and Keelan and I could slip out the back door.

Brian approached the office door and rapped three times, a signal that he was there with me.

"Enter."

Fuck, fuck, fuck. Here we go.

Brian opened the door, took my arm, and we walked inside. Near the back of the room, my father and Arthur sat on two black leather chairs, smoking cigars, with a round glass table between them. Smoke hung heavy in the room, the only ventilation coming from the slightly open window. Both men wore expensive black suits, with their hair styled to arrogant perfection. I had forgotten how much Keelan looked like his father. He had the same facial structure and toned body, but Arthur, though he had a few tattoos on his arms and chest, wasn't fully covered like Keelan. The one feature that separated these two was the stark difference in their hair color. Keelan inherited those beautiful raven locks from his mother.

"Brian, lock the door behind you," my father said. My body froze like a deer in headlights. God, it was like I was staring at the Devil himself.

"Sadie," he breathed. "Thank God you're alive."

Yeah, I bet you're thrilled to have your little punching bag back.

"Hey, Dad," I said, taking a few steps closer. "I'm sorry I ran away, but I was afraid. If Keelan had found me ..." I took a deep, heavy breath, trying to settle my nerves. "It was all I could think to do back then."

My bastard of a father smiled, taking another long drag of his cigar before blowing the smoke into the air. My nose wrinkled slightly. I always hated the smell of cigars because it reminded me of him. "But you're not afraid of him now, though. Right?"

I winced at those words. "I can explain—"

"Save it," he growled, his eyes growing dark. "I'm surprised, honestly. After everything Keelan did to you, and then kidnapping you from your little haven, you would fuck him again."

"Finn!" This time, Arthur stepped in, intent on defending his son. "That's enough." Arthur's eyes turned to me. "The last we heard, Keelan was heading to the storage building. Where is he now?"

"After my men shot him, he grabbed Aisling and took off," Brian explained. "We had already removed Sadie from the location. They're searching for him now."

My father cursed under his breath. "Let's just hope bringing her here draws him out. Arthur's men are keeping watch on the grounds while cameras monitor every person entering the house."

"I'm not sending my son back to prison, Finn. You and I had a deal. If he shows up, you take Sadie, I take my son, and our families are done with this arrangement."

Arthur turned back to me and looked at my mouth, his eyes narrowing on my lip.

"What happened there?" Arthur asked.

I turned to Brian and gave him a stern look. "Brian took his job very seriously."

Father took a moment to study me while putting out his cigar in a crystal ashtray. "Well," he said. "When you're a whore like your mother, you can't expect a man to behave."

My skin burned with fury, but before I could respond, he looked at Brian. "You're relieved of this assignment." My father took his phone from inside his jacket and tapped a few buttons on the screen before standing and approaching us. Brian released my arm and reached into his pocket, pulling out a small neon green Post-it.

"Transfer it to that account," Brian instructed.

My father looked down at me as he transferred the money he had promised Brian. He was so close to me that cigar smoke smelled cloying. My stomach churned with anxiety and disgust. I didn't like that look in his eye—the look of a wolf savoring the fear of his prey.

"Sadie," my father said. "I have a surprise for you. Think of it as a welcome home present."

What the hell does that mean?

Brian cleared his throat before casually sliding his hands into his pants pocket. "Finn, I suggest you keep a low profile for a while now that the deal is done. You know the feds have launched an investigation into your company, and I have to play by the book starting from here on out."

"By the book, huh?" my father mocked, and I prayed Brian had already pressed the recorder on. We had to get this confession on tape before the feds came swarming in. Otherwise, no one would be able to protect me.

"Dad?" I said, drawing his eyes away from Brian. "I have something to ask you. Something that's been bothering me for a long time."

"And what's that, sweetheart?"

I swallowed. "Patrick's death."

He blinked at me. "What about it?"

Anger flared in my gut, but I kept my voice calm and soft. "I know the reports said it was a suicide. They said he used a nine-millimeter handgun with his right hand to shoot himself in the chest."

"Your point?" he asked, clearly annoyed.

"Patrick was left-handed."

My father's mouth parted a little. *It figures the asshole forgot Patrick's dominant hand.*

Taking a breath, I took the leap into further danger. "Why did you hire Richard Wertz to kill Patrick? He was your son."

There was a heartbeat of silence before my father grinned in that way that always made my skin crawl. "Hire Richard to kill my own child? Sadie, that's quite the accusation. I'd mind that fucking tongue of yours."

"Alright, enough," Brian said. He started to move to get between my dad and me, but he and Arthur drew their guns. Father grabbed my arm and yanked me away from Brian, pressing the barrel into my side.

Oh, shit.

This had escalated far too quickly. He already had me back; Brian was paid....

"Stop!" I cried out. "You're hurting me."

Brian's eyes went wide with shock, darting between the two men before settling on my father's grip around my arm.

"What the hell is this? This isn't part of our deal. I delivered your daughter. There's no excuse for manhandling her. Let her go, or I'll arrest you."

"Arrest me?" my father snorted derisively. "I'm the goddamn mayor of Los Angeles and president of a major tech company, Brian. You can't touch me." He smiled. "Oh, isn't this interesting? Did you fall for my daughter during this last year while you were fucking her?"

"Dad! Stop it!" I tried to wrench free from that iron vise of his. Arthur, hearing a tap at the door, walked past us to open it. Another man entered the room. That was when I saw a horrifyingly familiar face step into the light.

Alex Thatcher.

"Gentlemen," he said, his brown eyes focused on me as he walked toward us. "It seems I've arrived on time."

The last time I saw Alex, he sat beside my parents during the trial when I testified against Keelan. His slick black-and-silver hair was longer now, brushing the bottom of his ears. He shaved off his entire beard, revealing a square jawline and a wicked smile as he came closer.

"What is he doing here?" I asked. Panic started crawling up my spine. Jesus, that man gave me the creeps growing up.

"I see you remember Alex," my father said, keeping his gun on Brian. "He certainly remembers you."

"Finn, what the fuck is going on?" Brian said through gritted teeth.

"Where are the files, Brian? You said you found where my son hid them." He dug his nails deeper into my skin. I winced but didn't move. I couldn't risk my dad shooting Brian. Arthur was leaning against the bookshelf, silent as a corpse, and his gun pointed almost lazily in our direction.

The bastard is loving all of this chaos. My eyes drifted to Brian's other pocket, where the signal was to notify Keelan if anything went wrong.

"I'll take you to the files as promised, but you should let Sadie go. Killing your daughter is going to get the feds on your ass. I can't cover that up."

My father raised the gun higher, pressing the barrel against his forehead. "I just paid you. Tell me where the files are. Now."

"Dad, stop!"

My father was going to kill Brian, and then I would be completely helpless.

"Alright, fine. I put the box in the trunk of my car. I was going to bring you to them after everyone left the house. Here." Brian slowly reached into his left pocket and removed his car keys.

Dad kept the gun trained on Brian's head as he shoved me backward to grab the keys, and I fell right into Alex's hands. "Miss

Sadie Ryan," Alex whispered in my ear, low and deadly. "You've truly grown into such a beautiful woman."

I felt him lean close and inhale the scent of my hair. My body froze, and a cold sweat collected on my spine. The weight of his body pressed on my back made me want to vomit.

"Get your hands off me," I cried, but he only squeezed my arms tighter.

"I'm glad you two are getting reacquainted," my father said. "I would have sent him to collect you in Vermont, but I couldn't risk you running off again. So, I sent Brian instead to monitor you and then bring you home once he found the files. Now that you're back, Alex and I can complete the long-term deal we made. Patrick found out about the transaction when he went snooping around the company files to take me down and tried to stop it once he discovered that I had bigger plans for his little sister."

Transaction?

"As you know, Alex has been an investor in our family's operations since you were fourteen. He's brought us more clients than all our associates combined. With each reference, Alex got quite a generous cut."

Bitter fear burned my throat.

"Sadie, he's been vying for a *different* form of payment since you were fifteen. Of course, we couldn't risk you falling in love and leaving the family to parts unknown. So, when you turned twenty, we handed you over to Arthur's son, who you hated. Keelan would have no idea it was all a plan to break you in for a year until it was time to hand you off to Alex. Alex may have a taste for younger women, but he doesn't fuck virgins."

Stunned and speechless, I could only shake my head. *This can't be happening. No fucking way.*

"Patrick found out I sold you off, and he couldn't mind his fucking business. He wanted to play the 'noble brother' by bringing down both families to protect you," my father explained. "When I found out he betrayed me, it was easy to arrange his death. God, he was such a damn fool to believe I'd let that slide."

Alex's hand moved from my right arm and gripped my chin, forcing my face to turn to look at him. His brown eyes glittered with dark lust, making my instincts scream to run. "Soon, my dear Sadie, you're going to know what it's like to have your tight pussy fucked by a real man. That'll make you nice and obedient."

The taste of bile filled my mouth as Alex twisted me around, grabbing my wrists in his hand. He pulled a pair of handcuffs from his pocket with his free hand. A ferocious terror filled my body. I had to fight. I had to fight for my fucking life until Keelan came. Brian was shouting but couldn't move as he was still being held at gunpoint by my father.

Alex tried to snap the metal bracelets over my wrists, but I stomped on his foot as hard as I could and then kicked him in the kneecap. His grip loosened, and I turned to make a run for it. But Alex recovered quickly, and his arms wrapped around my waist, yanking me back. I forcefully head-butted him, but he showed no reaction to the blow. That's when I started screaming. I screamed at the top of my lungs, but Alex's hand covered my mouth, muffling my cries for help.

There was a loud crack as the office door broke free of its hinges. Arthur swiftly turned, but the door forcefully swung open and slammed into his arm. There, in the doorway, was Keelan, and a wave of relief crashed over me. His eyes were like twin blue flames of Death's promise. Keelan was wearing gloves and rushed into the room, grabbing his father's suppressor from the floor. Before anyone could react, Keelan raised the gun and pointed it at Alex, firing off a shot. There was no need for me to duck as the perfectly aimed bullet went past my head and struck him dead center in between the eyes. Fortunately, because of the suppressor mixed with the loud music blaring down the hall, it drowned out the sound.

Alex's arms jerked, and then his lifeless body collapsed onto the expensive rug, blood slowly leaking into the fibers. My father's eyes widened with shock. Arthur lunged for Keelan, but he drew back his arm and slammed his elbow into Arthur's nose. The man dropped to the ground, blood pouring between his fingers.

"You fucking bastard!" my father roared, his eyes wholly fixed on Keelan. Brian charged at him, taking advantage of his distraction, and slammed his shoulders into my father's chest. The two went to the ground, and Dad lost his grip on the gun, which skidded a few feet away. Brian reared back and punched my father three times in the face. Thankfully, he went slack from the force of the blows.

Brian stood and quickly retrieved the gun.

"Control your fucking son, Arthur!" My father spat out a mouthful of blood on the floor. Despite feeling terrified, I laughed, almost hysterically, at seeing my big, violent father reduced to a heap.

Arthur looked at his son, hands raised. "Don't be stupid, Keelan. You have no idea what you're doing—"

"Shut the fuck up!" Keelan snarled. "You were about to take my wife away from me."

"Keelan, my dad arranged to have me sold to that man you just killed," I explained. "That's why he had Patrick murdered. He found out I was being sold like cattle, stole the files, and was going to release them to stop him from doing it."

Keelan's eyes widened slightly, and a mixture of sadness and rage flickered across his face. He raised the gun at my father's head, but his eyes looked at me. "Sadie, what do you want me to do?"

I moved away from Alex's body and crossed the room to Keelan, my eyes fixed on my father's face. As he was lying there on the floor, blood on his face and chest heaving. Rage burned within my heart. He should not only be held responsible for the horrific abuse my mother and I endured but also for taking the life of my older brother, Patrick, who had always tried to protect me despite his flaws. Finn Ryan had too much power. He had too much control over the many players who would work to keep him free from prison. If he lived, it would never end.

"Sadie, don't you fucking dare do this," my father hissed. "You stupid, worthless child."

"Stop!" I spat back. "Your ego has ruined you ... *Finn*. The people you were meant to love and protect will be the ones to destroy your empire. Keelan saved my life in more ways than just being engaged to him. Your selfishness delivered my freedom from you. As much as rotting in prison would be nice, I think it's time you burn in hell. Shoot him."

Without a word, Keelan shot my father in the head. I gasped as he slumped back to the ground. I stared at him briefly, reassuring myself that my father was dead.

"Fucking hell," Arthur murmured, his arms slack at his sides. Keelan threw the gun at his father's feet. Arthur picked it up and looked down at the weapon with confusion.

Keelan gently placed his hand on my waist, turning me away from my dead father. He then cupped my face in his warm hands, running his thumb over my lips. "You're safe, baby," he whispered. "They can't hurt you anymore."

"Keelan," Arthur said, holding the gun up toward us. "Are those files really in the agent's trunk?"

"That gun's unloaded, Dad," Keelan said, not even glancing over at him. "I emptied the chamber and ejected the magazine already. The feds that are waiting outside have the files. I submitted them last night. By now, they've gotten a warrant and are searching Finn's house and office as we speak."

Arthur's eyes widened, and he looked at my father's body.

"It's over," Keelan said. "Everything you tried to hide in those files will take you all down, including Aiden and Logan. Now that you've killed your business partner and your associate, you're going to prison for life."

Realization seemed to pull Arthur from his haze as he looked down at the gun—the gun that had his fingerprints on it. A slight smile formed on his lips, as if he was proud of his son's clever tactic. He'd taught Keelan well.

Arthur placed the gun on his desk and walked back to his leather chair, stepping over the cooling blood puddle before sitting back down. His cigar still lay in the ashtray. Arthur reached into his pocket and took out a lighter, reigniting the cigar before taking a long puff.

"I guess it doesn't surprise me that this is the outcome," Arthur mused through the smoke. "You were the smartest one out of all of us. But I'm still so disappointed in you."

Keelan pulled me closer to his body. "What else is new?"

"Take care of Mia. She's going to be an incredible artist, just like you."

In the distance, police sirens drifted through the open window.

"You need to get out of here now," Brian said. "My agents just informed me they apprehended your brothers at the airport. That means the window to escape is closing fast. Go out through the back door."

I mouthed "thank you" to Brian and took Keelan's hand before we rushed out of the office and toward the back of the house. Brian would stay behind, recounting what he had witnessed: Arthur shot and killed both Finn Ryan and Alex Thatcher, nearly killing him as well before he could grab his weapon.

We were free ... for now.

An hour later, we reached the Burbank airstrip. Brian had done his part by securing us with fake identifications and a flight out of California. This plane would take us to our first stop, and then from there, it was up to us to disappear. He would help build the case to take down Arthur and his two sons while Keelan and I escaped to freedom.

Gavin and Mia had snuck out of the party right before the police arrived. They were going to meet his parents, Byron and

Serena, in an undisclosed location. I wasn't sure where Lily was, but hopefully, she would be reunited with her daughter soon.

My heart ached because I wasn't sure when I would see my mom again. Maybe once the dust had settled, she could reach me, as she said.

We entered the small plane and sat beside each other. One of Brian's pilot contacts was flying us. Keelan reached into his pocket and pulled out a small sheet of paper.

"Is that the account number?" I asked, and he nodded. Once Keelan logged in, we looked at the balance my father had transferred to Brian with wide eyes. Brian had gifted it to *us*. To him, it was blood money. To us, it was a nest to help us escape and stay hidden.

"Holy shit," I said, looking at the amount and then back up at him. "That's what my father paid Brian to sleep with me?"

My father had transferred ten million dollars to the offshore account Brian had set up for us under my and Keelan's new identities. It was all ours.

"Well," I said. "I guess we can get that beachfront property I've always wanted." I smiled and reached out my hand for him to take. "One with a white picket fence to grow old in."

Keelan placed his hand on my knee and glided his fingers up my thigh until they reached between my legs. His breath was hot against my neck as he kissed me softly. "You're safe, Sade. You'll always be safe with me. Understand?"

I leaned into him and cradled my head into his shoulder. "I do now," I said gently. "Even though you're a complete psycho … I've never felt more safe in my entire life."

Keelan lightly bit the side of his bottom lip. "Even after kidnapping you?" he teased.

I let out a small laugh. "Especially after kidnapping me."

Keelan pulled me in close with one hand and squeezed my thigh with the other still resting between my legs. "You were never meant to stay hidden from me, princess. We had a contract. And I take that very seriously."

I barked out a laugh that time. "Fuck that contract." I reached up and placed my hand on his cheek. "At least I know now that you're in love with me, so if I did walk out the door or run away from you again someday ... you'd let me go. Right?"

Keelan tucked a strand of hair behind my ear, and his gaze darkened. "... Never."

Epilogue

Sadie

Aore, Island in Vanuatu, Six Months Later

The coolness of the sand caressed my feet as I sank them deeper into the soft ground. Leaning back in my chair, I stretched my arms over my head and stared out at the sparkling, deep-blue water. There was nothing more perfect than this.

As I closed my eyes to allow the sun to hit my cheeks, a little furry weight jumped on my leg.

"Hey, sweetie," I said to Poe, watching him climb up and plop down on my chest. I ran my hand over his soft fur, listening to him purr loudly, as if he knew it would help to lull me into a relaxed state. The sight of him filled me with bittersweet joy.

My mind returned the moment I got him back. I was grateful that Mason decided to take care of my cat after he had called the police, keeping him until it was safe for us to return. I didn't want to put him in danger, so Keelan broke into his home while he was at the bookshop, stole my cat back, and left another nice little Post-it note. It was just enough for him to know it was me, but not enough information where he'd have to lie to the authorities if they ever searched for us.

Keelan sat my drink on the little table beside me and leaned down, kissing me on the forehead. "Here," he said, handing me his phone. "Take a look."

I sat up quickly but wrapped my arms around Poe so he wouldn't leap off my lap. The LA Times was on the screen. Right at the top was a photo of Keelan and me from when we got engaged, along with an article about how I was missing and presumed dead.

It was a risk we took, but it was a necessary one. Before we had met with my father, I had given Brian a few vials of my blood. We had staged the scene perfectly on my father's boat, which he kept inside the Cabrillo Marina.

According to the article, they found the yacht floating idling off the western coast, with my blood, Keelan's DNA, and a handgun with his fingerprints. On the edge, they discovered a torn shirt, where police believed Keelan Blake shot himself after murdering Sadie Ryan, daughter of the disgraced Los Angeles mayor, and fell into the water. The sea claimed both bodies, and the Ryan and Blake families mourned their deaths.

Though necessary for our escape, I hated that the world believed he would ever do that to me.

After escaping under new identities, we found a small home on the island, away from death and crime. There was always fear that the authorities would come to find us, though. But for now, Brian held up his end of the deal, and we could live in peace.

"Brian did one more thing for us," he said. "Well, one more thing for someone I knew."

"Who?"

Keelan took the phone from me and opened another article. The story was posted without a photo but with a headline stating that Andrew Wright, a former FBI agent, had been exonerated after new evidence surfaced and cleared him of wrongdoing. Shawn Daniels investigated the case, arresting the corrupt agents involved in framing him.

Keelan explained that it was Daniels who picked up the files at the cemetery.

I turned to look at him. "See," I said. "You're not as much of a monster as you pretended to be back then. You care about people, Keelan Blake."

Keelan rolled his eyes and brought his bottle of beer to his lips. "I can show you much how I care," he said seductively, biting his bottom lip.

God, why are men like this?

I placed Poe on the sand and watched him stretch before curling up into a ball under the beach umbrella by the coconut tree. Surprisingly, Poe enjoyed the beach, which some might think was odd for a cat, but we never had to worry about him wandering off to the ocean. He made his home here just like we did.

Keelan stood up and walked over to me, his body blocking the sun and creating a shadow over my face. "Stand up," he ordered, and I very much obliged.

He sat on my lawn chair, and he pushed down his swim trunks, pulling his cock free and pumping it a few times.

"Ride it," he demanded, and I shook my head.

"Keelan," I said as my cheeks flushed. My lips parted, but I was quick to recover and remember that we weren't alone. No matter how much I wished we were. "We still have neighbors we share a beachfront with."

Keelan's eyes turned dark. Clearly, he cared about our surroundings far less than I did. "I said ride my fucking cock, princess."

Now it wasn't just my flushed cheeks reacting as my stomach flipped and my core ached for him to slide inside.

I looked around the beach, ensuring no one else was outside watching the show. We were alone—for now, at least. I moved on top of his lap, pushing my bikini bottoms to the side. To any potential by-passers, we would've likely looked like a couple exchanging affection at this point. I positioned myself above him, straddling his hips and gradually moving down over his hard cock, his hand gently helping him slide inside. My brows furrowed as he filled me up, stretching me out with his size. He felt so damn good from this angle, rubbing up against all the sweet spots.

"That wasn't so hard, was it?" he teased, leaning in and kissing the bridge of my neck and gliding his tongue to my ear as I began to bounce up and down his length. My hands gripped his shoulders, using them for additional support as I moved against him. My breaths were heavy already as the tip of his length hit so fucking deep, causing a trail of goosebumps to move up my back. "That's my good fucking girl. Ride my cock, just like that."

Keelan gripped the straps of my bikini top and pulled them over my shoulders. He leaned forward and exposed one of my breasts before putting it in his mouth and sucking. His tongue lashed against my nipple mercilessly, only intensifying the pleasure that was already coursing through me.

"Keelan," I cried out, throwing my head back. One of my hands drifted upward, knotting in his hair and yanking him closer to ensure he didn't pull back. He nipped at my breasts, just enough to cause me to wince and moan at the same time with a mix of pleasure and pain.

"God, your pussy was made for me," he praised, the words coming out muffled against my skin. "So fucking tight. So fucking beautiful."

This time, he took my entire left breast in his hand, sucking, squeezing, and teasing as he thrust up to push himself deeper inside me. His hands rested on my hips, helping to guide my pace. He had me right where he wanted me. I moved faster now, my pussy clenching around him, having to brace myself on his shoulders to keep from falling. The chair below us squeaked against the sand, threatening to snap under the force of our movements.

"Don't slow down," he said, lifting his hips again while I rode him faster. His eyes were almost pleading, filled with so much lust. "Don't fucking slow down, Sadie. Fuck, your pussy feels so goddamn good around my cock. Just like that, baby."

"Keelan, I can't—" I stammered, wanting to let him know I was close. *So* close to the point where I couldn't hold it back anymore. I could no longer hold in my cries, either, as I practically shouted his name, quickly burying my face into his neck to stifle any more sounds threatening to leave my lips. The neighbors were absolutely getting a show now.

I came hard and fast, soaking his cock in my arousal, my entire body shaking as I struggled to breathe. Keelan still kept a firm grip on my hips, thrusting himself upward to ram his cock inside me. "So needy, aren't you? You need to come all over me more than once ...."

"Keelan—" I gasped for air, still shaking. My pussy was throbbing as he continued to fuck me, to where I could practically feel my insides shake with his force. "I can't—"

"Oh, you can. My dick was made for you, princess," he said soothingly, still guiding my body against his. Every time I bounced on him, a tingle of pleasure shot through my entire body. I wasn't sure how long I would last this time, but I wanted to hold on for him. I wanted us to come together. My teeth sunk into my bottom lip, my eyes rolling back into my skull as I leaned back slightly. Keelan placed his hand between us, slipping his thumb against my wetness and circling my clit, stimulating me further. *Fuck. Fuck,* that felt too good.

Our bodies slapped together as my breathing became heavier all over again, and I was hanging on by a thread.

Keelan's other hand gripped my thigh tighter as I slowed, unable to take the pleasure, directing me to roll my hips into his slow yet rough touch.

"I want to feel you come all over my cock again, Sadie," he murmured, watching himself slide in and out of me, our juices soaking the fabric of my bikini. "Are you going to be a good girl and give me what I want, baby?" Before I had the chance to respond, he pulled me close, so he could bite down on the skin of my neck. This time, he clamped down, hard and feral.

Oh, my fucking God. It only spread another wave of pleasure through me, pushing me closer to that point of no return—so painful that I was sure he had broken my skin, and I loved every second of it as he marked me.

Marked me *again.*

"I'm going to come. You feel way too fucking good," he said as Keelan lifted his lips from my skin. It was as if those words gave me one last push of energy, making me desperate to reach that peak with him. I sped up, using my knees to brace myself on the chair. After a few more thrusts, my orgasm hit, and a wave of euphoria washed over me. My lips parted, but no sound would come out as I shook on top of him. Keelan released his grip on me and quickly wrapped his arms around my body. He yanked me even closer while I whimpered and quivered against him, drowning in pleasure.

"Fuck yes," he groaned. "Drench my cock again, baby." Keelan didn't last much longer after that, his head falling back into the chair as he came, filling me up as our pleasure dragged on—neither of us could breathe properly.

I didn't immediately move off him as we both came down but leaned into him instead, resting my chest against his as he reclined in the chair. His cum dripped down my thigh, and honestly, I didn't care. I was too spent even to consider moving or standing up.

The only sounds now were our heavy breaths and waves crashing against the shore.

"I'll never get bored of this," Keelan said, running his hand over my sweat-coated hair.

"Fucking me like this in front of our neighbors? Someone actually might call the police on us, Keelan," I pointed out, and he chuckled.

"God," he murmured, brushing my hair from my face. "I can't believe you're mine, Sadie. You're actually mine."

I looked up and placed my left hand on his chest, running my fingers in circles over his tattoos, the pink diamond ring glittering in the sunlight. "I've always been yours, Keelan Blake. My body is branded by your marks, remember?"

It was as if those words stirred something feral within him. He threaded his hands through my hair and tightened his grip. Even through the pain, he was everywhere at once. He had marked my body and soul, making me his in all senses of the word. He kissed me, and my heart felt whole.

I bore his sinful marks—stained by darkness and pain—branded by obsession and unconditional love. Keelan Blake was my destruction and my empowerment. He was my captor and my savior.

He. Was. Mine.

About D.L. Blade

D.L. Blade has always been passionate about creative writing, with a particular focus on poetry during her younger years. One night, after having a vivid dream, she was inspired to pick up her pen and write her debut novel, *The Dark Awakening*.

Initially, Blade had focused on writing young adult fiction, but she has since shifted her focus to adult fantasy, paranormal, and dark romance. Through her stories, she takes readers on a journey into a world of unconventional love, morally gray men, and villains who get the girl.

When she's not writing, Blade enjoys reading, spending time with her husband and two children, attending rock concerts, and exploring new restaurants in Denver. She dreams of continuing to create exciting novels for her readers, taking them on a journey through the magical realms that spill from the pages of her books.

About C.M. Locke

C.M. Locke is a passionate writer who has been crafting short stories and poems for many years. Though she is a first-time author in the book world, she has already honed her skills through her love of writing.

Reading is one of her favorite pastimes, and she has likely read over 100,000 pages throughout her lifetime. Whenever she has free time, she loves to curl up on the couch with a cup of peppermint tea and dive into a well-loved book or a brand-new novel.

Originally from Colorado, C.M. Locke currently lives in rural Missouri with her boyfriend and three beloved kitties.

Made in the USA
Middletown, DE
18 January 2026

27256315R00250